D1174835

PRIDE'S HARVEST

by the same author

YOU CAN'T SEE ROUND CORNERS
THE LONG SHADOW
JUST LET ME BE
THE SUNDOWNERS
THE CLIMATE OF COURAGE
JUSTIN BAYARD
THE GREEN HELMET
BACK OF SUNSET
NORTH FROM THURSDAY
THE COUNTRY OF MARRIAGE
FORESTS OF THE NIGHT
A FLIGHT OF CHARIOTS
THE FALL OF AN EAGLE
THE PULSE OF DANGER
THE HIGH COMMISSIONER
THE LONG PURSUIT
SEASON OF DOUBT
REMEMBER JACK HOXIE
HELGA'S WEB
MASK OF THE ANDES
MAN'S ESTATE
RANSOM
PETER'S PENCE
THE SAFE HOUSE
A SOUND OF LIGHTNING
HIGH ROAD TO CHINA
VORTEX
THE BEAUFORT SISTERS
A VERY PRIVATE WAR
GOLDEN SABRE
THE FARAWAY DRUMS
SPEARFIELD'S DAUGHTER
THE PHOENIX TREE
THE CITY OF FADING LIGHT
DRAGONS AT THE PARTY
NOW AND THEN AMEN
BABYLON SOUTH
MURDER SONG

JON CLEARY

Pride's Harvest

WILLIAM MORROW AND COMPANY, INC.
NEW YORK

First published in Great Britain in 1991 by HarperCollins Publishers

It is the policy of William Morrow and Company, Inc., and its imprints and affiliates, recognizing the importance of preserving what has been written, to print the books we publish on acid-free paper, and we exert our best efforts to that end.

Library of Congress Cataloging-in-Publication data has been ordered.
Cleary, Jon.
PRIDE'S HARVEST
ISBN 0-688-10408-8

91-30582
CIP

Printed in the United States of America

First U.S. Edition

1 2 3 4 5 6 7 8 9 10

for Isabel

Collamundra is a dozen towns.
Each character in the story is a dozen people.
A novel is the only cocktail I know how to mix.

ONE

1

'You should take a week's leave and come out here,' said Lisa. 'It's so restful, just what you need.'

That had been the day before the murder; Lisa's timing, usually so reliable, had been way off. Scobie Malone, missing his wife and children, already weary after only four days of getting his own meals, making his bed and trying to iron his shirts so that they didn't look as if he had pressed them by sleeping on them, had hung up the phone and thought seriously of applying for a week's leave. Murder had taken one of its rare holidays in the city and now would be as good a time as any to ask for a few days off. Then the very next day the routine telexed report had come in of the murder at Collamundra and later that afternoon there had been the telephoned request to Regional Crime Squad, South Region, in Sydney, asking for assistance.

Malone was the acting officer-in-charge of Homicide and he had assigned himself to the case without mentioning to any of his superiors at Police Centre that his wife and family were staying in the district where the murder had occurred. He had learned one thing, amongst others, from crims he had interviewed: the less police, especially superior officers, know, the better.

'We'll leave first thing in the morning,' he told Russ Clements.

'We flying or driving?'

'We'll drive. Another day won't matter, and I'd rather have our own wheels out there than borrow some. The tracks are probably cold, anyway. They didn't mention any suspects.'

'Collamundra. Isn't that where Lisa and the kids are staying?'

'Keep your voice down. Why do you think I want to load myself with a homicide out in the bush? The last time we went bush the local cops were as unco-operative as the cow cockies.'

'This is a Jap cow cocky who's been murdered. Does that make any difference?'

'He wasn't a cow cocky, he was the manager of a cotton farm and gin. Yeah, that does make it interesting.'

'So seeing Lisa and the kids wasn't what interested you?'

'Are you kidding?'

'Are you taking your laundry with you? You're beginning to look like me, a bachelor.'

Now Malone and Clements, in their unmarked police car, were approaching the end of the four-hundred-kilometre drive from Sydney to Collamundra. They had left early this Thursday morning, come over the Blue Mountains through the charred landscape of the summer bushfires, down the western slopes and out here to the rolling country that, beyond Collamundra, became the vast flat terrain of the western plains. The holdings hereabouts were not as huge as those farther west, but they were big enough; this was rich country and men had made comfortable fortunes on as little as five thousand acres. The landscape had begun to open out, unfolding till the eye could not take it all in without turning the head, and the sky had become immense, not anchored as it was on the coast by city skylines but dropping away behind the distant horizon to what one knew was eternity.

'You know anything about trees, one from another?' Malone was a city boy and sometimes he was ashamed at his ignorance of the native flora. Australia was still at least ninety per cent open space and he was almost as ignorant of it as the most recently arrived immigrant from over-crowded Europe and Asia. Crocodile Dundee, though the creation of a city-bred comedian, would have turned his back on him.

Clements was no more bucolic: 'I know some shed their leaves and some don't. But I wouldn't know a river-gum from a Wrigley's, so don't ask me.'

Malone felt better: ignorance is an acceptable bond if nothing better offers.

As he had on previous sorties into the bush, he remarked the seeming absence of any livestock. The broad paddocks, dotted with (though he didn't know their names) clumps of white cypress pine or kurrajong for shade, seemed to be raising more timber than sheep or cattle. The grazing paddocks were on one side of the main road, brown-tinted and dusty from summer; thin stands of yellowbox lined the road and behind them was the broad stock route, not used as much today as in the old heyday of droving when sheep flowed in slow motion along these tracks to the rail-head stockyards or, in time of drought, looking for better pasture. On the other side of the road were the wheatfields stretching away to a low line of hills that was no more than a wavering of the flat line of the horizon. It was now mid-April, the long drawn-out tail of a long hot summer, and the harvest out here would have been finished by late January, early February; the harrows were at work now, raising dust that drifted away as a grey-pink haze in the westering sun. A flock of galahs rose up from the fields, looking for a moment like a thickening of the haze. In the distance two kangaroos loped along, a jumping nervous tic in the tired eye.

A little later Clements said, 'That's where it must've happened.'

For some time they had been noticing the sprinkling of wisps of cotton on either side of the road, like a scattering of last year's snow; except that no one had ever known snow to fall out here. Now they were passing the cottonfields, which stretched away into the distance on both sides of the road. Amidst the white glare the mechanical cotton-pickers moved like top-heavy houseboats on a broad white lake; the operators sat up front in their air-conditioned, glass-sided cubicles, remote and bored-looking. Trailers stood in access tracks beside the rows of cotton, waiting to be loaded by the pickers. Two trailers were being hauled by small tractors to a long low truck that would take the cotton, now compressed into modules, to the big steep-roofed shed at which Clements had nodded.

'That's the gin, I guess. You wanna call in there now?'

'No, let's go into town. I'm buggered. We'll start tomorrow.' He also wanted to stick by protocol: you did not land unannounced in another cop's territory and start your investigations at once. No bird, animal or Cabinet minister enforces the territorial imperative more than does a policeman with rank.

They drove on, came to the edge of town, drove in past the wheat silos and the railway siding with its empty stockyards, past the BP and Shell service stations, the used car lots and the farm equipment sales yards, and then they were in the main section of town. They had passed a sign that said: 'Collamundra, Pop. 9400'; and it seemed that the 9400 Collamundrans, give or take a few, were a civic-minded lot of voters. It was not a pretty town, it was too flat and sunbaked for that, but it was attractive; or had been made so. They passed a pleasant tree-shaded park; beside it, amidst sun-browned lawns, was a large community swimming-pool. They went round the war memorial standing in the middle of an intersection. The memorial was a bronze Anzac on a marble plinth, staring up the street into the distance, his bayonet-topped rifle held up threateningly against any invader. It struck Malone that the Anzac was gazing eastwards, towards Sydney, home of the State government and city Homicide cops, as if the enemy was expected to come from there.

'This is Rural Party country,' said Clements, as if reading his mind. 'That guy with the bayonet was probably a local party secretary. Our friend Mr Dircks comes from here.'

'Oh crumbs,' said Malone, to whose tongue stuck some of the phrases of a childhood more innocent than today's; his mother had been a great believer in mouth-washing with soap and he could still taste the bar of Sunlight she had shoved down his throat when, in a moment of anger and forgetfulness, he had told the kid next door to *fuck off*! Dircks was the Police Minister, a bigger handicap to the Department than a cartload of corrupt cops. 'I'd forgotten that.'

Clements spotted a marked police car parked on the corner of a side street and he swung the Commodore over alongside it. Malone wound down his window. 'Where's the station, constable?'

The young officer, slumped behind the wheel, looked at him without much interest; then his eyes narrowed. 'You the guys from Sydney?'

'Yes,' said Malone and thought he had better establish rank at once. 'Detective-Inspector Malone and Detective-Sergeant Clements, from Regional Crime Squad, South Region. You're in that Region – just, but you're in it. Your name is – ?'

The young constable decided he had better sit up straight. 'Constable Reynolds, sir. If you'd like to follow me . . .'

They followed his car down the main street. It was a wide street, cars and trucks angle-parked at the kerbs on both sides. The stores were the usual one- or two-storeys, the fronts of almost all of them shaded by corrugated-iron awnings; they were characterless, stamped out of the mould of country-town stores all over the State, as if no architect had ever found it worth his while to come this far west. There were four banks, two of them solid as forts, built in the days when men took time to build with care and pride; the old names were cut into the stone just below their cornices, still there as defiant mockeries of the new names, dreamed up by corporation image makers, on the brass plates by the doors. The other two banks were new structures, as unimposing as a depositor's shaky credit rating.

Clements had not been impressed by the young constable's attitude. 'Do you think we're gunna be welcome?'

'They sent for us. But we're outsiders, don't forget that. Be diplomatic.'

'Look who's talking.'

They turned into a wide side street after the car in front. The police station was a cream-painted stone building that had been erected in 1884; the date was chipped out of the stone above the entrance; this, too, had been built by men who took time and pride. It was a good example of the solid public buildings of the period: nothing aesthetic about it, squatting as firmly on its foundations as Queen Victoria had on hers. Behind it had been added a two-storeyed brick building, painted cream so that it would not clash too much with its parent. There was a side driveway leading to a big yard and a row of garages and a workshop at the rear. A peppercorn tree stood on the width of thin lawn that separated the police station from the courthouse, another Victorian building on the other side from the driveway. It was a typical country town set-up, the law and justice keeping each other company. It wasn't always that way in the city, thought Malone.

Clements waved his thanks to the young constable, who drove on; the Commodore swung into the side driveway and went through to the rear yard. Clements parked the car by a side fence and he and Malone got out and walked back down the driveway, aware of the sudden appearance of half a dozen heads from the doorways of the garages, like rabbits that had smelled ferret on the wind. Not frightened bunnies, but hostile ones.

'You feel something sticking in your back?' said Clements. 'Like, say, half a dozen ice picks?'

They went in through the front door, asked the constable at the desk for Inspector Narvo and were taken along a short hallway to a large corner office that looked out on to both the street and the courthouse next door. There was a fireplace, topped by a marble mantelpiece, above which was a framed colour photograph of the Queen; its glass, unlike that on most portraits in public offices where the Queen was still hung, was not fly-specked but looked as if it were washed every day. The grate and ornamental metal surrounds of the fireplace had been newly blackened. On the wall opposite the fireplace was a manning chart, as neatly ruled and lettered as an eye chart; there were no erasures, as if a new manning list was put up each day. Between the two windows that looked out on to the street was a desk and a man seated behind it, both as neat as everything else in the room. Malone, sweaty and rumpled from the long drive, felt as if he were about to be called up for inspection.

'I'm Hugh Narvo.' The man behind the desk stood up, his immaculate uniform seeming to creak with the movement. Malone had only ever met one cop as neat as this man and that was Police Commissioner Leeds. Narvo was as tall as Malone, rawboned in build and face, with dark brown eyes under thick brows, dark hair slicked down like a 1920s movie star and a mouth that looked as if it might have trouble sustaining a smile. Malone judged he could be the sort of officer-in-charge who would never be popular with his men nor attempt to be. 'What plane did you get in on? I'd have had someone out there to meet you.'

Narvo was studying the men as carefully as they were studying him. Cops in the New South Wales Police Department, like crims, do not take each other at face value; it is a legacy of the old days, still there in pockets, when corruption started at the top and filtered down like sewage. Narvo looked at these two strangers, whom he had sent for only on the insistence of his detective-sergeant. He saw two tall men, Clements much bulkier than Malone. The latter, whom he knew by repute, was the one who engaged him. He was not given to thinking of men as handsome or plain or ugly: he looked for the character in their faces. Malone, he decided, had plenty of that: tough, shrewd but sympathetic. He wished, in a way, that they had sent him a bastard, someone he could turn his back on. Malone had a reputation for integrity, for not caring about repercussions, and that, Narvo decided, was going to make things difficult.

'We drove,' said Malone. 'Russ likes driving.'

'Do I?' Clements grinned.

But Narvo didn't seem to see any humour in the small joke. 'You must be expecting to stay here a while. It's a long way to drive just for a day or two.'

'You expect it to be cleared up as soon as that?'

'We hope so. You probably know how it can be in a town like this – we don't like a homicide hanging over our heads. Especially with so many visitors in town.'

'What's on?'

Narvo looked mildly surprised. 'I thought you'd have known – but then, why should you? It's the Collamundra Cup weekend, the big event of the year.'

'Russ is the racing expert. Did you know about it?'

Clements shook his big head. He looked even more sweaty and rumpled than Malone; but that was almost his natural state. 'I'd forgotten about it. I never bet on bush races.'

'Don't let the locals hear you call it a bush race.' Narvo for an instant looked as if he might smile. 'They think the Collamundra Cup is a cousin to the Melbourne Cup and the Kentucky Derby.' Then he said abruptly, 'I'll get Sergeant Baldock in here, he's in charge of my detectives.'

He spoke into his phone and almost immediately, as if he had been waiting outside for the call, Sergeant Baldock appeared. He was a burly man in his mid-thirties, already bald, hard-faced, ready to meet the world square-on. Yet he seemed friendly enough and put out a hand that looked as, if closed into a fist, it could have felled a bullock.

'Jeff will look after you,' said Narvo; and Malone, his ear, as always, sensitive to a new environment, thought that Narvo spoke with relief. 'I have to go over to Cawndilla first thing in the morning to see the District Super. I'll tell him you're here. Will you want to see him?'

No cop in his right mind ever wanted to see a District Superintendent, especially one who might resent strangers on his turf. 'I don't think so.' Out of the corner of his eye he saw Baldock grin and nod appreciatively. 'Just give him my respects and tell him we won't kick up too much dust.'

'He'll be glad to hear that. We all will, won't we, Jeff?' Baldock seemed to hesitate before he nodded; but Narvo was already looking back at Malone. 'We've booked you into the Mail Coach Hotel. We were lucky to get you a room. You don't mind sharing?'

'So long as we don't have to share the bed. Does it have a bathroom or do we have to queue up down the end of the hall?'

He knew there were still some country hotel owners who thought they were spoiling their guests if they gave them too many amenities. If the explorers Burke and Wills, starving to death on their last ill-fated expedition, had chanced to stop at one of those hotels they would not have been fed, not if they had collapsed into the dining-room after eight p.m.

The Collamundra cops looked as if local pride had been hurt. Baldock said, 'It has a bathroom. Narelle Potter, the owner, likes to stay on side with us. It can get a bit rowdy down there sometimes. You know what country pubs can be like, especially when everyone comes in from out of town.'

'I'd like a shower before I go out to see my family.' Malone enjoyed the look of surprise on both men's faces, especially Narvo's. 'My wife and kids are staying out at Sundown, the Carmody property – or rather, they're staying with Mrs Waring, Carmody's daughter. My wife and her are old friends, they worked together down in Sydney.'

He wondered why he was telling them so much about a relationship that was no concern of theirs. But he had noticed how both Narvo's and Baldock's faces had closed up, as if they were abruptly suspicious of him.

'Well,' said Baldock, 'you'll get all the dirt on the district out there. Old Sean Carmody's not one of your back-fence gossips, but he can never forget he was a journo, a big-time foreign correspondent.'

'He's probably got the Sagawa murder already solved,' said Narvo. 'Enjoy your stay, Scobie. Russ.' But he said it without conviction, as if he knew there would be no enjoyment for any of them.

Malone and Clements went out with Baldock and up to the detectives' room on the first floor of the rear building. It was an office in which there had been an attempt at neatness, probably under Narvo's orders, but it had failed; this was a room which would have more visitors than Narvo's, many of them obstreperous or even still murderous, and neatness had bent under the onslaughts. There was one other detective in the room, a short, slight dark man in a suit that looked a size too large for him.

Baldock introduced him. 'Wally Mungle. He was the first one out to the crime scene. A pretty gory sight, he tells me.'

'Gruesome.'

Now that they were standing opposite each other, Malone saw that Mungle was an Aborigine, not a full-blood but with the strain showing clearly in him. He had a beautiful smile that made him look younger than he was, but his eyes were as sad as those of a battered old man.

He held out a file. 'Maybe you'd like to see the running sheet.'

'We don't run to computers here in the detectives' room,' said Baldock. 'We're the poor cousins in this set-up. Both computers are downstairs with the uniformed guys and the civilian help.'

Again Malone had a feeling of something in the atmosphere, like an invisible shifting current. He took the file from Mungle and flipped through it: so far it was as meagre as the report on a stolen bicycle:

> *Kenji Sagawa, born Kobe, Japan, June 18, 1946. Came to Collamundra August 1989 as general manager South Cloud Cotton Limited. Family: wife and two children, resident in Osaka, Japan.*
>
> *Body discovered approximately 8.15 a.m. Tues-*

day April 12, by Barry Liss, worker in South Cloud cotton gin. First thought was accidental death due to body being trapped in cotton module travelling into the module feeder. Later inspection by Dr M. Nothling, government medical officer, established that death was due to gunshot wound. (Medical report attached.)

'That's all?'

'The bullet has been extracted,' Mungle said. 'Ballistics had a man sent up from Sydney last night. He left again this morning. The bullet was a Twenty-two.'

'What about the cartridge?'

'No sign of it.'

Malone frowned at that; then glanced at the file again. 'This is pretty skimpy.'

Mungle said almost shyly, 'It's my first homicide, Inspector. I've only been in plainclothes a month.'

Malone decided it wasn't his place to teach Mungle how to be a detective. He nodded, said he would see Mungle again, and he and Clements went downstairs and out to their car. Baldock followed them.

'Wally will do better. He's the first Abo cop we've had in this town. He's done bloody well to make detective.'

Malone decided on the blunt approach; he was tired and wanted the picture laid out for him. 'Tell me, Jeff, do you coves resent Russ and me being called in?'

'It was me who called for you. And call me Curly.' He took off his hat and ran his hand over his bald head. 'I get uptight when people call me Baldy Baldock. My mates call me Curly. Does that answer your question?'

Malone grinned and relaxed; he was surprised that he had begun to feel uptight himself. Several uniformed men, in their shirt-sleeves, two of them with chamois washcloths in their hands, had come to the doors of the garages again and stood in front of the cars and patrol wagons they had been cleaning. There was a stiffness about all of them that made them look like figures in an old photograph. Through a high barred back window of the two-storeyed rear building there came the sound of a slurred voice singing a country-and-western song.

'One of the Abos in the cells,' said Baldock. 'Today's dole day. They start drinking the plonk as soon as the pubs and the liquor shop open and we've usually got to lock up two or three of 'em by mid-afternoon. We let 'em sober up, then send 'em home.'

'How do they feel about Constable Mungle?'

'He's an in-between, poor bugger. But it's a start. Come on, I'll take you down and introduce you to Narelle Potter. She's a good sort, you'll like her. She's a widow, lost her husband about five years ago in a shooting accident. Let's go in your car. You may need me to make sure you get a parking place.'

'How do you do that out here in the bush?' said Clements, the city expert.

'Same as you guys down in Sydney, I guess. I give some poor bugger a ticket, tell him to move his vehicle, then I take his place. What do you call it down in the city?'

'Emergency privilege. Makes us very popular.'

But miraculously, just like in every movie Malone had seen, there was a vacant space at the kerb in front of the Mail Coach Hotel. Clements squeezed the Commodore in between two dust-caked utility trucks. Some drinkers on the pavement, spilling out from the pub, looked at them curiously as the three policemen got out of their car.

'It's the most popular pub in town,' said Baldock. 'Especially with the races and the Cup ball coming up this weekend. There may be a brawl or two late in the evening, but just ignore it. We do, unless Narelle calls us in.'

The hotel stood on a corner, a two-storeyed structure that fronted about a hundred and twenty feet to both the main street and the side street. It was the sort of building that heritage devotees, even strict teetotallers, would fight to preserve. The upper balconies had balustrades of yellow iron lace; the windows had green wooden shutters; the building itself, including the roof, was painted a light brown. It was one of the most imposing structures in town, a temple to drinking. The congregation inside sounded less than religious, filled with piss rather than piety.

Baldock led Malone and Clements in through a side-door, past a sign that said 'Guests' Entrance', a class distinction of earlier times. They were in a narrow hallway next to the main bar, whence came a bedlam of male voices, the Foster's Choir. In the hallway the preservation equalled that on the outside: dark polished panelling halfway up the cream walls, a polished cedar balustrade on a flight of red-carpeted stairs leading to the upper floor. Mrs Potter, it seemed, was a proud housekeeper.

Baldock returned with her from the main bar. She was a tall, full-figured woman in her mid-thirties with dark hair that looked as if it had just come out from under a hairdresser's blower, an attractive face that appeared as if it had become better-looking as she had grown older and more sure of herself. She had an automatic smile, a tool of trade that Malone knew from experience not all Australian innkeepers had learned to use. Narelle Potter, he guessed, could look after herself, even in a pub brawl.

'Gentlemen –' She had to adjust her voice from its strident first note; the gentlemen she usually addressed were those in her bars, all of them deaf to anything dulcet. 'Happy to have you. We'll try and make you comfortable and welcome.'

She looked first at Malone, then at Clements, who gave her a big smile and turned on some of his King's Cross charm. It worked well with the girls on the beat in that area; but evidently Narelle Potter, too, liked it. She gave him a big smile in return.

Baldock left them, saying he would meet them tomorrow out at the cotton farm, and Mrs Potter took them up to their room. It was big and comfortable, but strictly hotel functional; the heritage spirit ran dry at the door. There were three prints on the walls: one of a Hans Heysen painting of eucalypts, the other two of racehorses standing with pricked ears and a haughty look as if the stewards had just accused them of being doped.

'You like the horses?' said Clements, whose betting luck was legendary, at least to Malone.

'My late husband loved them, he had a string of them. I still have two, just as a hobby. One of them is running in the Cup.' She looked at Malone. 'You're here about the murder out at the cotton gin?'

Malone had put his valise on the bed and was about to open it; but the abrupt switch in the conversation made him turn round. If Mrs Potter's tone wasn't strident again, it had certainly got a little tight.

'That's right. Did you know Mr Sagawa?'

'Oh yes. Yes, he was often in here at the hotel. He was unlike most Japs, he went out of his way to mix with people. He tried too hard.' The tightness was still there.

'In what way?'

'Oh, various ways.' She was turning down the yellow chenille bedspreads.

'Do you get many Japanese out here?'

'Well, no-o. But I've heard what they're like, they like to keep to themselves. The other Jap out at the farm, the young one, we never see him in here.'

'There's another one?'

'He's the trainee manager or something. I don't know his name. He's only been here a little while.'

'So you wouldn't know how he got on with Mr Sagawa?'

She paused, bent over the bed, and looked up at him. He noticed, close up, that she was either older than he had first thought or the years had worked hard on her. 'How would I know?'

He ignored that. 'Did Mr Sagawa have any friends here in town?'

'I don't really know.' She straightened up, turned away from him; he had the feeling that her rounded hip was bumping him off, like a footballer's would. 'He tried to be friendly, like I said, but I don't know that he was actually *friends* with anyone.'

'Is there any anti-Japanese feeling in the town?'

She didn't answer that at once, but went into the bathroom, came out, said, 'Just checking the girl left towels for you. Will you be in for dinner?'

Now wasn't the time to push her, Malone thought. Questioning a suspect or a reluctant witness is a form of seduction; he was better than most at it, though in his sexual seduction days his approach had been along the national lines of a bull let loose in a cow-stall.

'Sergeant Clements will be. I'm going out of town for dinner.'

'Oh, you know someone around here?' Her curiosity was so open, she stoked herself on what she knew of what went on in the district. She'll be useful, Malone thought, even as he was irritated by her sticky-beaking.

'No, I just have an introduction to someone. I'd better have my shower.'

He took off his tie, began to unbutton his shirt and she took the hint. She gave Clements another big smile, swung her hips as if breaking through a tackle, and went out, closing the door after her.

Clements's bed creaked as he sank his bulk on to it. 'I don't think I'm gunna enjoy this.'

Malone nodded as he stripped down to his shorts. He still carried little excess weight, but his muscles had softened since the days when he had been playing cricket at top level. So far, though, he didn't creak, like an old man or Clements's bed, when he moved. He tried not to think about ageing.

'Get on the phone to Sydney while I have my shower, find out if they're missing us.'

When he came out of the bathroom five minutes later Clements was just putting down the phone. 'Another quiet day. Where have all the killers gone?'

'Maybe they've come bush.'

'Christ, I hope not.'

2

It was almost dark when Malone got out to Sundown. The property lay fifteen kilometres west of town, 20,000 acres on the edge of the plains that stretched away in the gathering gloom to the dead heart of the continent. On his rare excursions inland he always became conscious of the vast loneliness of Australia, particularly at night. There was a frightening emptiness to it; he knew the land was full of spirits for the Aborigines, but not for him. There was a pointlessness to it all, as if God had created it and then run out of ideas what to do next. Malone was intelligent enough, however, to admit that his lack of understanding was probably due to his being so steeped in the city. There were spirits *there*, the civilized ones, some of them darker than even the Aborigines knew, but he had learned to cope with them.

He took note of the blunt sign, 'Shut the gate!', got back into the car and drove along the winding track, over several cattle grids, and through the grey gums, now turning black no matter what colour they had been during the day. He came out to the open paddocks where he could see the lights of the main homestead in the distance. His headlamps picked out small groups of sheep standing like grey rocks off to one side; once he stamped on the brakes as a kangaroo leapt across in front of him. Then he came to a second gate leading into what he would later be told was the home paddock. Finally he was on a gravel driveway that led up in a big curve to the low sprawling house surrounded by lawns and backed to the west by a line of trees.

Lisa was waiting for him at the three steps that led up to the wide veranda. 'Did you bring your laundry?'

'We-ell, yes. There's some in the boot –'

'I thought there might be.' But she kissed him warmly: he was worth a dirty shirt or two. He looked at her in the light from the veranda. She was blonde, on the cusp between exciting beauty and serenity; he tried, desperately, never to think of *her* ageing. 'Oh, I've missed you!'

Then their children and the Carmody clan spilled out of the house, a small crowd that made him feel as if he were some sort of celebrity. He hugged the three children, then turned to meet Sean Carmody, his daughter Ida, her husband Trevor Waring and their four children. He had met Ida once down in Sydney, but none of the others.

'Daddy, you know what? I've learned to ride a horse!' That was Tom, his eight-year-old. 'I fell off, but.'

'Have you found the murderer yet?' Maureen, the ten-year-old, was a devotee of TV crime, despite the efforts of her parents, who did everything but blindfold her to stop her from watching.

'Oh God,' said Claire, fourteen and heading helter-skelter for eighteen and laid-back sophistication. 'She's at it again.'

Malone, his arm round Lisa's waist, was herded by the crowd into the house. At once he knew it was the sort of house that must have impressed Lisa; he could see it in her face, almost as if *she* owned it and was showing it off to him. This was one of half a dozen in the district that had seen the area grow around it; a prickling in his Celtic blood told him there would be ghosts in every room, self-satisfied ones who knew that each generation of them had made the right choice. Sean Carmody had bought it only ten years ago, but he had inherited and cherished its history. This was a *rich* house, but its value had nothing to do with the price real-estate agents would put on it.

'I live here with Sean,' Tas, the eldest of the Carmody grandchildren, told Malone over a beer, 'I manage the property. Mum and Dad and my brothers and sister live in a house they built over on the east boundary. You would have passed it as you came from town.'

He was a rawboned twenty-two-year-old, as tall as Malone, already beginning to assume the weatherbeaten face that, like a tribal mask, was the badge of all the men, and some of the women, who spent their lives working these sun-baked plains. His speech was a slow drawl, but there was an intelligence in his dark-blue eyes that said his mind was well ahead of his tongue.

'He's a good boy,' said Sean Carmody after dinner as he and Trevor Waring led the way out to a corner of the wide side veranda that had been fly-screened. The three men sat down with their coffee and both Carmody and Waring lit pipes. 'Ida won't let us smoke in the house. My mother's name was Ida, too, and she wouldn't let my father smoke in their tent. We lived in tents all the time I was a kid. Dad was a drover. He'd have been pleased with his great-grandson. He's a credit to you and Ida,' he said to Waring. 'All your kids are. Yours, too, Scobie.'

'The credit's Lisa's.'

'No, I don't believe that. Being a policeman isn't the ideal occupation for a father. It can't be ideal for your kids, either.'

'No, it isn't,' Malone conceded. 'You can't bring your work home and talk about it with them. Not in Homicide.'

'The kids in the district are all talking about our latest, er, homicide.' Trevor Waring was a solidly built man of middle height, in his middle forties, with a middling loud voice; moderate in everything, was how Malone would have described him. He was a solicitor in Collamundra and Malone guessed that a country town lawyer could not afford excess in opinions or anything else. Especially in a district as conservative as this one. 'I noticed at dinner that you dodged, quite neatly, all the questions they tossed at you. I have to apologize for my kids. They don't get to meet detectives from Homicide.'

'I hope they don't meet any more. You said the *latest* murder. There've been others?'

'We've had three or four over the last fifteen or twenty years. The last one was about – what, Sean? – about five or six years ago. An Abo caught his wife and a shearer, up from Sydney, in bed together – he shot them, killed the shearer. They gave the Abo twelve years, I think it was, and took him to Bathurst Gaol. He committed suicide three months later, hung himself in his cell. They do that, you probably know that as well as I do. They can't understand white man's justice.'

'Are there any Aborigines linked with the Sagawa murder? You have some around here, I gather.'

There was no illumination out here on the side veranda other than the light coming through a window from the dining-room, where Lisa and Ida were now helping the housekeeper to clear the table. Even so, in the dim light, Malone saw the glance that passed between Waring and his father-in-law.

'I don't think we'd better say anything on that,' said Carmody after puffing on his pipe. 'There's been enough finger-pointing around here already.'

Malone was momentarily disappointed; he had expected more from Carmody in view of Baldock's description of him. The old man was in his late seventies, lean now but still showing traces of what once must have been a muscular back and shoulders, the heritage of his youth as a shearer. His hair was white but still thick and he had the sort of looks that age and an inner peace and dignity had made almost handsome. He had lived a life that Malone, learning of it from Lisa, envied; but he wore it comfortably, without flourish or advertisement. Despite his years abroad he still had an Australian accent, his own flag. Or perhaps, coming back to where he had grown up, he had heard an echo and recaptured it, a memorial voice.

'The police haven't pointed a finger at anyone. Not to me.'

Occasional confession to the public, though it did nothing for the soul, was good for a reaction.

'The police out here are a quiet lot.' Carmody puffed on his pipe again. 'But you've probably noticed that already?'

'You mean they don't like to make waves?'

Carmody laughed, a young man's sound. 'The last time we had a wave out here was about fifty million years ago. But yes, you're right. Maybe you should go out and see Chess Hardstaff. He rules the waves around here.'

'Chess Hardstaff? Not *the* Hardstaff?'

Carmody nodded. 'The King-maker himself. He owns Noongulli, it backs on to our property out there –' He nodded to the west, now lost in the darkness. 'The Hardstaffs were the first ones to settle here – after the Abos, of course. He runs the Rural Party, here in New South Wales and nationally. They call him The King to his face and he just nods and accepts it.'

'I'm surprised he's not Sir Chess,' said Malone.

'His old man was a knight, same name, and Chess wanted to go one better. He didn't want to be Sir Chester Hardstaff, Mark Two. He wanted a peerage, Lord Collamundra. He should've gone to Queensland when the Nats were in up there, they'd have given him one. But he'd have had to call himself Lord Surfers' Paradise.'

Carmody said all this without rancour; it was an old newspaperman speaking. He had left his life as a youthful shearer and drover, gone to Spain, fought in the civil war there on the Republican side, begun covering it as a stringer for a British provincial paper, moved on to being European correspondent for an American wire service, covered World War Two and several smaller wars since and finally retired twenty years ago when his wife died and he had come home to take over Sundown from his mother, who was in her last year. It had been a much smaller property then, but he had added to it, put his own and his dead wife's money into it, and now it was one of the showplaces of the district, producing some of the best merinos in the State. He was a successful grazier, running 12,000 head of sheep and 500 stud beef cattle, having achieved the dream of every old-time drover (though not that of his father Paddy, who would have remained a drover all his life if Sean's mother had not been the strong one in the family). He was all that, yet he was still, deep in his heart, one of the old-time newspapermen, the sort who brushed aside the quick beat-up, who would dig and dig, like ink-stained archaeologists, to the foundations of a story. Malone, recognizing him for what he was, decided he would take his time with Sean Carmody.

'Did you know Kenji Sagawa?'

'Not really. I've never been interested in cotton. My dad would never have anything to do with grain – wheat, barley, sorghum, stuff like that. He was strictly for the woollies. I'm much the same. They approached me, asked me if I wanted to go in with them on raising cotton and I said no. They never came back.'

'Who?'

'Sagawa and his bosses from Japan. Chess Hardstaff introduced them.'

'Is he involved with the cotton growing?'

'Not as far as I know. As I said, he just *rules*, that's all.'

'Did you know him, Trev?'

Waring took his time, taking a few more puffs on his pipe before tapping it out into an ashtray. He was like an actor with a prop; he didn't appear to be at all a natural pipe-smoker. If he thought it gave him an air of gravity, he was wrong; there was a certain restlessness about him, like a man who wasn't sure where the back of his seat was. Trevor Waring would never be laid back.

'He was unlike what I'd expected of a Japanese, I'd been told they liked to keep to themselves. He didn't. He joined Rotary and the golf club and he'd even had someone put his name up for the polo club, though he didn't know one end of a horse from another and it only meets half a dozen times a year.'

'So he was popular?'

'Well, no, not exactly. For instance he was rather keen on the ladies, but they fought shy of him. You know what women are like about Asians.'

'*Some* women,' said Carmody, defending the tolerant.

'Er, yes. Some women. He came to see me last week at my office. He said he'd got three anonymous letters.'

'From women?'
'I don't know about that. I didn't see them. They told him Japs weren't wanted around here. I told him I couldn't do anything, the best thing was to go to the police.'
'Did he?'
'I don't know. You'd better ask Inspector Narvo about that. He and Ken Sagawa were rather friendly at the start, I think it was Hugh Narvo who put him up for the golf club.'
'Friendly at the start? Did something happen between them?'
'I don't know.' Waring shrugged, did some awkward business with his pipe. 'They just didn't seem as – well, as close as they had been. Not over the last few weeks.'
'There's a second Japanese out at the farm, isn't there? What's he like?'
'Tom Koga? He's young, rather unsure of himself, I'd say. I should think this, the murder, I mean, would make him even more jumpy.'
Sean Carmody sat listening to this, his pipe gone out. Now he said, 'This isn't a *simple* murder. Am I right?'
'Most murders aren't,' said Malone. 'Even domestics, which make up more than half the murders committed, they're never as simple as they look. Sometimes you have to peel off the layers to find out why the murder happened – you hate doing it. You realize you're going to make a lot of people unhappy, the family usually, who are unhappy enough to begin with.'
Then Ida Waring came out on to the veranda. 'Time to take the kids home to bed, Trevor.'
She was in her early forties, two or three years older than Lisa. Her mother, Cathleen, had been half-Irish, half-Jewish, a featured player on the MGM lot in Hollywood in the 1930s. She had gone to Berlin looking for her Jewish mother, who had disappeared, and there, in the last month of peace in 1939, she had met Sean. Cathleen had been successful in her search and the two women had escaped to England, where she married Sean, who had managed to get out of Germany in October of that year. Sean had become a war correspondent and Cathleen had gone back to New York, where, instead of returning to Hollywood, she had gone on the stage and become a minor

Broadway star. Ida had been born in 1947 and she had been twenty-three, already married and divorced, when Cathleen died of cancer. Unhappy in New York, she had been glad to accompany Sean back to his homeland. She had her mother's beauty, most of her fire and all of her father's love of the land. It was difficult to guess what sort of love she had for her husband. All Malone felt was that it did not have the passion and depth that he and Lisa had for each other. But then married love, like politics, came in so many colours.

'We'll take all the kids in the Land-Rover. Lisa can ride back with Scobie. You'd like that, wouldn't you?' She gave Malone a half-mocking smile.

He smiled in return, liking her, but wondering if he would come to know her properly in the short time he would be here. He was all at once glad of the Carmody clan: they might prove to be the only friendly oasis in the Collamundra shire.

While Lisa was helping to put all the children into the Warings' Land-Rover, Malone waited by the Commodore for her. Sean Carmody came across to him, moving with the slow deliberation of a man who now told time by the seasons and no longer by deadlines or the clock.

'Take things slowly, Scobie.'

'Don't make waves, you mean?'

'No, I don't mean that at all. Certain things around here need to be changed and Mr Sagawa's murder may be the catalyst.'

'If things have needed to be changed, Sean, why haven't you tried it before?'

'Do you know anything about opera or musical comedy?'

It was a question that came out of nowhere; but Malone was used to them. He had faced too many high-priced barristers in court not to know how to be poker-faced. 'No, I think I'm what they call a Philistine, even my pop-mad kids do. I like old swing bands, Benny Goodman, Artie Shaw, all before my time.'

'Mozart was before *my* time.' Carmody smiled.

'The only thing that saves me, according to Lisa, is that my favourite singers are Peggy Lee and Cleo Laine. Lisa's an opera fan, but she likes them, too.'

'Benny Goodman and Artie Shaw used to be favourites of

mine when I went overseas before the war. *My* war, that is. There have been a dozen wars since then, but it's still the one I remember . . .' He stopped for a moment; then shook his head, as if he did not want to remember after all. 'In Vienna and Berlin I started going to the opera – I heard Gigli and Schmidt and Flagstadt.' He paused again, nodded. 'Just names now – and echoes. Anyhow, there's an operetta called *Die Fledermaus*, by Johann Strauss, the younger. It's lightweight, but its theme song is "Happy is He who Forgets what Cannot Be Changed." You want me to sing it?'

'No, I get the message.'

'No, Scobie, you get only half the message. It was *my* theme song for quite a while after I came home. But lately . . . If I can help, come out again. Any time.'

Driving back to the Warings' house Lisa said, 'I'm glad you're here. I missed you.'

He leaned across and kissed her, almost hitting a tree stump as he took his eyes off the winding track. 'I've missed you, too. I didn't realize how big a queen-sized bed is till you're in it alone.'

'Just as well we didn't get a king-sized one. You haven't invited anyone home to fill up the space, have you?'

'Just three girls from the Rape Advisory Squad. How are the kids making out? You'd better keep an eye on Tom. He could hurt himself falling off horses.'

'Don't be so protective. They're all right. Claire's fallen in love with Tas.'

'She's only fourteen, for God's sake! Tell her to get that out of her head!'

'You tell her. You'll be more diplomatic and sympathetic than I would. Relax, darling. She's going to fall in and out of love ten times a year from now till she's twenty-one. I know I did.'

'I never did ask you. How old were you when you lost your virginity?'

'It's none of your business. And don't you ever ask Claire a question like that. That's *my* business.' They were out on the tarmac of the main road now, running smoothly; she leaned back against the door of the car and looked at him. 'How's the investigation going?'

'We haven't really started yet, but it's already beginning to look murky.' He noticed in the driving mirror that another car was behind them, but he gave it only a cursory look. A semi-trailer hurtled towards them, front ablaze with rows of small lights, so that it looked like the entrance to a travelling strip show. It went by with a roar, the wind of its passing rocking the Commodore. 'Bastard!'

'How long do you think you'll be out here?'

'Your guess is as good as mine. A coupla days, maybe more. Depends on what Russ and I dig up.'

'What's Russ doing this evening?'

'I don't know. I wouldn't be surprised if he's investigating Narelle.'

'Who's Narelle?'

'She owns the pub where we're staying. A very attractive widow.'

'Does she have a queen-sized bed?'

'I wouldn't be surprised. I'll ask her.'

'Never mind. I'll ask Russ.'

'Mind your own business. This where we turn in?'

They drove up another long track, this one straight and lined on either side by what looked, in the darkness, like poplars. He pulled up in front of another large one-storeyed house, but this one more modern than the main Sundown homestead. The lights were on in the house and the Land-Rover had been taken round to a garage at the back. Off to one side the wire netting surrounding a tennis court looked like a huge wall of spider's web. Malone wound down the car window and listened to the silence.

'It's so peaceful,' said Lisa.

He said nothing, thinking of Sagawa lying dead in the silence.

But Lisa could shut out the world from herself and him. 'Every time I'm away from you for even a night, I realize how much I love you. It's not so bad when I'm home in our own bed, I can feel you there beside me even when you're not. I've even had an orgasm in my sleep.'

'Sorry I wasn't there.'

'But in a strange bed, it's so *empty* . . .' The Commodore had bucket seats; detectives were not encouraged to embrace each other, even those of the opposite sex. But the Malones managed to reach for each other and their kiss was as passionate as if they were back in Randwick in their own bed. At last she drew away from him, taking his hands off her. 'That's enough. I don't want to have to call up one of your girls from the Rape Advisory Squad. Will you be out tomorrow night?'

'I'll try. I'd like some time with the kids. Keep an eye on Claire and Tas.'

'You want to leave your Smith and Wesson with me?'

He loved her for her sense of humour; it kept him anchored. They kissed again, then she got out of the car and he drove off down between the poplars. He went through the main gate, closing it after him, and turned on to the main road leading towards town. He had the feeling of leaving a harbour: town was where the wild waves broke. Or would, if he and Clements stirred them up.

He had gone perhaps a mile before he realized there was another car behind him, not attempting to overtake him but keeping a steady distance between them. He frowned, wondering where it had come from, certain that it had not come out of another gate along the road. He slowed down, but the car behind also slowed; the distance between them remained constant. Then he speeded up again, but this time the following car dropped back, though it continued to trail him.

He was not afraid, just curious. He went into town, slowed as he came to the main street. He looked in the driving mirror, saw the other car slow, then make a quick turn into a side street. He caught a glimpse of it, a light-coloured big car, a Mercedes or the largest Ford, before it disappeared.

He parked the Commodore, locked it and set the alarm and went into the Mail Coach Hotel. The bars were still open and full, but he wasn't looking for company; he just wanted to go to bed and dream of Lisa and the kids. But first to lie awake and wonder why anyone should drive all the way out of town and sit in their car and wait for him to return to town, as if they wanted to account for every minute of his movements. That was the sort of surveillance that, usually, only police or private investigators went in for.

TWO

1

'You must've got in pretty late last night,' he said to Clements over a country breakfast of sausages and eggs and bacon, toast, honey and coffee. 'Did you learn anything?'

'A few things. Nothing to do with the case, though.'

Malone refrained from asking if what he had learned had come from Mrs Potter. 'Well, we'll get down to work this morning. We'll go out to the gin. Get what background you can out of the workers, those in the fields as well as the gin.' He looked up as the waitress came to offer them more coffee. 'We'll be in for lunch, say one o'clock. Can you keep us this table?'

'I'm afraid it's taken for lunch.' She was a stout cheerful woman who liked her job; she gave better service than many of the more highly trained waiters and waitresses Malone had met in Sydney. 'Gus Dircks is in town. He's the Police Minister, but then you'd know that, wouldn't you?'

'We'd heard a rumour.'

She laughed, her bosom shaking like a water-bed in an earth tremor. 'Yeah, you would of. Anyhow, when he's in town he comes in here every day for lunch. He sorta holds court here by the window, if you know what I mean. You gotta vote for him.'

'Why's that?'

'Well, there's no one else, is there? Not even the sheep would vote for Labour, around here. You're not Labour, are you?'

'He's a Commo,' said Clements.

The waitress looked doubtful. 'Well, I wouldn't broadcast that around here. You oughta get someone to tell you what they done to the Commos in this town back in the nineteen-thirties.'

She looked at them, suddenly dark and secretive. 'But don't say I suggested it.'

Later, driving out to the South Cloud cotton farm in the Commodore, Malone said, 'I'm beginning to think this district has got more secrets than it's got sheep droppings.'

'You mean about the Commos? Narelle was hinting at a few things last night. Not about the Commos, she never mentioned them, but just gossip. I gather there was quite a lot of it when her hubby was killed.'

'It was a shooting accident, wasn't it?'

'Yeah. She hinted people said other things about how it happened, but it's all died down now. Then she suddenly shut up. I'd picked the wrong time to pump her. We – well, never mind.'

Malone could guess what would have been the wrong time; Clements had probably been intent on pumping of another kind. Sensible, experienced women don't let their hair down, not figuratively, the first time they go to bed with a stranger; and Narelle Potter was a sensible, experienced woman if ever Malone had seen one. 'Don't get yourself too involved. This is your commanding officer speaking.'

Clements grinned. 'You sound just like my mother.'

They bumped over the cattle grid at the entrance gates to the cotton farm and Clements pulled up. Four cotton-picking machines were moving slowly down the rows, plucking the cotton locks from the bolls and dumping them into a large basket attached to each machine. As soon as a basket was filled, the picker moved along to a second machine – 'That's a module maker,' said Clements – where the cotton was compressed. When sufficient baskets of cotton had been deposited in the module maker, a module was completed.

'I read up on it last night while I was waiting for dinner,' said Clements; and Malone knew that, with his usual thoroughness, he would have absorbed all the information available to him. 'Those modules are approximately thirty-six feet by eight by eight – there's about eleven tonnes of seed cotton in each one. If one of 'em fell on you, you'd be schnitzel.'

Malone grimaced at the description.

'Those loaders you see, they call 'em module movers, load them on to those semi-trailers, who take 'em up to the gin, where they're off-loaded by what they call a moon buggy.'

'How long does the cotton harvest go on?'

'I don't know when they expect to finish here. It usually begins late March and goes till the end of June.'

'This is one harvest they won't forget.'

Sergeant Baldock and Constable Mungle were waiting for them at the cotton farm's main office. The weather was still reasonably warm and Baldock had discarded his jacket. In his tattersall-checked shirt, wool tie, moleskin trousers and R. M. Williams boots, he looked more like a man of the land than a detective. As Malone and Clements drew in alongside him, he put on a broad-brimmed, pork-pie hat, completing the picture in Malone's mind of a farmer on his way to market, more interested in crops than in crime.

'Here comes Mr Koga, the assistant manager,' Baldock said.

A young man, slim and taller than Malone had expected of a Japanese, came out of the office and approached them almost diffidently. He had a thin, good-looking face, a shy smile and wore fashionable and expensive tinted glasses.

'Some senior executives are coming down from Japan at once.' He had a thin piping voice, made thinner by his nervousness. He had come to this country, which he had been told was xenophobic, at least towards Asians, and after only a month he was temporarily in charge, only because his immediate boss had been murdered. Xenophobia could not be more explicitly expressed than that. 'I don't suppose you can wait till then?'

'Hardly,' said Malone as kindly as he could. He had never been infected by racism, though his father Con had done his best to tutor him in it, and he was determined to lean over backwards to avoid it in this particular case. 'Who discovered the body, Mr Koga?'

'Barry Liss.' Koga had difficulty with the name. 'He is over at the gin now. We shall go over there, yes?'

'Sergeant Clements would like to talk to the men out in the fields. Could you take him out there, Constable Mungle?'

Clements looked out at the white-frothed fields stretching into the distance, said, 'Thanks, Inspector,' then he and Mungle got back into the Commodore. The Aboriginal cop, in fawn shirt and slacks and broad-brimmed hat, looked like a Boy Scout against the bulk of Clements.

Malone followed Koga and Baldock over to the gin, aware as they drew closer of the faint thunder within the huge shed.

'He's probably inside,' said Koga and opened a door that immediately let out a blast of noise. They went inside and Malone knew at once that there would be no questioning in here.

The thunder in the hundred-feet-high shed was deafening; maybe a rock musician would have felt at home in it, but Malone doubted it. He was not mechanically-minded and he could only guess at the functions of most of the machines, which he noted were all American-made, not Japanese as he had expected. The seed cotton seemed to move swiftly through a continuous cleaning process, streaming through from one type of machine to another. He stood in front of one which Koga, screaming in his ear like a train whistle, told him was a condenser. Behind large windows in the condenser he saw the flow of now-cleaned cotton, like thick white water out of a dam spill. Behind him a supervisor stood at a console, watching monitor screens; Malone looked around and could see only three other workers, a man and two girls, in the whole building. All four workers wore ear-muffs and seemed oblivious of Koga and his guests. It struck Malone that if Kenji Sagawa had been killed in this shed during working hours no one would have heard the shot.

Koga and the two detectives moved on, past blocks of solidly packed cotton coming up a ramp to be baled; the two girls were working the baling machine, unhurriedly and with time for one of them occasionally to glance at an open paperback book on a bench beside her. The man, Barry Liss, was marking the weight of each bale as it bumped down on to an electronic scale. He looked up as Koga tapped him on the shoulder and nodded towards the exit door. He handed his clipboard to one of the girls and followed the three men out of the shed, slipping off his ear-muffs as he did so.

'I understand you found Mr Sagawa's body,' said Malone when he had been introduced to Liss.

'Jesus, did I!' Liss shuddered. He was a wiry man, his age hard to guess; he could have been anywhere between his late twenties and his early forties. He had black hair cut very short, a bony face that had earned more than its fair share of lines, and a loose-jointed way of standing as if his limbs had been borrowed from someone else's torso and had not yet adjusted to their new base. 'It was the bloodiest mess I ever seen. I don't wanna see anything like it again. But I told you all this, Curly.'

'I know you did, Barry. But Inspector Malone is in charge now.'

Malone looked at Baldock out of the corner of his eye, but the local detective did not appear to imply anything more than what he had simply said. Malone looked back at Liss. 'Where did you find him, Mr Liss?'

'Over here. He was packed in one of the modules that had been brought in and he finished up against the spiked cylinders in the module feeder. It made a real mess, all that blood. Ruined that particular load.'

'I'm sure it did,' said Malone, who wasn't into cotton futures.

Liss led the way over to the huge machine that was inching its way along a length of track, eating its way into the long, high compacted cotton that stood, like a long block of grey ice at the open end of this annexe to the gin shed. A long loader was backing up to the bulked cotton, adding more to the supply.

'These moon buggies bring the cotton in,' said Liss. 'Maybe Mr Sagawa's body was in one of the loads, I dunno. I only found him when his body jammed the cylinders.'

'Was the module stack as long and as high as this the night before you found the body?'

'No, it wouldn't of been more than, I dunno, four or five metres.'

'So the body could have been brought in in one of those trailers from out in the fields?'

Liss looked at him, shrewdness increasing the lines on his face. 'You don't miss much, do you?'

'We try not to. How long was the stack when you started up this machine Tuesday morning?'

The lines didn't smooth out. 'Bugger! I didn't think of that.' He looked at Baldock. 'Sorry, Curly.'

'It's okay,' said Baldock, but looked as if he had asked the question, and not Malone.

Malone said, 'What was your first reaction when you found the body?'

Liss shook his head, shuddered again. He looked tough, as if he might have seen a lot of blood spilled in pub brawls, but obviously he had never seen anyone as mangled as Sagawa must have been. 'I thought it was some sorta incredible bloody accident – how the hell did he get in there? Then that night, the night before last, they told me the Doc had said he was murdered. Shot. If they'd shot him, why let him be chewed up like that? If they knew anything about the works here, they'd have knew his body was never gunna go right through the system and be chopped up like the green bolls and the hulls and that.'

Malone's smile had no humour in it. 'That's pretty graphic.'

'Eh? Oh yeah, I guess it is. I just think it's a bloody gruesome way to get rid of someone, that's all. There was nothing wrong with him, he was a good bloke. He expected you to work hard, but you wouldn't hold that against him. Most of us work hard out here in the bush, right, Curly?'

'Right,' said Baldock; then saved the face of the city bludger. 'But down in Sydney the police are flat out all the time. Right, Scobie?'

'All the time,' said Malone.

'Well, I guess you would be,' said Liss. 'From what I read, half the population of Sydney are crims, right?'

'Almost.' Malone wasn't going to get into a city-versus-country match. 'Well, thanks, Mr Liss. We'll be back to you if we have any more questions.'

'Be glad to help. Hooroo, Curly. Give my regards to the missus.'

Liss went back into the gin, adjusting his ear-muffs as he opened the door and the noise blasted out at him.

'He's all right?' said Malone.

Baldock looked surprised. 'You mean is he a suspect? Forget

him. He's a tough little bugger, but he'd never do anything like this.'

'Who's the government medical officer? He got a mention in the running sheet.'

'Max Nothling. He's got the biggest practice in town, but he doubles as GMO. He's Chess Hardstaff's son-in-law. He told us he'd had Sagawa's body on the table in the hospital mortuary for an hour before he woke up there was a bullet in him, that it was the bullet in his heart that'd killed him, not the chewing-up by the spikes in the module feeder.'

'I'd better have a talk with him.' Malone looked at the huge module feeder slowly, inexorably eating its way into the slab-sided glacier of cotton. He did not like coming on a trail as cold as this; he preferred the crime scene to be left as undisturbed as possible. 'Did your Physical Evidence Section get everything before you let them start up the gin again?'

'We got the lot, photos, everything. They sent a Fingerprints cove over from District Headquarters. Their reports are on my desk back at the station, they came in just before I left.'

'You said there was no sign of the cartridge.'

'The Ballistics guy went through the office, all around here, right through the gin, he went through the lot with a fine-tooth comb. He found nothing.'

'Who was he?'

'Constable James. Jason James.'

'There's only one man better than him at his job and that's his boss. Who, incidentally, is three-parts Abo.'

Baldock didn't react, except to say, 'It's a changing world, ain't it?'

Not out here, thought Malone.

They walked away from the gin shed towards the office a couple of hundred yards away. It was a silver-bright morning with patches of high cloud dry-brushed against the blue; one felt one could rub the air through one's fingers like a fine fabric. A moon buggy rumbled by with another load of cotton, raising a low, thin mist of dust. Life and work goes on, Malone thought: profits must be made, only losses of life are affordable. Crumbs, he further thought, I'm thinking like a Commo: I wonder what they would have done to me in this town fifty years ago?

'You got any suspects?'

They had reached the police vehicles and Baldock leaned against his car. 'None. Or a dozen. Take your pick. It'll be like trying to find a particular cotton boll in one of those modules.'

'Any Jap-haters in the district?'

Baldock hesitated, then nodded. 'Yeah, but I think they're a bit too obvious to go in for murder. There's Ray Chakiros. He's president of the local Veterans Legion.'

The Veterans Legion all over the nation harboured a minority of ex-servicemen who were still consumed by a hatred of old enemies; they got more media space than they deserved and so were continually vocal. Moderation and a call to let bygones be bygones don't make arresting headlines or good sound bites.

'Chakiros?'

'He's Lebanese, but he was born here in Collamundra. His old man used to run the local café back in the days when we had only one. Now we've got coffee lounges, a McDonald's, a Pizza Hut, a French restaurant, a Chinese one. Ray Chakiros owns the McDonald's and one of the coffee lounges and he's got the local Mercedes franchise. He's got fingers in other pies, too – you know what the Wogs are like.'

Baldock wasn't embarrassed by his prejudices; he was one of many for whom they are as natural as dandruff.

'What's he like?' said Malone, wondering about Chakiros's prejudices.

'He runs off at the mouth about Japs or any sorta Asians, but I don't think he'd pull a gun on any of 'em. He's all piss and wind. He served in World War Two in New Guinea, but they tell me he never saw a Jap till the war was over. I've interviewed him, but I think he's in the clear.'

'Anyone else?'

Again Baldock took his time before answering. 'There's an Abo kid they had working here, but Sagawa sacked him last month. Wally Mungle knew him, they're cousins. Then maybe there are half a dozen others, but we've got nothing on any of 'em.'

'Where do we start then?'

Baldock shrugged. 'Start at the bottom and work up.'

'Who's at the bottom?' But Malone could guess.

'The Abo, of course.' Baldock said it without malice or prejudice. It struck Malone that the local sergeant was not a racist and he was pleased and relieved. Baldock might have his prejudices about Wogs, but that had nothing to do with race. Malone did wonder if there were any European Jews, refugees, in Collamundra and how they were treated by Baldock and the locals. He hoped there would be none of those on the suspect list.

'His name's Billy Koowarra,' said Baldock.

'Where can I find him?'

'At the lock-up. He was picked up last night as an IP.' Intoxicated Person: the all-purpose round-up lariat.

Malone saw Clements and Mungle come out of the office, where they had been questioning the office staff. He said delicately, a tone it had taken him a long time to acquire, 'Curly – d'you mind if I ride back with Wally? You go with Russ.'

Baldock squinted, not against the sun. 'Are you gunna go behind my back?'

'No, I promise you there'll be none of that. But you've had some trouble with the blacks out here, haven't you? I read about it in a quarterly report.'

'That was six or eight months ago, when all the land rights song and dance was going on. All the towns with Abo settlements outside them had the same trouble. It's been quiet lately, though.'

'Well, I think Wally will talk more freely to me about his cousin Billy if you're not listening to him. Am I right?'

Baldock nodded reluctantly. 'I guess so. He's a good bloke, Wally. It hasn't been easy for him, being a cop.'

'It's not that easy for us, is it?'

Baldock grinned. 'I must tell him that some day.'

Then Clements and Mungle arrived. At the same time Koga, who had gone back into the gin shed, came out and walked towards the policemen. He was wide of them, looking as if he wanted to avoid them; his step faltered a moment, then he went on, not looking at them, towards the office. The four policemen looked after him.

'How did he get on with Sagawa?'

'We don't know,' said Baldock. 'I asked Barry Liss about that, but he said he couldn't tell. He said the two of them were like most Japs, or what he thought most Japs were like. Terribly polite towards each other. I gather Koga never opened his mouth unless Sagawa asked him to.'

'Is he on your list?'

'He will be, if you want him there.'

'Put him on it.' Then Malone turned to Clements. 'Well, how'd you go?'

'Bugger-all. Nobody understands why it happened. None of the drivers saw anything unusual in any of their loads, not when they brought the loads in from the fields.'

Malone glanced at Baldock. 'Did the Physical Evidence boys find any blood on any of the trucks or buggies?'

'None.'

'What time do they start work here?'

'The pickers start at seven in the morning,' said Mungle in his quiet voice; it was difficult to tell whether he was shy or stand-offish. 'The gin starts up at seven thirty. If the feeder was stopped at eight fifteen or thereabouts, that means the body must of been in the first or second load brought in the day before the murder. No one can remember who would have been driving that particular buggy.'

'Our only guess,' said Clements, 'is that he was shot during the night and the killer scooped out a module, put the body in and re-packed the cotton again. They tell us that would be difficult but not impossible.'

'He could have been brought in by the murderer in a buggy,' said Malone. 'Wally, would you ask Koga to step out here again?'

Mungle went across to the office and while he was gone Malone looked about him, faking bemusement. Baldock said, 'What are you looking for?'

'Media hacks. Down in Sydney they'd be around us like flies around a garbage tip. Don't you have any out here?'

'There's the local paper and the radio station. They were out here Tuesday morning, getting in our way, as usual. They'll be making a nuisance of themselves again, soon's they hear you're taking over.'

'I thought they'd have heard that anyway,' Malone said drily. 'I don't want to see 'em, Curly. This is your turf, you handle them. You're the police spokesman, okay?'

Then Koga, diffident as before, came back with Wally Mungle. 'You wanted me, Inspector?' The thin, high voice broke, and he coughed. 'Excuse me.'

'What sort of security do you have out here, Mr Koga?'

'None, Inspector. Mr Sagawa and I live – lived over there in the manager's house.' He pointed to a farmhouse, a relic of whatever the farm had once been, a couple of hundred yards away. 'We were our own security. It was good enough, Mr Sagawa thought . . .'

But not good enough, Malone thought. 'Where were you Monday night?'

The question seemed to startle Koga; he took off his glasses, as if they had suddenly fogged up; he looked remarkably young without them. 'I – I went into town to the movies.'

'What did you see?' Malone's voice was almost too casual.

Koga wiped his glasses, put them back on. 'It was called *Sea of Love*. With Al Pacino.'

Malone looked at Baldock and Mungle. 'I saw that down in Sydney at Christmas.'

'It's already been on out here,' said Mungle. 'They brought it back – by popular demand, they said. I think the locals were hoping the cop would be bumped off the second time around.'

Malone looked at Clements. 'I thought you said this was a conservative district?' Then he turned back to Koga, who had listened to all this without really understanding the cops' sardonic acceptance of the public's attitude towards them. 'Was Mr Sagawa at the house when you got back from town?'

Koga shook his head. 'No, he did not come home at all that night.'

'Did that worry you?'

'Not really. Mr Sagawa liked to –' he looked at Baldock; then went on, '– he liked to gamble.'

Malone raised an eyebrow at Baldock, who said, 'Ray Chakiros runs a small baccarat school out at the showgrounds a coupla nights a week, Mondays and Thursdays. We turn a blind eye to it. It never causes us any trouble.'

Malone wondered how much money had to change hands for no trouble to be caused; but that wasn't his worry. 'All right, Mr Koga, that'll do. Thanks for your time.'

Koga bowed his head and Malone had to catch himself before he did the same; he did not want to be thought to be mocking the young Japanese. Koga went back to the office and Malone turned to the others. 'Righto, let's go back to town. Russ, you take Curly. Wally can ride with me.'

Clements was not the world's best actor, but he could put on an admirable poker face. Wally Mungle's own dark face was just as expressionless. He got in beside Malone and said nothing till they had driven out past the fields and on to the main road into town. As they did so, Malone noticed that all the cotton pickers, the trucks and the buggies had stopped and their drivers were staring after the two departing police cars. He looked back and saw that Koga had come out on to the veranda of the office and was gazing after them. He wondered how far the young man, with his thick glasses, could see.

Mungle said, 'Are you gunna ask me some questions you didn't want Sergeant Baldock to hear? I don't go behind his back, Inspector.'

'I'm glad to hear it. No, Sergeant Baldock knows what I'm going to ask you. It's about your cousin Billy Koowarra.'

'Yeah, I thought it might be.' Mungle nodded. He had taken off his hat and a long black curl dangled on his forehead like a bell-cord. He was a good-looking man, his features not as broad as those of a full-blood; his nose was straight and fine, and Malone wondered what white man had dipped his wick in tribal waters. He knew, from his experience in Sydney, that the mixed-bloods were the most difficult to deal with. They saw the world through mirrors, all of them cracked.

'How long have you been a cop, Wally?'

'Four years.'

'Any regrets?'

Mungle stared ahead of them down the long black strip of macadam, shining blue in parts as if pools of water covered it. A big semi-trailer came rushing at them and he waited till it had roared by. 'Sometimes.'

'They treat you all right at the station?'

'I'm the token Abo.' He smiled, as much to himself as to Malone. 'No, they're okay.'

There had been a recruiting campaign to have more Aborigines join the police force, but so far there had been a scarce response. Every time Malone saw a TV newsreel of police action in South Africa, he was amazed at the number of black Africans in uniform, many of them laying into their fellow blacks with as much enthusiasm as their white colleagues. That, he knew, would never happen here.

'What about amongst your family and the other blacks?'

'My mum's proud of me. I never knew my dad.' He offered no more information on his father and Malone didn't ask. 'The rest of the Kooris –' He shrugged. 'Depends whether they're sober or not. When they've had a skinful, some of 'em get real shitty towards me.'

'What sort of education did you have?'

'I got to Year Eleven. One time I dreamed of getting my HSC and going on to university.' He was a dinkum Aussie: he had said *haitch* for H. It was a characteristic that always brought a laugh from Lisa, the foreigner. 'We Kooris are supposed to live in the Dreamtime. Some of us have different dreams to others.'

Malone could think of nothing to say to that; so he said, 'What about your cousin Billy?'

'Is he a suspect?'

'I don't know. What about him?'

'He's a silly young bugger, but that's all I'm gunna say about him. We Kooris stick together, Inspector. Anyone will tell you that, especially the whites.'

Malone abruptly pulled the car into the side of the road, just opposite the grain silos on the edge of town. 'Wally, let's get one thing straight from the start. I've got my faults, but I'm not a racist. I don't care what yours or Billy's or anybody else's skin is like, I treat them with respect till something happens to make me change my mind. But whatever changes my mind, it has nothing to do with the colour of their skin. Now can you get that through your black skull?'

Wally Mungle, like most Aborigines Malone had known, had a sense of humour. He suddenly smiled his beautiful smile. 'Fair enough.'

Malone started up the car again. 'Before we see Billy, take me down to the black settlement. I don't want to talk to anyone, just look at the conditions there.'

'I don't live down there, y'know. My mother does, but I don't.'

'Where do you live?' Malone put the question delicately. Twice in fifteen minutes he had had to be delicate: it might lead to cramp in a tongue that, too often, had got him into trouble.

'I've got three acres over the other side of the river. I live there with my wife and two kids.'

'Is she black?'

Mungle looked sideways at him. 'Does it matter?'

They went round the war memorial; it seemed to Malone that the Anzac was ready to swivel on his pedestal, his bayonet at the ready. They drove down the main street, which was full now with cars and trucks parked at an angle to the kerb. It seemed to Malone, imagination working overtime, that people coming out of the stores stopped to stare at him and Wally Mungle. In the shade of the stores' awnings men and women stood motionless, heads turned in the unmarked police car's direction, ears strained for Malone's answer.

They had reached the far end of the main street before Malone said, 'No, it doesn't matter if she's black. But I'm a stranger here, it's a whole new turf to me, and people around here don't look at things the way I'm used to. I've learned that just since I got in last night.'

'Fair enough. Yeah, Ruby's black. She's a mixed-blood, like me. We would of been called half-castes in the old days, but that's out now. Ruby's what the Yanks call a quadroon, or used to. She's got more white blood than me, it shows.'

'She got white relatives around here?'

A slight hesitation, then a nod: 'Yeah, but they'd never admit to it. She doesn't press it, she's quite happy with things the way they are. By the time our kids grow up, things will have changed – we hope. They'll be white enough to be accepted.'

'What are they, how old?'

'A boy, six, and a girl, three. Nobody would know they're Kooris, they could pass for Wogs.'

'Is that what you want for them when they grow up, to pass for Wogs?'

'No.' He said it quietly, but his voice was emphatic. 'I want 'em to be Kooris. I just don't want 'em discriminated against because of the colour of their skin. I've had enough of that. You got any kids?'

'Yes. Pure white, all three of them. The only discrimination against them is that their father is a cop.'

'My kids have got that, too.' But he smiled his beautiful smile again. 'Okay, turn off here.'

They were just beyond the edge of town, coming to a two-lane bridge over the river, the Noongulli. Malone turned off on to a red-dirt track that led parallel to the river and soon came to the Aboriginal settlement. At first glance the location was idyllic. There was a wide bend in the river and a small beach of flood-washed sand on the far side of the grey-green stretch of slow-moving water. Red river-gums, their trunks blotched like an old man's skin, hung over the river as if looking for fish to jump to the bait of their leaves. Shade dappled the ground under a stand of yellowbox and on the far side of the river Malone could see the white rails of the racecourse seeming, at this distance, to hover above the ground like a giant magic hoop that had become fixed without any visible support. A white heron, looking in the reflected sunlight from the river almost as insubstantial as if it were made of no more than its own powder-down, creaked in slow motion up towards the bridge. Then Malone saw the reality.

The settlement, standing back about fifty yards from the river bank, was a collection of tin shacks flung together without any pattern, as if the shacks had been built where the corrugated iron for the walls and the roofs had fallen off a truck driven by a drunk. Four abandoned cars, stripped of their engines, wheels gone, lay like dead shrunken hippos between a patch of scrub and the shacks. The cars' seats rested in a neat row under two yellowbox trees, seats in a park that had been neglected and forgotten. Two drunken Aborigines lay asleep on two of the seats, just as Malone had seen other, white drunks in inner city parks in Sydney. The track through the settlement was a rutted, dried-out morass of mud in which half a dozen raggedy-dressed children played as he had seen his own children play in the sand on Coogee beach. The shacks themselves, some of them supporting lean-tos roofed over with torn tarpaulins, looked ready to be condemned. The part of the settlement's population that Malone could see, perhaps thirty or forty men and women of all ages, did not appear to have anything to occupy them. They sat or lolled on shaky-looking chairs, against tree-bolls or on the ground, just waiting – for what? he wondered. Wine flagons were being passed around, unhurriedly, without comment, every drinker waiting patiently for his or her swig. None of the boisterousness of white beer-swillers here: these blacks were prepared to take their time in getting drunk. And maybe *that's* what they're waiting for, he thought: to get drunk, to have the mind, too, turn black. He couldn't blame them and never had. It was just a pity they could make such a bloody nuisance of themselves. But that was the cop in him, thinking a policeman's thoughts.

'Well, that's it,' said Wally Mungle, making no attempt to get out of the car; silently advising Malone not to do so. 'Dreamtime on the Noongulli.'

'How did you get out of it?'

'Because I *wanted* to.'

'What about the others?' He tried to sound uncritical, but it was an effort.

Mungle didn't appear to resent the implied criticism. 'Most of 'em are full-bloods. I think they've given up the fight. This district has always had a pretty bloody attitude towards us Kooris. It's hardly changed in a hundred and fifty years, ever since Chess Hardstaff's great-grandfather came out here and started Noongulli Station. There was a massacre here, right where we're sitting, in eighteen fifty-one – a dozen Koori men and half a dozen women were shot and killed. There was a trial, but nobody went to gaol for it. The shire council showed a lot of sensitivity when they nominated this spot for the settlement – they thought they were doing us a favour, giving us a river view. It was put up twenty years ago when there was a conservative government in and when Labour got in, they did nothing about moving it from here. Now we've got a conservative coalition again and there's been promises about improvements, but so far there's been bugger-all.'

'Does everyone here live on the dole?'

'Practically everyone. In the old days, when I was a kid, some of the men got work at shearing time, but now the shearing teams come in from outside and none of the local graziers want to have anything to do with the Kooris.'

'What about Sean Carmody out at Sundown?'

'Well, yeah, him and his grandson take on a few. But they're looked on as radicals. His son-in-law, Trevor Waring, who lives next door, doesn't take on any.'

'What about out at the cotton farm? Billy worked there.'

'He was the only one. Practically all the work there is mechanized – these guys here ain't trained for anything like that. Billy was just a sorta roustabout out there. The token Abo for the Japs.'

'Why was he sacked?'

Mungle said nothing for a long moment; then decided to be a cop and not just a Koori: 'Billy likes the grog a bit too much. If he had a hangover, he wasn't always on time for work. Sagawa didn't like that, so he fired Billy. I don't blame him.'

'Does Billy blame him?'

'You better ask him that. You seen enough out here?'

Malone looked out at the depressing scene once more. The three or four circles of drinkers, aware all at once that their kin, Wally Mungle, was in the car with the stranger, had stopped passing the wine flagons and had all turned their heads to look at the two cops in the Commodore. Their faces were expressionless, mahogany masks. Sitting in their shapeless clothes in the dirt, surrounded by squalor, they still suggested a certain dignity by their very stillness.

'Christ!'

'I don't think He wants to help,' said Wally Mungle. 'The

God-botherers pray for us Kooris every Sunday, but it goes right over the heads of their congregations. I think Jesus Christ has given up, too.'

'Are you religious?' Malone remembered it had been bush missionaries who had first brought education to the Aborigines.

'I used to be. Not any more, though.'

Malone started up the car, swung it round and drove back along the river and up on to the main road. He and Mungle said nothing more to each other till Malone pulled the car into the yard behind the police station.

'Do you want to come in with me while I question Billy?'

Mungle hesitated, then shrugged. 'I better. I can't go on dodging the poor bugger.'

Malone wondered how many other Kooris he had dodged in the past. It struck him that, even in his mind, he had used the word Koori, the blacks' own name for themselves.

The lock-up cells were clean and comfortable, but that was all that could be said of them. There was an old-fashioned lavatory bucket in one corner, two narrow beds and that was it. These were for one-night or two-night prisoners; they weren't meant as home-from-home for long-term inmates. Malone had been told that remand prisoners were taken over to Cawndilla, the District headquarters town. There was a steel door to the cell, with a small barred opening in it; a small window high in the outer wall also had bars on it. Malone guessed that dangerous crims would not be locked up here, but would be taken immediately to District. Five minutes with Billy Koowarra told Malone that the boy was not dangerous.

He was nineteen, stringily built, with long curly hair and a sullen face that at certain angles made him look no more than a schoolboy who had just entered high school, one that he hated. He nodded when Mungle introduced Malone and stood leaning flat against the wall, like someone waiting to be shot.

'This the first time you've been locked up, Billy?'

The boy looked at Mungle, who gave him no help; then he looked back at Malone. 'Nah. I been in here, I dunno, two or three times.'

'Drunk each time?'

'That's what they said.'

Malone decided to hit the boy over the head, shake him out of his sullenness. 'Billy, what do you know about Mr Sagawa being murdered?'

The boy's eyes opened wide in sudden fright, as if he had just realized why this stranger from the city was in here to question him. He looked at Mungle, then leaned away from the wall as if he were about to run; but he had nowhere to run to. 'Jesus, Wally, what the fuck is this? Why'd you bring him in here, let him ask me something like that?'

'Take it easy, Billy. If you dunno anything about Mr Sagawa's death, just say so. Inspector Malone isn't accusing you of anything.'

'I wanna get outa here!' Koowarra looked around him in panic. 'Shit, all they locked me up for was being drunk! I ain't done nothing!'

'We're not saying you have,' said Malone. 'When did you last see Mr Sagawa?'

Koowarra had begun to shuffle along the wall, his back still to it. 'This fucking place is getting me down, Wally! Get me outa here!'

'I can't do that, Billy, not till Inspector Narvo comes back. This is the fifth time you've been in here, not the second or third. You'll probably have to stay here another night, I dunno. But that's the worst that's gunna happen to you. Now why don't you tell us? When did you last see Mr Sagawa?'

Koowarra had stopped shuffling, was flattened against the wall again. He looked from one detective to the other, then he said, 'Monday. I went out to see him, I dunno, about seven o'clock. I was gunna apologize and ask for my job back.'

Malone had not expected such a direct answer, but he knew that often a prisoner being questioned told the truth, or what sounded like the truth, in the hope of a favourable reaction from his questioner. Out of the corner of his eye he saw Wally Mungle frown as if he, too, hadn't expected such a frank answer.

'That was all you had in mind, Billy? Just to apologize and ask for your job back?'

The boy suddenly seemed to realize that he might have been

too honest; his face abruptly got older, seemed to become wooden and darker. 'What else would I wanna see him for?'

Malone shrugged, careful not to press too hard. 'I don't know, Billy. What did he say when you apologized?'

'I didn't see him. When I got out there –'

'How did you get out there?'

'I walked. I don't own no wheels. I tried to thumb a lift, but nobody around here gives a Koori a lift, not after dark. Right, Wally?'

'Right.' Mungle sounded even quieter than usual.

'Why didn't you get to see Mr Sagawa? Wasn't he in his office or anywhere around the gin?'

'I think he was in his office. His car, he's got a blue Toyota Cressida, was parked outside.'

Malone looked at Mungle. 'Was the car still there the next morning, when they found his body?'

Mungle nodded. 'It was still there. The car keys were in the ignition.'

'Any prints on the car?'

'The Crime Scene fellers didn't find any. Not even Sagawa's.'

'Didn't you find that queer? The owner's print nowhere on his own car? You didn't mention that in the running sheet.'

Mungle worked his mouth in embarrassment. 'I forgot, Inspector. I thought it was queer at the time, but I didn't make a note of it. Sorry.'

Malone wasn't going to tick him off any further, not in front of a prisoner, even if the latter was his cousin. He looked back at Billy Koowarra. 'Why didn't you go in to see Mr Sagawa?'

'There was someone with him, I think. I waited about twenty minutes, but nobody came out. So I started walking back to town.'

'What time was this?'

'I dunno, about seven thirty, I guess. Mebbe eight o'clock, I dunno. I don't own a watch.'

'Was there another car there?'

'Yeah, a fawn Merc.'

'You recognize whose it was?'

The boy shook his head. 'I didn't get close. I stayed, I dunno, about a hundred yards away, by the kurrajong tree near the inside gate as you come up from the road.'

'How many Mercedes in the district?' Malone asked Mungle.

'Half a dozen, I guess. Ask Billy, he's the car man.'

For a moment there was a spark of – something: a dream, a hope? – in the boy's dark eyes. 'Yeah, I can't wait till I get a car of me own –' *We Kooris are supposed to live in the Dreamtime. Some of us have different dreams to others.* 'There are seven Mercs around here. Not all the same model, though.'

'Did the car pass you when you were walking back to town?'

Koowarra spread his hands, almost an Italian gesture. 'I dunno. There was half a dozen cars passed me, maybe more, and a coupla semi-trailers. One of the cars was a Merc, but I dunno whether it was the one out at the gin.'

'You didn't hear any row going on in the office?'

'No, I was too far away. I told you,' he added petulantly. He was edgy again, pressing himself back against the wall. Somewhere in another cell a man's voice, a little slurred, had begun to sing: *Like a rhinestone cowboy . . .*

Malone looked enquiringly at Mungle, who said, 'Another cousin. He knows all the country-and-western ballads.'

Malone wanted to ask why the other cousin had to borrow his sad songs from another culture; but didn't. Instead, he said, 'Righto, that'll do for now, Billy. When you're released, don't leave town. We'll need you as a witness.'

'Shit, where'm I gunna go? I'm stuck here, like everyone else.' He banged the back of his head against the wall, then leaned towards Mungle, grabbing the front of the latter's shirt. 'Get me outa here, for Chrissake! I can't stand being locked up no more!'

Mungle gently pulled the boy's hand away, said quietly, 'Billy, there's nothing to be afraid of. Nobody's gunna do anything to you.'

'What about him?' Koowarra jerked his head at Malone.

'Inspector Malone's not charging you with anything. You'll just be needed as a witness, that's all.'

'I'm still gunna be locked up!'

'Only till Inspector Narvo gets back. He'll probably authorize bail, maybe fifty bucks or something, then you'll have to wait till the magistrate comes in, he's due in town for the Cup. Just one more night in here, Billy, that's all.'

'You're on their fucking side, ain't you?' The dark eyes blazed: not with hatred of his cousin, the cop, but out of sheer frustration and despair. Malone had seen it before, even amongst the city Kooris.

Wally Mungle sighed. 'Don't start that again, Billy. Can we go now, Inspector?'

Without waiting for Malone's assent, he went out of the cell. Koowarra stared at the open door, looked for a moment as if he might make a break for it; then he looked at Malone, all the fury and frustration draining out of his face. All at once he looked as old as some of the elders Malone had seen down at the settlement by the river.

'It's fucking hopeless, ain't it?'

Malone had heard the same complaint from nineteen-year-old whites on the streets of King's Cross; but he had had no answer for them, either. 'Make the best of it, Billy. I've got no authority here, otherwise I'd have you released on bail now. I'll see you tomorrow. Just remember – when you do get out, don't leave town.'

He went out, pulling the door gently closed behind him, not wanting to slam it on Billy Koowarra. Along the corridor the Koori rhinestone cowboy was still singing softly to himself.

Upstairs in the detectives' room Clements, Baldock and Mungle were waiting for him. He took off his jacket and slumped down in the chair Baldock pushed towards him. Baldock then went round and sat behind his desk, the presiding officer. Malone wondered if Baldock had stage-managed the placing of the chairs, but he didn't mind. He would observe protocol, be the visitor on Baldock's turf. He wanted as many people as possible, few though there might be, to be on his side.

'Well, what d'you think?' said Baldock.

'He's in the clear, he's too open. You agree, Wally?'

Mungle, standing with his back to the wall just as Koowarra had done in his cell, nodded. 'Billy's not a killer.'

'Wally, did the Crime Scene fellers go right over Sagawa's car for prints?' Mungle nodded again. 'It hadn't just been washed, had it?'

'No, but it was pretty clean. Sagawa kept his car like that. Billy used to wash it for him every coupla days. But there were no prints *inside* the car. On the steering wheel, on the dash – nothing. It had been wiped clean, the Fingerprint guy said.'

Malone looked at Baldock. 'What does that suggest to you?'

'That someone had driven the car in from somewhere else. Then wiped his and Sagawa's prints off everything.'

'Did they go over the car for bloodstains?'

'Nothing,' said Mungle. 'They've got the car over at Cawndilla. I was talking to them yesterday – they've found nothing. I don't think Sagawa was killed in his car or that the killer brought the body back to the farm in it.'

'So it could've been brought back in the Merc that Billy saw. Assuming Sagawa was dead by then. What time did the GMO put as the time of death?'

'He was guessing,' said Baldock. 'Doc Nothling said the time of death was probably somewhere between ten and twelve on Monday night. Sagawa had eaten, there was food still in the stomach.'

'Well, whoever was in the Merc that Billy saw might not have had anything at all to do with Sagawa's murder.' He looked at Clements in mock despair. 'Let's go home, Russ.'

Clements munched on his lower lip. 'Wally's been telling me about that Merc. He says there are seven in the district. Let's start running 'em down. Who owns them, Curly?'

'Off the top of my head, I can name four of 'em. Chess Hardstaff, Narelle Potter, Trevor Waring, Ray Chakiros. Oh, and one of the local graziers, Bert Truman. He's a Flash Jack, plays polo, wants his own plane next, I'm told. He's a ladies' man.'

'What about Doc Nothling?'

'He drives a Ford Fairlane. Or is it an LTD? Anyhow, it's a Ford. Chess Hardstaff doesn't want a son-in-law who tries to match him in everything.'

That was one good thing about a bush investigation: gossip flowed like an irrigation channel. Malone said, 'Rustle up the names of the other owners. Check on where they all were last Monday night.'

'You want me to check with Mrs Potter?' Clements's face was absolutely straight, virginal.

Malone kept his own face just as straight. 'No, you're coming with me.'

'Where are you going?' said Baldock, trying to hang on to a rein on his own turf. 'You want me to come with you?'

'I think it'd be better if you didn't, Curly. We're going out to see Mr Hardstaff.'

Baldock got the message: when this was all over, he'd still have to go on living here. 'Sure. You can't miss his place, Noongulli, it's out past the Carmody place, about another five kilometres to the turn-off. You want me to ring and say you're coming?'

'I don't think so. Surprise is the spice of a policeman's life.'

'Who said that? Gilbert and Sullivan?'

'No, Russ did. He's Homicide's resident philosopher.'

The resident philosopher jerked a non-philosophical thumb.

2

Chester Hardstaff poured two stiff whiskies and soda, handed one to his guest and took a sip of his own. He usually had nothing to drink before lunch, but this morning he took his visitor's habit as his excuse for breaking his own. Gus Dircks was a man who would accept a drink any time of day, but Hardstaff could not remember ever having seen him drunk.

'It's not good for the district, Gus.'

'I know, I know. That's why I came up a coupla days early, Chess. I wasn't going to come up for the Cup till Saturday morning. But when I heard they were sending up two Homicide blokes from Sydney, I thought I better get up here and see what you thought of the murder.'

'I don't like it, Gus. It's upset the whole district. It's dampened everyone's spirit.'

'I hadn't noticed that. You been into town since it happened? Everybody's talking about the murder, but I don't think you could say it's dampened anyone's spirit. Nobody's going to stay away from the Cup because of it.' Lately he had begun to think that Chess Hardstaff had lost his touch, that he had become too unbending even to notice what was happening at the grass roots.

Most people's names go unremarked; it is just the sound signature for who a person is. Most of them have lost their original meaning: Johnson need no longer be John's son, he can be Bert's son or, if the father is insignificant, Doreen's son. But some names do retain their meaning, have their warning: Hardstaff was one of those names. It suggested mastership, discipline; the Weakreeds of the world would bend before it. Even the diminutive of Chester Hardstaff's first name fitted the man: Chess never made a move solely on instinct. Except once . . . And Gus Dircks didn't know about that.

Hardstaff had said nothing and Dircks grew uncomfortable in the silence. He sipped his drink and said, 'This is a nice drop.'

'I buy only the best,' said Hardstaff, though he sometimes wondered if he could say that about some of the candidates he bought for the Party. Especially the purchase sitting opposite him in his office now.

Australia has never bred any aristocrats, though more than a few of the natives have aspired to the stud-book. Chester Hardstaff was one of them: he thought of himself as better bred than any of the champion merinos he raised. His great-great-grandfather had come to the colony of Sydney with the First Fleet, a midshipman scion of a middling wealthy farming family from Yorkshire. The midshipman's son, Chess's great-grandfather, had come west in 1849 and taken up the Noongulli run; at one time it had covered 150,000 acres, but now it was down to 50,000 acres, or almost 25,000 hectares, a measure he never used. The homestead, a showpiece of colonial architecture, had been built in 1870, a fit dwelling for a pastoral aristocrat. Chess Hardstaff felt at home in it and he had decided that, when he passed on (for he was of the sort who would never just *die*), his ghost would come back to see that it remained in the family. He had no doubt that he would be master of his own movements in the next world: the Rural Party, like all conservative parties, believed it had been made in Heaven.

Chess Hardstaff *looked* an aristocrat; or what the popular conception was of such a rare breed in this flat land of flat social levels. There was something un-Australian about his looks; as if his eighteenth-century forebear had risen from the grave to provide the clay for him. He was seventy-five years old, but carried himself like a much younger man: tall, straight-backed, silver head held high. He gave some lesser men the impression that he was gazing down his handsome nose at them, an impression that was correct. Arrogance was a virtue in his eyes and he polished it till God Himself would have put on dark glasses against the shine of it. He looked every other inch the patrician he thought he was; but the alternative inches hid the son-of-a-bitch his enemies thought he was. He had many enemies and would have been disappointed if he hadn't; he had no time for people with neutral feelings. He had always been a passionate man, but always controlled. Or had been except for one occasion.

'We've got to keep this played down, Chess.'

Augustus Dircks looked the very opposite of Hardstaff. In his late fifties, short, nuggety, blunt-faced and with close-cropped ginger hair, he looked as if he could be the foreman of a shire road gang. He was, instead, a reasonably wealthy wheat and wool farmer; his family had been in the district since the turn of the century and he had been the Rural Party's member for the electorate of Noongulli for the past twenty years. He had been an odd and bad choice for Police Minister, but Coalition politics and Chess Hardstaff had got him the job when the joint conservative parties had deposed the long-time Labour government in the recent State elections. He had never had an original political thought in his life, but that has never been a handicap to any politician anywhere in the world. Dircks's saving grace was that he knew his limitations: without his mentor, he would be a nobody. It hurt, however, to have heard the New South Wales police call him Gus Nobody. It is one thing to know your own limitations, it is another to have everyone agree with you.

'What are these detectives from Sydney like? Busybodies?'

'I don't know much about them, I didn't have time to look into 'em. Except that Malone, the inspector, is supposed to be dogged, he doesn't give up easily. He's solved one or two tough cases the last coupla years.'

'Will he solve this one?'

'Who knows?' Dircks sipped his drink; then said carefully, 'Do we want it solved?'

Hardstaff had been gazing out the window at the garden that surrounded the house; Mick, the Aboriginal gardener, was cutting back the rose bushes. But at Dircks's question, he turned round and sat down at his desk. It was a large desk, an English antique that had come from the original family home in Yorkshire; the leather top had had to be replaced, but the wood of the desk had a patina to it that pleased him every time he looked at it. Had it been possible, he would have totally avoided the new. Only the old, the tried and true, could be trusted.

'What do you mean by that, Gus?' His deep voice was toneless, as unhurried as ever.

'Well, we don't know what's going to come out, do we? We want the Nips to stay here, don't we?'

'Yes.' Though Hardstaff had invested no money of his own in the consortium that had set up South Cloud Cotton, it had been he who had persuaded the Japanese to come in as major partners. 'We want more foreign investment in this country and the Japanese are our best bet.'

'Sure. But they're not going to feel too bloody welcome if it turns out one of our locals is out to murder them.'

'What makes you think it's one of the locals?'

'Who else could it be? I saw Hugh Narvo last night, he told me they haven't found any trace of strangers hanging about out at the gin.'

'Does Hugh think it's a local who's the murderer?'

Dircks shrugged. 'You know him, he never commits himself. Not even to the Police Minister.' He laughed: it sounded like a sour joke.

'Is he still in charge of the case? Or are these outsiders from Sydney taking over?'

'Nominally, he should be in charge. But I don't know that he wants to be. He seems to be leaving everything to Curly Baldock.'

'I think you'd better have a word with Hugh.' He looked up as his housekeeper, a stout middle-aged woman with glasses that kept slipping down to the end of her snub nose, came to the door of the office. 'Yes, Dorothy?'

It had taken him a long time to be able to say her name without thinking of his dead wife, that other Dorothy.

'There are two detectives here, Mr Hardstaff.' She sounded puzzled; she pushed her glasses back up her nose, squinted through them at him. 'From Sydney?'

Hardstaff rose from his desk, not looking at Dircks. 'I'll see them in the living-room. You'd better come too, Gus.'

Dircks lifted his bulk from his chair, breathing heavily: it was difficult to tell whether he was overweight or over-anxious. 'They didn't take long to get out here, did they?'

'Leave them to me,' said the King-maker, who could break as well as make men.

3

When Clements had switched off the engine of the Commodore, Malone sat for a moment looking at Noongulli homestead. 'Take a look at how the squattocracy lives.'

One didn't much hear the word squattocracy these days. It had been coined near the middle of the last century to describe the then colonial aristocracy, or what passed for it. The original squatters had been ticket-of-leave men, emancipated convicts, who, legally or otherwise, had taken up land in remote areas and prospered as much by rustling from neighbours as by their own sheep- or grain-raising efforts. Gradually the word squatter had gained respectability. All countries can turn a blind eye to the sins of their fathers, but none was blinder than that of the local elements. Men, and women, have killed for respectability.

Clements nodded appreciatively. He had been impressed as they had come up the long drive, half a mile at least, from the front gates; an avenue of silky oaks had lined the smoothly graded track and the fences behind them had had none of the drunken lurch one found on so many of the properties as large as this one. The gardens surrounding the house were as carefully tended as some he had seen on Sydney's North Shore; an elderly Aborigine stood unmoving in the midst of a large rose plot, gazing at them with stiff curiosity like a garden ornament. Trees bordered the acre or so of garden: blue-gum, liquidamber, cedar and cabbage tree palm, though Clements knew only the name of the liquidamber. On one side of the house was a clay tennis court and beyond it a swimming pool. The house itself, though only one-storeyed, suggested a mansion: there was a dignity to it, an impressive solidity, that told you this was more than just a *house*. This was where tradition and wealth and, possibly, power resided. Its owner was not to be taken lightly.

'Not bad, eh?' Clements said. 'I think I might've liked being a squatter. A rich one.'

'You'd have buggered the sheep. I don't mean literally. Russ, you couldn't raise a pup even if it gave you a hand. Lassie would have turned up her nose at you and gone home. Come on, let's go inside and see what we can get out of Mr Hardstaff.'

He had seen Hardstaff on television, but he was not prepared for the *presence* of the man in person. He fitted the dignity of his home; it was a proper setting for him. Dignity is not an Australian characteristic, the larrikin element is too strong in the national psyche. Hardstaff stood in the middle of his living-room, a heavily elegant chamber, and looked at the two larrikin intruders.

Malone introduced himself and Clements and was greeted by, 'You might have telephoned me first to let me know you were coming.'

'We slip up sometimes on politeness,' said Malone; and looked at the Police Minister. 'It's Mr Dircks, isn't it?'

'Yes,' said Dircks. 'I think Mr Hardstaff has a point. You shouldn't come charging in here, you don't have a warrant, do you?'

'No, sir. I wasn't aware we were charging in. You're the Minister, you'd know we'd get nowhere if we stuck to protocol all the time.' Oh crumbs, he thought, there goes the Malone tongue again. He glanced to his right and saw Clements looking around as if seeking a way out of the room before the roof fell in.

Dircks's face reddened, but Hardstaff was not going to have a Police Department row in his home. 'Let's start again, Inspector. Why did you want to see me? Sit down.'

Malone and Clements lowered themselves into armchairs. This was a *man's* living-room, leather and tweed and polished wood; there was no chintz or silk. Brass glinted at various points around the room and the paintings on the walls were bold and challenging, though not in any modern style: de Kooning or Bacon or Blackman would have finished up in the marble-topped fireplace. The challenge was within the subject of the paintings: a hold-up by bushrangers, a horse-breaker trying to tame a buckjumper. There were, however, vases of flowers on side tables around the room, the only soft touch, like that of a ghostly woman's hand.

Clements had taken out his notebook and Hardstaff gave him a hard stare. 'You are going to take notes?'

'Only if necessary.'

'Will it be necessary?' Hardstaff looked back at Malone.

'I don't know, Mr Hardstaff, not till I start asking the questions.' He plunged straight in, freezing though the water might be: 'Can you tell us where you were Monday night, the night Mr Sagawa was murdered out at the cotton gin?'

'Jesus!' said the Police Minister. 'What sort of question is that?'

'A routine one,' said Malone. 'It's normal police procedure in cases like this. Where were you, Mr Hardstaff?'

Hardstaff had shown no expression at the question. His long handsome face could turn into a stone replica of itself; he turned his head slightly and, in a trick of light, his pale blue eyes seemed suddenly colourless. A classicist might have described him at that moment as a Cæsar in his own museum. But Malone was no classicist, just a cop who had learned to read stone faces, no matter how faint the script.

'I was at a meeting of the Turf Club. I'm the chairman.'

You would be, thought Malone: you're probably chairman of everything with more than two members in this district. 'Where was that held?'

'At the Legion club. From seven o'clock till nine.'

'And after that?'

'After that I went to my daughter's home, the other side of town. I was there about an hour, I suppose. Then I drove home.'

'Alone?'

'Of course.' He didn't attempt to explain why *of course* he would drive home alone.

'What sort of car do you have?'

'A Mercedes, last year's model. A 500SEL.' He did not say it boastfully, but as if mocking Malone's questioning of him. He looked at Clements taking notes. 'Got that, Sergeant?'

'Colour?' said Clements.

'Beige, I think they call it. I don't have a good eye for colour, I'm colour-blind.'

'Does that apply to people, too?'

'Jesus Christ!' Dircks sat up in his chair. Hardstaff had left his drink in the study, but the Police Minister had brought his with him and now the ice rattled in his glass like dice. 'That's enough of that sort of insult, Malone! The interview's over!'

My bloody tongue again, thought Malone. But Hardstaff's air of arrogance, his apparent resentment that the police should interrogate him without making an appointment, acted on Malone like a burr in his pants.

Hardstaff did not appear disturbed by the question. He looked at Malone with new interest, as if the detective were an adversary who might prove hard to put down. Weak opponents bored him. Without looking at Dircks he said, 'It's all right, Gus. Perhaps the inspector has some point to his question?'

Malone saw that Hardstaff suddenly had some respect for him. 'Yes, there was a point to it. I've heard that there is some strong anti-Japanese feeling in the district.'

'Not from me, Inspector. I brought the Japanese investment in here. Mr Dircks will confirm that. He's one of the partners in South Cloud.'

Malone saw Clements's ball-point suddenly slip, scratching

across the page of his notebook. Then the big hand was steady again, waiting to make a note of Dircks's reply.

'I didn't know that, Mr Dircks,' Malone said.

'It's in the records. You'd have seen it if you'd looked at the books of the company.' But Dircks sounded as if he wished the connection hadn't been mentioned.

'We've only just started. There's a lot we still have to look into. Have you visited the cotton farm lately, Mr Hardstaff?'

'No, I have no financial interest in it.'

'Did you know Mr Sagawa?'

'Yes. He came to dinner once. And he came out once or twice to tennis parties we had. He was an enthusiastic tennis player. He was enthusiastic at everything, come to think of it. Everyone liked him.'

'Except the person who murdered him.'

'Christ, you're blunt!' said Dircks, a politician never known for his subtlety in parliament.

Malone stood up, ignoring the Minister's remark. 'Did you know anything about Mr Sagawa other than that he was enthusiastic and popular?'

The other three men were now on their feet. Hardstaff said, 'No, I don't believe I did. Perhaps the other Japanese out at the farm, the assistant manager, Mr Koga, might help you there.'

'You know Mr Koga? I thought you said you had no interest in the cotton farm?'

Hardstaff smiled, a crack in the stone. 'I'm interested in everything that goes on in this district, Inspector. This is my turf, I think is the expression.'

'Oh,' said Malone, letting his tongue have its way this time, 'I thought it was the Minister's.'

'Enjoy your stay, Inspector,' said Hardstaff, the crack widening. The bugger's enjoying this, thought Malone. 'Come and see me again if you have any more questions. Just telephone me first, that's all. I'm not always available to every Tom, Dick and Harry.'

'Scobie and Russ,' said Malone. 'Thanks for your time.'

As he and Clements went down the steps from the wide front veranda, Dircks came hurrying out the front door. 'Inspector!'

Malone turned. 'Yes, sir?'

'I heard you're staying at the Mail Coach.' *Narelle Potter would have told him that.* 'Have lunch with me there. One o'clock. Just you and me.' He didn't look at Clements.

'Yes, sir.'

They got into the Commodore and halfway down the driveway to the front gates Clements said, 'You've stirred up something back there. I think we could be on our way outa town by this evening. I was looking forward to going to the races tomorrow afternoon.'

'What are you going to put your money on? Narelle or her horse?'

'Okay, wipe the shit off your liver. It's just a bit of innocent nooky with her.'

'She hasn't been innocent since she got out of kindergarten.'

'Geez, we *have* got S.O.L., haven't we? You've let those two bastards get to you.'

Malone nodded morosely. 'You're right . . . Look, as soon as we get back to the station, get on to Sydney. Get Andy Graham, if you can. Have him contact the Tokyo police, I want a full background on Mr Sagawa – so far we know practically bugger-all about him. Tell him to phone you when he's got something, not put it on the computer.'

'We keep it to ourselves? Okay.'

'Tell him to tell the Japs it's urgent. I'd like it by Monday morning at the latest.'

'It's Friday now, for Chrissakes.'

'Let's see if the Japs are as industrious as I'm always reading. We work weekends, don't we?'

'Not tomorrow, I hope. Not while I'm out at the course, putting my money on Narelle's horse.'

'She's really conned you, hasn't she? Lisa's going to be disappointed when I tell her. She's still hoping she can marry you off to some convent virgin. What happened to that girl Sheila from Forensic Science?'

'She was too clinical. She wanted to take a blood sample every time we did it.'

'Excuses, excuses. You're just afraid of marriage.'

They drove back to town, being overtaken several times by cars hurtling towards the Big Weekend; there was no respect for the speed limit out here in the backblocks. They went by the entrance to Sundown and Malone wondered what Lisa and the kids were doing right now; maybe Tom was falling off another horse, Claire was still mooning over Tas Waring, Maureen was chatting away, careless of whether anyone was listening to her or not. All at once he wished he could retire now, while the kids were still young; perhaps they wouldn't need him by the time he got to retirement age. The thought suddenly saddened and frightened him.

They passed the racecourse, where workers were preparing the track for tomorrow's meeting. Bunting was being hung from the small grandstand and several marquees had been erected. In a small showground beside the course a travelling circus and carnival was setting up its tents and stalls; two elephants were being used as fork-lift substitutes, raising up a long thick pole. Clements slowed the car.

'You gunna bring the kids to the circus tomorrow?'

'I'll try. Depends whether we're working or not.' A day with Lisa and the kids would be a nice break. 'I might even watch the Cup and put a dollar or two on something.'

'Don't get rash. That's money you're throwing around.'

They drove on into town, which now seemed full of cars and utility trucks and four-wheel-drive wagons. The sleepy air of the town had disappeared; Collamundra looked as if it might be getting ready to get drunk. Some drunks were already evident, but Malone noticed from the police car, slowed by the traffic, that they were mostly Aborigines. He wondered if Cup weekend was a cause for celebration for them or whether this was how they marked every weekend.

One of the drunks stepped off the footpath, walked unsteadily to the middle of the road, then stopped, facing the traffic. Clements slammed on the brakes. The Aborigine was middle-aged, thin but for a bloated belly; he wore a tweed cap, with his hair sticking out on either side and curling up like the horns on a Viking's helmet. He grinned foolishly at the two strangers in the Commodore, raising his hand and giving them a slow wave.

The traffic had banked up behind the police car and horns were being sounded in temper. The Aborigine leaned sideways, slowly, without moving his feet, and peered past the Commodore to the cars behind. He gave their drivers the same slow wave, still grinning foolishly.

'Jesus Christ,' said Clements, 'is it any wonder people have no time for the stupid bastards?'

Malone was smiling back at the Aborigine. 'This might be his only happy moment in the whole week.'

Clements turned his head. 'Don't be a bloody bleeding heart. Down in Redfern you'd have been out of the car in a flash and grabbed him if he'd done that to us.'

Malone opened the door of the car, got out, the chorus of car horns still hooting behind him, and walked up to the Aborigine. He took the man by the arm.

'Come on, Jack. You're going to get sun-struck standing out here in the open.'

The man giggled. 'Sun-struck?'

'Sun cancers, too. Your complexion's all wrong. Come on, back in the shade.'

The man didn't struggle. With Malone still holding him by the elbow, he walked unsteadily back to the footpath and stood under a shop awning. A small crowd had gathered, all whites, men and women; they were silent, their faces full of a hostile curiosity. *He's a cop, why doesn't he arrest the drunken Abo?*

Malone looked over their heads, searching for another Aborigine, saw two young men standing in a doorway. He raised his hand and beckoned them over. They hesitated, looked at each other, then came towards him, the crowd opening up to let them through.

'Take him home,' Malone told the two young Aborigines. Then to the drunk: 'Go with them, Jack. Otherwise I'll have to lock you up.'

'You're a copper?' The man's look of surprise was comical. He looked around at the crowd, shaking his head in wonder. 'Wuddia know! He's a copper!'

He grabbed Malone's hand, giggled, shook his head again, then let the two young men lead him away. As Malone stepped off the kerb to get back into the Commodore, which Clements had pulled out of the way of the traffic, a thickset farmer, a redneck if Malone had ever seen one, said, 'You're wasting your sympathy, mate. They're just a bloody nuisance when they're like that, to 'emselves and everyone else.'

'Maybe you're right,' said Malone. 'But you don't have to play at being a cop, do you?'

As he got into the car beside Clements a man's voice said from the back of the crowd, 'Why don't you go back where you belong?'

'Drive on,' Malone said quietly and Clements pulled the car out into the traffic again.

They said nothing more; then Clements was pulling the Commodore into the police station yard. As soon as they got out of the car they were aware of the tension amongst the half a dozen uniformed men in the yard. At first Malone thought they were waiting to say something to him and Clements; he stiffened, seeking some sort of answer to a question he hadn't yet heard. Then, as they reached the steps leading up to the back door of the rear annexe, Baldock, hatless, his face tight and red as if he were holding his breath, came out through the doorway. He stopped abruptly on the top step and looked down at the two Sydney men.

'Billy Koowarra's just hung himself.'

THREE

1

'Looks like he did it, don't you reckon?' said Dircks.

He and Malone were at lunch at the reserved table by the corner window. The dining-room was crowded, mostly with men but also with a few women. Narelle Potter had refurbished the big room, but its restored old-time charm fought a losing battle against the rough, loud bonhomie of the male diners. The women guests tried hard, but they were just whispers in the chorus of shouts, laughter and loud talk. Malone, as sometimes before, wondered how people could manage to eat and yet still make such a hubbub.

He caught what Dircks had just said in the moment before it was lost in the noise. 'What?'

'He's the obvious suspect. I'm not saying shut the book on Sagawa's murder, but it might be better if we just let it die quietly.'

You're the one who's obvious. 'Why do you think Koowarra's the one who did it?'

'I didn't say that. I'm just suggesting you take advantage of what's happened.' Dircks dipped his handkerchief in his glass of water and sponged a spot of gravy off the lapel of his expensive suit. Everything he wore was expensive, but he didn't look comfortable in it, as if his wife or perhaps a daughter had bought his wardrobe and each morning he just put on what was laid out for him. He didn't look comfortable at the moment and Malone wondered if Chess Hardstaff had laid out instructions for him. 'His suicide is tantamount to a confession. Use it. We know he'd been sacked, there was bad feeling between him and Sagawa.'

'How do you know that?'

'I *know.*' Dircks finished his wet-cleaning, picked up his knife and fork again. Whatever he felt about the two deaths, the murder and the suicide, his appetite had not been affected. He began to chew on a mouthful of steak that would have satisfied a crocodile.

'No court would accept a case built on that. There was no note of confession, he didn't say a word to any other prisoner or any officer.' Malone cut into his rack of lamb. The menu was written in English, no fancy French handles to the dishes, and the chef, Malone guessed, probably cooked with the Australian flag hanging over his stove. The dessert list, he had noted, contained such local exotica as bread-and-butter pudding, sherry trifle and lamington roll; somehow the national dish, passion-fruit pavlova, had missed out. 'Frankly, Mr Dircks, I don't think Koowarra killed Sagawa and I'm not going to waste my time following that line.'

Dircks picked up his napkin to wipe his mouth, noticed it was wet and gestured to a passing waitress for a fresh one. Malone had remarked that only he and the Minister had crisp linen napkins; all the other diners, including the women, had paper ones. Narelle Potter herself brought the fresh linen, flipped it open and spread it on Dircks's broad lap.

'You're still as careless as ever, Gus. I thought Shirley would've smartened you up, down there in the city, now you're a Minister. Look at Inspector Malone. Spotless, and he's just a policeman.'

Malone, just a policeman, said, 'Thanks.'

She gave him her hotel-keeper's smile, as dishonest as the collar on a badly-poured beer, and went away. Dircks looked after her admiringly. 'Nice woman. One of my best campaign workers when an election's on . . . Malone, I don't think you understand me.'

The remark caught Malone a little off-balance; Dircks had still been looking after Mrs Potter when he said it. But now he turned to face Malone and there was no mistaking the antagonism in the small blue eyes. He could be authoritative, though in only two months as Minister he had already acquired a reputation for making wrong decisions. But the incompetent don't necessarily give up trying: it is why a few of them occasionally succeed and rise to the top.

Malone took his time, finishing his mouthful of lamb, then cutting some baked pumpkin in half. At last he said, holding his gaze steady against Dircks's, 'I understand you perfectly well, Minister. You want me to close the case, not make waves, just go back to Sydney and leave everything to the locals. Right?'

'Put as bluntly as that . . . Well, yes, that's the gist of it.'

'I'll have to talk to my superiors in Sydney.' He chanced his arm: 'It could go up to the Commissioner. He takes a personal interest in anything I'm working on.'

Dircks looked disbelieving, but also uncertain. In his short time as Minister he had come to know that the Police Department had its own way of working; more so, perhaps, than any other public service department. The men responsible for law and order, it seemed to him, had their own laws. The conservative coalition had not been in government for fifteen years and its ministers were learning that power, no matter what the voters might say about its democratic transfer, was an abstract, not something that could be handed over in a file. In the Police Department there was power at every level, something he had not yet come to terms with.

'The Commissioner and I get on very well together,' he said, though that was not strictly true; he hardly knew John Leeds, a reserved man. 'How come he takes a personal interest in what you do?'

'Past association,' said Malone and closed up his face, as if to imply there were police secrets, as indeed there were, that even ministers should not be privy to.

Dircks neatly backed down; weak-willed men are adept at a few things. 'Well, I don't want to bring politics into this – there was too much of that from the last government.' He waited for Malone to comment, but got no satisfaction. Then he went on, 'You have to realize, out here things are different from what you're used to, I mean in a community like ours. Everybody has to live with everybody else.'

'I understand that was what Mr Sagawa was trying to do. But

somebody didn't want to live with him.' Malone had finished the main course; he picked up the menu. 'Do you mind if I have dessert? I've got a sweet tooth.'

'So have I. I can recommend the bread-and-butter pudding, a real old-fashioned one. Yes, I never thought anything like this would ever happen to Sagawa.'

'There's Mr Koga. He could be next. Bread-and-butter pudding,' he told the stout waitress as she loomed up beside their table.

'The same for you, Mr Dircks?'

'No. No, I think I've had enough.' Dircks waited till the waitress had gone, then he leaned forward, his wide-set eyes seeming to close together on either side of the two deep lines that had suddenly appeared between them. 'Christ Almighty, I hadn't thought of that! You'd better stay, catch the murderer before he has the Japs pulling out of the district. They not only grow the cotton, they buy ninety per cent of the crop for their own mills.'

'Then you don't think Billy Koowarra did it?'

'Forget him! Just find out who killed Ken Sagawa.'

'Mr Dircks, you said you had an interest in South Cloud . . .'

Dircks remained leaning forward on the table for a long moment; then he eased himself back, said quietly, 'Yes. The shares are in my wife's name. It's common knowledge, you'll find it in the declaration of MPs' interests down at Parliament House in Sydney. There's nothing to hide.'

'I didn't suggest there was. But I think it might be an idea if you stayed at arm's length from me and the investigating team, don't you? You know what the media are like.'

'I own the local paper, the *Chronicle*. You don't have to worry about it.'

That would explain why no reporter had tried to by-pass Baldock to get to him or Clements. 'What about the radio station?'

'Chess Hardstaff owns that.'

I might have guessed it. 'I wasn't thinking so much of the local media as those down in Sydney.' He usually tried to keep the media at his own arm's length; but they were always useful as a weapon, especially with politicians. 'How much interest do you have in South Cloud? Or how much is in your wife's name?'

'Twenty per cent.' The answer sounded a reluctant one.

'Any other local shareholders?'

Dircks hesitated, looking at his front to see if he had spotted it with any more gravy. 'Well, I guess you'll look it up in the company register. Yes, there are two others. Max Nothling, Chess Hardstaff's son-in-law, and one of the town's solicitors, Trevor Waring.'

Malone didn't mention that he had already met Waring; but he wondered why Sean Carmody's son-in-law had said nothing about his interest in the cotton farm. 'How much do they hold?'

'Ten per cent each. The Japanese own sixty per cent.'

The waitress brought Malone his bread-and-butter pudding; it looked and tasted as good as Dircks had claimed. Dircks watched him eat, seemed undecided whether to say anything further, then went ahead, 'If you have to arrest someone for the murder, ring me first.'

Malone stopped with a mouthful of pudding halfway to his mouth; his mouth was open, as if in surprise, a reaction he never showed. 'Why?'

'I just don't want to be here when it happens. If it's someone I know – and chances are it will be – well . . .' He abruptly stood up; that did surprise Malone, though he managed not to show it. 'I think it'll be better if you and I don't see each other again, Inspector.'

Malone swallowed the mouthful of pudding. 'I couldn't agree more, Minister.'

'The bill's taken care of,' said Dircks and made it sound as if it had come off ministerial expenses and not out of his own pocket. He was not used to paying to be put in his place by one of his own minions.

He left on that, moving swiftly, jerking his head at greetings but not stopping to shake hands with any of those who hailed him, going against the grain of twenty years in politics: any hand ignored could be a hand that might vote against you. Malone was aware of the sudden hush that seemed to have fallen on the big room; the other diners were looking at him, as if to accuse him of upsetting their local member. He went back to finishing his bread-and-butter pudding, glad that something tasted good.

2

'I got in touch with Andy Graham,' said Clements. 'He's getting on to Tokyo right away. How did you get on with the Minister for Free Beers?'

When Dircks had first come to office he had put out three press releases a day, one of which stated that, to polish the New South Wales police's image as squeaky clean, no member of the force was to accept the occasional beer from a hospitable hotel-keeper, not even if dying of thirst. Hence his title, one of several bestowed on him by the squeaky clean.

Malone told him of the luncheon conversation. They were sitting at Baldock's desk in the detectives' room and he laid the conversation out word for word in front of the local man. He was still a little unsure of where Baldock's loyalties lay, but had decided that, if he wanted Baldock to trust him, he had to offer his own trust. He had found, in the past, that often it was the only way to pick the lock in a closed door.

Baldock nodded, not surprised by what Malone had told them. 'It figures, with Gus Dircks. I'd bet Chess Hardstaff put him up to it.'

'I didn't like his suggestion that we lay the Sagawa murder on Billy Koowarra.' Malone made the remark casually, but he was watching carefully for any flicker of expression in Baldock's eyes.

There was none, except for a frown of annoyance on the broad forehead. 'That would be too bloody easy. And it would raise a riot with the Abos, they'd tear the town apart. Jesus, some politicians are dumb!'

'Speaking of Sagawa,' said Clements, 'I went out to the cotton farm again and had a talk with Mr Koga. He told me that Sagawa had had two threatening phone calls a coupla days before he was murdered.'

'He didn't tell me that!' Baldock was genuinely annoyed.

Clements tried to soothe him. 'I don't think there's anything personal in this, Curly, but Koga doesn't trust any of the locals. He's scared out of his pants.'

'He doesn't have any cause to be. Not with me.' Baldock looked hurt, as if he had been a friend of Koga's for life.

'Is Koga still living out at the manager's house?' Malone asked.

Clements nodded. 'I gather a local woman comes in to clean for him, but he and Sagawa did their own cooking when they wanted Jap food. Otherwise they ate here in town, usually at the Chinese place. I got the idea that neither of them thought much of barbecued steak or sausages or a hamburger. I think Koga's stomach would be even more delicate since the murder.'

Clements's comments were rarely delicate. Malone said, 'What do you think about the threats, Curly? Trevor Waring told me last night that Sagawa had been to see him about some threatening letters he'd got.'

'For Chrissake!' Baldock ran his hand over his bald head, clawed at it as if wishing he had hair to tear out. 'Why didn't he come to us with those complaints? Why go to Trevor Waring?'

'Maybe because Waring, I gather, is the South Cloud lawyer. He's also a partner in it.' He saw Baldock frown again. 'Didn't you know that?'

'No. Why would I, if Waring didn't broadcast it? It's not a public company.'

'Sure, why should you? Why would Waring keep it quiet, though? Did you know Doc Nothling and Gus Dircks were also partners?'

'No, I didn't know Dircks was. But yes, I knew about Max Nothling – I think everybody in the district knew it. The Doc runs off at the mouth sometimes, especially when he's had a few.'

'Does he drink much?'

Baldock pursed his lips, then nodded. 'Too much for a doctor. We've had him turn up as GMO to pass on a corpse and I've had to talk one or two of the uniformed guys out of handing him a ticket for driving under the influence. He hasn't always been like that, only the last few years or so.'

'Why is he kept on as GMO?'

'It would be too much of a scandal to sack him. Chess Hardstaff would be down on Hugh Narvo like a ton of bricks if Hugh, or any of us, for that matter, put in a bad report on him. He's a good doctor, when he's sober. I have to say that's most of the time. He just lapses, that's all.'

'Did he come here to inspect Koowarra's body?'

'No, he was out at one of the properties on his rounds, I believe. Anyhow, he was somewhere else. Dr Bedi came and told us to move it to the hospital.'

'Who's Dr Beddy? How do you spell his name?' said Clements, always the note-taker.

'B-E-D-I, Dr Anju Bedi, and she's a she, not a he. An Indian, from somewhere in the Himalayas, I think. Not a bad sort,' he added. 'And a good doctor, too, so they tell me up at the hospital.'

'Would Doc Nothling be at the hospital now?'

Baldock looked at his watch. 'He should be, he's usually there from two till four. You want me to take you up there?'

'No, I'll walk up with Russ. I need the exercise – I had two helpings of bread-and-butter pudding.'

Baldock nodded appreciatively. 'Narelle serves a good meal, doesn't she? She serves a lot else, so my wife says. I wouldn't know.' The lechery in his eye made a mockery of the piety in his voice. 'She's a bit of a fool, Narelle, playing around the way she does. Everybody talks,' he said, seemingly unaware of his own contribution.

Malone felt, rather than saw, Clements shift uneasily in his chair. Not looking at his sidekick, he said to Baldock, 'Go down and see her, ask her to find a room for Mr Koga. I want him in the hotel with me and Russ.'

'But the pub's full up!'

'Curly, use your influence on Narelle. If she won't listen to reason, charge her with something. What's the one you use, Russ?'

Clements had regained his composure. 'Obscene language in a public place, abusing a police officer. It never fails, Curly.'

Baldock grinned. 'They talk about us bastards from the bush, but we're not a patch on you guys. Okay, I'll talk to Narelle, she can tell some poor coot who's booked in weeks ago for tonight and tomorrow night that she made a mistake, that she double-booked. She's – maybe I shouldn't say this, she's a good sort otherwise – but she's a bit of a bigot when it comes to non-whites, Asians and that.' Evidently he could forget his own prejudice about Lebanese and other Wogs.

'Tough titty – or maybe I shouldn't say that about a lady. But I want Koga in the Mail Coach with Russ and me. At least at night. I don't want us called out to the farm to find another body chopped up by those spikes. I'm sure you don't, either.'

Malone and Clements went down the stairs and out into the street. A slight wind had sprung up, coming from the south-west, cooling the town; but it was a dry wind, no hint of rain in it, and there was still the promise of a fine weekend. The main street and the side streets were now full of cars and trucks, many of them dust-caked. Today, instead of Saturday, was shopping day. Tomorrow everyone would be at the races; no one was going to allow the murder of a Japanese and the suicide of an Aborigine to spoil the Big Weekend. Yet as Malone and Clements walked the four blocks to the district hospital, they both remarked the total absence of Aborigines. In a town of this size the percentage of them would have been small anyway; yet Malone, in the drive into town yesterday afternoon, without looking for any of them, had seen groups loitering on almost every corner. This afternoon there was none in sight.

'Has someone told the boongs to get outa town?' Clements had his own prejudices, but it was usually in language rather than deed. The tongue is the loosest of cannons.

But when they got to the hospital a small group of Aborigines stood under a peppercorn tree in the hospital's small front garden. The building was a one-storeyed structure stretched across perhaps two hundred feet, with two wings running back to the rear. It was built of red brick, featureless and undistinguished, a monument to the dull creativity of government architects of the 1920s. An ambulance station, its doors open to expose two ambulances, stood on a narrow lot to one side.

Wally Mungle detached himself from the group as Malone and Clements came in the open front gate. 'You after me, Inspector?'

'No, Wally, we came over to see Dr Nothling. I'm sorry about Billy. Is that his family?'

'Yeah, his mum and dad, a coupla his brothers, an uncle and aunt. And my mum, she was an aunt, too.'

'I'd like to meet them.'

Mungle looked dubious for a moment; then he led the way across to the shade of the peppercorn tree and introduced Malone and Clements. The Aborigines just nodded, but none of them said anything. Malone and Clements were *police* and strangers into the bargain.

Mungle was embarrassed by the silence; but Malone was gazing at Billy Koowarra's father. He was holding his cap in his hands now, but his hair still stuck out on either side like a Viking's helmet horns; he was no longer drunk but he was still suffering the effects of his drinking bout. He stared back at Malone, but it was obvious he did not recognize the plainclothes cop who had gently steered him out of the way of the traffic in the main street. Shock had not only sobered him, it had shrunk him till he could take in only one thought: his son was dead.

'Uncle Les,' said Mungle, 'it wasn't the Inspector's fault Billy did what he did. He wanted Billy released.'

The father said slowly, not looking at all at Malone, 'Don't matter who's to blame. Billy's still dead, only nineteen.'

He had the voice one found so often in his race, deep and soft and sounding as if coming up through rough pebbles in his throat. He had a deeply lined, leathery face and eyes that had been affected by trachoma; no matter what he had looked like when drunk, he now looked old enough to have been Billy's grandfather. Sadness lent him a dignity he had not had this morning, but, Malone thought, it was a hell of a way to have earned it.

Malone nodded; he had no words that would not have sounded hollow and hypocritical in his mouth. He went up the steps into the hospital, followed by Clements and, after a moment's hesitation, by Wally Mungle. They found Max Nothling in the end office of the doctors' wing. With him was Dr Bedi, an attractive plump woman in her early thirties, with placid eyes and an air of patience that suggested nothing short of the end of the world would disturb her. Malone wondered what Indian catastrophes, floods, cyclones, religious riots, had prepared her for life here in this unexciting Australian outback town.

'Ah, the gendarmes!'

Nothling rose from his chair and put out his hand as Mungle introduced the two Sydney men. The doctor was not quite as tall as Malone, but he was bulkier than Clements. Most of his weight was lard; there might have been muscle under the fat but it wasn't easily discernible. He had thick, greying hair and a two-chinned face in which the effects of his drinking showed like a watermark, except that he usually drank something much stronger than water. He was fifty years old; he looked the sort of man who might catch a glimpse of old age but die before reaching it. Surprisingly, the hand that took hold of Malone's had a lot of strength within its fat. Malone just wondered how strong and steady it would be performing any surgery.

'Well, to what do we owe the pleasure of this visit?' He had a loud, fruity voice; his phrases, it seemed, were also fruity. 'The late lamented Mr Sagawa or our departed Abo friend? Sorry, Wally,' he added, as if for the moment he had forgotten Mungle was in the room. 'No offence.'

'I don't think Billy cares very much now what he's called,' said Mungle. 'Abo, boong, coon, anything.'

'No, I suppose not,' said Nothling, taking the rebuff better than Malone had expected. 'Well, which one is it, Inspector?'

'Billy Koowarra is not our case. Sergeant Clements and I would like to ask a few questions about Sagawa. You examined the body out at the gin?'

'Well, no. No, I didn't, actually. I was otherwise occupied.' He didn't look at Dr Bedi, and Malone wondered if it had been a hangover that had otherwise occupied him. 'Dr Bedi went out to the scene of the crime. Anju often helps out, don't you, old girl?'

Anju, old girl, gave him a tolerant smile. 'Just occasionally. Yes, I inspected the body, Inspector. Then I gave instructions for it to be brought in here to the hospital morgue.'

'Did you prepare the report?'

'No, I have no official standing as a GMO. I just instructed them to bring the body in here and then left it to Dr Nothling. He was here at the hospital by then.'

'I took over right away,' said Nothling, taking over now. 'The body was a mess, not a pretty sight at all.'

'How long did it take you to find out Sagawa had been shot?'

'Well, actually –' Nothling glanced at the Indian doctor, who just returned his gaze with what looked almost like a half-smile in her eyes. She's mocking the pants off him, Malone thought. 'Well, actually, Anju discovered that. I was called away, an emergency here in one of the wards, and Anju went on with the examination.'

'You hadn't noticed the bullet wound when you first examined the body out at the gin?'

Dr Bedi shook her head slowly; all her movements were unhurried. She was dressed in skirt and blouse and white coat, but one could imagine her in a sari, the silk floating like a drifting mist around her slow grace. 'I wasn't looking for anything like that, Inspector. The damage done by the spikes of the roller would have been enough to kill him.'

'So how did you come to find the bullet wound?'

'Sheer accident.'

There was something in the air that made Malone uneasy, a friction that rubbed almost indiscernibly against his own awareness. It was a moment or two before he remarked that Nothling and Anju Bedi were not looking at each other, as if deliberately avoiding each other's gaze, while she spoke. Had there been some professional negligence, had Nothling not been present in the morgue at all and she was covering up for him?

'Do you do many autopsies, Dr Bedi?'

She was unhurried, taking time to fold her long white coat over her plump knees. 'No, I don't. Dr Nothling usually does those. I'm just the staff doctor here at the hospital. He is the senior surgeon.'

There was an edge to her voice that was unmistakable, and Malone all at once wondered just how placid she really was. The tension between her and Nothling was like that of lovers who were trying to keep private their quarrel.

'You called Dr Nothling at once?'

'Of course. He came as soon as he could get away from the – from the emergency in the ward.'

Malone looked at Nothling. 'What was your reaction to the news, Doctor?'

'Oh, astonishment, old chap, absolute astonishment. Anju will tell you, I just stood there shaking my head.'

'You're not used to seeing murder victims who have been shot?'

Nothling's eyes narrowed just a little; almost as if, for the first time, he was taking Malone seriously. 'We don't get that many murder victims out here, Inspector.'

'No, I guess not. Things are different where Sergeant Clements and I come from. So you're satisfied that death was due to the gunshot wound?'

'Oh yes, yes.' Nothling appeared to relax again. 'It was right through the heart, dead centre. Oh, the bullet killed him, all right.'

'Did the bullet lodge in the heart?'

Nothling looked at Dr Bedi, who said, 'Just. It didn't break through the wall of the heart – it was in the right atrium. It entered the body near the spine.'

'Near the spine? You mean he was shot in the back?'

'Yes. I don't know much about guns –'

'Why should you, old girl?' Nothling interrupted. 'That's the Inspector's trade, right, old chap?'

'Yes,' said Malone, old chap.

'The murderer probably hoped we wouldn't find it, that we'd think the spikes on the roller had killed him.'

'Why try to hide it?' said Clements, who had been taking his usual notes. 'After he'd killed him, why put him in the module feeder? He must've known the body wouldn't be chewed up. It wouldn't be like feeding bits of a body into a sausage grinder.'

Nothling looked at Clements as if he were a gate-crasher; then he looked back at Malone. 'The sergeant has a vivid imagination. Or is something like that an everyday occurrence in your trade?'

'Not everyday. But we did have a case like that once, a butcher minced a girl in a supermarket. Business at the supermarket fell off for a while. But you see Sergeant Clements's point? The body was never going to finish up any further than the roller.'

Nothling shrugged, a major displacement. 'I'm no detective, Inspector, no talent for that sort of thing at all. Every man to his last, eh?'

'I guess so. When will the inquest be?'

'You know how long these things can take. We don't have a resident magistrate here, he comes in from Cawndilla. When everything's ready, he'll probably do Sagawa and Billy Koowarra on the same day.'

Malone looked at Wally Mungle, who had been standing silently in a corner of the small office, like a patient waiting for the specialists to decide what to do with him.

'I think I better tell you now,' Mungle said, 'my uncle and aunt are gunna demand an inquiry into why Billy died.'

'Your uncle and aunt,' said Nothling, 'or those radicals down at the camp?'

'There's only two or three of them, Doc, and nobody takes much notice of 'em. But I don't think it matters. The noise is gunna be just as loud, no matter who complains. The deaths in police custody is a hot potato right now. I'm as much to blame as anyone for letting Billy commit suicide. I should've tried harder to get him released.'

'You couldn't have done anything more,' said Malone, though he knew he sounded unconvincing. 'Not while Inspector Narvo was away.'

'I hope those bloody hotheads aren't going to start any demonstration,' said Nothling. 'Not tomorrow, of all days. Think what the media will make of that, with the Governor-General up here for the Cup!'

'Is he going to be here?' said Clements.

'He's a friend of my father-in-law's. He's going to present the Cup to the winner. It won't look too good if he has to present it to me. I've got a horse running.' He smiled broadly; then sobered. 'But the G-G won't like it too much if there's a demo.'

Malone had seen the Governor-General only once in the flesh. He was an ex-diplomat, a little man who loved the trappings of his office and regretted that the days had gone when he would have worn the plumed hat, the epaulettes and the sword. It was said that he never turned down an invitation and had once been on his way to open a garage sale when his aide-de-camp discovered the mistake. Though he had been a diplomat he hated controversy and would probably out-run the horses if there was a demonstration tomorrow out at the racecourse.

'If there's going to be a demo, Wally,' said Nothling, 'tell 'em to keep it down at the courthouse, there's a good chap.'

'I'll try, Doc,' said Mungle, 'but I can't guarantee anything.'

Malone stood up, finishing the interview; well, almost: 'What sort of car do you drive, Dr Nothling?'

Nothling had been about to rise from his chair; but he paused, arms stiff, holding his bulk in mid-air. 'A Ford LTD. Sometimes I drive my wife's car.'

'What sort is that?'

'A Mercedes coupé. What's this all about, Inspector?'

Baldock hadn't mentioned *Mrs* Nothling and her Mercedes; but then she was Chess Hardstaff's daughter and there was no reason why she shouldn't drive the same sort of car as her father. Hardstaff surely wouldn't think that his daughter was competing against him.

'Where were you on the night of the murder?'

Nothling came right up out of the chair at that; his face suddenly went red and he seemed to sway, as if the sudden movement had made him light-headed. 'Jesus Christ, what are you getting at? What sort of stupid question is that? That's bloody outrageous!'

Malone glanced sideways at Dr Bedi. She was impassive, her eyes now seemingly black and opaque. She caught his glance, but her expression didn't change.

Malone looked back at Nothling. 'Just a routine question, Dr Nothling. A car was seen outside Sagawa's office early on Monday evening, a fawn Mercedes. We're just checking on all the Mercedes in the district.'

'Who saw the car?'

'That's confidential.' But Malone knew all at once that he now had no witness at all; he couldn't produce Billy Koowarra. 'Were you visiting Sagawa Monday evening? I understand you're part of the partnership that owns South Cloud.'

Nothling had regained his composure; the colour drained out of his face. 'Yes, I'm a partner. No, I wasn't visiting Ken Sagawa. I was at home with my wife all Monday evening. I was worn out. I had been in the theatre all afternoon. Dr Bedi can confirm that.'

'Fair enough,' said Malone, choosing his moment to depart. Always leave them hanging, preferably by their thumbs: it was an old police trick. He had upset Nothling with his last few questions and he was certain that it was not just because the doctor had found their inference insulting. 'Thanks for your help. You too, Dr Bedi.'

Outside the hospital the Koowarra family still stood under the peppercorn tree. What are they waiting for? Malone wondered. Billy's resurrection? Then it occurred to him that waiting seemed to be a natural part of the Aboriginal existence, especially among the older blacks; it was as if life had come to a standstill for them and they would just wait for extinction instead of hurrying towards it. But that, he knew, was not how the radicals thought: most of them had just enough white blood in them to spark some hope; or anyway, rebellion. He could blame neither branch for their attitude.

'I'll stay with them,' said Wally Mungle.

'Sure.' But Malone hoped he would not just stand around waiting; Mungle had too much promise in him for such hopelessness. 'Wally, is there anything going between Nothling and Dr Bedi?'

Mungle looked puzzled for a moment, as if he had missed the meaning of the question; then he shook his head. 'I don't think so. He wouldn't be good enough for her.'

'How do you mean?'

'She's very uppity, thinks she's a cut above most people. And he's a drunk and a slob. Most people don't know how his wife puts up with him.' He sounded almost garrulous; and he seemed all at once to realize it. 'Sorry, I'm getting as bad as everyone else. Gossiping, I mean.'

'Never knock gossiping, Wally. Not if you want to make things easier for you as a detective.'

'There's a difference between listening to it and saying it.'

Malone changed tack a little: 'How well do you know Dr Bedi?'

Mungle waved his hand in a so-so-gesture. 'She's colour-conscious.'

'You're kidding!' said Clements.

'No, I'm not. I told you she's uppity. She's middle class and she's fairly light-skinned, you saw that. I think she puts most of us Kooris on a par with the Indian Untouchables. Why?'

'She knows something about Nothling. I don't know what it is, but it's *something*. I was hoping you might be able to get it out of her.'

'Because we're both coloured?' Mungle saw the instant flash of anger in Malone's face and he hastily said, 'Sorry, Inspector. I'm not feeling the best this morning.' He glanced towards the family group, nodded reassuringly at them. 'My mum's taking this as hard as Billy's mother.'

Malone looked towards the stout, prematurely grey-haired woman to whom he had been introduced. She was holding the hand of Billy's mother, her sister, and they were like a mirror image of each other. It struck him that there was no shock in their faces, more a look of old pain that had been years coming to the surface.

'I understand,' he said quietly. 'Forget it, Wally.'

'No, I'll see what I can do. But don't count on it.'

'Play it by ear. If she's going to be uppity towards you, back off. I'll get Russ to work on her. He's the lady's man.'

'I'm working on Narelle,' said Clements. 'Isn't that enough?'

'It might be more than enough,' said Malone cryptically.

As the two detectives stepped out of the front gate of the hospital a fawn Mercedes coupé drew up, its rear tires skidding a little on the gravel at the side of the road. A dark-haired woman got out, slamming the car door behind her and making no effort to lock it: things are different in the bush, Malone told himself. Yet this woman looked more city than country, would not have been out of place in the kill-'em-dead chic of Double Bay; or perhaps would have been more at home in the don't-let's-even-mention-it chic of Mosman. She was in her forties, he guessed, but money and care of herself had held back the years; she was handsome rather than beautiful, a woman who had made the most of what she had. She had a good full figure and a well-chiselled face and she wore her country casual clothes with the confidence of a model.

'Mr Malone?' She came striding towards them. 'I'm Amanda Nothling-Hardstaff.'

It was the first time he had heard the double-barrelled name; to everyone else she had been Amanda Nothling. But, obviously, she bore the Hardstaff like a sceptre or whatever it was that queens carried.

'*Inspector* Malone. This is Detective-Sergeant Clements.' Sometimes it was politic to broadcast rank; it drew the boundaries of the playing field, level or otherwise. 'We have just been interviewing your husband.'

She nodded at Clements without really looking at him; she kept her gaze on Malone, the *inspector*. 'My husband is terribly upset by the – the murder of Mr Sagawa. We all are,' she added, but it sounded like a polite afterthought. Then she noticed the small group of Aborigines standing by the peppercorn tree. 'What are *they* doing here? Have you been interviewing them?'

'About the murder? No. Should we?'

She looked back at Malone, her pale blue eyes hardening. 'I don't know, Inspector. Like most of the people around here, I know nothing about police investigation. But I am interested in the welfare of the blacks.'

'One of the young blacks committed suicide this morning, hung himself. Billy Koowarra. I thought everyone would know by now,' he couldn't help adding.

She shook her head, looked genuinely upset by the news. Then Max Nothling came out on to the veranda of the hospital, pulling up sharply when he saw Malone and Clements with his wife. He hesitated, then came down the few steps and across to the gate, not even glancing at the Koowarra family. Malone guessed they had been waiting to see Nothling, but now they didn't move, waited for him to come to them.

'Hello, sweetheart. Something wrong?'

'No, Max.' She looked at him carefully, as she might check him after he came out of the operating theatre to see that he had washed himself clean of blood. 'I just introduced myself to Mr – *Inspector* Malone and Sergeant – Clemson?'

'Clements,' said the sergeant and, with the eye that was hidden from her, winked at Malone.

'The Inspector tells me one of the black boys hung himself this morning?'

'In a police cell. The gendarmes are having a bad time lately with all the deaths in custody. Nobody's fault, of course. Certainly not Inspector Malone's, right?' He looked at Malone and smiled with bad taste that Malone, somehow, hadn't expected from him. *The bugger's a bundle of nerves.*

'I think you – *we* should go and speak to the family,' said Amanda.

'Yes. Yes, I suppose one should.' Nothling looked across at the Aborigines, as if their patience was proving a magnet he could not resist. 'Yes, that'd be a good idea. Afternoon, Inspector. You know where to find me if you want me. Don't know how much I can help, though. Coming, sweetheart?'

He held open the gate, as if he wanted something to do with his hands; it was already pushed back almost as far as it would go. Amanda nodded at Malone and Clements, went through and took one of her husband's hands, as she might have taken the hand of one of his patients who was unsure of himself. Together they moved across to the Koowarra family, all of whom seemed to be as unmoving as the trunk of the tree under which they stood.

3

The two detectives left the hospital and started their walk back to the police station. Malone said, 'What d'you reckon?'

'About Mrs Nothling-Hardstaff or both of them?'

'Both.'

'She wears the pants and signs the cheques, I'd say. Probably drawn on a Hardstaff trust fund, since she seems dead set on hanging on to the family name. As for him, he's got something on his mind and she knows it.'

'You think he knows who killed Sagawa? Or he's made an educated guess that's got him shit-scared?'

'Do we start leaning on him?'

'Not yet. Let's take it softly, softly for the moment. We start chucking our weight around the day after we get here, kicking the arse of the town's leading doctor and son-in-law of King Chess, what happens if we find out we're barking up the wrong tree . . . ? What's the matter?'

'I'm trying to sort out all those mixed metaphors.'

'You taken up night school again?' But he grinned, glad he had Clements here with him in Collamundra, where more than just metaphors were mixed.

As they waited at a traffic light in the main street, a slim arm inserted itself into Malone's. 'Hello, sailor.'

Malone kissed his wife on the cheek. 'Book this woman for soliciting, Russ.'

Lisa kissed Clements on the cheek. 'There, that takes care of you. You don't know Ida Waring, do you?'

Clements raised his hat, smiling expansively; he always seemed to open out, like one of the rougher wild-flowers, when in the company of good-looking women. Ida returned his smile, asked if the men had time for a cup of coffee. She seemed intrigued by the presence of two Homicide detectives, and Malone wondered if Lisa had told her of his work on past murders. Ida took them along the main street towards the Buona Sera coffee lounge, leading the way with Clements while the Malones brought up the rear.

'Where are the kids?' Malone asked.

'Out on the property. Tas has taken all of them with him for the day, they're having a picnic lunch. He's shooting some kangaroos that are making a nuisance of themselves.'

He looked sideways at her. 'You said that like someone who's been on the land all her life. No sympathy at all for the poor bloody 'roos.'

'Maybe it's being married to a Homicide detective. You get

callous after a while.' He glanced at her again; but she was only joking. Or he hoped she was. 'How's the case going?'

'Round and round. We lost one of our witnesses this morning. A young Abo committed suicide in his cell at the station.'

Ida stopped sharply. 'Oh no! Who?'

'A young feller named Billy Koowarra, he used to work out at the cotton gin.'

'I knew him. Oh God!' Ida resumed walking.

'I think we're going to be here longer than I expected,' Malone told Lisa.

'Good. Maybe you can find an hour or two for me. We might even find somewhere to make love,' she whispered.

'Here we are,' said Ida and led them into the coffee lounge.

It was run by an Italian couple, who obviously knew and admired Ida. They brought cappuccinos and carrot cake piled high with thick cream. Malone said, 'Is there a coffee shop anywhere now that doesn't serve carrot cake? Whatever happened to lamingtons? Or chester cakes?' He remembered the lumps of lead-in-pastry of his schooldays.

Ida sipped her coffee, decided it was too hot and looked across the Laminex-topped table at Malone. 'Why did Billy Koowarra commit suicide?'

'Who knows?'

She thought a moment, then nodded. 'Yes, who does? It's not always easy to understand why *white* people commit suicide.' She tried her coffee again; then said, 'So who murdered Mr Sagawa or aren't I supposed to ask?'

'You can ask all you want,' said Malone, smiling at her. He liked this pleasant, forthright woman and wished that more of Lisa's women friends were like her. Lisa had an unfortunate habit of befriending women she thought were lonely or unhappy with their husbands. Then, like an unexpected itch, he wondered how happy Ida was with Trevor Waring. It was a thought that was somehow ungracious towards her and he put it out of his mind. 'Right now, we don't have any answers.'

'Everyone hopes it was some itinerant,' she said. 'Someone none of us knows. But I suppose you've guessed that.'

'How long have you lived here, Ida?' Clements, it seemed,

was giving her more than just a policeman's attention. *Eat your carrot cake*, Malone told him silently, *and think of Narelle*.

'I came home with Dad in nineteen seventy.' Ida was giving Clements as much attention as he was giving her. 'But I'm still a newcomer to some of the people around here, especially since they never met my mother. The Hardstaffs, for instance. They look on anyone who arrived after nineteen hundred as week-enders.'

'Has there been much scandal in the district?' Malone said.

'Oh yes, several times. What place doesn't have a scandal or two? There was a divorce that surprised everyone – a happily-married couple who, we found out, couldn't stand each other. A couple of affairs that had everyone talking. The well-known family, I shan't name them, their son came back from the Gold Coast a heroin addict. Oh yes, we've had them.'

Malone looked out at the main street, busy in a slow, deliberate way with traffic and people. It seemed to him that, in their short walk up here to the coffee lounge, he had noticed a change in the atmosphere of the town, the heavy brittleness one felt before a summer storm. The people had come out of their houses here in town and in from the big station homesteads and the small farmhouses, they had come in and brought the main street alive; they had come in for groceries or to pay bills or place bets for tomorrow's races with the SP bookies or the TAB or just to gossip; but whatever had brought them in to this wide sun-baked street with its shops sheltering in the shadows of their corrugated-iron awnings had been forgotten or put aside in the absorption with the deaths, the murder and the suicide, which had been flung at them and which they resented, as if the bodies had been dropped from the back of a truck right there in the middle of the main street. The atmosphere had not been in the air this morning: the murder, the greater crime, had somehow been accepted, almost as if it could be ignored till the Cup meeting was over. Then Billy Koowarra, the Abo, had piled it on by suiciding in the town lock-up: that, it seemed, was too much.

Malone had noticed the townspeople watching him and Clements and Lisa and Ida as the four of them had traversed the hundred yards from the corner of the cross-street to the coffee lounge; some of them had nodded to Ida, but most of them had just looked at them without turning their faces, their glances sidelong, in the same way crims had looked at him when he had gone out to the State prison at Long Bay to question a prisoner who had decided, after two years in jail, to turn informer on a gangland killing. But those had been crims, wary of any cop. The Collamundra elements were ordinary law-abiding citizens, people who claimed, with some justification, whenever there were State or Federal elections, that they were the production rock on which the nation was built, that they were the ones who voted for law and order and proper Christian values (for there were no Jews or Muslims or Buddhists here; and if there were any heretics, there was no room on the voting card for them to say so). He knew in his heart that the great majority of them were hard-working and honest and unhypocritical; yet they had looked at him and Clements, not with hate but with suspicion and resentment, though some of them did look shamefaced about the way they felt. It seemed to him that he and Clements were even more unwelcome than Sagawa's murderer, if he were known, would have been. Without the two city detectives, the townspeople of Collamundra would have solved their own problems, buried them neatly with the bodies, and settled back into their steady, unhurried ways, troubled by nothing more than drought, crown-and-root disease in the wheat, and sheep hit by fly-strike. Their conscience might have worried some of them for a time, but public conscience is like public goodwill: it has to feed on itself and that is no sort of sustenance at all.

He turned his gaze away from the street outside and looked at Ida, who had just said something. 'What?'

'And there were the two murders,' said Ida.

'Two? I heard about only one. About five or six years ago – your father told me about that one. Some Aborigine shot his wife and a shearer he caught in bed with her. What was the other one?'

'Seventeen years ago, three years after Dad and I came home.' Ida drank the last of her cappuccino. 'Chess Hardstaff's wife was murdered.'

FOUR

1

'I thought you knew,' said Curly Baldock. 'It would've been on the reports sent down to Sydney.'

'Did you see it?' Malone asked Clements.

The latter shook his head. 'I wasn't in Homicide then. You were away overseas and I was working on something with Special Branch, I'd been seconded to them. I think it was those suspected Croat terrorists.'

'It was nineteen seventy-three, towards the end of the year. November, I think. You were overseas, you say?' Baldock sounded envious; all the plums fell to the city boys. 'What on, a course?'

'No, my honeymoon. My wife was kidnapped while we were in New York.' He had no trouble recalling the year; he had not yet reached the age when all the past years merged into one long calendar. That year would always stand out.

'Oh, sure! I remember reading about that.' Baldock looked expectant, but Malone didn't elaborate: that was another story, one he preferred not to re-run. It had been a terrifying start to their marriage, his wife and the wife of the Mayor of New York kidnapped by two anarchists, and he and Lisa never discussed it. The children knew nothing of it and he hoped it would be a long time before they did learn of it.

'Does anyone talk about the murder of Hardstaff's wife now?'

Baldock shook his head. They were in the otherwise empty detectives' room, the windows open to the late afternoon sun; two galahs sat in the peppercorn tree next door, pink-and-grey blooms against the drooping green. Wally Mungle had not yet come back from the hospital and the other two detectives were on 'routine enquiries' down at one of the pubs, getting tips not on crime but on tomorrow's Cup. It was almost as if the Sagawa investigation had been put on hold by the locals.

'It's history,' said Baldock. 'They managed to play it down when it happened. The local rag ran a front-page story on it the day after it happened, but the next edition after that it was somewhere on the inside pages. I know it sounds hard to believe, but Gus Dircks owned the paper even then and he did what he was told.'

'Who told him – Chess Hardstaff?'

'Not *our* Chess. His old man. The old bloke, *Sir* Chester, was still alive then and he ran the district just like Chess does now. It didn't get a great spread in the Sydney papers, either, but I think that was because Chess wasn't the big shot he is now, he was just Old Chess's son. There's a difference in country districts.'

'There's a difference in other places, too,' said Malone, but he doubted that he would take second place in people's minds to Con Malone. And, as he often did, he felt sorry for his father, the battler who had never won but still didn't know he had been defeated. 'What happened?'

'She was strangled, as I remember it. I was never on the case, I was stationed over in Cawndilla then – I'd just joined the force. You ask Hugh Narvo, I believe he was on it.'

'Would the report and running sheets still be in the files?'

'I've never seen them. But then I never went looking for 'em.'

'Anyone ever arrested for it?'

'Never. As far as I can remember, it went down as by "person or persons unknown". The guess was that it was someone passing through, someone who tried to rob her. Ask Hugh, he knows more than I do.'

'Is he back yet?'

'He came in about an hour ago. The Billy Koowarra business brought him back. He's bloody ropeable about that. How were the boys down in the lock-up to know Billy would string himself up? It's never happened before, not out here.'

Malone remembered the shouted agitation of Billy Koowarra,

a boy bursting out of his nerves; but all he said was, 'Sure, who'd have known?'

He stood up, saying he would go down and see Hugh Narvo; but he stopped at the door. 'Curly, is young Tas Waring Trevor's son?'

Baldock looked up, surprised. 'Why do you ask that?'

'Just something Ida Waring said this afternoon. It hadn't struck me before, but I was told last night that Tas was twenty-two, yet Ida said she came back here with her father in nineteen seventy . . .'

'No, he's her son by her previous marriage. I gather he took the Waring name by deed poll. He's always been known as Tas Waring, as long as I've known him.'

'How does he get on with Trevor?'

Baldock chewed on the ballpoint he had picked up. 'Not too well, I hear. That's why he lives with his grandfather.'

'They seemed okay together last night, Tas and his stepfather.'

'Well, we're all good at putting on a face for outsiders, aren't we? I mean, if we have to.'

He gazed frankly at Malone: *make what you like of that.*

Malone said nothing, just nodded. He left Baldock and Clements to work up today's running sheet, not that there was much to add, and went downstairs to Narvo's office. He passed several uniformed men and they nodded and one or two smiled; they were slowly coming to accept him and he wondered how much influence Curly Baldock had had on them. But the latter's remark about putting on a face for outsiders had made him begin to doubt the bald-headed man again.

'Yes?' Narvo looked up impatiently as Malone paused in the doorway. He was seated at his desk and a typist, a blonde girl in her mid-twenties, was standing beside him, leaning over to point out something in some letters laid out in front of Narvo. There was an intimacy about their closeness, but Narvo looked uncomfortable about it. Despite his stern look, he was a good-looking man with a suggestion of controlled virility about him, and Malone could imagine a young girl being attracted to him. He shuffled the letters together and handed them to the girl. 'We'll finish this later, Janine.'

Janine went out past Malone as he stood in the doorway, giving him a frank stare but no smile. She was just the right side of plainness, but there was a sexuality about her that one knew she would be aware of as much as any man would.

'I'm busy, Scobie.' It was difficult to tell whether Narvo's rudeness was deliberate or not. 'This bloody suicide . . . I'm going to string someone up for this –' Then his rudeness fell away from him. 'Sorry, I didn't mean to put it like that. I'm upset for where this puts Wally Mungle. He's my protégé, you know.'

'I didn't know.' It surprised Malone; somehow he hadn't expected the starched station chief to have a protégé, least of all an Aborigine. 'I saw him out at the hospital, with Billy's family. The poor bugger's caught in the middle.'

Narvo sat back in his chair, waving to Malone to sit down. Whatever had been keeping him busy, he had evidently decided to forget it. 'How are things going on the Sagawa case?'

'Round and round,' said Malone, remembering he had told Lisa the same thing less than an hour ago. 'Hugh, what can you remember about the murder of Chess Hardstaff's wife?'

It was as if Narvo suddenly coated himself in a thick glaze. 'What has that got to do with the Sagawa case?'

'Nothing, as far as I know. I'm just curious.'

'Who mentioned it to you?'

'I just heard it. I've queried Curly Baldock on it, but he couldn't tell me much. Is the file still available?'

'No.' Narvo was still stiff and cold behind the glaze.

'Where could I find it? Over at District at Cawndilla?'

There was a slight hesitation; then: 'No, I don't think so. Look, why do you want to go into this? Have you got something on Chess Hardstaff?'

'I've got nothing on nobody so far,' he said and smiled at his double negative; but Narvo was in no mood for humour, weak or hilarious. Malone paused, looking steadily at the uniformed man opposite him. 'Hugh, let me tell you something about the way I work. I don't believe any crime starts the moment it happens, not even a so-called crime of passion. The start of it is buried somewhere inside the person who commits it. My wife, who is the educated one in our family, once told me that some Greek philosopher said that a man's character is his own fate. So I start looking into the past when I come into a case, because that's where the present began.' He had enough modesty to hope that he didn't sound pompous; pomposity has sunk more wisdom than ridicule ever has. 'I'm not saying, or even thinking, that Chess Hardstaff had anything to do with his wife's murder or Sagawa's. I just want to know what makes the man tick, why everyone in this district seems to genuflect whenever his name's mentioned. I don't know, but he may have influenced the one who killed Sagawa. If I have to go back to interview him again, I want to know everything I can about him. And if his wife was murdered, I want to know about that, too.'

There was silence in the room. In the outer offices there was the murmur of voices; at the front desk someone shouted, as if wanting to start an argument. At last Narvo said, 'Are you going to go into the background of everyone around here? Go back and dig up their past?'

'If I have to. You'd better face it, Hugh – I'm going to make waves.'

'Jesus!' The glaze broke. Narvo sat silent for a while; Malone did not hurry him. Then the uniformed man sighed resignedly. 'Okay, I guess it can't be avoided – making waves, I mean. Maybe we should never have called you in on the Sagawa business.' He said it without resentment and Malone didn't take offence. 'I was a very junior constable back then. I was the cop who first saw Dorothy Hardstaff's body.'

'Was she a local woman?'

'No, she was from Sydney.'

'Prominent family? These silvertails usually marry their own kind. The same school, that sort of thing.'

'No, she wasn't, not as far as I remember. She was never a favourite of old Chester Hardstaff's, she was a nobody as far as he was concerned.'

'What happened?'

'She was strangled with her own nightgown.'

'Raped?'

'No, there was no sign of that. There were one or two things that didn't add up . . .' He got up, came round from behind his desk and closed the door of his office. Then he went back and sat down, again lapsing into silence for a while. Somehow or other he looked less neat now, though there was no sign of disarray in his uniform or his precisely combed hair; the neatness had gone from his control. 'There was no sign of a struggle, she looked as if she had been strangled in her sleep – she was lying on the bed, the nightgown around her neck. There were bruise marks on her throat, they looked like fingermarks, but they weren't mentioned in the GMO's report.'

'Who was the GMO then? Doc Nothling?'

'No, it was an old chap named Postle, he's dead now. Max Nothling didn't come here to Collamundra till after the murder. His wife Amanda wanted to come home after her mother's death. They'd been living in Perth, where Nothling comes from.'

'Any other Hardstaff kids?'

'Another daughter, I've forgotten her name. She lives in London, never comes home. They say she's a lesbian, but no one knows. That's about the worst they can say about anyone in a district like ours, that someone's gay. It upset all the locals when the Department of Agriculture put out a piece that said cows could be lesbians.' For the first time Narvo cracked a smile, though it was only a tiny crack and looked more like an easing of tension than an expression of humour. 'The Country Women's Association, the local branch, said it was disgusting things like that should be said about animals.'

Malone returned the smile, hoping for some level of accord with this stiff, tightly-controlled man. 'Did you query the omission in the GMO's report about those fingermarks on Mrs Hardstaff's throat? And no sign of a struggle?'

Narvo nodded. 'I also mentioned in the running sheet that there was no sign of forced entry into the house, though it wasn't unusual back then for doors to be left unlocked. It's different now,' he added.

'Where was Chess Hardstaff?'

'He was out on the run, he'd left at daybreak. They were putting in a new dam out on the far boundary and he'd gone out to do the preliminary marking-out of where he wanted it. He got back at breakfast time and by then the body had been discovered by the housekeeper. Old Chester was still alive then, he lived in another wing of the main house, and he'd already called the police. I was the first one out there, I was coming in from Cawndilla and I took the call on the radio.'

'So what happened after you queried those omissions?'

'I was transferred, right out of the blue.' His hand strayed to his desk, re-arranged the already neatly arranged papers, the leather cup that held half a dozen pens, the diary. Malone wondered if he had always been so ordered, if he had been just as corseted as this when he had been a junior constable and naive enough to ask unwanted questions. 'I was sent to Murwillumbah.'

That was six hundred kilometres from Collamundra, just inside the border with Queensland, the edge of the world. 'Is that why your memory is so good on the details?'

'You're sharp, aren't you? You mean because I still hold a grudge? I don't know why I'm telling *you* this – but yes, I still think I got the dirty end of the stick.'

'Who was in charge of the investigation?'

'Peter Dammie. He's now the Superintendent over at Cawndilla. The coroner's verdict was that it was done by person or persons unknown.'

'I think that's what a lot of people would like to think about the Sagawa murder – person or persons unknown. No cop likes that on a file, not if he's honest.'

'I was young then, I thought if you helped solve a murder case, you'd be marked for promotion . . . There'd been a few blokes in the district at that time looking for work. We used to get families who'd pull up here for a couple of months, camp out by the river and do some casual work, then head south for the Riverina, down by the Murrumbidgee and around there, for the fruit harvest. It could've been one of them, though nothing was reported stolen, no money or jewelry. Anyhow, that was the verdict.'

'But you were never called as a witness?'

'They weren't going to bring me all the way down from Murwillumbah. Peter Dammie gave all the police evidence.' He leaned back in his chair, pushing himself back with his hands on his desk and leaving them resting on its edge. The starch had gone out of him, but he hadn't wilted. 'Scobie, forget it. There's no evidence at all that anyone locally did it. You make waves and Chess Hardstaff will have your arse kicked in and you'll finish up at Murwillumbah like I did.'

Malone grinned. 'Tibooburra is the new threat.' Tibooburra was in the far north-west of the State, as remote as one could get from a city posting, out where the kangaroos considered themselves the rightful voters and the only politician ever to visit the place had fainted from lack of attention. 'Righto, I'll paddle quietly. But if I wanted to look up the Hardstaff file, where would I find it?'

'You wouldn't. Just out of curiosity, I asked Peter Dammie about it a year or so ago. He told me it had been lost. It was a bald-faced lie, but Peter's good at those. After that, I decided to mind my own business. Some day I may be District Superintendent, if I tread carefully. Maybe I'll look for it then. But officially, I'll let it stay lost.'

The two men were silent for a while, a sudden bond established between them that had been undetected in the making. Narvo got up and went and opened the door again; the sounds of the station once more could be heard. Based at Police Centre in the city, Malone had almost forgotten the atmosphere of a local police station. Now there were snatches of noise, like daubs on an abstract painting: a drunk being hauled in, a woman shouting abuse, the chiacking amongst some cops as they came in from the beat. Out at the front desk he knew there would always be some citizen asking questions, demanding rights, paying fines: the duty officer would be doing his best to be polite, though bored almost to unconsciousness by the same-every-day routine of it. Normally a country police station would be relatively quiet, but today's activity seemed to reflect the atmosphere outside in the rest of the town: the beginning of what might prove to be a wild weekend. The annual Cup meeting, a murder, a suicide: all the ingredients were there.

'Are all your men going to be on duty this weekend?'

'They'll need to be. You're not going to ask for one or two, are you?'

'No, Curly and Wally Mungle will do. Who do you get in town on a weekend like this? Pickpockets, hookers, stuff like that?'

'No pickpockets, not that I know of. Some hookers, but they are mostly casuals, not full-time. They come in from some of the bigger towns, they're no real problem. We never pick them up, unless we get complaints about them. When we do, we just run them out of town.'

Life, it seemed, was normally so simple here in Collamundra; except for the occasional murder. Malone stood up, at ease now with Narvo. 'If I want to use the computer, is it okay?'

'Sure, just tell Janine. She'll fix it.'

'What's it connected to?'

'District Headquarters, Police Central in Sydney, shire registry, the motor registry.'

'The hospital?'

Narvo frowned, sensing waves again. 'Yes. It's not usual, but the hospital board okayed it. It happened three years ago when we had the bad floods through here, and we haven't been disconnected.'

'Where will I find Ray Chakiros?'

Narvo looked at his watch. 'He'd be down at the Legion club, he's always there this time of day. Is he on your list?'

'Of suspects?' Malone shook his head. 'I haven't even talked to him yet. But he owns a Mercedes, doesn't he?'

'What's that got to do with it?'

'Billy Koowarra told me he was out at the gin the night Sagawa was murdered. He saw a Mercedes parked alongside Sagawa's car. There was no mention of that in the running sheet. There's been some pretty sloppy work on this one, Hugh. I'm not going to report anyone, but you can't expect me to continue the sloppy work. I think I can guess what happened on Billy's evidence about the Merc. Wally Mungle probably interviewed Billy and decided the less Billy knew about the case, or *showed* what he knew, the better. Billy was his cousin and a Koori, he was going to look after him. I don't condone it, but it's understandable – I've known cops who look after each other.' He waited for some reaction from Narvo; but there was none. He went on, 'You spoiled things, Hugh, when you invited Russ and me in.'

For a moment it looked as if the glaze might set in again; but then once more there was the slight crack of a smile and Narvo nodded. 'Go ahead and talk to Ray Chakiros. Or go ahead and listen. He'll do all the talking.'

Malone went back upstairs to the detectives' room. The drunk, still shouting, was being led along to the cells in the lock-up; Malone felt some relief that he was a white youth and not a Koori.

Clements was adding to the running sheets as Malone came into the room. 'How'd it go?'

'Narvo's on our side, up to a point. He won't like us making waves, but he's not going to stop us. Go down and see Janine in the office – she's a blonde who should stir up a red-blooded feller like you. Ask her to plug in the computer to the hospital, tap into their records and get all you can about Doc Nothling and Dr Bedi. Where's Curly?'

'Wally Mungle rang in. A coupla Abo stirrers have come up from Canberra. They didn't know about Billy Koowarra's suicide till they got here, but Wally thinks they're gunna make something of it.'

'Where are they?'

'Out at the blacks' settlement. Curly's gone down to hear their pitch before the uniformed guys move in. I gather some of the young uniformed blokes wouldn't mind a bit of a stoush with the young Abos. It's been building up.'

'Well, that's none of our business. Go down and see what you can get out of the hospital computer on Nothling and Bedi. I'm going to ring Greg Random.'

Random, newly promoted, was the Commander, Regional Crime Squad, South Region. He and Malone had worked together in the old Homicide Squad before regionalization and they knew the limits and strains of each other's field. He greeted Malone's call with, 'What are you doing out there – having a holiday?'

'Never had it so good. Greg, this job has got – what used the kids say? – vibes.'

'I never listened to my kids when they talked like that.' Malone knew that in lots of ways he himself was old-fashioned, but

Random could be turn-of-the-century; yet he was a good cop, one of the best. 'What sort of – *vibes*?'

'I dunno, I can't put my finger on them. But trying to get information out of some of the locals here is like trying to get it down in Chinatown or out in Cabramatta amongst the Vietnamese. Did you know this is Chess Hardstaff's territory? I mean *his territory*?'

'I knew he lived out there, I never knew how much clout he had.' In the days of the Labour government, country politicians, elected or otherwise, had had little effect on the Police Department. Then the Premier, Hans Vanderberg, The Dutchman, had also been the Police Minister and he had brooked no interference from the hayseeds. Now one of the hayseeds was the Minister and the Department was having to change focus.

'He's King out here, Greg. He's told me to phone first for an interview.'

'I hope you didn't tell him what I know you're capable of telling him.' Random was as dry as a salt-caked creek-bed. 'Is he involved in the case?'

'I don't know. That's the trouble – I don't know much at all at the moment. It's like trying to catch scraps of paper in the wind –'

'Very literary. Cut out the bull and tell me what you want.'

'I want to stay out here – and keep Russ with me – till I can wrap it up.'

'If you do wrap it up, is it going to make waves?'

'Crumbs, you sound just like the locals. Yeah, I guess it will. Does it matter?'

'Simmer down. It might matter. Our much-admired Police Minister has already been on to the Commissioner, who's been on to an Assistant Commissioner, who's been on to me. The gist of it all is that Mr Dircks wants to know why you can't be sent to Tibooburra to direct traffic or arrest kangaroos or something.'

'Are you sending me there?'

'No. But just go carefully and get it over and done with as soon as you can. Things are still quiet down here, but it can't last. If it does, we'll all be out of a job.'

Malone hung up. Murder, he knew, was like the common cold: no one had yet discovered a cure for it. He was not often philosophical, but he sometimes wondered how the world would have gone if Abel had managed to sweet-talk Cain out of killing him.

2

The Veterans Legion had for years been one of the jealously guarded domains of men who had served overseas. At one time its political clout had had the fire-power of a division of howitzers; politicians who had opposed its ultra-conservative views had been blasted off the map; only discretion from more sensible members had stopped the national committee from emblazoning these victories beside their wartime battle honours. Time passed and so did many of the old members: age did not weary them nor the years condemn, as the Legion's prayer said, but death did not listen and took them anyway, just as it did the conscientious objectors, the communists and all the other enemies. Eventually the Legion, to survive, had to open its doors to virtually all and sundry. Well, sundry, perhaps, but not all. There were still candidates for membership who found themselves blackballed and not just because they might be Aborigines. There were no blacks from the river settlement who were members of the Collamundra Veterans Legion Club.

The club was a solid red-brick building built from the proceeds of the club's poker-machines; the one-armed bandit was now a national icon, along with the long-gone two-armed bushrangers. The club's conservatism was flexible.

The car park was full and Malone had trouble finding a space for the Commodore. Once inside the club he had trouble finding space for himself; it was thronged with men and women, the latter out-numbered ten to one. The hubbub seemed to be the human equivalent of the noise he had heard out at the cotton gin; he had to shout at the top of his voice into a nearby ear when he asked where he could find Ray Chakiros. The ear leaned away from him and a fist, holding a foaming glass, came up and waved towards the back of the big main room.

Malone pushed his way through the crowd, aware that some men, recognizing him, made no effort to make way for him; he brushed by them, once feeling a shoulder thump against his own. Though it was only five o'clock, many of the men already looked close to being drunk, as if they had been drinking all afternoon; red faces turned towards him, mouths opened and beer fumes enveloped him as if he were swimming through a brewery vat. But he was used to it: he was a beer drinker himself and this was not the first time he had had to make his way through a crowd intent on getting a skinful. He had never been that sort of drinker, but he had learned to tolerate them. Except when they got outside and got into their cars and drove out to endanger other people. He sometimes wondered how tolerant he would be as a highway patrol officer if, after the carnage of a bad accident, he had to arrest a drunken driver. He had, occasionally, been more sympathetic towards a premeditated murderer, a wife, for instance, who had shot her brutal husband, than he might have been towards the involuntary killers.

He slipped out of the crowd, went through a doorway into a short hallway and found Ray Chakiros in his office at the end of it. There were two other men with him: all three men looked much the same, in their late sixties, plump and well-fed and prosperous-looking, businessmen and not farmers. They all looked at him with the same mixture of suspicion and puzzlement: what was he doing here in the club uninvited?

'Can I see you alone, Mr Chakiros?' He wasn't sure which was Chakiros, but took him to be the grey-haired man with the thick moustache behind the desk. 'I'm Detective-Inspector Malone.'

'As if we didn't know,' said Chakiros and smiled at the other two men, neither of whom smiled in return. 'D'you mind, George? Les? We can continue our business later. Come in, Inspector, sit down.'

The two men got up and without a word went out of the office, leaving a faint chill behind them. But Malone was used to that; he had walked into as many chill winds as an Antarctic explorer.

'I'm on the Sagawa case, Mr Chakiros. But you probably know that, as well.'

'Naturally, naturally. There's practically nothing that goes on in this town that I don't know about, Inspector – that's part of being president of such a club as ours. We're the biggest in the district – bigger than the golf club or the bowling club –' He was ready to run on, his tongue full of running, but Malone cut in:

'That's why I came to you, Mr Chakiros. What did you know about Mr Sagawa?'

The club president sobered. 'All that I needed to know – which wasn't much. He was a Nip.'

'Yes, I've established that.'

But Chakiros was impregnable to irony; it bounced off him as off an anvil. He had been a handsome man in his youth and there were still hints of it under the plump cheeks and the jowly jaw-line; but his sense of humour had always been shallow, had not deepened with the years. He laughed a lot, but it was an empty sound, like canned TV laughter.

'How did you meet him?' said Malone.

'He came here, he wanted to join the Veterans Legion as an associate member. They tell me he was a great joiner – the golf club, the bowling club, he tried the lot. The bloody hide of him! A Jap, not even a veteran, wanting to join the Legion!'

The room had now started to impress itself upon Malone. It was a tiny museum to patriotism; not that he was against that sentiment, but this seemed overpowering. The walls were covered with photos of heroes, decorated men in uniform; furled flags stood in corners waiting to flutter in the breeze from unseen trumpets. Large prints of paintings of the Queen and the Duke of Edinburgh hung behind Chakiros; there were no photos or paintings of the Governor-General or the Prime Minister; patriotism, evidently, should not be too localized. Yet, on a level and of a size with the Queen and the Duke, there was a painting of Chester Hardstaff, Past President of the Club.

Malone said, 'It would have been worse, wouldn't it, if Mr Sagawa had been a veteran? Say he'd fought against you in New Guinea?'

Chakiros's eyebrows were not grey like his hair and moustache, but were black, almost as if they had been charcoaled; they came down now in a thick dark line that almost met across the bridge of his nose. 'You're not pro-Jap, are you? Don't get me wrong – I'm not *anti*-Jap.' His acting was terrible; he wasn't even a good hypocrite. 'I just don't think they should be buying up the country the way they are.'

'I don't believe Mr Sagawa was buying up the country. He was just the general manager of South Cloud.'

'Same thing. He represented the buyers. They're gobbling up the country, buying up the farm.'

'Who's selling it to them? Selling the farm is like doing the tango – it takes two to do it.'

'I can see you're a city feller, it sticks out all over you. Everything is a business deal down there.'

'Not in the Police Department.'

'Oh? You could've fooled me, from what Gus Dircks has told me. I understand he's really cleaned up the Department. I don't mean you to take that personally.'

'I'll try not to. Speaking of Mr Dircks, I understand he's a partner in South Cloud, that he sold off part of his farm to them. Is he pro-Japanese?'

The eyebrows came down again. 'You better ask him.'

'And your past president –' Malone nodded at the portrait of Hardstaff. Whoever had painted it had been inspired, or instructed, first to study the portraits of Spanish kings; all that was missing from Chester II was the breastplate and the sword on which to rest the royal hand. 'Didn't he introduce the Japanese to the district?'

Now only the nose separated the eyebrows from the moustache; the dark eyes were almost hidden. 'You better ask him, too.'

Malone decided it was time to change tack. 'Do you own a Mercedes, Mr Chakiros?'

The eyebrows climbed again. 'Yes. I'm the local distributor – you wouldn't expect me to drive a Jaguar or something, would you? Why?'

'What colour?'

'Beige. I think there's a fancy name for it, but that's what it is, beige.'

'Seems a popular colour out here.'

'It doesn't show the dust. We do a lotta travelling on gravel roads, not like in the city. Some money spent on roads out here wouldn't go astray.'

'Maybe Mr Dircks will be able to fix that for you, now he's a minister.' Malone chanced his arm, an old fast bowler's ploy: 'I'm sure Chess Hardstaff is working on him.'

Again the irony bounced off Chakiros; he saw the world in black and white, preferably white. 'That's what governments are for, to look after the people who put them in.'

Cronyism: but Malone stopped his tongue from going too far. 'Were you driving your car last Monday night?'

'I drive my car every night. I come here to the club every night, never miss. I don't always stay, the wife'd complain if I did. Women don't always appreciate the value of a club like this.'

'Where do you live, Mr Chakiros?'

'Right here in town, in River Street, the best part of town. Why d'you want to know was I driving the car Monday night? That was the night the Nip was murdered, right? Do you think I had something to do with that?'

'Mr Chakiros, all I'm doing is making enquiries. At the moment I've got no theories at all.'

'Well, you're making a bloody good fist of sounding like you got a theory!' Chakiros slapped a big plump hand on his desk. 'Jesus Christ, you come in here, shoving your nose in –'

'We don't shove our noses in unless we're invited.'

'I didn't invite you in here to badger me like this!'

'No, that's true. Are you saying you're refusing to answer any questions I want to put to you?'

The bluster went out of Chakiros; he backed down. 'No. Well, no, I'm not saying that. I'll answer your questions. Except if they get too personal.' But he didn't define what he meant by too personal; and he was not sure himself. He was a man of finite wisdom, not even approaching the boundaries of himself. He lived on dreams which had turned into false memories; he had wanted to be a hero, but had been denied the opportunity. The war had finished too soon for him: he was still fighting it, though he had never really got into it. He had cousins in Beirut, relatives in a city he had never visited, who had seen far more of war than he ever had. 'Stick to Sagawa and what happened to him.'

'Did you ever go out to the cotton farm?'

Chakiros hesitated. 'Yeah, I did. Once.'

'When?'

Again the hesitation; he tugged nervously at his moustache, as if it were no more than a cheap disguise he wanted to remove. 'Monday night.' Then the tongue began to roll: 'He was getting – assertive. Yeah, that's the word, assertive. He'd been to Chess Hardstaff and told him I'd said he couldn't join the club. He was carrying tales.'

'Did Chess Hardstaff want him admitted to the club?'

'No. Chess is an old Digger, like m'self. Well, not a Digger, exactly. He was in the air force, a fighter. He got a DFC and bar.' He looked up at the portrait. 'We wanted him painted in his uniform with decorations, but he wouldn't have that. He's modest about those sorta things.' He said it wistfully, as if he wished for those sorta things himself.

'I'm sure he's modest about other things,' said Malone; and wondered if Hardstaff would be offended if he knew that he was considered modest. 'Did he tell Sagawa that he wasn't wanted in the club?'

'Yes, he did. Chess doesn't pull punches, he tells you exactly what he thinks. He's never – *ambivalent*. Yeah, that's the word, ambivalent.' Malone had always thought of ambivalence as a two-eyed stance in a one-eyed batting line-up; he would never have taken Hardstaff for anything but one-eyed. It might be the only thing on which he and Chakiros would agree. 'He rang me to tell me Sagawa had been to see him. I went out there to the gin to tell *Mister* Sagawa to keep his complaints to himself, that we didn't want any discrimination talk around here.'

'But there is, isn't there?'

'What?'

'Discrimination.'

'Well, there's a bit of that everywhere, isn't there?' He had known it in his youth; and so had his father, even more so. The town's Dagoes: 'Wog' hadn't yet come into fashion. But he never mentioned that now, not even to his own son. 'Not least in the police force. You read about it in the papers, what the police are like towards the darkies over in West Australia or up in Queensland. It's only natural, no one's a hundred per cent bloody Christian, kissing the arses of black, brown or brindle.' He could taste the bile of long ago. 'Sure, there's bloody discrimination, it's a fact of life.'

Malone thought of his father Con, who didn't mind the blacks but couldn't stand a bar of the brown or brindle. Con still believed in White Australia and cursed all the politicians and do-gooders who had muddied its waters with their immigration policies. But Con's prejudices went even further: he would never join any Veterans Legion club, couldn't understand anyone who had gone away to fight for King and Country. For Country, all right; but not for the bloody King of England. Con was Irish to the core and Malone sometimes had to struggle against the Irish in himself. Heritage has its prickles.

'Did you see Sagawa?'

'No, I didn't. His car was outside the office, but he wasn't around anywhere. I went looking for him, but couldn't find him.'

'What time was this?'

'Ten o'clock, ten thirty, somewhere around then. After I left here.'

'That was a bit late to go visiting him, wasn't it?'

'I – I just wanted to make sure no one was around when I talked to him.'

'Did you go to the manager's house?'

'No. That other one, that Koga, would've been there. I didn't want to talk to Sagawa in front of him, just in case things got a bit sticky. You know what the Nips are like, they've got this bloody losing face thing that means so much to them.'

It might yet become an Australian thing, thought Malone: so many local high flyers had lost face recently. He suspected that Chakiros would hate to lose face, but would brazen it out. 'Were the lights still on in the office?'

'Yeah, that was why I thought he was still around the gin somewhere. But he wasn't.'

'No other car there?'

Chakiros shook his head, the black line forming above his eyes again. 'No.'

'You're sure? Come on, Mr Chakiros, don't fart-arse with me. I'm getting a bit bloody tired of running up against brick walls in this town. Make it easier for yourself. Because as sure as Christ, I'm gunna get to the bottom of this, no matter how high you build the wall!'

Chakiros looked genuinely surprised at Malone's burst of temper; he had been fooled by the detective's low-key, almost casual approach. He flushed, suddenly looking very dark in the dusk of the small office. He got up and switched on the light. He came back to stand behind his desk, but didn't sit down again immediately. He stood for a moment looking out through the window to the car park; standing up, he was surprisingly short, a barrel of a man. At last he turned and sat down.

'There wasn't another car outside the office, but one passed me as I drove up from the gate on the main road, up the gravel track to the office. That's a coupla hundred yards, I'd say. I saw its lights coming down towards me and I dipped mine, but he didn't dip his. He seemed to speed up when he was about, I dunno, about fifty yards in front of me and he went past me like a bat outa hell, plastering my car with gravel. It's chipped all down one door. I couldn't see a bloody thing because of his lights, he was on high-beam, and I went off the track. I was bloody lucky I didn't turn over.'

'Did you catch a glimpse of the car as it went past?'

'How could I? I was blinded by his lights.' A few bricks of the wall had been removed, but now they were replaced. 'If you're gunna ask me did I recognize the car, no, I didn't. That's all I'm saying.'

'Was it a Mercedes, light-coloured like yours?'

'No.' But the lie was plain in the dark, uneasy eyes.

3

When Malone got outside to his car he found the front and rear doors on the passenger's side had been bashed in; they had either been kicked in by heavy boots or thumped with a solid object. Whoever had done it could have worked without being seen from the club; the Commodore was hemmed in on both sides by other cars. There would have been some noise, but if anyone had noticed it, it had brought no one to the scene.

He looked about him; he could feel eyes watching him, but he could see no one in the car park. Then he looked over the roof of his car towards the club and saw the line of faces, flushed but frozen, stupid with malice, in the long windows that faced out on to the car park. He felt himself flush, with anger not drink; but he was not going to let them dent him further by showing it. He got into the Commodore, backed it out of the line, swung it round and drove sedately out of the car park: to burn rubber would only show his anger. He could imagine the faces in the windows breaking like cracked plates as they laughed; but he didn't look back. He had been subjected to treatment like this before, it was part of a policeman's lot, but he could not remember ever having been as angry as this. He slowed down when, out in the street, he realized he was driving almost blind.

To give himself time to cool down before he went back to the Mail Coach and probably more open aggression, he went looking for the shire library. He found it on the other side of the courthouse from the police station, a cream building almost a twin of the station. It was still open, the lights now on, but it was virtually empty. There was an old man with a beard sitting at a table in a far corner reading a newspaper file; and the librarian sitting at the front desk filing some cards. She looked up as Malone stood in front of her.

'We're just about to close –'

He showed her his badge and introduced himself. 'I'd like to look at the editions of the local paper for November nineteen seventy-three. You have them on file, I take it?'

She looked at him carefully, taking off her glasses as if to get him into focus. She was young, in her late twenties, pretty, with big short-sighted eyes and a small mouth that detracted from her prettiness. She pursed it now.

'It's already out. You'll have to wait till that gentleman down the back has finished with it. I gave it to him about twenty minutes ago.'

Malone looked towards the old man, but decided not to approach him. 'I'll wait.'

'I'm waiting to close,' the librarian said primly. Were all librarians prim? he wondered; or was that just their best way of dealing with unwelcome borrowers? She got up from behind her desk, went and locked the front doors and came back. 'All my staff have gone home, I'd like to do the same. It's Friday night.'

He smiled, hoping to break through her primness. 'I'm sorry, Miss – ?'

'Mrs.' She had a low pleasant voice, not prim at all. 'Mrs Dircks. Veronica Dircks.'

He showed no surprise; but felt some. Then remembered that in country districts it was not unusual to have large clans. 'Any relation to Gus Dircks?'

'His daughter-in-law. My husband is editor of the Collamundra *Chronicle*.'

It seemed that Gus Dircks, indirectly, had a finger in every information pie in the district. He mentally put Gus Dircks's son on his visiting list, if only to see how much freedom the press enjoyed in Collamundra.

The old man came up from the back of the library to the desk, laid down the file, said, 'Thank you,' went to the front doors and tried to open them, but failed. He looked back at Mrs Dircks. 'You've locked me in,' he said and sounded shocked, almost a little panic-stricken.

'No, just pull back the bottom lock,' said Mrs Dircks, not moving to help him.

The old man stared at her, not looking at Malone at all. He was tall and thin, with a long thin face half-hidden by a white beard; his clothes were stained and patched, but he was wearing what looked to be brand-new black boots. He carried a battered old broad-brimmed hat in a gnarled hand and, for all his trampish appearance, looked clean and had a certain presence. But the locked door seemed for the moment to have unsettled him; then he recovered and pulled back the bottom lock. 'Thank you,' he said again and went out into the gathering evening.

'Who's he?' asked Malone.

'I don't know. A stranger – the town's full of them this weekend. It's odd you both wanted to see the same edition of the *Chronicle*, one so old.' Seventeen years old: that would make her no more than ten or eleven when the paper had run its story on the murder of Dorothy Hardstaff. 'What happened then?'

Evidently the Hardstaff murder was never discussed in the Dircks family circle. 'You don't come from Collamundra?'

'No, I'm from Queensland.' Another country, some said another planet. A murder, even of the daughter-in-law of a prominent man, in one State rarely raised a ripple of interest in another State; there is a federalism of curiosity as well as of politics. It would, of course, be different if Chess Hardstaff's wife were murdered today; he was now a national figure, far more so than his father had ever been. 'Do me a favour, Inspector – hurry up. I have an appointment with my dressmaker. There's the Cup ball tomorrow night.'

He took the file across to a nearby table, sat down and opened its thick cardboard covers. The *Chronicle* was a twice-weekly newspaper, Tuesdays and Fridays: ten pages of agricultural news, stock and grain prices, local news and gossip and six pages of classified advertisements. It took him less than a minute to discover that the story he had come to check was missing; the two editions that had run the murder story had had the relevant pages torn out. He was on his feet at once, running for the door.

'What's the matter? Where – ?'

But he was out in the street and heard no more of what Mrs Dircks said. He stood on the top of the library steps looking both ways up and down the street; but there was no sign of the bearded old man. Dusk had folded into night; the street-lights were on. But they didn't spotlight the stranger.

He went back into the library. Mrs Dircks stood just inside the doors, puzzled and a little frightened. He smiled at her to put her at ease; frightened women always troubled him. 'It's all right. Come over here.'

He led her towards the table where he'd left the newspaper file. 'I wanted to look up a particular story which I know the *Chronicle* ran. The pages have been torn out.'

She put on her glasses and looked at the ragged edges of the strip that had been left on the foldover of the paper. She was ragged-edged herself; she hated the thought of anyone's coming into her library and defacing her stock, even old newspapers. She looked sideways at him, not at all frightened now. 'What story was on those pages?'

'The murder of Chess Hardstaff's wife.'

'Do you think the old man tore out those pages?'

'I don't know, but I'd guess so. Has anyone asked for that file in the past day or two?' *Since I came into town*: but he didn't add that.

'I wouldn't know. We don't enter up anything on a book or newspaper that is not taken out of the library. I could check with my staff.'

'Do that, would you, please?' He noticed that she had made no comment on the Hardstaff murder; had she, too, been warned not to talk about it? 'You know about the murder?'

There was a pause before she said, 'Yes. We're getting together a history of the district – there's never been one written.'

Malone wondered why: most country towns or districts had an enthusiastic historian, amateur or otherwise. 'Why was that?'

'I think there are certain things in the past that the town doesn't want remembered.'

'But you're going to take the risk?'

All her primness had gone; she was relaxed and trusting. She took off her glasses again, as if aware that they spoiled her looks; but she was not coquettish, it was no more than a small vanity in the company of a man. He always felt uncomfortable with feminists who made an aggression of looking as unattractive as possible: all he wanted to do with women was meet them on equal terms. Especially when on police business.

'*You* take risks, don't you?'

'Yes,' he said. 'A good deal of the time.'

He had taken too many risks in his career, not all of them physical; bullets and knives and iron bars were only part of the danger. He was not recklessly adventurous, but to live without risk was never to get one's feet off the ground. He never thought of himself as idealistic, but there were certain essentials for which one occasionally had to jump off a cliff: truth, justice, personal judgement. He smiled at Mrs Dircks and wished her well here in Hardstaff territory.

'It's always worth it,' he said and picked up his hat from the table. 'I'm keeping you from your dressmaker. Enjoy the Cup ball tomorrow night.'

'Will you be coming?' She switched off the lights and opened the front doors.

'I doubt it.' But Lisa, always protective of him, not wanting him to wear out his detective's nose on the grindstone, had suggested they go to the ball with the Warings.

At the bottom of the outside steps Mrs Dircks turned to him. 'You're trying to find who murdered Ken Sagawa, aren't you? What connection has that with the murder of Mrs Hardstaff all those years ago?'

'None, as far as I know. But it was hushed up and I've got the feeling some people in town would like the Sagawa murder hushed up, too. That may be the only connection. That's off the record, of course.'

'What do you mean?'

'Well, your husband's a newspaperman, isn't he? I wouldn't want him publishing a remark like that.' But he hoped she would at least tell her husband what he had said: anything to throw a little grit in the works.

He saw her small mouth purse, and he knew he had put a taste on her tongue that she could not wait to spit out to someone: perhaps even Gus Dircks himself. He had taken another risk, a small one, and it gave him a certain pleasure.

'Will you be okay, going home on your own?'

Her eyes widened. 'Why not? This is a safe town, Inspector.'

'I'm sure it is. Except that, as you said, there are a lot of strangers around this weekend. You never know . . . If that old man comes back to the library, will you call me at the station? Sergeant Baldock will pass on any message to me. Goodnight. Oh, and don't forget – ask your staff who took out the *Chronicle* file in the past week.'

When he got back to the Mail Coach Hotel the two bars were bursting at the seams. The noise boomed out at him as he got out of the Commodore; brewers have never over-estimated the stamina of Australian drinkers. Groups of men, foam-fisted, loud-voiced, blocked the footpath outside the hotel; they made no effort to get out of Malone's way, but he manoeuvred himself through them without causing any ruction. He remarked that there were no Aborigines in sight.

Except Wally Mungle, who stood inside the narrow entrance hall with Koga, the Koori looking as alien as the Japanese. With them was Mrs Potter.

'I'm doing this under protest, Inspector,' she flung at Malone as soon as she saw him; it seemed to him that she was speaking for the benefit of the crowd of drinkers just behind him. 'I've had to cancel –'

'Can we go upstairs?' said Malone and without looking back led the way up to his room.

Koga stood aside to let Mrs Potter go first; so did Mungle. The Japanese gave a slight bow of his head to her; but the Koori showed no expression at all. The three of them followed Malone up the stairs and at once the hallway below was crowded with drinkers spilling in from the street and from out of the bars.

'Give us a yell if you want us, Narelle!'

'We're right behind you, love!'

Clements was in the bedroom in his shirt-sleeves, putting down the phone as Malone walked in. 'I've been on to Andy Graham. Nothing from Tokyo yet . . . Hello, Narelle. You look fussed.'

'That's a polite word for it! I've got to turn over a double room to – to –' Malone waited for her to say *this Jap*; but she stopped herself: 'to Mr Koga here. Everyone's crying out for a hotel bed and there'll be one going to waste in his room –'

'No, there won't,' Malone interrupted. 'Detective Mungle will be staying with Mr Koga. Is that right, Wally?'

'Yes, sir.' There was still no expression on his face.

'Who's going to pay?' demanded Mrs Potter, getting her priorities right: profit before prejudice.

'The Police Department,' said Malone.

'Cash.'

Malone shook his head, trying to retain his good humour; or at least make a pretence of it. 'Have you ever heard of the government paying cash for anything? I'll sign for it and I'll guarantee you are paid.'

'Why can't you pay for it and then claim it?'

'You know the rumour – a policeman never pays for anything.'

'The room's a hundred dollars a night, same as yours.' She was profiteering, taking advantage of the demand, but she was brazen about it. Malone grudgingly conceded that Narelle would never be two-faced about anything.

The New South Wales Police Department paid a daily allowance of ninety-eight dollars to cover food and lodgings when away from home, and threw in an extra thirty-five cents in case some over-extravagant officer, usually not a native-born one, wanted to leave a tip. 'You'll get your money, Mrs Potter.'

'Will they be eating in the dining-room?' She hadn't looked at Koga or Mungle since they had all come into the bedroom.

'No. I think it'd be better if they ate in their room.'

'I don't have the staff for room service.'

'Then Detective Mungle will come down and get their meal. Thanks, Mrs Potter, for all your help. I'll write you a Police Department commendation.'

His voice was flat; but the sarcasm coated the room's sudden moment of silence. Narelle Potter glared at him, then turned and went out of the room like a dark fury. Malone went to the door, called after her, 'Which is their room?'

'Number Twelve!' she shouted, without looking back at him, and was gone down the stairs to a roar of welcome from her battalion below.

Malone turned back to Koga and Mungle. 'That's next door. I think it'd be advisable, Mr Koga, if you stayed in your room at night over this weekend.'

Koga nodded reluctantly. He took off his glasses and polished them; again there was the impression that he was no more than a bewildered schoolboy. 'Sergeant Baldock explained. How long is it going to be like this, Inspector?'

'I honestly don't know.' Perhaps the antagonism towards any Japanese who came into the district would never cease. Not while there were people like Ray Chakiros and Narelle Potter to stir the pot.

Koga said nothing, standing immobile for a long moment. Then he looked at his glasses, as if wondering whether to put them on again: perhaps the world would, miraculously, look better without them. Then he sighed, put them on carefully, bowed his head to Malone and Clements and went out of the room towards Number 12. Malone looked at Mungle.

'Well, Wally? You've got something on your mind.'

Mungle glanced from one to the other of the two Sydney men before he said, 'Why me, Inspector? Jesus, a Koori looking after a Jap in this town!'

'I don't know, Wally. I guess Sergeant Baldock must've detailed you for the job.' But he wondered why. 'I'll talk to him. Is he still at the station?'

'I think so. He was finishing up the week's paper work.'

'Righto. Wear it for tonight, Wally. I'll see what I can do about the rest of the weekend.'

Koga came back to the door. 'I do not like to complain, Inspector, but there is no television in our room.'

'Narelle must have had them take it out,' said Clements, who up till now had been silent. 'She really is a bitch, isn't she?'

'You can come in here and look at ours,' said Malone. 'Sergeant Clements and I are going out to dinner. We'll be out at Trevor Waring's place, Wally. Call us there if there's any trouble. We'll be back about eleven.'

Wally Mungle shrugged resignedly; it seemed that he was used to resignation, as some people are to a minor chronic illness. Then he glanced at Koga. 'We'll look at *The Golden Girls*.'

'I do not know the programme.'

'It's about three middle-aged American biddies looking for men to go to bed with. Maybe you and me can call 'em up.'

Then he and Koga went along to their room.

Malone looked at Clements. 'Wally will survive.'

'What about Koga?'

Malone shrugged, but not with resignation; it wasn't in his nature. He had been quicker than most Australians of his and older generations to understand how most foreigners thought, particularly Europeans; Lisa, sometimes deliberately, more often by example, had coached him there. Asians, however, for the most part baffled him. Which put him in the exalted company of certain presidents and prime ministers. 'Who knows what a Japanese thinks? Do you?'

'Sometimes I wonder if I know what *anyone* thinks.'

'It always takes you a while to wake up to what women think.'

'You mean Narelle? Don't rub it in. I've been listening to gossip about her down at the station – the uniformed guys, well, some of 'em, are talking to me now. Up till her husband died, Narelle evidently was a mousey little wife – in public, anyway. Then after he was gone, about two or three years ago, she started to play around. Anyone and everyone, so long as he wasn't married and was from out of town. I gather she wouldn't know Tom's dick from Harry's. Jesus, for all I know I could of got AIDS!' The thought startled him and he looked down at his zipped-up fly.

Malone gave him no sympathy. 'Then you won't mind if I use the shower first?'

Fifteen minutes later the two of them were ready to leave. Malone went along to Number 12, tapped on the door and opened it. Mungle and Koga were sitting on twin beds facing each other, like prisoners from separate wars who had finished up in a neutral cell.

'The TV's all yours. I'll see you at breakfast.'

When Malone and Clements went downstairs the hallway was crowded and the two big men had to push their way through the crush. Again no one made way for them and Malone, once more, felt his temper rising. Across the heads of the drinkers he saw Narelle Potter in her small office. She stared at him as if he were – a foreigner?

Driving out of town he said, 'Did you find out anything more about Nothling from the hospital computer?'

'He was born in Rangoon in nineteen forty. He got his medical degree at Guy's Hospital in London. He's an FRCS, London. He practised in Perth for five years before coming here.'

'Nothing else?'

'Nothing personal about him, just the bare facts. Hospital computers never say as much about doctors as they do about patients. That's against medical ethics.'

Malone grinned at that. They crossed the river and passed the showground where the carnival and circus were in full swing; coloured electric globes swung against the darkness like a conflagration of fireflies and, through Clements's half-opened window, there came the sawing of raucous music. Malone had to slow to pass the traffic turning into the showground.

Once clear again he said, 'What about Dr Bedi?'

'Born in Simla, India. She got her degree at St Mary's in London. Five years in hospitals in India, Bombay, Simla. She came out here a year ago.'

'None of that tells us much.'

'No. I think we're gunna do better listening to gossip.'

Which wouldn't be the first time they had gone down that track looking for clues.

They turned in at the Waring gates and drove up towards the house. The car's headlights heralded their approach; the Malone family was on the front steps waiting for them. Neither Malone nor Lisa had siblings and the Malone children had adopted Clements as Uncle Russ: he was as welcome as their father. More so, since he always brought them something. Malone kissed Lisa and waited for the kids to greet him; but they had greeted him last night, hadn't they, and they were too busy with Uncle Russ. He had brought small gifts for them and the Waring children: he was the ideal uncle.

Lisa kissed him. 'You're wasted, Russ. You should be a father.' She had been trying to marry him off ever since she had first met him. 'While you're out here we'll try and find you a nice country girl.'

'Don't!' screamed Maureen. 'He's better as an uncle! He doesn't want kids of his own!'

Clements agreed: marriage was for braver men than he. They all went into the Waring house, which was built in the colonial style but couldn't have been more than ten or fifteen years old. It looked as if it might originally have been furnished from the pages of *House and Garden*; but the rooms in that magazine have never had a child pass through them, let alone live in them. Children and dogs had worn the edges off the Waring furniture; a lively family had autographed every room. Ida, who had invited Clements to come to dinner with Malone, greeted him with the same warmth as she had shown towards him this afternoon. Malone, senses sharpened now by every nuance, wondered again at the state of the Warings' relationship.

But Trevor Waring's welcome was just as warm as that of his wife. 'Glad to meet you, Russ. A beer or a whisky?'

'Better take one or the other,' said Sean Carmody, seemingly as much at home here as in his own house. 'Trevor has no respect for men who drink wine before a meal.'

'Humphrey Bogart once said he wouldn't trust a man who didn't drink.' Waring did not look like the sort of man who collected the wise sayings of film stars.

'I'd never trust the intelligence of a man who said that.' For a moment father-in-law and son-in-law looked as if they might cross swords; then Carmody smiled and looked at Malone. 'How are things going, Scobie?'

Waring, in the process of pouring beers for the two detectives, paused and glanced over his shoulder. Malone said, 'We're learning a lot. I don't know how useful it's going to be.'

'Learning what?' said Waring, bringing them their beers.

'Just who and what makes things tick around here. Cheers.' He raised his glass. The two women had gone out to put the last touches to the dinner and the children had retreated to another room. 'Tas not here tonight?'

'He's in town with some of his mates,' Waring said offhandedly. He was still standing, his whisky glass in his hand.

'Does he have a girl?' Malone made sure that Claire was not at the door listening to him.

'Half a dozen, maybe a dozen,' said Carmody. 'I shouldn't say this in front of his father, but I think Tas is busier at the weekends than any of the rams we've got here on the properties.'

'Boys will be boys,' said Waring, trying to look like a father-of-the-world. 'The girls know how to look after themselves these days.'

Not my Claire, thought Malone, shotgun on shoulder.

'So you're not getting very far?' Waring was still standing, feet planted firmly in the middle of the room. A lawyer for the defence? Malone wondered. But who would he be defending?

'Do the police get very much co-operation around here?' he said.

'Depends what the police are investigating.' Waring sounded cautious and Malone, once again with ears too sharp, wondered if he were letting his imagination get the better of him.

'Who's not co-operating?' said Carmody.

'Practically everyone.' Malone looked directly at Waring, but his host had turned back to the sideboard to refill his own glass.

Waring, still with his back to them, said, 'Most people think Sagawa was murdered by someone who doesn't belong around here.'

'I keep hearing that, I'm waiting for someone to put it to music.' He couldn't help the acid in his voice; Carmody gave him a sharp look. 'There are a lot of strangers in town for this weekend, I keep hearing that, too. I saw one in the library tonight. An old cove, tall and thin, with a beard.'

'What were you doing in the library?' Waring turned round, at last sat down in a green leather wing-backed chair, obviously Father's Chair.

'Looking up background. I met the librarian, Gus Dircks's daughter-in-law.'

'Was *she* co-operative?'

Malone was aware that Sean Carmody was watching him and Waring, sitting very still in his chair. Even Clements seemed to sense that Waring's question was not an idle one.

'Up to a point. More than her father-in-law has been. But that's off the record. Police are not supposed to make political comments, especially about their own Minister. Is he a friend of yours, Trev?'

'No.' Waring took a long sip of his drink.

Carmody relaxed, slowly swallowed a mouthful of his own whisky. 'Any comment would be water off a duck's back with

Gus. He's got a hide like ironbark. Did Mrs Dircks know the old feller in the library?'

'No. But I think she'd like to find him. So would I. He tore some pages out of the *Chronicle* that I wanted to check.'

'Who would want to tear anything out of the *Chronicle*? It's duller than *Pravda*.' Carmody smiled. 'Sorry. I'm airing my experience. It's a tiresome habit in old men.'

Waring was holding his glass steady with both hands. 'Pages on what? What did he tear out?'

'The old Hardstaff murder.'

Waring's bland face took on character with his puzzlement. 'Why on earth were you looking up that?'

'Curiosity,' said Malone, finished his beer and stood up as Lisa, displaying that impeccable timing that wives sometimes achieve to their husbands' satisfaction, came to the door. 'You want us for dinner?'

The day's tension eased out of Malone during dinner. His family around him gave him not only pleasure but a sense of security; the innocence of his children, and of the Waring brood, was a reminder that the world had not yet surrendered entirely to intrigue and skulduggery and murder. But he himself was not so innocent (or rather, naive) as to believe that their innocence was not vulnerable to those assaults. Still, he took comfort in it, no matter how impermanent it might prove to be.

Lisa, of course, was the bedrock of his security. After dinner he took her outside for a walk in the garden. The nights were cooling now and the day's breeze, which had dropped at sunset, had cleared the air of the last of the dust. A full moon, low and golden, threw shadows from the trees and bushes; but out beyond the garden, the paddocks were greenish-gold, like a wash of verdigris on a vast copper table; the tree shadows there were a tiny distraction, like black pigmentation marks. Somewhere down towards the distant front gates a boobook owl called, its mournful morepork cry emphasizing the immense silence.

'It's so restful,' said Lisa, arm in his.

'That's what you said on the phone, the day before Sagawa was murdered.'

She did not miss a step, but looked at him sideways. She could read his moods, controlled though they were, as if she saw them under a Police Ballistics macroscope; she had learned to handle them without getting too excited or depressed by them. Except, of course, when he was in danger; then she was ready to declare war. 'It's not going well?'

'Bloody terrible. Don't let's talk about it.'

'Whatever you say. Hold me.'

They stopped and he took her in his arms. She was wearing his favourite perfume, Arpège; it cost an arm and a leg, by his tight standards, but he bought it for her every Christmas, no matter what other gift he gave her. He kissed her, their hunger for each other in every nerve-end.

'Have you ever made love in someone else's front garden?' she said.

'No, and I'm not going to start now. I'd be impotent for the rest of my life if the kids came out and caught me on top of you.'

They resumed their walk, she within the circle of his arm. He said as casually as he could, 'Are Ida and Trevor happy?'

Again she looked at him without turning her head. 'Why do you ask?'

'I don't know. I just get a feeling . . .'

'You're a better cop than I thought. No, they're not too happy, Ida told me. They try to keep it from her father and the children, but I think Sean's on to it. They're sleeping in the same room while we're here, but in separate beds.'

'Whose fault is it? His or hers?'

'Both. Or neither. Ida doesn't know, she's candid about that. Trevor has had a couple of affairs, I gather. Not here in Collamundra, but down in Sydney or somewhere.'

'Who with? Local women?'

'Ida thinks that Mrs Potter could be one of them. I gather she's a good time girl. She's what Ida called a girl who's perpetually *moist*.'

'She got her hooks into Russ last night.'

'Not Russ!'

He was sorry he had told her; he backtracked: 'I think he held her off. Russ is no fool.'

'You're all fools when it comes to an easy piece of it.'

'I hope you don't talk like that in front of the kids. You think I'd be a fool and take on Narelle if she offered me a piece of it?'

'You'd certainly be impotent for the rest of your life if you did. I was down at the stockyard today, watching how they turn bulls into bullocks.'

He winced, pressed her shoulder and kissed her. Then he said, 'Has Ida ever mentioned that Trevor owns part of the cotton farm and gin?'

'No. Do you want me to ask her?'

'No! You stay out of it!'

She stopped walking. 'All right, don't get excited. But if he owns something of the cotton farm, does that mean he has something to do with the murder?'

'I hope not –' The net was widening, even if it was full of holes. 'I don't know at this stage. All I've got so far are bits and pieces that don't add up to anything.'

'Oh God! I hope for Ida's sake and the children's that he didn't have anything to do with it. Why would he?' She sounded demanding, like another lawyer for the defence; but Malone knew she was really only defending the Warings. 'Don't press it, darling –'

'You don't mean it – asking me to do something like that.'

She stared at him in the moonlight, saw the pain in his face; then she leaned her head against his chest. 'I know. But you know how I feel about families, about children . . .'

'Don't you think I feel the same?' He wrapped his arms round her and held her to him. Somewhere in the night the boobook owl repeated its mournful cry.

They went back inside. At the door he turned and looked back over his shoulder. The moon had climbed higher, was less golden, was turning hard and bright. It seemed to him that the night had suddenly got colder.

When he left he kissed Claire, Maureen and Tom a little more tenderly than usual. Then he looked at the Waring children, a girl Claire's age and twin boys a year younger; and hoped that, somehow, he could protect them. But he knew in his heart that their protection was not up to him.

He kissed Ida on the cheek, then shook hands with Waring.

'Will you be in town tomorrow morning, Trev? I'd like to see you.' He avoided looking at Lisa. 'Just a few questions about Sagawa.'

There was a deep frown between Waring's eyes; his face was taking on character the more he appeared concerned. 'How about eleven o'clock? We're going to the races tomorrow, but I can meet you at my office.'

'Sure, eleven will be fine.' Malone tried to make the date sound as casual as possible.

'They've asked us to the races with them,' said Clements. 'Are we gunna take the afternoon off?'

'Yeah!' yelled Maureen and Tom. 'We want Uncle Russ to come with us! He's gunna teach us to bet!'

'Just what you need to know,' said their father. 'Righto, if nothing crops up we'll be there.'

Sean Carmody walked over to the Commodore with them. 'Is it just curiosity that's got you interested in the Hardstaff murder or do you really want to know what went on?'

'Do you know what went on, Sean?'

Carmody's gaze was direct. 'No, I don't. But I'm like you, I'm curious. I'm an old journo, remember? I guess old cops feel the same. You are always curious. Even when I'm dead, I'll be wondering what they've said in my obituary.'

'Can you remember what the *Chronicle* said about the Hardstaff murder?'

'No.'

'We can have someone look it up down in Sydney,' said Clements from the other side of the car. 'There should be a copy on file at the State Library.'

'What did Mrs Dircks say about the chap you saw in her library this evening?' said Carmody.

'Nothing, except that he was a stranger to her. He looked to me like an old-time swaggie, except that he was a bit better dressed. He could be a worker with the carnival that's out at the showground. I'll check on him tomorrow morning.'

4

As they turned out of the Waring gates on to the main road, pausing a moment to let a semi-trailer go thundering by, Clements said, 'What's worrying you about Trevor Waring?'

'Was it that obvious?'

'I think old Sean caught it, too. Have you dug up something about him?'

'Nothing, except that he has a share in South Cloud and he didn't bother to mention it.'

Clements nodded, saying nothing further. A car passed them, travelling at high speed towards town, and he cursed it. They had gone about three or four kilometres when, with a glance in the driving mirror, he said, 'We're being tailed.'

Malone looked back. 'I wonder if it's the same cove who tailed me last night? Slow down, see if he passes us.'

Clements dropped the speed; but the other car did the same. Clements speeded up again; so did the other car. Then all at once it came right up on the Commodore, tail-gating it; its lights were on high-beam and Clements had to flip up the driving mirror to block the blinding glare. He touched the brakes and as the brake lights came on, the other car also had to brake, skidding on the road-shoulder as it swung to the side on the gravel. At once Clements put his foot down hard on the Commodore's accelerator and almost immediately they were fifty yards ahead of the car that was chasing them.

Up ahead Malone saw another brightly-lit semi-trailer approaching, coming round a bend a kilometre or so away, moving against the darkness like an illuminated advertising sign. They passed a notice: 'Single Lane Bridge'; and he said, 'Make the bridge before that semi-trailer!'

'Jesus, you wanna get us killed?' But Clements pushed his foot hard on to the floor.

'Swing in behind the semi as soon as you pass and pull up!'

They hit the slight ramp of the bridge and the car was airborne; it landed halfway across the bridge and they went over the wooden planks with a rattling sound like machine-gun-fire. Then they were swamped by lights and the scream of the big truck's siren-like horn. Malone felt everything inside him curl into a tight knot; he opened his mouth to yell in protest as he died. Then they were off the bridge, the truck went past them like a huge blazing wind and for a moment he thought it was going to jack-knife on to them. Then it was past and Clements had skidded the Commodore to a head-jerking stop.

Malone tumbled out, trying to get his stomach unravelled, drew his gun and went running back across the bridge. The semi-trailer was disappearing into the night, its horn still bellowing the driver's anger, and the car that had been following the Commodore was pulled over to the side of the road, its engine still running. Malone reached the car, put his gun in against the driver's cheek and said, 'Turn off the engine!'

The driver did as he was told as Clements, gun drawn, came up on the other side of the car. 'Out! All of you – *out*!'

There were four of them, all youths, none of them looking much more than twenty, if that. They were all overweight, the driver already with a beer belly, dressed in jeans and either sweaters or leather jackets; they looked to be town boys, not farm boys, too close every night to the pubs. They got out of the car and stood silent and sullen while Malone frisked them. Malone could smell the fear on the driver, who had almost fainted when the gun had been pressed against his fat red cheek. All four had been drinking and the smell of beer was strong, but Malone recognized the other smell.

'Righto, what's this all about?'

'What's what about?' That was the youth, slightly older-looking than the others, who had been sitting beside the driver. He was shorter than the other three, black-haired and swarthy, intelligence, or shrewdness, marked in his olive-skinned face. 'We were just out for a drive.'

'Do you all drive?' said Clements. 'Let's see your licences.'

The four of them produced wallets, took out their licences. Clements took them and went round to study them in the car's headlights. Then he jerked his head at Malone. 'Come and have a look at this, Scobie.'

Malone said, 'Don't any of you think of running off into the scrub. You'll get a bullet in your leg if you do.'

'Shit!' said the black-haired youth. 'Is that what you Sydney cops do, shoot guys who just go joy-riding?'

'All the time,' said Malone.

He went to the front of the car, took the licence Clements showed him. He looked at the photo, then stepped aside from the beam of the lights. 'You're Philip Chakiros?'

'Yes,' said the black-haired youth; his manner changed: 'What have we done wrong, Scobie? Come on –'

'Inspector Malone.' Then for the first time he saw the three-pointed star on the front of the car. 'Does your old man let you take his Merc. out on joy-rides? Does he know you let your half-drunk mates drive it?'

Philip Chakiros was suddenly sullen again; then he shook his head. 'He doesn't know I've borrowed it.'

You're a liar, thought Malone. 'Did you borrow it last night, come out here and follow me back to town?'

'No.' This time Malone could not be sure whether the boy was lying or not. Even if he had been standing in the bright dazzle of midday, the youth's face wouldn't have given anything away. This kid, Malone now knew, was experienced at being interrogated; he had fallen into character, an invented one, maybe, but one that he knew how to play. 'I was in town all last night.'

Clements had reached in behind one of the other youths and taken a rifle from the floor of the car behind the front seat. 'See this, Inspector? A Twenty-two.' He held it up, went to the front of the car and looked at it in the headlights' glare. 'A Brno Twenty-two, magazine fully loaded.'

Malone decided to ignore young Chakiros, turned instead to the driver. He was a beefy boy, with long red hair, a weak imitation of a moustache and pale, unintelligent eyes. He would never get anywhere on his own, he would always need others to show him the way; yet one knew that, fifty years down the track, he would still be lost, still not getting anywhere. 'What were you doing with the gun?'

'We've been out shooting kangaroos,' said Philip Chakiros quickly.

'I didn't ask you,' said Malone, not looking at him. 'What's your name, son?'

The red-headed one swallowed. 'Stan Gruber.'

'Is that what you've been doing, Stan – shooting kangaroos?'

'Yeah. Yeah. We didn't have no luck, but.'

Clements lifted the barrel of the rifle to his nose. 'It hasn't been fired tonight. Not unless you sat out there in the bush cleaning it, deodorizing it. I'd say it hasn't been fired since – well, how about last Monday night?'

The four youths looked at each other, like contestants in a TV quiz game for not-very-bright students. Then they caught the point of the question and three of them looked startled. Only Philip Chakiros remained unmoved. 'That's stupid,' he said. 'We weren't even in town last Monday night, we were all over in Bathurst.' That was a couple of hundred kilometres east. 'You can ask anyone. We went over to a country-and-western concert. James Blundell and Deniese Morrison were singing. You can check.'

It was almost too pat: Malone waited for him to name the songs that had been sung. But again there was the doubt as to whether Chakiros was lying. Already Malone could see that this boy had a mind twice as sharp as his father's. Behind Chakiros the other three heads bobbed up and down in almost ridiculous corroboration.

'Yeah,' said Gruber, 'James Blundell we saw, and –'

'I just told him, Stan,' said Chakiros. 'Leave it to me.'

'We'll check,' said Malone. 'In the meantime we're confiscating the gun. You can get it back from Sergeant Baldock at the station, if he doesn't want it for evidence.'

'Curly knows me.' Phil Chakiros, it seemed, was on first-name terms with everyone.

'Does Chess?'

'What?'

'Nothing,' said Malone, feeling a small malicious satisfaction at the sudden puzzlement on the boy's face. 'Who has the licence for the gun?'

There was no reply from any of them. A car came over the bridge and slowed; but Clements stepped out into the middle of the road, still holding the rifle and his own gun; in the glare of the headlights he looked threatening. The car came to a halt and a frightened elderly couple stared out at him.

'Police. Just keep going, please. Drive carefully.'

The car picked up speed again and disappeared into the night. Clements came back and stood beside Malone. 'Isn't anyone gunna talk?'

There was silence: bush silence, stretching out from the small group beside the car to the immense darkness. Malone then stepped close to the driver, put his gun up against the fat cheek again. 'Come on, Stan. Who owns the gun?'

Gruber's eyes looked like marbles about to be fired from his pink face. 'It's Phil's father's –'

'Shit!' said Philip Chakiros.

Malone turned to him. 'Did your father know you'd borrowed the gun?'

'You got no right to do that to Stan! Holding a fucking gun at his head, for Chrissake!'

A bush lawyer: Malone loved them, though this was the first time he had met one actually in the bush. 'You have a point there. You want to argue it in front of the magistrate when he puts in an appearance? Because if you prefer it, we can book you and hold you till we have the gun checked down in Sydney whether it's the one that fired the shot that killed Mr Sagawa.'

Chakiros stared at him: he showed no sign of fear, just sullen anger. 'I'm not gunna say any more, not till I've got my lawyer.'

'Who's your lawyer?'

'Trevor Waring.'

FIVE

1

As they sat down to breakfast next morning at the table by the window Malone said, 'We'll see Curly Baldock first thing, have him send the Twenty-two down to Ballistics. There's a plane at midday. Tell Ballistics I want a report by tomorrow morning.'

'Do you think it's the gun that killed Sagawa?'

'Your guess is as good as mine. But if it is, young Chakiros would be bloody stupid to be carrying it around with him. He's not that dumb. Besides, there must be at least a hundred Twenty-twos in this district.'

Wally Mungle and Koga came into the dining-room and everyone stopped eating; even the out-of-town strangers. Malone had recognized the latter: the ones who didn't know the waitresses. The Mail Coach dining-room was a place where the regulars were like family, where the waitresses practically told the diners what to eat and not to spend too much time over it. The service fitted the dining-room decor: heritage Australian, lucky that even a semblance of it had been preserved.

Narelle Potter came out from behind her small counter, said something to them, gestured at the room and shook her head. Malone stood up and waved to Mungle and Koga. Both men hesitated, then came towards the window table, threading their way through barbed-wire territory. Narelle Potter followed them.

'I didn't think you'd want to be disturbed –' Her smile was as false-looking as the fake antique of the brand-new stone-washed jeans she was wearing this morning. Her top was encased (that was the word, Malone decided) in a tight blue sweater and he wondered why she was displaying herself like this, especially this morning of all mornings. Unless she was looking for some interest from one of the several unattached male out-of-towners.

'Why not? We're used to it. Would you mind bringing a coupla extra chairs?' He might have been speaking to a trainee constable only a day on the job.

'I'm not one of the waitresses,' she said, giving as good as she'd got, and walked away, her tightly-encased behind challenging him but not in a provocative way.

Two men stood up at the next table, having finished their breakfast, and Clements reached across and dragged their chairs to his and Malone's table. 'Okay, Wally, Mr Koga, sit down. If we're not served within two minutes, I'll create a disturbance.'

'He's good at that,' said Malone.

'It'll make an impression on the visitors to town. Oh Marge –'

The stout middle-aged waitress stopped in mid-stride beside him. 'I'm busy, Sergeant. I'll get one of the other girls –'

Clements held her by her apron-strings. 'Marge, don't be like that. If you don't take our orders, we'll go out to the kitchen and lay a complaint to the local health inspector about the cockroaches and the ratshit we found there –'

'There's nothing like that in the kitchen! It's as clean as my own!'

'It won't be when we've finished looking at it, Marge. Now would you like to take our orders? Detective Mungle and Mr Koga first, they're our guests.'

She gave him a suspicious glare, glanced across the room at Narelle Potter, then took her pad from her apron pocket. 'Narelle ain't gunna like this –'

'I'm sure she isn't.' Clements looked across at the stiff-faced Narelle and gave her a smile that made the women in the dining-room wonder if this wasn't the next-morning taste of a one-night stand. But the four men at the table, the three detectives and the young Japanese, knew it was far more than that.

As they began to eat Malone said, 'Did anyone trouble you last night, Wally?'

'Nup. There were some galahs shouting down in the street after closing time, but that was all.'

'Are you going out to the gin this morning, Mr Koga?'

The young Japanese was eating only fruit, cutting an apple into delicately thin slices; Malone would not have been surprised if he had made some sort of decoration with them on his plate. He was as awkward with Koga as Wally Mungle must have been last night.

'The gin and the farm will be closed for the weekend: I don't know what my bosses will think – they arrive on this morning's plane from Sydney. They expect us to work seven days a week when we're harvesting.'

'They obviously don't realize the importance of the Collamundra Cup. Were they coming anyway, before Mr Sagawa's death?'

'No. They had great faith in him. I thought everyone did,' he added; then looked down at his plate, as if embarrassed by saying the wrong thing.

Poor bugger, thought Malone: I wonder how I'd feel in a country town in Japan where nobody wanted me? 'We'll try and get someone to go out there with you.'

Mungle looked up from his bacon and eggs, but said nothing.

'No, Inspector,' said Koga. 'I shall be all right. Today, anyway. Everybody will be at the races.'

'Where are your bosses going to stay?' asked Clements. 'How many of them are coming?'

'Three. They will stay in the house out at the farm. It will not be what the president of our corporation is accustomed to, he is a very rich man, but I think it will be – be safer. Perhaps they will not listen to me, I am so junior. But where else can they stay?'

Malone had a mischievous idea: 'I'll talk to Mr Dircks, if I can catch him. He owns twenty per cent of the company – or his wife does. Maybe he can put them up.'

Clements grinned; and even Wally Mungle smiled. Koga looked at the three of them, then he, too, smiled. People nearby, still watching them covertly, wondered what the joke was that two Sydney cops, an Abo and a bloody Jap could share. Multiculture was going bloody mad.

'No,' said Koga. 'I shall stay with them at the house. We shall be okay.'

Later, when all four of them walked out of the hotel, they

found Koga's car had all four doors heavily bashed. The young Japanese closed his eyes behind his glasses and went pale; then he opened them and looked at Malone. 'Why? It is so stupid.'

'Drunks last night, probably.' Malone hoped so. Drunks could be dangerous enough, especially in a mob, but cold-blooded harassment was far worse: that could lead to more killing. He had seen it down in Sydney with the neo-Nazis at work on newly-arrived Asians. 'You still want to risk it on your own today?'

Koga nodded; he was not without courage. But Malone hoped he was not filled with some sort of kamikaze spirit. 'I shall be all right, Inspector. But perhaps you will come out to the gin and explain the police situation to my bosses.'

'If I can't get there, I'll have Sergeant Clements meet them. In the meantime, Mr Koga, keep your head down.'

Koga bowed his head and Malone heard a voice nearby say, 'Christ, look at that – bowing to a mug copper!'

Malone ignored whoever had said it, stood with Mungle and Clements and watched Koga drive away up the main street. Then they got into the Commodore and drove round to the police station. Clements parked the car in the yard, took the Brno Twenty-two rifle out of the locked boot, and followed the other two into the station and up to the detectives' room. Baldock was doing paper work at his desk. He sat back, saw the rifle in Clements's hands and looked enquiringly at Malone.

'We picked it up last night.' Malone explained what had happened. 'It belongs to Ray Chakiros. I want the gun and the bullets on the midday plane for Sydney. Russ will call Ballistics and tell 'em they're on their way.'

Baldock didn't move.

'*Now*,' said Malone.

Baldock raised himself slowly from his chair. He looked at Mungle. 'Wally, I've put a note on your desk about those two radicals out at the settlement. Have a look at it, will you?'

Mungle took the hint and moved down the room to a desk at the far end. Then Baldock looked at Malone and Clements. The hair that grew along the sides of his head stood out like tangled wire; the top of his scalp shone as if he had been polishing it for the last hour. His round face seemed to droop, as if all the muscles had gone slack.

'Scobie, I've already had two phone calls. One from Ray Chakiros, the other from Gus Dircks.'

Malone was not surprised. 'None from Hugh Narvo?'

'He's not coming in till midday, otherwise he'd have been on to me, too.' He nodded at the rifle, which Clements had laid on his desk. 'Do you really think that's the gun that killed Sagawa?'

'I don't know, Curly. But let me tell you something. Our Commissioner doesn't have much time for our Minister. If I went back to Sydney and John Leeds got to hear that I'd let myself be pressured by Gus Dircks, I could find myself back here, taking your job. The Commissioner had twelve years of political pressure from the last mob when they were in government and he never stood a bar of it. He won't stand any of it from this crowd, either. And he'd get very stroppy if I or anyone else bowed to it. You've got a long way to go to your pension, Curly. Don't hurry it up.'

Baldock considered this, working his mouth like a wine-taster; then decided today was not a vintage day. He picked up the rifle. 'Pity we can't do our own testing. You got anyone in particular you'd like to be the target?'

Malone could have let that one rub him up the wrong way; but he just smiled. 'Half the town. One more thing, Curly. Why did you pick Wally to look after Koga last night? Wasn't that asking for trouble, especially with Narelle Potter and her prejudices?'

'Scobie –' Baldock sounded weary. 'There was no one else. I went downstairs and the duty sergeant just said a blunt no when I asked for a uniformed guy to take Koga down to the Mail Coach. He said all his men would be too busy trying to keep the peace in town. The truth is, half of them would have turned their backs and walked away if anyone had gone for the Jap.'

'Jesus!' Malone threw up his hands and looked at Clements. 'I thought that only happened up in the bush in Queensland or over in WA.'

Clements said nothing, just chewed his lip; but Baldock said, 'We're all Aussies,' and walked away down the room and out the door, carrying the rifle as if he were looking for a target, *any* target.

Malone glanced down towards Wally Mungle, but if the Aborigine had heard anything he wasn't showing it.

Then a young uniformed constable came to the door, looking cool and neat in shirt-sleeves and, it seemed to Malone, totally uninterested in anything that might be going on up here in the detectives' room. Regionalism could operate even within a police station.

'Someone to see you, Inspector.'

It was Sean Carmody, dressed in collar and tie and moleskins, a houndstooth-checked jacket over his arm, a broad-brimmed hat in his hand. He looked like landed gentry, this man who had started life as a drover's son. 'I thought I'd catch you at the hotel, but you'd left.'

'What is it, Sean?'

'I did some thinking last night after you left. About that bearded stranger you saw in the library. I called in at the carnival and circus on the way in. They've had an old cove with a beard working for them, but he came into town yesterday afternoon and they haven't seen him since. One of the men said he thought he might have got drunk. Evidently he likes the bottle.'

'Sean, are you playing detective?' Malone couldn't help the irritation in his voice.

Carmody smiled. 'No, I'm playing newspaperman. Don't get excited,' he said as Malone and Clements exchanged looks. 'I'm not going to write anything. I'm just curious about the Hardstaff murder, that's all.'

'You're not curious about the Sagawa murder?'

'What does that mean, Scobie?' The smile faded.

'Nothing.' It would be time to ask other people about Trevor Waring after he had questioned Waring himself. 'You any idea where the old bloke might be now?'

Mungle came down from the other end of the room. 'I heard what you were saying. The other day when I was out at the settlement, I saw an old bloke with a beard down along the river. He was sitting there on his own, drinking plonk, it looked like.'

'You speak to him?' said Malone.

'No. I had other things on my mind.'

Malone didn't ask what they were. Any Koori cop going into a black settlement, where everyone either resented or suspected him, would always have things on his mind.

He turned to Clements. 'Russ, get on to Andy again, ask him if he can hurry up Tokyo. Then go out and meet the plane that's bringing in those Japs. Stay in the background, there's no need to introduce yourself to them just yet. Just see who meets them.'

'Care for a ride out to the airport, Wally?' said Clements.

'I'd prefer it,' said Mungle. 'But Curly wants me to go out to the settlement and check on those nongs who've come in from Canberra.'

'Give Mr Carmody and I time to get out there ahead of you,' said Malone. 'I don't want to be involved in that ruckus . . . Sean, would you take me out to the river and we'll see if we can dig up the stranger?'

'Are you encouraging my curiosity?'

It was Malone's turn to smile. 'No, maybe I'm going to indulge my own.'

Carmody looked at him skeptically; then led him downstairs and out to his car. It was a silver-grey Volvo.

'I'm glad it's not a beige Mercedes,' said Malone, 'otherwise you'd be on my list of suspects.'

'I met Hitler, Goebbels and Stalin and hated their guts.' Carmody settled in behind the wheel. 'Why should I want to kill a harmless little Japanese?'

Malone, who was no expert in history but knew about murder, could have told him that four out of five murder victims were harmless, no matter what their nationality.

Driving out of town in the thin stream of traffic already heading towards the racecourse, Malone said, 'Did you cover many murders when you were a newspaperman?'

'Only the big ones and somehow you never thought of them as murders at the time. They were too big for the word *murder*. I was in Dallas when Jack Kennedy was shot and in Los Angeles when Bobby Kennedy got it. I was never a police roundsman, if that's what you're asking me.'

'But you're playing at being one now?'

'Not *playing*, Scobie. I don't mock other people's tragedies.'

'Sorry, Sean. I didn't mean it to sound like that.' He liked this old man too much to want to offend him. He changed tack: 'What do you know about Narelle Potter?'

Carmody glanced at him without turning his head; unlike most elderly men, he didn't appear to have lost any of his peripheral vision. 'Very little, other than what gossip I've heard. Why do you ask?'

'She's a woman with a chip on her shoulder against all minorities and most foreigners, particularly if they're not the same colour as her. She has no time for blacks or Japs. She doesn't appear to have much time for me, either.'

'Are you a minority?'

'Russ and I are, in this town, anyway. Did you know her husband?'

'Better than I know her, yes. He was older than her, twenty years at least, I'd guess. He didn't have much interest outside of his pub, his horses and his shooting. He was always out shooting – 'roos, dingoes, rabbits, anything. He had the biggest collection of guns in the district.'

'Yet he accidentally shot himself?'

Carmody did turn his head this time. 'Who told you that?'

Malone considered. 'Nobody, now I come to think of it. I just assumed it.'

'I took you for the sort of cop who'd never assume anything . . . It was his wife who shot him. Her gun went off as she was getting through a fence. I gather from the gossip that she's never touched a gun since.'

'I wouldn't blame her,' said Malone, but even in his own ears he sounded noncommittal, as if he were passing an opinion on someone he had never even met. And maybe he had not met the *real* Narelle Potter, not yet.

They turned out of the traffic, down the track that led past the blacks' settlement. There was some activity there this morning, the women and children in one large group, the men in another. The men stood in a circle around a young Aborigine who was haranguing them; it looked like a two-up school, but Malone, smelling trouble in the still morning air, knew a different sort of gamble was being planned; more than two pennies would be thrown in the air before the day was out. It was none of his business: let Hugh Narvo and his uniformed men deal with it. He just hoped that Wally Mungle would not have to take sides.

'There could be trouble,' said Carmody. 'Probably tonight. I think it would be a good idea if we all went straight home after the races. You can come back later for the ball – I'm baby-sitting. You're going to the ball?'

'Lisa wants to. I'll probably do what I'm told.'

Carmody smiled. 'Ain't it always the way? What's the difference between being in love and being henpecked?'

'Don't risk your neck by asking Lisa that.'

They drove on perhaps half a mile beyond the settlement, came to another bend in the river where willows trailed their green petticoats, brown-streaked with autumn, in the shining water. The bearded stranger from the library, thin and naked, with coat-hanger shoulders and saddlebag buttocks, was knee-deep in the water washing himself.

Malone got out of the Volvo and slid down the bank to the edge of the water; Carmody remained at the top of the bank. 'Cold?'

'Not as cold as some of the charity around here.' The old man grinned, gap-toothed, through his wet grey beard. 'That what you expected me to say?'

'Why would I expect you to say that?'

'Us old swaggies, you think we're all bush philosophers, the wisest men in the land outside those gurus you hear on the wireless.'

'You don't claim much wisdom?'

'Not much. What can I do for you?'

'I hear you work for the carnival and the circus over there.' Malone nodded across the river. 'When did you last carry your swag?'

'I carry it all the time. I work only when it pleases me.' He came out of the water and began to dry himself by standing in the sun and running his palms down over his bony body and legs. He seemed unconcerned that he might not make a hopeful sight for a younger man who didn't want a glimpse of the future for himself. 'You're a copper, ain't you? Who's your mate?' He looked up at Carmody. 'You're not the Police Commissioner, are you?'

'Hardly. I'm Sean Carmody, one of the locals.' His face was relaxed with amusement and – *something else*. A glimpse of what once might have been his own future, one he had avoided?

'Carmody? Carmody? You any relation to Paddy Carmody?' Then he slapped a bare hip. 'Of course, I know you! You own that place out along the road. You his son? Geez, how time flies!'

'You've been here before?' said Malone.

'On and off.' He pulled on some droopy, patched underpants that looked like old-fashioned women's bloomers with the elastic gone from the legs. 'I was born here.'

'What's your name?'

'Fred Strayhorn.'

Malone looked up at Carmody. 'You heard of him?'

Carmody shook his head. 'It's an unusual name.' Then, with an old-time newspaperman's memory for names, but a memory that dated him, he said, 'There was a Billy Strayhorn played with Duke Ellington's band. I've seen his name on some records I have at home. It's the only time I've ever seen it.'

'No relation.' The gap-toothed smile appeared once more in the beard, which he was now drying with his fingers. 'I can't even play a gum leaf.'

Malone said, 'What are you doing over on this side of the river? Why not over there at the carnival?'

Strayhorn pulled on his trousers, nodded at two empty wine bottles. 'When I get on the red-eye I like to keep my shame to m'self. I'm a shameless old bugger, except about my drinking.'

'I saw you last night in the town library.'

'I know you did.'

'You were sober then. What made you go on the plonk? Was it something you read in those pages you tore out of the local paper?'

Strayhorn paused as he was about to pull on the shirt he had slept in. He looked distinctly less clean and neat than he had last night. 'I didn't tear out the pages. They were already gone.'

Malone looked out at the river. In the slowly moving water a fish jumped, creating a small silver explosion. A spoonbill flapped its way down the opposite bank, taking its time going nowhere. The scene could not have been simpler and more peaceful, yet he could feel currents in the air that bore something far heavier than an aimless bird.

'What were you looking for?'

'The same as you, I reckon.' The old man was shrewd, even if he disclaimed any wisdom. He sat down, began to pull on socks, neatly darned, and the new black boots he had been wearing last night. 'The Hardstaff murder.'

'What's your interest in that?'

'I was here when it happened.' He squinted up at both of them, looking at Malone and Carmody in turn. 'What d'you think of that?'

'Where? *Here*? In town? Where?' Malone, for the first time, felt a tiny lift of excitement: maybe here was someone who, after all, would talk.

Strayhorn tied his bootlaces, got slowly to his feet; his joints cracked and he grinned. 'I'm not as spry as I used to be. I'm getting on . . . I was out at the Hardstaff place the morning it happened.'

'You were working there?'

'I'd been there a week. I was building a coupla dams for old Sir Chester.' He looked up at Carmody. 'You remember him?'

'Not very well. I met him a few times, but I didn't like him. He reminded me of a few dictators I'd met, only on a smaller scale.'

'He was an arrogant old bastard, worse than his son. And he's bad enough.'

Canned music came drifting across from the showground beside the racecourse: carnival music, all brass and oompahpah. It and Strayhorn's harsh comment soured the morning air.

'Did anyone question you about the murder?' said Malone.

'Sure they did.' He took a comb, as gap-toothed as his own gums, from a pocket and ran it through his hair and beard; it was as if he were applying respectability to himself bit by bit. 'But Chess Hardstaff, the young 'un, that is, he vouched for me.

He said I was out at the dam at the time of the murder, that he was there with me. The police let me go. I didn't finish the dams. Old Sir Chester paid me off, gimme more than I was entitled to, and I left town next day.'

'Why did he pay you more than you were entitled to?'

Strayhorn picked up the two wine bottles and put them in a thin plastic bag that had been lying under one of them. 'I'm not one of them new Greenies, I always cleaned up after me long before I knew what the environment meant. Any good swaggie did . . . He paid me because I *was* out at the dam the time of the murder and young Chess wasn't.'

He stood a moment looking hard at Malone; then he picked up his old jacket and hat and clambered up the bank. Malone didn't move, just turned his head to stare up at Carmody.

'Did you know that, Sean?'

'No.' Carmody took his time before he went on: 'But then I don't think anyone knew much about it. The local police didn't send for anyone down in Sydney, not as I remember, not like they've done with you and the Sagawa murder.'

Strayhorn, two or three inches taller than Carmody and looking taller because of his thinness, looked at the other old man, then down at Malone. He gave the impression that he was a man who would take his time assessing other people, would never make a rushed judgement. 'You're on that one, too, Inspector?'

'I'm on that one on its own. The Hardstaff case is closed.'

'Then why are you so interested in me?'

Malone climbed the bank, stood beside Strayhorn; they were virtually the same height, but again the old man looked the taller because of his thinness. 'When did you get into town?'

Strayhorn laughed, a surprisingly robust sound. 'You think I might of killed the Jap? Nah. We come into town Wednesday afternoon. I joined the carnival over in Cawndilla. I been in my fair share of brawls and stoushes, but I'm not a murderer.'

'You said you were born here. Why did you leave? You got any family still here?'

'I think it's time I went to work,' Strayhorn said abruptly and turned away.

Malone put out a hand and held his arm. 'Not yet, Fred. We'll give you a lift over to the carnival. But first, I'd like to know a little more about you and the Hardstaffs.'

'All right. Let go my arm.' He didn't look at either of the two men, but gazed down at the river. 'I used to swim here as a kid, right at this very spot. The Noongulli. It was a much bigger river than this, once. Not in my time, though. It ran all the way down to the Murrumbidgee. The first wool crops from around here used to go down the river by boat, back in the sixties and seventies. The eighteen-sixties and -seventies, that is,' he said with a smile to Malone. 'I used to dream of them days when I'd sit here as a kid. There was plenty of time for dreaming when I was young. When you're young and when you're old, that's the only time for dreaming.'

Malone waited, knowing, in some odd way, that the old man was slowly working his way round to a confession of some sort. Across the river the music had changed: the brass band was waltzing its way along 'The Sidewalks of New York'. 'Are they still playing that?' said Carmody in genuine wonder. 'They used to play that on the merry-go-round when I was a kid.'

'Rock'n'roll don't sound the same on a merry-go-round,' said Strayhorn, and for a moment Malone felt outside the circle of the two old men. 'There was a circus and carnival here in Collamundra the day they kicked us outa town. Only they were both closed for the day because in them days the wowsers wouldn't let anything open on a Sunday.'

They had now walked across to the Volvo. 'They kicked you out of town?' said Malone. 'Who were *they*?'

'The Old Guard. Before your time, son. But you'd remember them, wouldn't you, Mr Carmody?'

Carmody nodded, but a little doubtfully. 'I remember the *New* Guard. It was one of them, a Captain de Groot, who opened the Sydney Harbour Bridge – unofficially. He was in uniform and he rode up on his horse and slashed the ribbon with his sword before Jack Lang, the Premier, had a chance to cut it with his scissors. I was nineteen then, droving sheep with my mum and dad somewhere up near Walgett, so I only read about it. It was a big story,' he said almost wistfully, as if he wished he had covered it. All his reporting experience had been overseas, he had never filed a story on an Australian event.

'I remember de Groot,' said Strayhorn.

The two old men were locked for a moment in a common memory and once again Malone was outside their circle.

'That happened in March nineteen-thirty-two,' Strayhorn went on. 'The Depression. Christ, them was hard times! But I'm talking about the *Old* Guard. The New Guard got all the publicity, they were a flash lotta fascists, but the Old Guard was the real danger. They stayed outa the papers, but they had more big names than the New Guard ever did. Plenty of knights – Sir This, Sir That. They had the money and the power and they were shit-scared they were gunna lose it!' For the first time he was showing some passion, his voice taking on an edge. 'Colonial Sugar had some of their top men in it, the Bank of New South Wales lent it money, the Veterans Legion was behind it . . . Christ!' He had to stop, spittle suddenly showing on his beard round his mouth.

Carmody looked at Malone. 'Your generation probably will never understand how much fear there was of socialism and communism.'

Strayhorn stiffened, his head coming forward on his neck, his eyes sharp with suspicion. 'You didn't feel that way, did you?'

'Fred,' said Carmody patiently, 'four years later I went to Spain to fight for the Republicans. Franco would have had me shot against a wall if I'd been captured.'

Strayhorn stared at him, as if trying to see in this image of a wealthy squatter another, dimmer image: that of a young rebel who had fought for the socialist cause in another land. Then he nodded. 'You'll do . . . My old man was a Commo. He worked on the railways out here as a ganger and he thought Karl Marx and Lenin were direct descendants of Jesus Christ. There was him and three other railway blokes, all Communists. The Collamundra Communist Party, four men and my old man's red kelpie. A real bloody menace to democracy, four men and a dog!' He laughed. 'I was only fourteen years old then and all I can remember them doing was talk.'

'Go on,' said Malone.

'The Old Guard was dead scared there was gunna be a socialist revolution, especially if Jack Lang stayed in power as the Labour Premier. He was a fiery old bugger, a real autocrat, but he was for the workers. The Old Guard set up command posts all over the bush. Up in Scone, Molong, Parkes, all over the place. They had one here in Collamundra and Old Man Hardstaff – he wasn't Sir Chester then – he was the leader. They held a meeting one Sunday in the old Legion hall, they must of got two hundred to it. They come into town with their guns – you'd of thought the bloody Yellow Peril was just a coupla miles out there in the mulga. It never occurred to me they was afraid of my dad and his mates, the all-mighty Collamundra Communist Party! I remember my dad reading out something to my mum from the *Chronicle* that week – it didn't name Dad and his mates, but it said something about, I've never forgotten it, "parasites and pariahs, the scummunists". My old man a parasite and a pariah! Christ, nobody worked harder than a railway ganger in them days! There was none of this sharing the work like you see now, one bloke working and four overseeing him.'

'Nobody works today,' said Carmody, another voice from the past.

Malone, one of today's workers, held his peace.

Strayhorn leaned on the roof of the Volvo, as if the strength had started to leak out of him with his venom. For a moment it looked as if he was not going to say any more; then he went on, speaking more quietly now, 'Anyhow, they come down, all two hundred of 'em, marching down the street to the beat of a drum, to the four railway cottages down by the line. I remember the Cawndilla Mail went through, it didn't stop here on Sundays, and the passengers leaned outa the windows and waved to those bastards with their guns. You'd of thought they were cheering off another lot of Anzacs to another war. Then Old Man Hardstaff come up to our front door, knocked on it and when my dad answered it, he told him we had ten minutes to pack everything and get outa town and never come back.'

Malone could taste the bitterness of all those years ago. 'Where were the wowsers, the ones who wouldn't let the carnival be open on a Sunday?'

'Most of 'em, the men anyway, were there in the mob with their guns.'

'What did you do?' asked Carmody.

'What could we do? We packed what we could – we didn't have much. A ganger's wages was rock-bottom, but at least Dad had a job and we had a roof over our heads. We didn't have much, like I said, but have you ever tried to pack up your life in ten minutes and leave the place where you were born and you'd lived all your life and never come back? My dad come from Narrabri, but my mother was born and bred in Collamundra. She never got over it. Some of the more decent blokes helped us carry what we took with us over to the line and put it on a trike, one of the hand-trolleys we used to ride on. There were three of 'em and four families somehow squeezed on to 'em and I stood up with my father and we worked the levers up and down and that's how we left Collamundra. As we did, the drummer and some fellers with bugles began to play "God Save The King". And "Advance Australia Fair". Dad looked back and said, "There they go with their tunes of glory," and when he looked back at me he was crying, the only time in all my life I ever saw him do that.'

He paused, tears in his own rheumy blue eyes, and the other two men stood silent while far across the river the band played a meaningless song, one that was faintly familiar to Malone but the name of which he couldn't recall.

After a moment he said, 'What happened then?'

Strayhorn recovered. 'We went all the way down to Cawndilla. I dunno what happened to the other families, they just stopped there. Maybe they finished up down in Sydney. Commos weren't exactly popular down there, either, but there was more of 'em and nobody tried to drive them outa town.'

'Where did you go from Cawndilla?'

'We just went on, switching lines, and finally we finished up down in Wagga. Down there the police come and tried to arrest Dad for stealing the trike and he stood there in front of me, there was just me and him, Mum wasn't there, and he was holding a cut-throat razor – he'd been shaving when the police come. And he said if they laid a hand on him, he'd cut his throat.

And he would of, too. He'd reached the end of his tether by then. The revolution, for what it was worth, was over.'

Malone and Carmody looked at each other, both of them with the Irish imagination for the melancholy. They saw the Strayhorns, a man and a woman and a boy, on that small railway trolley, the man and the boy working the levers up and down, the woman sitting, wrapped in misery, on their miserable belongings, travelling along the never-ending glittering tracks under the high uncaring sky, a tiny tragedy in the vast flat and pitiless landscape.

Malone said, 'What would your father think of today, in Europe and Russia?'

Strayhorn shook his head, smiled through his beard and his memories. 'I dunno. I think he's in the best place for idealists to be – dead. We buried Dad's illusions with him.'

Malone, with a conscious effort, forced pity out of his mind. 'Why did you take Old Man Hardstaff's money and not tell the police the truth about where Chess was?'

'I didn't know where Chess was. He just didn't turn up at the dam site to meet me, like he was supposed to. I wasn't gunna point the finger at him.'

'Would you now?'

Strayhorn was suddenly cautious. 'I'd have to think about it.'

'Was Chess there that Sunday afternoon you were run out of town?'

'Yeah, he was there. He wasn't very old, maybe eighteen or so, I dunno, but he was there, all right. His old man told him to help us carry our things outa the house, but he made out he didn't hear him and he walked away. He was arrogant even then.'

'Did he recognize you when you came back to work on the dam site?'

'No. Forty-two years had gone by. His father, he was Sir Chester by then, he had one foot in the grave. Each time I come back here, after the war, in the fifties, then again in the sixties and then in nineteen seventy-three, I never used my real name – it was too unusual, someone would of recognized it. As it was, they didn't know me from Adam.'

'Would anyone recognize you now?'

'No, I've grown this beard in the last four or five years.'

'So what are you planning to do?'

'I thought I might try and bump into Chess this afternoon and tell him who I really am. It might scare the shit outa him.' He smiled at the thought, the beard opening up like a nest out of which a bird might fly at any moment, one with a sharp attacking beak. 'I've always wondered if he knew who killed his wife.'

'Who do you think killed her?' Malone avoided looking at Carmody.

Strayhorn shrugged his bony shoulders. 'Who knows? It might of been the bloke she was having an affair with – they said there was another man in her bed. Or there had been. Maybe both Chess and his old man knew who killed her, but they were more afraid of the scandal than they were upset by the wife's murder. I never seen two men so wrapped up in themselves. Like father, like son. Now how about giving me that lift you promised? I better go and do some work or I'm gunna look like a modern bludger. I'm always telling the young coves over at the carnival they dunno what real work is. They don't, do they, Mr Carmody?'

'It's another world,' said Carmody, who had seen more worlds than most men but somehow didn't look or sound totally disillusioned: he wouldn't want his illusions buried with him. Meeting men like him, thought Malone, gives me hope.

They got into the Volvo, Carmody swung it round and they drove back along the river track, past the blacks' settlement where the men and women had now gathered into one large group. The young man still stood in the centre of the circle, no longer haranguing but asking questions. Beyond the adults the children were dancing to a quickstep drifting on the still air from the showground, their spindly legs shimmering like black drumsticks as they created their own dance.

'There'll be trouble tonight,' Carmody said again.

Malone, turned halfway round in the front seat, noticed that Strayhorn, who had become very quiet since getting into the car, hadn't even glanced at the settlement. He wondered if the old man now regretted having told as much as he had.

They dropped him at the entrance to the showground. Malone said, 'When does the carnival and circus leave town?'

'We pack up Monday morning.'

'You thinking of leaving before then?'

'That'd look like I'm running away, wouldn't it?' Strayhorn's mocking grin was evident even through his beard. 'Don't worry, Mr Malone. I'll be here for the rest of the weekend. Unless Chess Hardstaff runs me outa town again when I tell him who I am.'

I'd like to be there, thought Malone. But the Hardstaff case wasn't his concern: he had to forget it. 'Take care. And stay off the grog. The lock-up is going to be full enough tonight.'

Strayhorn tipped his hat to both of them, an old-fashioned gesture that surprised them, and went into the showground. He paused and dropped his plastic bag with its contents into an empty oil drum that doubled as a refuse bin, took off his hat to a young girl who passed him leading an elephant, and disappeared behind one of the carnival tents.

'A dying breed,' said Sean Carmody. 'My father would have finished up like that if my mother hadn't scrimped and saved and bought some land and made him settle down.'

'Was your dad happy when he died? Did they bury his illusions with him?'

'I don't know,' said Carmody, somehow not surprised at the question. 'I wasn't there to ask him. He died in November nineteen sixty-three. I was in Dallas then. You'd have been very young when Kennedy died.'

'I was old enough to come pretty close to tears. A lot of very young people did.'

'I cried,' said Carmody without embarrassment. 'But not for Jack Kennedy, though that was sad enough. For my father. He had a dream, but I don't think he even knew what it was. Not clearly, anyway. He envied me, I think. He was a wanderer and I got to wander much further and wider than he had ever dreamed about.'

'A free spirit?'

'I was never that. And I don't think Fred Strayhorn is. He will always remember what happened to his mother and father here in Collamundra.'

'I just wonder why he didn't point the finger at Chess Hardstaff when he had the chance.'

'Maybe we'll never know how much pressure was applied to him.'

'By the police or by Chess's father?'

Carmody said nothing. He all at once seemed to be driving more carefully, concentrating, as the traffic coming out to the racecourse and the showground had thickened.

Malone said, 'Sean, are the cops in this town corrupt?'

They were entering the outskirts of town. Carmody remained silent till he pulled the car up outside the police station. He switched off the engine and turned to face Malone.

'No,' he said flatly. 'I don't think you'd find one of them who would take money. They might bow to a bit of pressure, but that's a different thing. This isn't a big town, Scobie. Maybe everyone doesn't know everyone else by name, but they know them by sight. The police, like everyone else, have to live in it. They have family, friends, neighbours – they *belong*. It's not like the city. Where are you stationed?'

'Police Centre, in Surry Hills.'

'Where do you live?'

'Randwick.'

'A suburb, another part of the city altogether. You get my point? Have you ever had to question or arrest anyone who lives in your street or just around the corner? Don't be too harsh on the locals, Scobie. They do their job as best they can. They may not treat the blacks as well as they might and if ever there was a Gay Mardi Gras out here, some of them might act like Stormtroopers, the sort I saw in Germany in the nineteen-thirties. But that's par for the course in Australia. We've never been as tolerant as we claim. We delude ourselves as much as the Brits or the Americans or the French or anyone else. The only ones, I think, who don't delude themselves are the Chinese. Or maybe it's because they're so inscrutable, we can't tell.'

'What about the Japanese? Aren't they inscrutable?'

'Maybe you'll know more about that when you get deeper into the Sagawa murder.'

It was very oblique, but Malone caught a note of criticism in Carmody's tone: you're being sidetracked from what brought you here. He thanked the older man for the lift and got out of the car.

'Where are you going now?'

'To see Trevor.'

Carmody raised an eyebrow. 'I can drive you there.'

'I don't think so, Sean. Thanks, though.'

He turned and went into the station before he had to explain to Carmody why he didn't want him there when he questioned his son-in-law. He went upstairs to the detectives' room and was relieved to find Baldock was not there, though he wasn't quite sure why he felt that way.

Clements looked up from his preparation of the running sheet. 'I just got back from the airport. The three Nips came in. Gus Dircks and Koga were there to meet them.'

'Not Doc Nothling or Trevor Waring?'

'No. Gus Dircks was all over them – I was surprised he hadn't brought flowers.'

'Did he see you?'

'It's a small airport, mate. It's pretty hard to get lost in it. He didn't speak to me, just gave me a hard glare and turned his back.'

'What about the Japs?'

'They all look alike to me. They were well-dressed and the one who seemed to be the boss, he looked as if he was used to being considered important. I nearly fell over when Gus actually bowed his head to him, Jap-style.'

'You can start practising – your manners need a shake-up. Anything from Tokyo yet?'

'Andy Graham got off the phone about five minutes ago.' He sorted out some notes he had jotted down. 'There's nothing much to add to what we already know. He did his technical training in cotton farming in the US, in Alabama and Arizona. He's got no criminal record, not even a traffic ticket. Tokyo just said, "More to follow." Whatever that means.'

'It could mean they're following up a lead. I wonder if his bosses could tell us anything? Make a date for us to see them late this afternoon, after the races.' He looked at his watch. 'I'm running late to see Trevor Waring.'

'Then we're going to the races this afternoon?' Clements looked eager. He was not an eclectic gambler, he was not interested in cards or baccarat or flies crawling up a wall. But horse-racing drew him like a magnet, he would have laid bets with the Man from Snowy River on which brumby would finish in front of their wild horse chase.

Malone sighed, beginning to feel the weariness brought on by a mind that was becoming increasingly cluttered almost by the minute. Reason, and his usual orderly approach to a case, told him he should wipe the Hardstaff murder and the suicide of Billy Koowarra from his thoughts: he was here to find the murderer of Kenji Sagawa and nothing else. But the net he had thrown kept getting caught on unseen obstacles in dark waters.

'I think we might. Everyone else in town is going to be out there. Unless –' The net caught again. 'Unless you think we ought to keep an eye on Koga and his bosses just in case the killer wants to try his luck again?'

'I think that's someone else's job, don't you?' Clements's face showed nothing. 'After all, they were met by the Police Minister himself out at the airport. If he can't look after 'em, who can?'

Malone grinned, nodding appreciatively. 'You should be our Foreign Minister. You'd have the country at war in five minutes . . . I'll meet you back here at twelve thirty.'

He went out to meet with Trevor Waring, taking the net with him.

2

Waring's office was in a small two-storeyed complex of professional offices just off the main street. The building looked no more than three or four years old, built probably when developers, swept along on the surface of a boom, thought prosperity could only get bigger and better. Now the boom was over, wool and grain prices were down, developers were on the dole and the nation's belt was starting to feel like a tourniquet. As Malone crossed from the other side of the street he saw two 'For Sale' notices in upstairs windows of the block, like commercial Band-Aids.

The solicitor's rooms were on the ground floor, the largest office in the complex. Malone remembered the old saw: smart lawyers and smart accountants could always keep themselves busy. In good times they helped the successful reduce their taxes, in bad times they facilitated bankruptcies. They had learned how to harness an ill-wind.

Waring was waiting for him; anxiously, it seemed. There was no one in the outer office, but as soon as Malone knocked on the door and entered, Waring came through from his own office, hand outstretched. Like meeting a new client for the first time, Malone thought. He had all policemen's suspicion of lawyers and their intentions: it was there between the lines of a policeman's swearing-in oath.

'Come in, come in, Scobie! Coffee?' There was a coffee percolator on an electric hob in the other office. 'Sugar? Milk?'

Ease off, Malone silently advised him. He took the china cup and saucer, none of your thick mugs or styrofoam cups here, and followed Waring into the latter's office. It was a room for a successful lawyer, though not as richly furnished as some that Malone had visited down in Sydney; but down there the fees made those of country solicitors look like pension cheques. Still, Waring had done well, as a solicitor, a cotton farm investor or a part-time grazier. Malone sat down in a chair upholstered in genuine leather, none of your antique vinyl, and looked at Waring across the leather-topped desk.

'How's the case coming along?' said Waring with genuine interest.

Which one? Malone had to bite back the question; and determinedly pushed the Hardstaff murder to the back of his mind.

'Sagawa? We're making progress.' You were always 'making progress', even if sometimes it was the generals' strategic retreat. Never confess, especially to a lawyer, that you didn't know where the hell you were going. 'Trevor, why didn't you tell me the other night, when we first met, that you had shares in South Cloud?'

Waring stalled. 'I thought you might ask me that.'

'Yeah, you're a lawyer, I guessed you might.'

'Would you believe me if I said I just didn't think it was important to mention it? That it slipped my mind entirely?'

'No.'

There was a set of four pipes in a rack on the desk. Waring reached for one, but didn't attempt to fill it; he looked at it, as if wondering what he should do with it, then he put it back in the rack. He looked at Malone. 'Why not?'

Malone sipped his coffee. It was excellent: Lisa, the coffee expert, with her Dutch conceit that the Dutch made the best brew in the world, would have approved. 'What happens to your share of the company if the Japanese decide to pull out of the whole venture? Which they might do, if they think there's too much anti-Jap feeling around here.'

'They have invested too much to want to pull out.'

'From what I've read, the Japanese will always cut their losses if it means losing face. They are economic imperialists, but they don't want to start another war, even a small local one, to prove it.'

Waring smiled. He picked up a pair of square, gold-rimmed glasses from the desk, put them on, looked carefully at Malone, then took them off and put them back on the desk. Malone sat, patient: he had been scrutinized by the best, from Supreme Court judges to top crims.

'I don't mean to sound offensive, Scobie, but you're a smart cop. Or are all the cops down in Sydney experts on economic imperialism?'

'We take courses in it now, instead of pistol practice.' *Come on, Malone. You sound like some tough private eye.* Philip Marlowe and Lew Archer would have struggled against the dry wit and arid skepticism he had heard from the native crims. 'Trevor, let's cut out the fencing. No offence, but I think I've had more practice at it than you, even though you're a lawyer. I've been in the ring with –' He named two of Sydney's top Queen's Counsels and then two of the nation's top criminal elements. 'No bullshit, Trev, just a friendly talk man to man.'

Here in his office Waring did not seem anywhere near as bland as he had in his own home; his eyes, indeed his whole face, took on a shrewdness that Malone hadn't detected before. He picked up his glasses again, but didn't put them on; then he leaned back in his chair. 'Am I a suspect of some sort?'

Malone pursed his lips as if he were thinking over the proposition; but he had already decided. 'Yes, I think you might be. You and at least a couple of dozen others. In a murder case, Trev, I never rule out anyone except myself and the corpse.'

Waring smiled and the smile seemed to relax him a little. 'I see your point. I don't suppose I can plead that I'll say nothing without my lawyer being present?'

'Not unless you believe that old one, that a lawyer who defends himself has a fool for a client?'

Waring shook his head, smiling again. 'No, I don't think I'm a fool, Scobie. And I think I'm a good lawyer, though maybe I haven't been tested as much as those QCs you mentioned . . . Okay. To answer your question as to what would happen to my shares in the company if the Japanese pull out – well, we'd try to raise the money to buy them out.'

'Try to raise it?'

'It wouldn't be easy. It'd take a lot – at least by local standards.'

'How much?'

Waring hesitated; though he was not unsophisticated, he had none of the city lawyers' glib approach to large sums of money.

'About ten million dollars, if all the outstanding options were to be taken up. That's a five-stand gin out there and we have twenty thousand hectares cleared, with eight thousand hectares already under crop. There's an option on another fifty thousand hectares that has to be taken up in the next three months. The original plan was to make this the largest cotton project in Australia. If we don't take up the option and clear the land, then we've put too much cash into what we've already developed.'

'Could you raise sufficient money for a buy-out, I mean locally?'

'I don't know. I doubt it. People around here are strapped for cash now – interest rates, poor crop prices, things like that. Normally this is a rich district, but already this year there have been six farms taken over by the banks.'

'Who would buy in, then?'

'A Yank syndicate. Or some of the big money that's still down in Sydney or Melbourne, despite the slump. I'd be pushed out.'

'And you don't want that?'

'Scobie, we grow cotton here that's the equal of any grown anywhere in the world. We sell every bale we pack. I got in at the jump – why would I want to be bought out now, just when it's all coming to fruition?'

'Had any offer been made before Sagawa's murder, to buy out the Japs?'

A slight hesitation; a hand fiddled with the glasses. 'Just a tentative one.'

'Who proposed it? The outsiders? Or someone local?'

'Like who?'

The tongue gave out the name, not the mind: 'Chess Hardstaff, maybe?'

Waring put on his glasses. 'We-ell, yes. He was the one who told us there was outside interest.'

'Yet he was the one who got the Japs here in the first place? Why didn't he invest then?'

'I wouldn't know. Chess plays everything close to his chest. Max Nothling said something one night when he was half-drunk. That if ever they open Chess up for heart surgery, they'll find his thorax packed tight with secrets. They won't have to slice open his sternum, there'll be a combination lock on it. I don't think anyone in the district knows what makes Chess tick, not even his daughter.'

'What about Max Nothling? Would he know?'

'Him least of all, probably. Chess and Max have never been close. Not till lately, that is.'

'What do you mean by that?'

Waring spread a hand, as if surprised by what he had just said. 'I don't know, frankly. It just struck me then that lately I've seen them together more than ever before. It may be just coincidence, with the Cup meeting coming up. I just don't know.'

'Could Nothling raise enough money to share in the buy-out?'

'I doubt it. His wife, Amanda, has most of their money. She inherited quite a bit from her grandfather, old Sir Chester. She was his favourite.'

'Gus Dircks's wife also owns shares. Would they have enough to buy into the takeover?'

'You're asking me to divulge clients' confidential affairs. They're all clients of mine.'

'Forget I asked the question, Trev. You've just answered it.' Malone put down his empty cup, waved away Waring's offer of a refill. 'The other night you said Sagawa had been to see you about threats. Did he show you the letters?'

'No.'

'You're a lawyer, he came to you for advice and you didn't ask to see the letters he was complaining about?'

'He didn't bring them with him. I never saw him again after that.'

'Your name isn't mentioned in the running sheet. Didn't any of the investigating officers come and question you?'

'No.'

'Where is South Cloud's registered office?'

'Care of this office.' Waring still wore his glasses; there was a pinched look to his face now, as if his eyes were suffering from focusing so carefully on Malone. 'Look, if you're thinking of accusing me of murdering Ken Sagawa, I think I'll choose not to answer any more questions. Your family come to stay with mine, you come out to my house for dinner . . . Christ Almighty!' For a moment Malone thought he was going to burst into tears.

Malone stood up. 'Trevor, I don't think you murdered Sagawa. You were happy with the status quo, with the Japs running things, am I right?'

Waring nodded, knowing there was still something to come.

'But –' Malone picked up his hat. 'But I still think you know more than you've told me. Without knowing it – or, I dunno, maybe even knowing it – you could be an accessory before or after the fact. Think about it.'

He went out, the net still trawling in dark waters.

3

He went back to the police station and brought his own additions to the running sheets up to date. It looked like a weather forecast: waves were beginning to rise.

Then Clements came in and Malone said, 'Let's go to the races.'

Driving out of town Clements said, 'How'd you get on with Waring?'

'You ever feel you wish you hadn't started something?'

'I was with a girl once. She talked all the way through it, about what a month of aerobics would do for my agility. I was flat out being agile and there she was under me talking about aerobics. But I was too far in to stop, if you know what I mean.'

Malone laughed, feeling some of the tension and weariness slip away from him. Once he had come into the dressing-room at Adelaide Oval, having spent the whole day in the field and having bowled thirty-two overs while the temperature had hovered around the old hundred degrees F. mark; the dressing-room attendant had handed him a long cold beer, he had downed it in one long slow swallow, and living had become bearable again. Clements sometimes, as now, had that effect on him.

'I didn't get much out of Waring, nothing really concrete.'

'Just suspicions?' Clements nodded. 'I know what you mean. But where would we be without them?'

'Pull in at the carnival first. I said I'd meet Lisa and the kids there.'

Lisa and Ida Waring and their respective children were waiting for them; with two exceptions. 'Where's Claire?' said Malone.

'Tas is looking after her for the day,' said Lisa.

He looked at her teasing smile. 'On a day like this, I thought he'd like to be with his mates.'

'Relax, Scobie,' said Ida, also smiling. A conspiracy of mothers, he thought: how can you lick 'em? 'Tas is a gentleman

– or at least I know he is towards Claire. He's also trying to show he's independent. One of the local girls, he's taken her out a couple of times, is talking as if she has an option on him.'

Malone looked at her, suddenly no longer concerned for his daughter's moral safety: concerned, instead, for Ida and her family. How will I ever be able to face her if Trevor turns out to be implicated somehow in Sagawa's murder? Will she look on me as a gentleman if I have to arrest her husband?

'Where's Trevor? He's not here yet?'

'No, he rang to say he had a meeting with Max Nothling. Probably to do with the cotton farm, now the Japanese bosses have arrived.'

'Probably,' said Malone, trying to sound convinced.

Clements took the children off to the sideshows, a rich uncle bursting to splurge. Malone fell in between Lisa and Ida, feeling that sense of pride that is common to most men when they are escorting two good-looking women; even the least conceited of men can't help such a vanity. Both women were smartly, without being over-dressed; casual elegance, Malone thought, might be the phrase. He himself would never trouble the ghost of Beau Brummel; he saw no reason why his wardrobe should not last as long as, say, his teeth or his hair, both of which were still in mint condition. Yet he never stopped admiring Lisa for always being well-groomed. Walking between her and Ida, he felt the day becoming better by the minute. Somehow, tonight he would find somewhere to make love to Lisa.

'What are you looking so pleased about?' Lisa could sense the sex rising in him as plainly as if he were walking about naked.

'Nothing. I've just decided to keep my mind empty for the rest of the day.'

'Good,' said both women and each of them squeezed his arms.

They strolled through the happy crowd. The merry-go-round spun its wild-eyed horses to a wheezy waltz and the spruikers at the stalls sang their siren songs in raucous voices that would have made a flock of cockatoos sound musical. The autumn sun beat down out of a cloudless sky and the smell of hamburgers, hot dogs, meat pies and greasy chips hung in the still air. There was death, too, in the air but no stranger would have known it and the locals looked as if they had forgotten it. Malone tried his best to do the same.

They passed a stall and Fred Strayhorn raised a bamboo ring to Malone and gestured he should try his luck to win a kewpie doll for the ladies. Malone grinned and shook his head and Lisa said, 'Just what I need, a kewpie doll. I thought they'd stopped making them.'

'This is a very old-fashioned carnival,' said Malone. 'Soon there'll be nothing like this left.'

'I think the Governor-General's just arrived,' said Ida. 'Let's go over to the course. Russ can bring the children over when he's had enough of spending his money on them. Look at him! He's getting into a Dodgem car with Tom. He's not very agile, is he?'

'He's working on it,' said Malone, laughing so freely that both women looked at him. He excused himself and went back to Strayhorn.

'Changed your mind, Mr Malone?' The old man had had someone trim his hair and his beard; he looked almost handsome. He fingered the beard when he saw Malone glance at it. 'I was gunna shave it off, but the girl who cut my hair, she told me not to. She looks after me and the elephants. She said all old fellers should look distinguished, we owe it to the young.'

'She's right. I'll try and remember that when I'm long in the tooth . . . Are you going to face up to Chess Hardstaff this afternoon?'

Strayhorn looked at him shrewdly. 'What's it to you, Mr Malone?'

'I'd like to be there to see it.' He couldn't keep the mind empty, no matter how much he might try.

'Righto. If I decide to do it, I'll give you the nod.' He spun a bamboo ring in his gnarled, scaly hands. 'I don't think it's gunna make much difference to what happened seventeen years ago, but. That's all ancient history now.'

'So is what happened back in the thirties, when he and his dad ran you out of town.'

Strayhorn shook his head. 'Ah no, Mr Malone. That'll never be ancient history, not with me.'

He turned away to sell some rings to a couple of youths and

their girls; Malone left him and caught up with Lisa and Ida. The former looked at him curiously.

'What was that all about?'

'Ancient history,' he said, and she knew enough not to ask any more questions about the bearded old stranger.

They went into the racecourse, into the paddock enclosure, which was the only section where admittance was charged. The small grandstand was almost full, but Sean Carmody stood up and waved to them to come up and join him where he had kept seats for them. The paddock, a trim green sward at city racecourses, was a dust bowl here; but it had not deterred the women from dressing up. This was *the* meeting of the year, to be celebrated. The wealthier, more social couples might go down to Sydney for the big meetings; or even further south for the Melbourne Cup, the feast day of St Bart and St Tommy and other Heaven-bound trainers and jockeys. The locals, however, the ones content with life in and around Collamundra, chose this day to bring out their George Grosses and their Covers, to tramp their Maglis and Jourdans through three or four inches of dust; hats were worn, though not by all, and some even wore gloves, reminding Malone of photos he had seen in his mother's collection of old, yellowed *Sydney Mails*. The women were given a certain grace by what lay about their feet: they drifted above a thin brown mist of dust like models in a couturier's nightmare. Some of the men wore their best suits, all trousers brown up to the knees no matter what the colour of the rest of the suit; but most men, sensibly, wore moleskins and tweed jackets and elastic-sided boots; most of them, Malone saw, were conservative enough to wear ties. Whatever they wore, the aim was to show that the Collamundra Cup was a special occasion.

Dr Bedi was there, elegant as a plump, brightly plumaged bird in a rich blue and cerise sari; she had the sense to stay out of the dust and remain seated in the grandstand. And Narelle Potter was there, too, gliding through the dust in a champagne-coloured knit that showed off her figure; she put on a dark sour look as an accessory when she looked up and saw Malone. She glanced past him and nodded and smiled at Sean Carmody and walked on towards where the horses were being saddled for the first race.

'Who's the lady with the figure?' said Lisa.
'Narelle Potter,' said Malone. 'Our hotel-keeper.'
'She's bandy.'
'It's an occupational hazard with her,' said Ida, smile thick with artificial sugar. 'And I don't mean her hotel-keeping.'
'I hope she doesn't make your bed,' Lisa told Malone.
Just along from the Carmody seats the Governor-General was settling himself into a cane chair in the tiny official section that had been roped off. With him were Gus Dircks, political smile working so hard it sometimes seemed to be coming out of the back of his neck; and Chess Hardstaff, looking and acting more like the G-G than the actual man from Canberra. He was still standing several minutes after the vice-regal representative had sat down, dipping his silver head in slight nods to greetings from people all around him. The Governor-General, a little man in a grey homburg that sat on his head like a tea-cosy, gestured peevishly to the chair beside him and at last Hardstaff sat down. It would probably be the last time the G-G would visit Collamundra, at least while Chess Hardstaff was alive.
The horses were now out on the track for the first race, breaking away from the strappers leading them out of the gate and beginning their canter down to the starting barrier.
Malone said, 'I thought there might have been some Kooris acting as strappers. They're supposed to be good with horses, aren't they?'
'Kooris?' Carmody looked at him quizzically, but made no further comment on Malone's use of the word. It was obviously not one he himself used; but then, like Fred Strayhorn, he was an old-timer, a generation that, without meaning real offence, had used words like 'blackfellers' and 'darkies'. Malone decided that he would not use 'Koori' again, realizing that it might sound affected; even patronizing, to the Kooris themselves.
'There usually are some of them out here, working as casuals,' said Carmody. 'Come to think of it, I haven't seen any of them at all out here today. Some of them might come up to the bookies to make a bet, but they don't mix. They usually stay together down there at the far end of the straight.'
Malone made no mention of the gathering they had seen in

the blacks' settlement this morning. He turned his attention to the first race, which an announcer, his voice crackling over a faulty public address system, said was about to start. Everybody looked across to the far side of the course, where the starting barrier was obscured behind a thin screen of trees.

Suddenly: 'They're off!'

But only one horse came out from behind the trees, galloping flat out at once, pulling hard as its jockey tried to jerk its head in and slow it down. It swept round the far side of the course, round the bend and down the straight, still pulling hard as its jockey tried to control it. The other horses had now come out from behind the trees, but were standing still, they and their jockeys staring after the runaway like dancers in a ballet where one of the corps had suddenly run amok.

The runaway's sides were a lather of foam; it went past the grandstand, its eyes wild and its mouth gaping, hell-bound for only the God-of-Bent-Bookies knew where. The crowd fell about laughing as the horse disappeared round the far curve, heading down the track again for the distant barrier, where the other horses patiently awaited the return of the stoned prodigal.

'False start!' crackled the announcer and it was difficult to tell whether it was static or laughter that was breaking him up.

Carmody wiped his eyes with a handkerchief. 'Doped to the eyeballs! They've given him too much!'

'It was Mulga Lad!' Ida was a shaking mixture of laughter and surprise. 'It's one of Trevor's!'

'Trevor's been got at,' said her father. 'Someone's double-crossed him.'

'Someone's double-crossed *me*,' said Lisa.

'Why?' asked Malone, the police mind working again.

'I don't know. I heard a bookie say he was thirty-three to one and that sounded like a good price to me, a bargain. So I backed him.'

Malone looked at her lovingly, his momentary concern put at rest; then he looked past her at Carmody. 'Normally she's the level-headed one in the family.'

'I wish I'd known you'd done that,' Ida told Lisa. 'I'll give you your money back. I don't think Trevor thought it had a chance

– it was probably the trainer who nominated it for the race and paid the fee. Trevor's other horse, Go Boy, is the favourite. He's two to one on.'

'Who's the trainer?' said Malone.

'A boy named Phil Chakiros, his father is –'

'I know him,' said Malone; and marvelled at his own lack of surprise. The skeins around here seemed to be as interwoven as those in a Chinese string puzzle.

'They're off!' yelled the PA system.

'What – again?' said a voice behind Malone.

The horses came out from behind the screen of trees, bunched in a moving floral bouquet, the jockeys' colours bright even at a distance. This first race was a maiden handicap; all these horses were scrubbers. They were the bottom end of a long line of descendants from the legendary Byerley Turk and other Arab stallions of the seventeenth century in England, the product of equine sperm that had finally run out almost to piss. They galloped with no enthusiasm, they had little or no desire to finish in front of another horse; if they had pricked their ears before they had started it was only because a bush-fly had stung them. They gave meaning to the term 'horse sense': winning might be the name of the game to football coaches and other egomaniacs, but these awkward nags knew better. They raced now with the jockeys shouting at them to get a move on, at least to put on a show; but no horse showed any inclination to break free to a clear lead, they were egalitarian, none wanted to show he was any better than the others.

Then, abruptly, a horse did break clear: it was Go Boy, the favourite. He came round the bend into the straight a good two lengths in the lead. Malone, using the spare set of binoculars Carmody had brought for him, could see the jockey looking anxiously over his shoulder and shouting, as if to urge the others to make a race of it and not leave him out here in this undemocratic position. The other horses, however, despite their jockeys' efforts, weren't interested. They plodded along, intent only on getting past the post and going home.

Then Mulga Lad, still foam-decked, came out of the pack. He caught up with Go Boy and the two horses came down the straight locked together. Malone, binoculars to his eyes, saw the favourite's jockey pulling hard on the reins, almost standing straight up in the stirrups to get more leverage. The two horses came to the winning post: they didn't exactly *flash* by it, but they did go past it. Mulga Lad was a neck in front, covered now in more foam than a blocked drain; Go Boy, mouth wide open from the pull on the bit, was a disgraceful second. Twenty yards past the post Mulga Lad went down head first, throwing his jockey; the boy, who must have been expecting it, did a professional tumble and picked himself up at once, dodging to one side as the other horses came cantering through. Mulga Lad lay still, obviously dead.

Everyone in the stand and the enclosure had begun to laugh; but now they were abruptly quiet. The race had been a joke; but it was no joke to kill a horse. They were country people and only an absolute bastard would treat a horse that way.

'Why did they let him run?' said Malone.

'You'd better ask the stewards that,' said Carmody. 'Ray Chakiros is the chief steward.'

Another skein woven. 'What'll they do?'

'They'll take a swab and send it down to the lab in Sydney. By then all the bookies will have paid out and be long gone. None of them are locals. Go down and collect your money, Lisa.'

'I can't. I couldn't bear to win money on a horse that died for it!'

Ida said, 'Go and collect, Lisa. Otherwise, it'll be only the bookies who win. For all we know, some of them were probably in on the scam.'

'What'll happen to Trevor as the owner?' said Malone. 'Both horses were his, and the favourite wasn't trying. Down in Sydney that jockey would get at least twelve months.'

'Trevor will be okay,' said Carmody. 'Nobody would ever suspect him of being a party to anything as blatant as that. Young Phil Chakiros will be the one they'll question, him and the two jockeys. And whichever bookie was in it with them. Go and get your money, Lisa.'

'I'll get it,' said Malone and took the ticket from Lisa, got up and went down to the betting ring. He had seen Chess Hardstaff stand up, face livid, and he wanted a closer look to see how the president of the turf club had taken this crude scandal. Even in a nation of gamblers, whose patron saint was a bushranger, it was not the sort of thing to be staged in front of the Governor-General. Though the Queen, a racing enthusiast, far away in Buckingham Palace, might laugh if ever she got to hear of it. She knew her Aussie subjects.

Hardstaff had come down from the official box and had reached the bottom step of the grandstand when Malone paused in front of him. 'Nice start to the meeting, Mr Hardstaff. Is it going to get better?'

Hardstaff, eyes sharp, saw the betting ticket in Malone's hand. 'Did you have a bet on the race?'

'I backed the winner. Pity he won't win any more races.'

'How did you know what to back?'

'Oh, I think I'll keep that till the inquiry, in case I'm called. There'll be one, I suppose?'

'Did you know something?'

'Nothing. I just bet on suspicion. It's a police habit.'

Hardstaff gave no answer to that. He brushed by Malone and went over towards the saddling paddock, where Ray Chakiros was snarling at his son. Malone glanced up at the Governor-General, who looked as if he were praying for a national emergency that would call him back to Canberra within the next couple of minutes. At least there the scandals were never so out in the open, they might politically kill an opponent but never in front of a grandstand crowded with voters. One Governor-General, sure, killed a *government*, but there had been no betting scam on that.

Out on the track a truck had already appeared and was dragging the dead horse down to the far end of the straight. In the small betting ring the bookmakers were wiping tears from their cheeks: it was difficult to tell whether they were from laughter or for the dead horse. Malone presented Lisa's ticket to a nuggety, walnut-faced man who could have been an ex-jockey. He was one of the game's battlers, not one of your expensively-suited bookies who had the rails stands at Randwick and Flemington. He wore jeans, a turtlenecked sweater and a hat whose brim had been greased by years of thumbing. He had the sort of eyes that had never been innocent, he would have winked knowingly at his father the first time he had been put to his mother's nipple.

He scrutinized the betting ticket, then Malone. 'I don't remember you, sport. Where'd you pick this up?'

Malone looked at the man's name on the bag hanging like a leather sporran in front of him. 'We haven't met, Mr Gissop. I'm Detective-Inspector Malone.'

Gissop's face went pale under his deep tan. 'Look, sport, I didn't have nothing to do with that out there –' He nodded out towards the track. 'I'd never kill a horse – Christ, I love 'em like me own kids –'

'I'm from Homicide,' said Malone, enjoying every moment.

'Jesus, mate, look, I told you – You're from *what*? Homicide? You're investigating a dead *horse*?'

Malone laughed, let the bookie off the hook and collected Lisa's winnings. He went back towards the grandstand feeling a little better. If he was still alive the day the world ended, he hoped he would find a laugh somewhere amongst all the wreckage.

He went up a different set of stairs, saw a vacant seat beside Dr Bedi and dropped into it, taking off his hat. She smiled, her big dark eyes glistening with amusement. It struck him that she was one of the few people he had met since coming to Collamundra who looked totally relaxed.

'You're always a gentleman, Inspector? Taking your hat off to a lady?'

'I always thought there was supposed to be more gentlemen in the bush than in the city.'

'Not around here. Not to me.' She was still smiling as if unperturbed by the lack of respect shown to her. 'But then Indian men are no better. Worse, perhaps. Unless one is a rich old maharani – then they bow and scrape like men everywhere.'

'I've never met a rich old maharani. Is there a Mr Bedi?'

'Yes. He is back in Simla, where I come from. He couldn't face the thought of outback Australia.'

She looked out at the local example of outback Australia. She was facing west, towards the plains stretching away forever. She would never become accustomed to the limitless flatness; she missed the mountains, the towering peaks against the Himalayan sky, more than she did her husband. She could close her eyes here in Collamundra and see, with heart-aching clarity, the view from the Mall in Simla in the early morning: the air so clear that one felt one could reach out and touch the glittering peaks a hundred miles away, the pennants of snow streaming from their tops in the winds, the silence, the voice of Himalaya, the snow abode. She turned back to Malone.

'My husband is a great cricket fan like so many Indian men. He was afraid that all Australian men would be like your fast bowlers, aggressive and vicious.'

'I was a fast bowler, once.'

She raised her eyebrows. 'A fast bowler *and* a policeman? Are you popular?'

'In Australia fast bowlers have always been more popular than policemen. Even the vicious ones. Dr Nothling's not here?'

'He is coming later, I understand. He is entertaining some Japanese gentlemen at the moment.'

There was no one seated near them; everyone was down in the betting ring or parading up and down in the dust bowl. He moved closer to her. 'Dr Bedi, did Dr Nothling examine Ken Sagawa's body at all?'

The amusement faded from her eyes; they became as opaque as he had seen them yesterday afternoon at the hospital. 'There is a question here, Inspector, of professional etiquette –'

'You mean one doctor won't point the finger at another? I understand you're all gentlemen in that respect, even the ladies.'

She studied him as if he were a specimen under a microscope. 'You're quite a mixture, aren't you? You can be rough-and-ready and other times you're as smooth as – as –'

'As a Macquarie Street specialist? Or the president of the AMA?'

Her eyes became a little less opaque, some light showing in them. 'You don't like doctors, do you, Inspector?'

'You don't like policemen. Or anyway, Dr Nothling doesn't. You haven't answered my question. Forget the professional etiquette. I'm trying to find a murderer, Dr Bedi, I'm not trying to send Dr Nothling or anyone else up before the medical ethics committee. Though I might do that if I had to.'

'My husband would think that was the fast bowler in you talking.'

'I bowled my share of bumpers at a batsman's head. I've never done it to a lady, but there's always a first time for everything.'

'Oh, I wish he were here – my husband, I mean . . .' But she did not wish that, not really. She re-arranged an already neat fold in her sari. 'All right, Inspector. The truth. No, Dr Nothling did not examine Sagawa's body. He came in, took one look at it, told me to stay with the examination and went away.'

'Not to an emergency in one of the wards?'

'No.'

'What had prevented him from going out on the original call to the gin to view the body? Was he on rounds?'

She hesitated, looking down to see if the fold needed re-arranging again. 'No. He was suffering from a hangover, the worst I've ever seen him.'

'Does he get drunk very often?'

'Lately, yes. Just the last couple of months. Twice he hasn't turned up for surgery and I've had to perform it. Fortunately, they were not major ops.'

'And nobody has complained?'

'No one on the staff, no. I think they're all afraid to.'

'What about the patients?'

'I heard one old lady complaining very loudly to him one day, but he charmed her out of it. He can be very charming when he likes. A little heavy-handed for my taste, but yes – charming. I don't think Mrs Nothling would ever have married him, otherwise.'

'I think Mrs Nothling-Hardstaff has arrived.'

Dr Bedi raised an eyebrow at his mockery of the double-barrelled name. Then she added her own mockery: 'In her pale-blue Givenchy or Montana and her big picture hat. She is the district's ball of style.' For just a moment the claws showed.

Amanda was looking up at Dr Bedi and Malone and he could see her clearly. She had some of her father's imperiousness about her, softened by the occasional smile she gave to passers-by, a smile that was both sincere and yet suggested a hand-out, like royalty on Maundy Thursday. Like her father she looked as if she would not suffer fools, gladly or otherwise.

'She looks sort of – regal.'

'Dr Nothling, when he was in his cups once, told me about a time they were down in Sydney, dining at the most expensive place in town. She kept turning her nose up at everything on her plate. The head-waiter knew who she was and he came across to their table and asked if everything was all right. And she just asked him in a loud voice if it was the chef's night off.'

'A real lady.'

'The funny thing is, she *is* a lady. Unfortunately, her father keeps coming out in her.'

'Is her husband under her thumb?'

'What an odd question! But yes, I think he is.' She returned the smile Amanda Nothling was giving her. Still looking down at the doctor's wife, without turning her head towards Malone, she said, 'I am not going to answer any more questions, Inspector. Whether you bowl bumpers at my head or not.'

'You've batted well, Dr Bedi. Your husband would be proud of you.'

'He always was,' she said, letting down her guard, 'till I left him and came to Australia.'

He had stood up; the crowd was starting to drift back into the stand. 'Are you sorry? That you came?'

'Yes and no. Mostly no. I may feel at home here in another twenty years. God knows where India will be in twenty years.'

He put on his hat, raised it like a country gentleman, one of the old school, and went back to Lisa, Ida and Carmody. He gave Lisa her hundred and seventy dollars and she tipped him five dollars.

'Thanks,' he said, and wanted to kiss her, right out there in the open, in front of all the spectators, giving them a grandstand view. But he didn't: the old Malone reticence about showing affection in public was too thick in his blood. He just pressed her hand; but he knew it was enough. The look in her eyes told him that. She knew he would never be a fool, not towards her.

'You seemed to be getting on very well with Dr Bedi,' said Ida, probing like a surgeon.

'We were talking cricket. She's afraid of fast bowlers.'

'Is she afraid of you?' said Lisa.

'I couldn't tell,' he said and changed the subject away from Anju Bedi.

There were three more races before the Collamundra Cup and Malone, never a racing fan, grew bored. Russ Clements, leaving the children at the carnival, came up to join them, squeezing into a space between Lisa and Ida.

'I've backed Doc Nothling's horse. I was told it would romp home.'

'If you backed it, it can't lose,' said Malone, and explained to Ida, 'He's legendary down in Sydney. He makes more money on a Saturday at the races than the Commissioner earns in a month.'

Max Nothling had just arrived with Trevor Waring. The latter came up into the grandstand and fitted himself in on the other side of Ida from Clements.

'You get all your business fixed up?' Ida said. 'How were the Japanese?'

'Very formal,' said Waring, avoiding the eyes of both detectives as they leaned slightly forward to glance at him.

'Max looks pleased about something,' Ida said.

Nothling had joined the vice-regal party in the official box. He looked flushed, as if he had been drinking, but he was steady on his feet and greeted everyone, including the Governor-General, with bonhomie that came close to back-slapping and kisses. As he sat down he ducked under the brim of his wife's hat to plant a kiss on her cheek, which she brushed away with a gloved hand as if it had been a fly-bite.

'Things went well,' said Waring and put his binoculars to his eyes, as if donning a mask.

The horses filed out on to the track and cantered away to the far side. The race, Malone had been told, was a two-miler; the horses would pass the grandstand twice. The crowd had come alive, as if the running of the Cup was the sole purpose of the meeting; which, indeed, it was.

'I think we can start heading home after this,' said Carmody. 'You've got nothing running after this one, have you, Trevor?'

'No. I've withdrawn our other entry, after what happened to Mulga Lad.'

'Have the stewards spoken to you yet?'

'No. Young Phil Chakiros is going to have some explaining to do. Silly young coot.'

'I'm sorry about your horse,' said Lisa.

'Yes,' said Waring; but showed no emotion. 'The children will miss him.'

But you won't, thought Malone; and wondered why he had not noticed this cold streak in the lawyer.

'They're off!' crackled the PA system and the horses, bunched together, came out from the screen of trees and headed for the first long bend. They settled down to a two-mile pace, bowling along at a good clip, the dust rising behind them in a long train. They came round the bend for the run down the straight for the first time. The crowd stood up, ready to cheer on their fancies as they swept past.

Then above the cheering and the shouting there came faintly the heavy beat of drums. Malone looked to his left, down to the other end of the straight. Marching up the middle of the track, a huge banner floating above them, were perhaps two hundred Aborigines, men, women and children. At their head marched three young men, each banging away on a big bass drum; later it would be learned the drums had been stolen from the local Boy Scouts' hall. The banner, limp at first as the two young men holding it veered towards each other, suddenly tautened as they drew apart. In large red and yellow letters on a black background was the demand:

NO MORE BLACK DEATHS!

There was a roar from the racecourse crowd, of horror and anger. The horses swept past, hoofs a steady thunder, but already the leading jockeys had seen the obstruction and they were desperately trying to slow their horses. Those behind, their view obscured, saw nothing till it was too late. Then they rose up in their stirrups, dragging hard on the bits, but the horses in the middle of the packed bunch hit those in front. They went down in slow motion, the jockeys going up in the air like tumbling acrobats, then falling ever so slowly, it seemed to Malone, down amidst the plunging hoofs. Some of the jockeys managed to swing their mounts wide of the mêlée, going right out to the outer rails and somehow scraping by the massed Aborigines, who had now come to a halt, the drums still being banged by the three young men but no one else moving. Horses were screaming, jockeys were yelling, the racecourse crowd was boiling with anger and the Aborigines, bunched tightly together now like a small dark island, stood mute and defiant.

'Oh Christ,' said Sean Carmody, his voice full of despair, 'what good do they think they've done for their cause?'

Chess Hardstaff, handsome face now ugly with fury, had stood up. He shouted, like a Roman emperor, 'Get rid of them!' and at once, as if they had been waiting for such an order, men erupted from the crowd, ran down and jumped the fence on to the track. Some were police in uniform, but most of them were civilians, middle-aged men, youths, even some young teenagers. They all wore a face Malone knew so well: the face of the mob, their skulls empty of everything but frenzy, their shouts an animal howl. He had seen it as a young cop in anti-war demonstrations in the early seventies, in a New Year's Eve riot in The Rocks area in Sydney, in an ethnic brawl at a soccer match. Let loose, it could kill like any animal.

He looked around for Hugh Narvo or some senior sergeant, but could see no one to take charge.

'Come on!' he said, and Clements was on his feet at the same time as himself. As he went down the steps he flung back over his shoulder at Lisa, 'Get the kids and take 'em home! Now!'

He and Clements pushed their way through the crowd, sometimes having to pull people apart to force a passage. They jumped the fence, Clements having a little difficulty in getting his bulk over it, then they were on the track, running through the fog of dust raised by some of the fallen horses that were still kicking but couldn't raise themselves on to all four legs.

The uniformed police had reached the Aborigines who still stood tightly packed together, still mute but fear now plain on their dark faces. Dust was settling on them, but rivulets of sweat gullied the dust, turning their faces into mockeries of corroboree masks. The police pushed at them, handling them roughly but not using their batons. Then the first wave of men and youths hit them from behind, pushing the police at the Aborigines, coming in with fists and boots swinging, hitting and kicking anyone with a dark face.

Malone pulled up, drew his gun and fired it twice in the air. Beside him Clements had also taken out his gun. The sound of the shots was a shock; at first no one seemed to know where they had come from. Then the police, the men and the youths swung round; a teenage boy fell over and knelt in the dust, looking up at Malone with wide, disbelieving eyes. For a moment it looked as if the mob was going to charge the two Sydney detectives. Malone brought his gun down, aimed it at the youth closest to him: it was Stan Gruber, fat face as suddenly full of fear again as it had been last night.

'All you men, except the police officers, back off. Hear me? Back off!'

The white men glared at him and for a moment he thought there was going to be a stand-off; he knew he would never pull the trigger on Stan Gruber. Then the fat youth walked unsteadily away, over towards where ambulance officers and several of the race strappers were doing their best to attend to the injured jockeys and horses. The others in the mob hesitated and Malone moved his gun round to point it at Max Nothling, whom he saw now for the first time.

'Go over and help the jockeys, Doc. That's your job, not bashing up people.'

Nothling didn't move, looking at Malone as if he hadn't heard aright. Then a voice behind Malone said, 'I'll take over now, Inspector. Thanks. Lead the way, Dr Nothling. The others will help you.'

Nothling flicked a glance at Narvo, but still didn't move; then the defiance abruptly ran out of him. But he paused long enough to say, 'What are you going to do with these black bastards? They could've killed some of the jockeys. And we're going to have to destroy at least half a dozen of the horses.'

'I'll attend to these people, Doctor.' Narvo was as punctiliously polite as if he had never met Nothling before. 'Just leave them to me. This is a police matter, not a medical one.'

Malone put away his gun as the mob of whites, muttering threats at the blacks, moved across to the carnage scene near the inner rail. He looked up towards the stand: Lisa, Carmody and the Warings had disappeared. Oddly, it was Waring that he wondered about: where had he gone?

The stand was half-empty, the people who had remained there standing in the seemingly same state of shock; all their faces had a faint resemblance, as if they had been captured in a wide-lens photograph of an extended family reunion. Except that no one was smiling: the resemblance was in the shock and horror as they all stared out at the jockeys still lying in the middle of the track like so many brightly coloured rag dolls and the horses screaming as they struggled, on shattered limbs, to get to their feet. It struck Malone that an animal's shriek of pain was, somehow, more frightful than a human's. Or perhaps it was that he was more accustomed to the pain-filled cries of humans.

The two detectives stood silent while Narvo gave orders for the Aborigines to turn round and go back to their settlement. 'Except for you two guys carrying the banner. You don't belong here. Where do you come from?'

'We come up from Canberra,' both said at once, as if rehearsed in answers to police questions. They had 'rebel' written all over them: Malone had seen their sort before in city demos, always up front, always shouting defiance, falling over themselves to get in front of the ever-obliging television cameras. He could never, in his heart, bring himself to blame them. They were just a pain in the arse; but what rebel hadn't been? God must have groaned when Lucifer first waved his banner.

'That where you live?' Narvo, like most country folk, had little time for Canberra. Politicians and protestors: they were both pains.

'No. Sydney,' both said again.

'Arrest them,' said Narvo, as if that were their final crime. He turned his back on them and looked at Malone. 'I'm sorry you had to do that, Scobie, take over like that.'

'I looked for you –'

Narvo grinned in embarrassment, something Malone would not have thought him capable of. 'I was caught short. I was sitting in a portable dunny out the back of the stand. Something I ate for lunch went through me like a firehose . . . Thanks, anyway. You too, Russ.'

The Aborigines had turned and were walking slowly back down the track, no longer a tight little island but a loose shoal, their anger and defiance no longer binding them. They had been harangued into something they had not thought through, they had caused a disaster that none of them had envisaged. Malone looked for Wally Mungle and the Koowarra family, but couldn't see them, and felt an immediate relief.

'Are you going to let them go?'

The three senior policemen turned round: Chess Hardstaff stood behind them, stiff with cold anger. 'I want them arrested and charged, every damned one of them!'

Out of the corner of his eye Malone saw a smartly dressed Aboriginal girl standing by the outer rail. As he looked at her she abruptly spun round and walked away, but not before a final glance back at – whom? Then Malone realized she was staring at Hardstaff, that her attractive, coffee-coloured face was a mixture of emotion that clouded and spoiled her attractiveness. Then she walked on and disappeared round the end of the grandstand.

'I'm not going to arrest them, not the lot of them.' Narvo was as polite as he had been with Nothling. Something had happened to him, he was prepared to make waves. 'Not at the moment, anyway.'

'I'll call Superintendent Dammie over at Cawndilla –'

'Do that,' said Narvo.

'You'll regret –' Then Hardstaff stopped, looked at the man who had appeared behind the three policemen and was standing there listening frankly to every word. 'Who are you?'

'I thought you might recognize me,' said Fred Strayhorn. 'But I guess it's been too long. Too much water under the bridge, eh? Or in the dam? I'm Fred Strayhorn. You and your old man and a lot of other fascist mongrels run me and my mum and dad outa town just on sixty years ago. You still got no time for Commos? You certainly got no time for the darkies, have you?'

'I don't remember you,' said Hardstaff, even stiffer now.

'You will,' said Strayhorn with certainty. 'The last time you saw me was seventeen years ago. I had a different name then, I can't remember what I called m'self. But we could look it up in the police files, if they're still around. I was the bloke who told the police you were out at the dam with me the morning your wife was murdered. You remember that?'

After a glance at Strayhorn, Malone had been watching Hardstaff. This had not been the best of days for the King-maker. There had been the farce of the drugged horse winning the first race; then the demonstration by the Aborigines and the disaster it had caused. Those had been enough, bringing out fury that Malone had never expected to see. Now he saw something else he had never expected to see on that cold, controlled face: fear.

But the exposure was only momentary; Hardstaff was granite-hard and granite doesn't give up its secrets easily. 'Yes, I remember now. You wanted to talk to me about it?'

'I think I might, just nostalgia,' Strayhorn said with an exaggerated drawl. For just a moment he flicked a glance at Malone, but Hardstaff caught it.

'You know Inspector Malone?' he said.

'Who? Oh, *him*. Never met him in my life. He a friend of yours? You always had friends amongst the coppers, didn't you?' He smiled a greeting at Malone; then looked back at Hardstaff. 'Come into town tonight, at the Mail Coach, and I'll buy you a drink.'

It was blatant insolence, but he got away with it. He turned and ambled off, only stopping when Hardstaff said, voice hard and cold as metal on metal, 'I shan't be in town. Come out to the property tomorrow morning, you know where it is.'

Strayhorn pondered a moment. 'How'll I get there? I'm still travelling on Shanks's pony.' Then he smiled, almost evilly. 'Does the railway line run past your place? Maybe I could borrow a trike.'

But Hardstaff had evidently forgotten that episode; or chose not to remember it. He said, 'I'll send one of my men in to pick you up. Where will you be?'

'Over at the carnival. I'm camped right next to the elephants.'

He walked away down the track, unhurried, not looking back: the biggest winner of the day, thought Malone, one I should have had my money on. Hardstaff stared after him, no expression showing on his face; but one could feel the anger, the fear, *something*, tearing at the insides of him. Malone, reluctantly, had to admire the autocrat's control.

The three policemen had stood silent during the stand-off between the two old men: Malone, for one, had learned more by being a spectator than by butting in. But now, chipping away at Hardstaff's foundations, he said, 'After you've talked with Mr Strayhorn, I'd like to talk to you. How about tomorrow morning out at your place?'

'What do you want to talk to *me* about?' The arrogance was back, it was second nature to him.

'I'll tell you when I see you. Eleven o'clock tomorrow morning, Mr Hardstaff, okay? You won't need me to confirm it by phone. Tom, Dick and Harry won't be coming – just me and Sergeant Clements.' He nodded to Narvo. 'I'll see you back at the station, Hugh. I guess the rest of the meeting's abandoned.'

'That's up to the chairman of the turf club,' said Narvo.

Hardstaff looked across the track, where some jockeys still lay in the dust, waiting for another ambulance to arrive. A strapper with a Twenty-two rifle stood by a prostrate horse that was still kicking weakly; he looked at the turf club's honorary veterinary surgeon, a young man with red hair and a stricken look, who nodded. The Twenty-two was put to the head of the horse, there was the sound of the shot, several men attending to the jockeys jerked upright, then the strapper moved on, put the rifle to the head of another horse, waited for the approving nod and pulled the trigger again. Most of the course crowd were still outside the rails watching the tragedy; there were gasps and a young girl's cry of grief as the horses died under the bullet. Hardstaff looked back at Narvo.

'I'll call off the last two races. But I'd still like to see you, Inspector. Here comes Mr Dircks, I'm sure he'd like to see you, too.'

Dircks, face red with exertion, came lumbering down the

track. He arrived puffed and sweating. 'I thought someone had better stay with the G-G. He'd have been pretty shirty if we'd all gone off and left him. An ugly business.' He shook his head. 'The demo, I mean. Christ Almighty, who put 'em up to such a stupid show?'

Malone stared at him with contempt. Dircks was a coward, morally and politically, the sort who would always dodge decisions that required courage. It had been far easier to stay with the Governor-General than come down here and face a political demonstration by a mob of angry Aborigines. Unlike politicians in more volatile countries he could not read the face of the mob. He preferred individuals, names, addresses, voters who could be relied upon. He had been spoiled, representing a safe seat for so long.

'I heard you fire your gun.' He was afraid to be aggressive; he sounded more aggrieved. 'Would you have shot any of them?'

'No. But that's the advantage of being an outsider.' Malone was aware of Hardstaff watching him. 'Nobody knows how far you'll go.'

Then he jerked his head at Clements and the two detectives walked away, leaving the locals to sort out their local troubles. Driving back to the police station through the traffic already beginning to stream towards town, Clements said, 'Do we still go to the ball tonight?'

'I'm not keen on it. But Lisa is. She thinks I need some relaxation. Who are you taking? Narelle?'

'You kidding?'

'Did you know it was her who shot her husband?'

Clements jerked his head round; the car wavered a moment on the road. '*She* shot him?'

'It was an accident, Sean told me. She tripped or something. The two of them were out shooting, 'roos or rabbits.'

'Did they ever investigate if it was an accident or not?'

'I don't know.' He didn't want to get caught up in *another* murder.

'Be interesting if it wasn't an accident.'

'Yeah, wouldn't it. You ever been to bed with a murderess before?'

Clements grimaced and said nothing more. When they reached the police station, Wally Mungle was waiting for them in the upstairs detectives' room. Outwardly he looked relaxed, but Malone at once could feel the tension in him.

'You heard what happened out at the course?'

'Yes, sir.' Everyone, it seemed, had become formally polite.

'You been here all afternoon?'

'I volunteered to be the duty man.' He had stood up as the two Sydney men entered; he had a respectful air about him without seeming to be obsequious. But Malone had a feeling he had stepped into a role, a policeman playing by the book. 'I've been here since one o'clock.'

'Wally –' Malone tried to make the question as gentle as possible. 'Did you know there was going to be a demo?'

The Aborigine stared at Malone, his dark eyes showing nothing; then he nodded. 'I didn't know for sure, but I guessed it.'

'Why didn't you report it to Inspector Narvo or Curly Baldock?'

'Inspector –' For a moment there seemed to be a spark of rebellion in his eyes; then he said calmly, 'I talked my mother and my uncle and aunt out of going along with any demo, if there was gunna be one. I figure I did enough, doing that.'

Malone was silent for a long moment; he felt Clements look at him for his answer. Then he said, 'I see your point.'

'I dunno that you do, Inspector. I tried to talk 'em out of it, but Kooris are like honkies – a lot of 'em don't listen.' He wasn't insolent, but he was less concerned now with appearing to be respectful. 'Those two stirrers who come into town this morning, they'd got 'em going. They didn't wanna listen to me, a cop, someone from the other side. Or anyway, halfway between. When you're halfway between, Inspector, most of the time you got nothing to stand on but quicksand.'

Malone offered him no more advice. For two hundred years the whites had been giving advice to the blacks and it seemed that neither side had profited. He just nodded, let the subject of the demonstration drop and said, 'Any messages for us?'

'Constable Graham called from Sydney. He asked if you could

call back to Police Centre before he left at six. He said it was important.'

Malone picked up the phone and dialled Sydney, asked for Andy Graham, who came on the line, all enthusiasm as usual. 'Bingo, Inspector! Tokyo has sent us something at last!'

Malone was patient. 'What have we got, Andy?'

'Kenji Sagawa – his old man was a war criminal!'

Malone, all at once feeling weary, tried not to sound unimpressed. 'I must be slow, Andy. What's the connection between Sagawa's murder and what his old man was –' Then his mind, the cogs of which had been slipping, was abruptly in gear. 'Did Russ tell you anything about the anti-Jap feeling out here?'

'Yes! That's what I mean!' Graham was shouting down the line. 'Maybe someone out there found out about it . . . Listen to this.' There was a rustle of paper at the other end of the line; then Graham began to read, or rather to declaim like a town crier:

'Chojiro Nibote, a permanent army officer, was wounded in action in Burma in 1942, declared unfit for front-line service. He was appointed commandant of Mergui prisoner-of-war camp in Siam. He was captured by British forces while trying to return to Japan at the end of hostilities in August 1945. He was indicted as a war criminal and executed on May 24, 1946. His wife, Tsuchi, reverted to her maiden name of Sagawa, gave it to her son and daughter and moved from Kobe to Osaka immediately after Chojiro Nibote's execution. Message ends . . . Jesus!' And Graham seemed suddenly to run out of steam, but had enough left to gasp, 'How'd it be, having a war criminal for a father?'

'You think it'd be any worse than having a serial killer for a dad?' But Malone didn't want to get into any discussion on degrees of crime, of the weight of the sins of the fathers. 'I didn't expect the Japanese to come up with anything as frank as that.'

'Neither did I!' Graham had regained his breath. 'I thought the Japs didn't take any blame for what happened during the war –'

'Maybe there's a whole new generation there now.' *Like there is here.* He and Andy Graham had not been born when the war ended; even the war crimes' trials had been history by then. 'Right, fax back our thanks, Andy. Take the weekend off. Russ will call you Monday, let you know how things are going up here. What about down there?'

'We had a murder this morning, out at Rockdale. Just a domestic.' A nothing crime, just a husband killing a wife or vice versa. *Grow up, Andy. Homicide isn't an adventure.*

'What are you doing for the weekend?'

'Tomorrow I'm going to the league. Balmain are playing the Gold Coast. It should be murder.'

'Enjoy it.'

He hung up and told Clements and Mungle what he had just heard. 'What do you think?'

'Do we go over to the Veterans Legion and ask for a list of the members who were POWs?' said Clements.

'Do you know anyone in the district who was a POW, Wally?'

Mungle shook his head. 'None, as far as I know. But maybe they wouldn't wanna talk about it. Not if they had a bad time.'

'I'll ask Ray Chakiros tonight. He'll be at the ball, you can bet.'

'Maybe you wouldn't have to be a POW,' said Clements slowly, 'to want to kill the son of a war criminal.'

'What are you getting at?'

'Doc Nothling was born in Burma. I wonder what happened to his parents? His old man, for instance?'

4

The gin manager's house had been the farmhouse on one of the original properties that had been bought up for the cotton acreage. It was an old timber, one-storeyed structure that had been renovated and re-painted; the small garden at its front had almost the neatness and formalism of a Japanese garden. The yards at the back had been cleaned up, but, with a bow to local heritage, some of the old, weathered buildings had been retained. The woolshed, not a large one, was still there; the machinery shed had been repaired, its missing timbers replaced, and now housed a Nissan Patrol wagon. The chutes, slippery as brown ice, still ran from the woolshed into the yards, but the yards themselves had been reduced in size, though their railings had been replaced. Even the outdoor dunny had been renovated and painted pale blue, a monument to the fact that men may come and men may go, but their waste goes on forever. Malone sometimes felt that half the nation's literary education had been taken in while sitting on a toilet seat. There was no rusting machinery lying about, the usual skeletons of a farmyard.

Koga and his three bosses were sitting in comfortable chairs on the front veranda when Malone and Clements arrived. Koga was on his feet at once; the older Japanese rose more leisurely.

Koga introduced them, deferential as a court page to both his executives and the two detectives. Malone felt like an ambassador presenting his credentials. 'I told Mr Tajiri you would probably be coming out to see him.'

Tajiri was the president of Okada Corporation, the parent company of South Cloud. He was in his mid-sixties but well preserved, with iron-grey hair neatly parted and brushed flat on his head, a firm square jaw and rimless glasses with gold sidebars. He wore a green golf shirt, a yellow cashmere cardigan, cavalry twill trousers and expensive walking shoes. Malone wondered if he had brought his golf gear with him.

'So you are investigating Mr Sagawa's death.' His English was as good as Koga's, perhaps a little more precise, as if he did not want to make any mistakes in front of a very junior employee. 'Very sad. We hope it will not mean the severing of our relations with Collamundra.'

The other two men, Hayashi and Yoshida, both in their mid-forties, as neatly and expensively dressed as their president but not as casually, nodded their neat heads. It was the neatness of all three and their smallness that made Malone feel that he and Clements probably looked like a couple of football oafs.

'Very sad,' said Hayashi and Yoshida, but none of the three executives appeared to be overwhelmed by Sagawa's death. Still, Malone told himself, he knew nothing of what emotion Japanese showed in public.

'Had he been with your company long?'

Tajiri looked at Hayashi, evidently the personnel man; or perhaps he had been a friend of Sagawa's, but first and foremost was a company man. That was supposed to be the big thing with Japanese . . . *Come on, Malone. You're jumping at judgements.*

'He came to us straight from high school. We sent him to university in Japan, then to university in the United States. He was a very valued worker.'

'Do you have a photo of him?'

Malone looked at Koga. It struck him that he had no idea what Sagawa looked like, not that it mattered now. He had not gone to the morgue to look at the body; when they had told him how it had been chopped up by the spikes, he had chickened out. He could still be squeamish at what could be done to what had once been living flesh.

Koga went into the house and Malone gestured to the other three Japanese to resume their seats. He and Clements sat on the veranda railing. All around them the fields stretched away, silent and deserted now, darker patches showing like sharp-edged currents where the harvesters had sailed through the white sea.

'Will you gentlemen be staying long?'

'Not long,' said Tajiri. 'We shall wait till Mr Sagawa's body is released to us, then we shall take it back with us to Japan for cremation. Those are his family's wishes.'

'You have tidied up all your business here? With your partners?'

The eyes were still for a moment behind the glasses. 'You know our partners?'

'Were they supposed to be secret? I didn't realize that.'

Tajiri lost his composure for just a moment; he said hastily, 'Oh no, not at all. I just had not appreciated the thoroughness of Australian police investigation.'

Wait till I tell you how thorough we can be . . . But he said nothing about that. He took the eight-by-six photo Koga had brought out. 'It was with his belongings, Inspector. I packed them all in his suitcase this morning. I took that photograph only two weeks ago.'

Malone held up the photo and Clements leaned close to him to look at it. Clements said, 'He's nothing like I expected.'

'Me, neither.'

They were looking at a full-length photo of a slimly-built man whose energy seemed to spring out at them; his head was thrown back and he was laughing, showing good-looking teeth in a broad good-looking face. His hands were on his hips and he seemed to be rocking backwards and forwards on the balls of his feet. He looked like a man who would have had a zest for life, who would never have had the patience for Zen or other ancient contemplations, who would have been thoroughly modern . . .

'The hair,' said Malone.

Tajiri glanced at Hayashi, who said, 'Ah yes, that did sometimes disturb us. It did not fit –' *our company image*: but he stopped before he said that. 'We turned a blind eye to it. He was too good a manager for us to quarrel over whether he went to a hair stylist or a plain barber.'

Malone looked at Sagawa again. He had seen pictures of young Japanese swingers wearing their hair like this: shoulder-length, blow-waved. But they would probably have been half Sagawa's age, rock musicians or in television, maybe a sanitized Tokyo chapter of Hell's Angels; but they would not have been cotton gin managers, field technocrats. Sagawa was not at all what the two detectives had imagined him to be; not that that mattered, either. He still was dead, murdered, blow-waved or short-back-and-sides.

Malone handed back the photo. 'Was he a good family man?'

The three older Japanese looked at each other at the question. Then Yoshida, who had been silent up till now, said, 'His wife never complained.'

'Do your employees' wives complain to the company if their husbands are not good family men?'

'No. It is not our custom. Do Australian wives complain like that?'

'No, Australian wives handle things like that in their own way.'

'How?'

'Sometimes they shoot them,' said Clements, the bachelor.

The senior men looked at each other, glad that Japanese wives were better behaved than that.

Then Malone said casually, as if he had only just thought of it, 'Did you know Mr Sagawa's father was executed as a war criminal?'

There was a long silence. The timbers of the house creaked as the warmth of the day went out of them in the gathering dusk. The veranda faced east and the house's fading shadow stretched away to take the colour out of the garden. A crow went overhead, heading home, its croak scratching the silence. When Tajiri spoke, his voice, too, sounded like a croak.

'Yes, we knew. I served under Major Nibote in Burma, before he was invalided back to take charge of a prisoner-of-war camp. I was a very junior officer and he saved my life in action.'

'So you sponsored his son as a sort of repayment for that?'

'It was a debt, Inspector. What we call *giri*.'

'Did Sagawa know what his father had been and how he died?'

'Yes.'

'Did he ever discuss it with you?'

'I would never have allowed it.'

Malone glanced at Koga. 'Did he ever mention it to you, Mr Koga?'

It was plain from the look on Koga's face that the revelation of Sagawa's father's execution was a shock. 'Never.'

Malone turned back to Tajiri. 'Sagawa was killed in the service of your company, Mr Tajiri. He would probably still be alive if he had not been sent here. Do you have a debt to *his* children?'

The three younger Japanese did not look at their company president; but Malone felt they were as interested in the answer as he himself was. Perhaps they had their own idea of what corporate debt was. Tajiri stared at Malone, looked away for a moment, then back at the detective.

'We shall take care of his family, Inspector. Just find his murderer.'

'You want him found?'

That shook Tajiri; his head reared back a little as if Malone had shoved something under his nose. 'Of course, Inspector. Why not?'

'Indeed,' said Malone, as formal as the four Japanese, 'why not?'

Clements, lounging on the veranda rail, as informal as a pub drinker except for the lack of a singlet and a pair of thongs, said, 'There's one thing, Mr Koga. I've been through everything Sergeant Baldock took into the station from Mr Sagawa's desk. There's no sign of a business diary.'

Malone loved Clements's little surprises, even if they were sometimes a surprise to himself. He always left the 'murder box' and its contents of general evidence to Clements: the big man was sometimes a magician in what he could produce from it.

Koga said, 'I noticed it was missing the day after Mr Sagawa was murdered. I looked for it to see if he had made any appointments that I would have to keep for him. When it wasn't there, I assumed Sergeant Baldock had taken it along with everything else.'

'What sort of diary did he keep?' Koga frowned and Clements went on, 'I mean, was it a meticulous one? You know, detailed entries for every day?'

'Oh very. Mr Sagawa was a most meticulous person.' The young man looked over his shoulder at his three superiors; Malone wondered if he was laying it on for their benefit. 'He would not only write down his appointments, but later would enter up his remarks on what had taken place. It was the basis for his monthly report.'

Clements looked at Malone. 'It looks as if the killer came back afterwards and pinched the diary. That means the chances are whoever killed him came to see him on business, otherwise his name wouldn't be in the diary.'

Malone nodded; then turned to Koga. 'Test your memory, Mr Koga. Write down the names of everyone who came to see Mr Sagawa the week before he died. Take your time, but I'd like it by tomorrow morning.' Then he glanced at Tajiri. 'You wanted to say something, Mr Tajiri?'

'If – *when* you catch the murderer, what will happen to him? Will he be hanged or electrocuted or what?'

'We don't have capital punishment in this country, Mr Tajiri. Sorry.'

Tajiri made a small deprecating gesture with his hand. 'Civilization has many modes. Major Nibote would be interested if he knew that his son's murderer would not be executed.'

'Yes,' said Malone, wishing he had a more telling answer. Then he said, 'I don't notice any security men around here today. You're not afraid the killer will come back?'

All four Japanese looked at each other; then Tajiri looked back at Malone. 'The thought had occurred to us, Inspector.' If it had, they had made a good job of concealing the thought. If Tokyo cops had to put up with Oriental inscrutability, Malone didn't envy them their job. 'But we don't want to turn the cotton farm into an armed camp.'

'I'll suggest to Inspector Narvo that he post a man out here, three of them doing eight-hour shifts.'

'Will that be popular with the townspeople? I understand the feeling . . .' His voice tapered off.

'The police have to do a lot of things that aren't popular with the voters, Mr Tajiri.' He stepped off the veranda and Clements followed him. 'Incidentally –' He paused. 'Just on sixty per cent of the people in this State are in favour of capital punishment. If that's any satisfaction to you.'

'Not really, Inspector,' said Tajiri, his face a blank page. 'But perhaps we are all much more alike than we think.'

SIX

1

The Cup ball was held in the only building at the showground. It stood just outside the showground itself, an iron-roofed, timber-walled structure that had begun life a hundred years ago as a woolshed, been added to and renovated and now was an all-purpose building. It served as a home crafts' pavilion for the annual Collamundra show; as the occasional display showroom for agricultural equipment salesmen; and as the venue for the monthly dances and the annual Cup ball. It was two hundred feet long and a hundred feet wide and tonight it was overflowing, despite the fact that a second dance floor had been laid outdoors on a hard, dusty patch between the hall and the carnival inside the showground proper. A six-piece band, Five Drovers and Their Dog, were belting out their version of 'Lola', while over at the carnival the horses on the merry-go-round were still waltzing to 'The Sidewalks of New York'. The circus elephants trumpeted; a lion roared, carnival spruikers shouted; young bucks, already well liquored, yahooed; girls screamed with delight and fake resistance as their panties came down ahead of schedule. Bedlam on the Noongulli: *It's so restful out here*, Lisa had said. Out in the scrub and timber the night-birds gave up and fled, wondering if the world had gone mad.

'I thought they might've called off the ball,' said Malone. 'Because of what happened this afternoon.'

'It was too late. Anyway, the proceeds are for the local hospital,' said Hugh Narvo. 'It'll need the money. It's full up right now. There are seven injured jockeys in there.'

He and Malone, each with a beer glass in hand, were standing outside the hall, out of the stream of guests coming and going between the outdoor dance floor, the hall and the portable toilets fifty yards away on the edge of the scrub. Narvo, like most of the men, even the young ones, was in black tie and dinner jacket; though the young men, by now, had taken off their jackets and piled them in a heap in the back of a nearby utility truck. Malone was in the only suit he had brought with him from Sydney, but he was not alone in being less than formally dressed; there were other men in shirt-sleeves and neatly pressed moleskins and elastic-sided boots. Still, conservatism ruled: all the men, no matter what their outer dress, wore ties. At least for now.

'There's another thing, Scobie,' Narvo went on. He seemed more relaxed than at any time since Malone had met him; as if he had crossed some sort of sand-bar and, out amongst the waves, had found he didn't mind them at all. 'This is not going to be a good year for people on the land.'

'It's not looking good for a lot of people in the city, either.'

'I guess so.' But Narvo sounded unconcerned for the city folk. 'Wool prices are down, wheat's down, interest rates are still up. If the farmers don't make money, the town doesn't. Things are going to get worse before they get better and everybody knows it now. Some of these people here tonight may be broke before the end of the year. This ball may be their last chance to kick over the traces. Nobody was going to cancel it.'

Malone looked around him. He rarely, if ever, went to a ball in the city; he had certainly never been to a country ball. He had heard how wild and woolly they could be; country folk worked harder and played harder than their city cousins. It was still relatively early, but the pitch and volume were rising; yet he could see no sign of desperate reaching for pleasure, of dancing while the bushfires raged. Not yet, anyway.

'What about cotton? Is that still selling?'

'Yes. But there's only the South Cloud farm and gin and they're not going to let anyone else in here. They're owned by the Japanese.'

'Not all of it. There's a forty per cent local holding.'

Narvo paused as he was about to take another mouthful of beer. 'You've got your facts.'

'I'm learning a few. If cotton prices are going to hold up, now'd be the time to buy into South Cloud, wouldn't it? Killing Sagawa would be a start to making the Japanese feel they weren't wanted.'

Narvo said, and it sounded admiring, 'You have imagination.'

'Ten or twelve years in Homicide and you have it, it sort of comes naturally. It helps to be part-Irish,' he grinned, and sipped his own beer, not particularly liking it. Under Lisa's tutelage he had developed a taste for European and even home-grown boutique beers, but he would not dare mention that out here, where it would be looked upon as a treasonable affectation. They might even think he was gay and run him out of town. 'You don't think anyone killed Sagawa for that reason?'

'That would narrow the list of suspects, wouldn't it?'

'There's something else that might narrow the list of suspects. Sagawa's father was executed as a war criminal. Some ex-POW might have heard of that and decided on his own extended revenge. Are there any ex-POWs around here?'

'None that I know of.' Narvo showed no interest in what Sagawa's father had been. 'Ray Chakiros would be the man to ask. He knows the war record of everyone back to the Duke of Wellington.'

'Was Chakiros at Waterloo?'

'You'd think so, to hear him talk.' Then a pleasant-looking blonde woman came out of the hall and put her arm in his. 'You haven't met my wife Monica.'

'Are you two talking police business?' she said.

Malone shook hands with her, liking her friendly smile. 'No. I've been admiring the way everyone dresses up out here. The races this afternoon, the ball.'

Monica Narvo looked down at her green evening dress with flounces that camouflaged her tendency towards plumpness. She had a practical air to her and he could imagine her making the dress, baking cakes for the ball supper, running the rock-solid sort of house that a policeman wished for.

'This is last year's dress. I'm not expected to keep up appearances, not like some of them around here.' She said it seemingly without malice; but Malone wasn't sure. 'Amanda Nothling, for instance. If she wore the same frock twice to a ball or a dance, everyone would wonder if she was short of money.'

'She and Amanda are the best of friends,' said Narvo, winking at Malone. 'There she is out there, dancing with her son. What's she wearing this year, Monny?'

'It's a Chanel by Karl Lagerfeld.'

'I thought it was,' said Narvo, straight-faced.

Malone looked at him first: this wasn't a Narvo he had met before. Then he looked towards the dance floor, saw Amanda Nothling, brilliant in a shimmering silver sheath, dancing with a boy of about sixteen who already was turning into an image of his father: thick unruly hair, red-faced, running to fat. On an impulse he said, 'Does she dance with out-of-towners?'

'If you genuflect first,' said Narvo and spluttered into his beer as his wife dug him in the ribs.

As he walked away from them, Malone noticed that Monica Narvo was questioning her husband. She, too, had evidently noticed the change in him.

Malone tapped the Nothling boy on the arm as he stepped up on to the raised dance floor. 'May I cut in and dance with your mother?'

The boy, relieved, relinquished his hold on her: it was embarrassing, having to dance with your own mother. 'Sure, sure, she's all yours. Thanks, Mum.' And was gone.

'I hope you don't mind me cutting in?'

'I don't mind, Inspector, so long as this isn't going to be an interrogation.' She was charming enough now, insinuating her body into his without being provocative. 'You dance well. Somehow one expects policemen to be heavy-footed.'

'No, just heavy-handed. I haven't seen your husband this evening.'

'Is that why you asked me to dance?' She didn't act coyly annoyed. This woman was as sophisticated as any he had met, there were no grass seeds in her immaculately done hair.

He smiled: he was no nightclub smoothie, but he could try. 'You know better than that, Mrs Nothling.'

She smiled back, accepting him. 'Max will be along. He's busy at the hospital. Some emergency ops on those jockeys who were injured this afternoon. I thought you handled those stupid blacks very well. Very dramatic, firing your gun like that. No one expected it.'

'I thought there was a lot of shooting around here, that they'd be used to it.'

She leaned away from him, but only from the waist; her pelvis remained against his. But she was not being provocative. She had her father's pale-blue eyes and, like his, they could turn to marble. 'What does that mean?'

'Nothing,' he said innocently. 'Do you want us to dance apart, like everyone is?'

'I don't do what everyone else does.' She eased back into his arms. They were both good dancers and they found their own rhythm to the beat of the music. 'Are you wearing your gun tonight?'

He wondered if she was going to crack the old Mae West joke; and was glad when she didn't. 'No, not tonight . . . Nobody seems upset about the shooting of Mr Sagawa.'

He had remarked that, so far, no one at the ball appeared to have brought with them the resentment that he and Clements had experienced during their two days in town. Perhaps an unspoken moratorium had been declared, but only for tonight.

She stiffened again in his arms, but only slightly. 'He – he was an outsider. The feeling would have been different if he had been a local.'

'I've gathered that, from a few others. How did you get on with him?'

'I told you I should only dance with you if it didn't turn into an interrogation. Enough, Inspector . . .' He waited for her to slide out of his arms; but she didn't. 'Does your wife mind you dancing with strangers?'

'Not so long as they're women. Why?'

'She's just come out of the hall with Ida Waring and your detective friend. She's very attractive. You're a lucky man.'

'I know.'

'She's looking daggers at either you or me. Is she jealous?'

'I don't know. I've never given her any cause to be.'

'Oh my, ain't we goody-goody! Faithful husbands – the conservationists should be looking into them, they're a dying species. I'm as jealous as hell.' Then she seemed to regret the admission, because she smiled and said, 'I'm joking. Jealousy never gets you anywhere, does it?'

He couldn't imagine her being jealous of the half-drunk slob she was married to; but maybe Nothling hadn't always been like that. 'No, not in the end.'

'Are you speaking as a policeman or a marriage counsellor?'

'Both.'

They smiled at each other and for a moment their bodies melded together like lovers'. Then the music ended and he let her go. Only then did he say, trying his best not to sound like an interrogator, 'Your father isn't here. Isn't he chairman of the ball committee?'

'You mean besides being chairman of everything else?' There was an edge to her smile, like a knife turned to the light.

He smiled, too, but with no edge. 'Yes, I guess I do.'

'No, he's not on the committee at all. I'm chairwoman – one Hardstaff is enough for any committee . . . My father is at home, he's entertaining some Japanese who arrived today. He doesn't like these sort of shindigs – they aren't decorous enough for him. He doesn't understand young people.'

'Wasn't he ever young himself?' Like sixteen or seventeen and running Commos out of their home town with guns: very decorous.

'Oh yes. From what I've heard he was the wildest boy in the district. But we all change when we grow older, don't we?'

'Were you wild when you were young?'

She smiled, took the hand he offered her as she stepped down off the dance floor. 'I still am, occasionally.'

'But never in Collamundra?'

'No, never in Collamundra. Thank you, Mr Malone. Enjoy your stay.'

She walked away; like father, like daughter, every other inch an aristocrat; or perhaps in her the percentage was higher. Malone looked after her, watching what seemed like a royal progress through the crowd. Then he went over to join Lisa, Ida and Clements, stepping over two drunken youths wrestling each other like playful infants in the dust.

'Enjoy that?' said Lisa. 'You looked as if you were feeling for every nook in Granny.' It was an old joke between them, the sort that married couples swap as shorthand, telling each other he or she has nothing to worry about.

'I don't think she's a granny.' He grinned at Clements. 'Who is it sings "Jealous Woman"?'

'Liberace?'

'Where's Trevor?' Malone said to Ida.

'He's coming later. He and Gus Dircks are out at Chess Hardstaff's place, having a conference with those Japanese. Russ has been looking after me.'

Malone was glad that she and Clements were not standing arm-in-arm; though, he told himself, it was none of his business. He wondered why Chess Hardstaff should be playing host to the meeting of the Japanese executives and two of the local partners in South Cloud, in which he himself was supposed to have no financial interest. Unless he was standing in for Max and Amanda Nothling. Maybe he should have asked Amanda about that.

Tas Waring, still in his dinner jacket, came by with a pretty auburn-haired girl in a green dress that showed as much bosom as Malone had seen all night. Though she was steady enough on her legs, she was clinging to Tas's arm as if she would fall over if she let go. Malone was glad that Claire was back at Sundown with the other children, all of them being baby-sat by Sean Carmody. Her fourteen-year-old heart couldn't have taken such opposition in its stride.

Tas gave the elders a smile and, behind the girl's head, raised his eyebrows in despair as he took her up on to the dance floor.

'Poor Tas,' said Ida. 'That's the girl who's already got her engagement ring, though he hasn't asked her yet. I hope he's not foolish enough to get her pregnant.'

'She's giving him every encouragement,' said Lisa. 'She's not wearing any pants under that tight dress.'

Malone looked at Clements. 'They're marvellous. With eyes like that, why do we pay hundreds of thousands of bucks for macroscopes in the Department?'

The band had struck up again, an old-fashioned quickstep for the benefit of the older guests, those born around the same time as Irving Berlin. Malone took Lisa across to the dance floor and they glided through their steps, natural partners, each with an easy grace and rhythm. As they moved round the edge of the crowd he saw Wally Mungle and a pretty, coffee-coloured girl come round the corner of the hall and stand, almost shyly, like guests who had just realized they had stumbled into the wrong party. Then Amanda Nothling, a wine glass in her hand, came out of the hall, saw them and stepped across to where they were. She talked to them for a minute or two, speaking more to the girl than to Mungle. Her smile was friendly, but she was aloof, though not condescending. She gave a final smile to the girl, said something to Mungle and walked away to join a group of well-dressed matrons, her own kind: well, almost. Even with them she looked a little aloof, though still friendly.

Ida and Clements, the latter no natural dancer but trying hard on his flat feet, came up beside them. Once again Malone was glad to see that there was nothing intimate between them; they were dancing as far apart as Amanda Nothling and her young son had been. And once again he told himself it was none of his business.

'Ida, who's the pretty girl with Wally Mungle?' He now recognized that she was the girl he had seen this afternoon at the racecourse. 'You know him, don't you?'

'Of course.' He should have known that: everyone in Collamundra would know the only Abo cop. 'That's his wife Ruby.'

'How would Mrs Nothling know her? Is she chairwoman of some welfare committee for the blacks?'

Ida laughed. 'Old Chess Hardstaff would never allow that. There is a welfare committee for them – but *he's* boss of that. Not that it ever seems to do much for them. No, Ruby grew up out at Noongulli station. Her mother was the Hardstaffs' cook.'

'Where's the mother now?'

'Dead, I think. Chess has a white housekeeper now. Why?'

'Nothing.'

'He's just interested in pretty girls, any colour,' said Lisa, and she and Malone danced on. 'What was that all about? You don't have to tell Ida.'

'But I have to tell you?'

'Please yourself. But you said the other night the case was going round in circles.'

The music had slowed: the band was playing a golden oldie, 'Memories Are Made Of This'. Malone looked across the drifting dancers, some young, some middle-aged, some elderly, all of them giving themselves up to the sentiment of the song. Even the band's drummer, a stick-thin young man with a bald scalp and long hair hanging from the sides of his head as if to protect his ears, looked as if he had just discovered that nostalgia wasn't as hard to bear as he had thought. Malone wondered who he was, one of the Five Drovers or Their Dog; he looked more like the latter, a human anorexic basset-hound. Even the band's name had a touch of nostalgia to it, though of course it should have been Five Dogs and Their Drover.

'This is beginning to look like one of those old Cecil B. De Mille movies we sometimes see on Bill Collins's TV programme. With a Cast of Thousands.'

'And who are you? The Hero, that actor with the rock face? Henry Wilcock?'

'Wilcoxon,' he said with his pedantic memory for names. 'No, I'm the poor bugger running around picking up the camel dung. Akim Tamiroff.'

'That's all you've got so far? Camel dung?'

'There's a more local word for it.'

'Keep it to yourself.' She pressed herself against him, imprinting her faith in him. 'It'll all come together in the end. I don't know anyone who knows more about camel dung than you do.'

'Thanks.' He kissed her on the lips, right out there in the open.

She opened her mouth and he could feel her tongue forcing his lips apart. Then she gurgled with laughter and drew back. 'You wanna go out in the scrub, sailor?'

He laughed, holding her to him; she was a tonic, his very own Medicare. 'When we get back to Sydney, we're going to bed for a week.'

'What'll we do with the kids?'

'I'll charge 'em with something and get them remanded to reform school.'

The dance finished and they stepped down off the floor and walked into the hall to the drinks' table. Wally Mungle and his wife were standing there, each holding a soft drink, both still looking as if not sure that they should have come. Malone introduced himself and Lisa to Ruby Mungle, got himself a glass of red wine and some cheddar and, leaving Lisa with Ruby, eased Wally Mungle outside again. They stood at the corner of the hall watching the young men, at least half of them now staggering-drunk, wrestling with each other like young de-horned bulls. Some were rolling in the dust, locked together, and their girl-friends, many of them flushed with drink, were urging them on.

'We get as pissed as that,' said Mungle, 'and they lock us up. For our own good, they say.'

'Why'd you come tonight, Wally?'

'Ruby insisted. She made that dress she's wearing special for the occasion, she said she wasn't gunna waste it.'

'Did you come to last year's ball?'

'No.' He sipped his Coke. 'We didn't pick the best night to start, did we? But, like I said, Ruby insisted. She said she's a policeman's wife, not some gin from out at the settlement.'

'She said that?'

'Well, no. Not *gin*. But sometimes . . .' His voice trailed off.

When you're halfway between, most of the time you got nothing but quicksand to stand on . . . 'I understand she grew up out on Noongulli station?'

'Yeah.' Mungle gave him a sharp glance, but didn't ask how he knew. 'She was sixteen before she had to move into town and live in the settlement.'

'Who made her do that?'

'Her mother died and Chess Hardstaff brought in the house-keeper he's got now, Dorothy Pijade. She's Yugoslav, she doesn't understand blacks, she says. Why they don't work, get their own business, be successful.'

'What does she think of you?'

'Oh, I'm okay. I'm a policeman, that's successful. She even has time for Ruby now. But not back then, not when she asked Chess Hardstaff to sack her.'

'And Chess did?'

Mungle nodded. 'Ruby will never talk about it, so I don't press it. I've never been much good at understanding women.'

'Who is?'

They stood there, the Koori and the white man, self-pitying in their ignorance of women. Malone looked across the wrestling youths, through the mist of the dust rising from around them, and saw two young girls, cold sober, standing gazing at the drunken, roistering brawl, their faces frozen in a mixture of puzzlement, sadness and a bleak hopelessness, gins in the white settlement. Somewhere in the tangle of drunks were their future husbands.

He felt his own sadness, for them. Then he snapped himself out of it; they would survive and so would the drunks. This district, rich as it was but still hard on the men who worked it, had not been built by hopeless louts.

He changed the subject: 'Where's Curly tonight?'

'He's riding herd on the Japs, wherever they are.'

'They're out at Noongulli.'

'Then Curly is probably sitting out on the main road in his car, listening to one of the country-and-western sessions.'

'On his own?'

'He thought he'd better do it himself in case some of those galahs . . .' He nodded at the youths who had finished their wrestling and were now sitting in the dust, grinning like gargoyles at each other and yelling at their girls to get more beers; the white gins ran off to do what they had been told. Malone, for the first time, noticed that neither young Phil Chakiros nor any of his mates were here at the ball. 'They might get it into their heads to go out and start something.'

'That's not a detective's job.'

'Inspector –' Mungle looked at him as if he were a raw recruit. 'Out here you do whatever has to be done. All the uniformed guys are in town waiting for the Kooris to come in from the settlement to start a riot.'

'Are they going to?'

Mungle shook his head, finished his Coke. 'This afternoon scared the shit outa them. My mum told me they didn't really know what they were getting themselves into.'

'What about the two city Kooris they've got locked up?'

'Fuck 'em!' He said it quietly but with as much venom as any white racist might have. 'We'll solve our own problems. It's the only way. They think different to us.'

Then Lisa and Ruby Mungle came out of the hall as the band struck up again. As they did so, Malone saw a light-coloured Mercedes draw up beside the parked cars at the side of the hall. Narelle Potter got out, followed by a tall, good-looking man in a dinner jacket. They walked by Malone and the others without looking at them and stepped up on to the dance floor and moved into each other's arms.

'Who's the man?' Malone said.

Mungle grinned. 'Bert Truman, the district playboy.'

'He plays the field, just like Narelle?'

'Birds of a feather,' said Ida, coming up behind them with Clements.

Malone turned to Ruby Mungle, who stood shyly on the edge of the small group. She wore a simply cut cream dress that looked more expensive than, he guessed, it really was; it complemented her café-au-lait complexion. Her black hair had only the slightest wave in it and was cut short in what he, no fashion expert, always thought of as the French style, though for all he knew it could have been Spanish or Italian or even Japanese. Only her shyness spoiled her from being striking, and he wondered how she had managed to screw up the courage to insist on coming to the ball tonight, especially after this afternoon's demonstration.

'Ruby, would you care to dance?'

She looked at her husband, as if seeking his approval to dance with a senior officer. He nodded, smiling; then he looked in surprise at Lisa, who said, 'I take it you dance, Mr Mungle? I'm a great admirer of the Aboriginal Dance Company.' Then she realized how condescending that sounded. 'Sorry.'

His beautiful smile forgave her. 'The last time I danced in a corroboree, they threw me out for jitterbugging.'

'Well, I don't know that I can jitterbug, that was before my time. Let's try something more sedate. Coming up again, Ida?'

'Why not?' said Ida and took Clements's arm as if she had decided he was her partner for the night. Watch it, Russ, thought Malone; and wondered if Lisa was as over-sensitive as he was. Don't start adding to the camel dung, he advised himself.

The band was either exhausted, had discovered that an old beat was music after all, or had spied an uncle or aunt amongst the dancers who would perhaps remember them in their wills. A fantastically ancient number, 'Three Coins in the Fountain', sprayed the night air.

'Who wrote that?' Malone heard a young girl ask her father as they danced by. 'Mozart? It's almost *fab*. I could grow to like it if, you know, I lived long enough.'

Malone looked down at Ruby Mungle, seemingly as fragile in his arms as if her bones were dried sticks. 'Is this your sort of music?'

'Do you mean do I – ?'

'Do I mean do you prefer didgeridoo music? No, I don't. Ruby, get the chip off your shoulder. I've already had to tell Wally that.'

'Sorry, Inspector. Yes, I do like it. I'm a romantic.'

He didn't ask whether her Dreamtime was in the past or the future. Those sort of questions were taboo. Tonight she was a policeman's wife, she wanted to be more white than black. He remembered something an old Chinese in Sydney's Chinatown had told him: *Same bed, different dreams*. It hadn't changed since Adam and Eve had started sleeping together.

Someone bumped into his back and he looked over his shoulder. It was Ray Chakiros, dancing with a slim, dark-haired woman who looked as if she would rather have been dancing with someone else.

'Sorry,' said Chakiros, obviously not sorry at all. 'I didn't see you.'

He looked down at the woman in his arms and smirked, but she just rolled her eyes and looked away.

Malone had been bumped by Sydney's best and he wasn't going to let this dumb bumpkin get his goat. 'It must happen a lot, Mr Chakiros. You've got such a narrow view.'

The woman threw back her head and laughed. Malone could feel the laughter start in Ruby's body and he danced her quickly away. 'Don't,' he said. 'Who's the woman with him?'

'Mrs Chakiros.' She stifled her laugh, danced a few steps, then said soberly, 'You can get away with a remark like that.'

'Why?'

'You're an outsider.'

And a white. 'I have the rank, too. That makes a difference.'

'Inspector Narvo would never say that.' Then she looked as if she wished she had not said *that*.

'I think you underestimate Hugh Narvo. This afternoon he even told Chess Hardstaff to mind his own business.'

She missed a step and he almost trod on her foot. 'You mean he actually stood up to Mr Hardstaff? Good on him!'

'Would you stand up to him?'

'Why?' She looked at him slyly this time, not shyly.

'I saw you over there at the track this afternoon. You looked for a moment as if you were going to jump the fence and join the demo.'

She hesitated, then said, 'I almost did. He acted as if he owned all those people in the demo, as if they had no right to be on *his* racecourse –'

'Ruby,' he said gently, 'they went about it in the wrong way. People might have been killed, including themselves.'

'Well, maybe they did! But –' Then she realized whom she was talking to and where she was; her body, which had become taut in his arms, relaxed. 'I'm sorry, Inspector. It's just –'

'Just what? Something that's been building up for years?'

She looked at him puzzled. 'What do you mean?'

'Ruby, if I had to call you as a witness . . .'

She went stiff again; for a moment he thought she was going to break away from him. He was aware of other couples glancing at them as they danced past; there seemed no apparent disapproval on their faces, just a curious blankness. Then he realized they were not looking at him but at Ruby. It was almost as if they had never seen her before, had never realized that she was so attractive.

'What sort of witness?'

'In a murder trial, for instance.'

He had taken a chance there; she stumbled again and this time he trod on her toe and she winced. 'You'd never do that! What murder?'

They were close to two other couples; all four heads turned sharply. He stared at them; after a moment they turned away and danced on, out of rhythm with the music. He looked down at Ruby.

'I'd like to talk to you about Mrs Hardstaff's murder.'

'No!'

She stepped away from him, pulling out of his arms; but he went after her, taking her by the elbow. 'Relax, Ruby. Don't make a scene. We're the outsiders, remember – both of us.' It was cruel to say it and it stung his tongue; but it made her pause, relax her arm in his grip. She turned and looked up at him and he saw the pain in her face. 'I'm sorry, Ruby.'

He helped her down off the dance floor and she said, still looking at him with the pain in her eyes, 'Why did you come to Collamundra?'

'I was sent for.'

'It's bad enough as it is, for Wally and me.' She looked down at her cream shoes, brown now with dust. 'Why did I wear this colour?'

He looked down at his own black shoes, now a dark beige, and grinned. 'I'm glad I didn't wear my Guccis.'

'*You* don't wear Guccis?' Then she somehow managed a smile. 'You're kidding me, aren't you?' He nodded. 'Inspector, why ask me to dig up something that happened when I was eleven years old?'

'I may not need to, Ruby. Not in public, that is. Will you talk to me about that day?'

'I'll think about it.' The music had finished, the other dancers were coming off the dance floor. She shook hands with him. 'Thank you, Mr Malone. Wally says you're on our side. I hope you are.'

Then she was gone before he could tell her that he really didn't want to be on anyone's side.

An hour later, when supper was served, he had grown tired of the ball, of the whole night and day. Standing in the hall against a wall, a plate of hot sliced beef and salad in his hand, a glass of red resting on a ledge near him, he looked over the guests lining up at the long serving tables. He saw the librarian Veronica Dircks, her new ball dress looking crumpled and stained, as if she had been caught in a beer shower. Beside her was a man he guessed to be her husband, the editor of the *Chronicle*, square as a butter-box, ginger-haired like his father, all foghorn voice and loud laughter. He caught sight of Malone watching him and his pink square face suddenly closed up; he turned and said something to the man behind him in the line, his father. Then both Dircks looked across at Malone, faces as belligerent as those of hobbled bulls.

Malone picked up his glass and, both hands full, moved along the wall to where Ray Chakiros stood behind a plate that was a meat-and-vegetable barricade. He froze, with his mouth full, as Malone stopped beside him.

The detective raised his glass, drank a toast to him, then put the glass down on a nearby table. 'Everyone seems to be enjoying themselves.'

Chakiros nodded, then swallowed, almost choking himself because he had not chewed the food he had in his mouth. 'Yeah,' he managed to say. 'You enjoying yourself?'

Malone grinned and shrugged. 'It's a bit noisy and crowded for me.'

'I thought you cops'd be used to noise and crowds.'

'I gave up football duty years ago. That's one of the good things about a homicide – all the noise and fuss is over before we're called in. Mr Chakiros, maybe you can help me . . .'

Chakiros lowered his plate, as if he had suddenly lost his appetite. 'How?'

'Is there anyone amongst your members at the Legion who was a POW of the Japanese?'

A thick crease spread across Chakiros's brow. 'A POW? No.

A coupla fellers were POWs of the Germans. But no, not the Japs. What're you getting at?'

'Just a thought.' *Don't paint Sagawa blacker than this man already has.* 'Young Phil not here tonight? I thought this'd be his scene. He's not in trouble, is he?'

Chakiros had been about to resume eating, but stopped again. 'Why would he be?'

'I understand he was the trainer of the horse that was doped this afternoon, the one that dropped dead. The stewards can't be too happy about that.'

'I'm the chief steward.'

'Oh?' Malone made a good job of pretending he hadn't known. 'That must be embarrassing. Does conflict of interest worry you or is that a phrase they don't understand out here in Rural Party territory?'

'You sound just like The Dutchman.' Like Hans Vanderberg, the Opposition leader, who made regular trumpetings about the cronyism of the Rural Party, ignoring his own years of jobs for the faithful. 'You vote bloody Labour, I'll bet.'

'No, I'm a Greenie.' Which he wasn't, but which would sound even worse to the likes of Chakiros.

The older man lowered his plate, looked for a moment as if he might throw it and its contents at Malone. 'You're a shit, Malone, you know that? You're gunna regret you ever come out here, I promise you!'

Malone looked at him steadily, then he nodded. 'I already regret it, Mr Chakiros. But I promise you something. Before I leave here there will be people who'll have bigger regrets than I'll have. Watch your plate. The gravy is dribbling on your shirt.'

2

Malone looked around for Lisa; the night, and the day, had gone on long enough. Some people have an infinite capacity to enjoy themselves; or anyway an ability to convince themselves of their enjoyment. He was not one of them.

He had seen Lisa go out of the hall with Ida and he went outside into the cool, if strident night air. The band had stopped playing, were taking time out for a beer and whatever else they needed to keep them going for the rest of the night; over in the showground the carnival had closed down, but a lion roared once, scaring the fur off the kangaroos out in the scrub. A drunk answered the roar and other drunks and near-drunks took it up, splintering the night with their yahoo-ing. Over in the car park a chorus of girls suddenly screamed in delight, as if pack rape had taken on a reverse meaning. At the corner of the hall a youth, held up by his girl-friend, was being violently ill. Older people looked away, not wanting to be reminded of their own youthful over-indulgence.

Clements was standing alone, a plastic glass of white wine in his hand. 'Did we ever behave like that?' He nodded, as if he had addressed the question to himself. 'Yeah, we did. Or I did. I dunno about you.'

'Where's Lisa and Ida?'

'Over in the bush, in the queue for the loo. There's a line of about fifty women over there, all standing with their knees tight together. There's something to being a man. All you have to do is take it out behind any bush and make sure you don't splash your shoes.'

Malone became aware of someone standing behind them, listening to their conversation. He turned round.

'Hello, Inspector,' said Veronica Dircks. 'I've been eaves-dropping, wondering what policemen talk about when they're together, especially Homicide detectives. The bladders of the sexes. Very interesting.'

She looked ball-worn; the night had proved too much for her. She was not drunk, but she had had enough drink to loosen her up; or down. There was no sign of the prim librarian, even if that impression of her had been Malone's mistake. Her new dress could have been last year's or even the year's before, stained and creased like a library book that had been taken out too often. Twenty dollars' worth of shampoo and back-comb was down over her ears and forehead. She was not wearing her glasses and occasionally she squinted, as if trying to get him into focus.

Malone introduced her to Clements. 'Mrs Dircks is writing a history of the district. We might smuggle her a copy of the running sheets when the Sagawa case is over.'

'What are running sheets?' she said.

'Sort of our own little history. The Literature Board is thinking of giving Sergeant Clements a grant, they reckon he's got such promise.'

'You're pulling my leg. Not that I mind.' She had had enough drink to be coy; it didn't suit her. She looked off, squinting even more. 'There's history being made, over there. Amanda Nothling and Narelle Potter being nice to each other.'

Malone turned his head, saw the two women halfway between the hall and the row of toilets at the edge of the scrub; standing a little aside from each other, as if they had been about to pass, then decided to speak. It was difficult to tell at the distance whether there was any tension between them.

'They don't get on?' he said casually.

She shook her head; more hair fell down. 'Mrs Potter doesn't meet Mrs Nothling's high standards. But then few of us do.'

Clements had been listening to her with mild amusement. 'Does Dr Nothling meet his wife's standards?'

She looked at him with exaggerated caution. 'Who knows what a wife thinks of her husband? Or vice versa? Supposing they have vices.' She looked around, as if trying to find her husband up to some vice or other; then she shrugged, gave up and looked back at the two detectives. 'If I knew the answer to that, my history would write itself. The personal bits, anyway.'

'You're having trouble with the personal bits?' Malone guessed that any historian could have told him that. Battles left their own mark, treaties were their own documentation, but who knew what Elizabeth said to Essex when they were alone, what Churchill called Stalin, even through an interpreter?

'Oh, am I! Am I!' She giggled. 'The Hardstaffs, for instance. A closed book. Well, almost closed.'

Malone saw Amanda Nothling now coming towards them on her way into the hall, her chin held up. He wondered if continually looking down one's nose gave one a squint.

He said quietly, '*Almost* closed?'

'Oh, I've found out a few things . . . Hello, Mrs Nothling. A lovely ball. As the eunuch said to the bull.' She was drunk now; the drink, it seemed, had had a delayed reaction. Or maybe spite had spiked it: 'No Doc Nothling here tonight? Missing again?'

'Lock her up,' said Amanda Nothling with a smile to Malone that said she knew what a pain drunks were. She passed on into the hall, all arrogant dignity, queen of the night.

Veronica Dircks looked after her, swaying slightly as she turned round; she put a hand out to steady herself, but there was nothing there. Clements put up a hand and she leaned against his arm.

'Smell that perfume? Two hundred dollars an ounce. It disinfects the air the rest of us contaminate.'

'Do you know where Doc Nothling is tonight?' said Malone.

She shrugged; her dress slipped down off one shoulder, but she didn't attempt to pull it up again. 'The Doc? The original Hippocratic Oaf? That's an old joke, but it fits him. Or it does now. I'm told he was much different when he first came here to live under the thumb of Chess Hardstaff. I could tell you a thing or two about Old Chess.' She winked; it looked almost lewd. 'Things I can't put in the history, so my hubby tells me. He's one of those journalists who's scared of the law of libel.'

'What could you tell about Chess Hardstaff, if there was no law of libel?'

'About his war record, f'rinstance.'

'I thought he had a good war record?'

'Oh, he had, he had. Decorations down to his navel, like one of those American generals. But you should ask Frank Kilburn. But you can't ask him, can you? He died just before Christmas.'

Suddenly, without warning, she crumpled. Her legs folded under her long dress and she went down like a collapsing circus tent. Malone and Clements, caught unawares, were slow to pick her up. Then, as they bent to do so, they were roughly pushed aside by her husband. He lifted her, holding her in his arms as if she were a child, and glared at them, looking like a more threatening version of his father.

'Leave her alone! What were you going to do – run her in?'

The two detectives looked at each other, shook their heads, laughed and walked away. They had had enough experience of domestic situations to recognize that Dircks was more angry at his wife for being drunk than he was at them; the best way to handle such a situation was to turn one's back; when Adam had his first row with Eve, even the serpent glided away. Malone guessed that Veronica Dircks's passing out would not be mentioned in the *Chronicle*'s report on the Cup ball.

'The trouble with drunks,' said Malone, when he and Clements were out of earshot, 'is that they always pass out before they get to the punchline. I wonder what she was going to tell us about Hardstaff and Nothling?'

Then Lisa and Ida came towards them, both smiling broadly. Lisa said, 'The last time I stood in a queue that long was when I took the kids to see *Back to the Future*. You ready to take me home?'

Malone looked at Ida. 'It doesn't look as if Trevor is going to turn up.'

'It won't be the first time.' Then she glanced at Clements, but the look was so swift Malone barely saw it.

'I'd take you home,' Clements said awkwardly, 'but Scobie has the car.'

'How will you get back to town?' Ida asked him.

'I'll get a lift. Some of them are so drunk they won't recognize me.'

'Not with Narelle, I hope.' She was smiling, but there was a sharp edge to her tone for just that moment.

Clements grinned. 'She came with some guy. I presume she'll be going home with him.'

'Not necessarily. Well, goodnight, Russ.' She gave him her hand, as if deciding that it would be indiscreet to give him even a peck on the cheek. 'I enjoyed the night, thanks to you.'

'Me, too.'

They might have been old lovers who had met again for the first time in twenty years, uncertain as to whether the old intimacy was still there. Malone, watching them closely, decided that Clements had decided to call it quits before both of them got too far out of their depth, before the wrong current took hold of them.

'I'll see you in the morning, Russ,' he said.

'You're coming to Mass with me and the kids,' said Lisa. 'Eight thirty.'

Malone sighed. 'She's getting to be worse than my mother. She washes my shirts in holy water.'

Waring had brought Lisa and Ida to the ball in his own car before going back to his meeting with Gus Dircks and the Japanese at Chess Hardstaff's place. Malone took the two women home in the Commodore, Lisa riding up front with him and Ida reclining, as if exhausted, in the back seat. Lisa chatted about the ball, but Ida remained quiet, out of character from what Malone knew about her.

He said off-handedly, not glancing back at her, 'I noticed that Gus Dircks turned up at the ball. I wonder what kept Trevor? Does he get on that well with Chess Hardstaff?'

'I don't know.' Ida sounded listless; or perhaps disappointed. He wondered if she had hoped for a better response from Clements. 'He never discusses business with me. I don't have a head for it.'

Malone felt Lisa's hand on his knee, pressing it warningly. He took heed of her and said nothing for the rest of the journey home. When they drew up in front of the Waring homestead Ida was asleep and they had to wake her. She stretched, sat up, leaned forward and kissed each of them on the cheek.

'Lucky people,' she said and got out of the car and went quickly into the house.

The Malones sat silent till they heard the front door close behind her. Then Lisa said, 'You almost put your foot in it tonight.'

'How?'

'Asking where Trevor was.'

'Was he with some woman somewhere?'

'I don't know where he was. He was in a bad mood all the way in to the ball this evening – it was damned uncomfortable being with them. He and Ida had a row before we left the house, a pretty fierce one. They kept it as quiet as they could, but I happened to pass their room . . .' She stopped, put her hand on his. 'I'm glad we're not like them. Their marriage is falling apart.'

'You want to get in the back seat?'

'No, it's too uncomfortable. I'm not going to tear a hamstring – or whatever it is all those marvellously fit sportsmen are always tearing.'

'You think love-making is a sport?'

'It is in the back seat of a car, unless it's a stretch limousine. A feel is as far as we go tonight.'

'You're disgusting.'

'You want to give me a ticket?'

They kissed; then he said, 'Do you think our marriage will ever fall apart?'

She stroked the back of his neck. 'Darling . . . No, I don't. But don't ask me questions like that – not with your hand down *there*. I'm practical about most things, but not about love. If anything ever went wrong between us – and I'll kill you if ever it does –'

'That would be something wrong for a start.'

'What?'

'Killing me.'

'Be serious . . . If something went wrong, I couldn't sit down and analyse it. When you have to analyse what went wrong with love, there isn't any love left.'

'You think that's what's wrong with the Warings?'

'I suspect so. There's probably fault on both sides, but she's more romantic than he is, so she feels it more. Women are supposed to be the stronger of the sexes, but I sometimes think we feel disappointment more than men do.'

'Is Trevor chasing another woman?'

'Maybe. I don't know. I think it's mainly business they argue about. Trevor wants to be rich, *really* rich. He's just got the bug in the last couple of years, just when so many others are going broke. Don't you ever get that way.'

His doubts about Trevor Waring came back. If Waring was so keen to be rich, would he kill for it? But now was not the moment to think about that possibility.

He pressed his head back against Lisa's loving hand. It was moments like this when he wished he was retired, when he would be able to spend every hour of every day with her. Then, he told himself, *he* would be rich.

Ten minutes later he left her, promising not to be late for Mass the next morning. He drove down the long drive to the front gate, pulled up and got out as the other car, its headlights suddenly snapped off, stopped on the opposite side of the gate. Malone felt the tightening in his belly and he cursed himself for not having taken his Smith & Wesson out of the car boot where he had left it during the ball. Clements's was in there, too.

He saw the man get out of the car; then he relaxed when he recognized Trevor Waring. 'You brought Ida home?' said Waring, opening the gate. 'Thanks. I went in to the ball, but they said she'd left with you and Lisa. Sorry I'm late.'

If Waring had been out at Noongulli all night with Chess Hardstaff, why hadn't he called in at his own place to check if Ida was home before going all the way into the ball? The doubts scratched away in Malone's skull again.

But he came at them from side-on: 'The Japanese giving you trouble?'

Waring stopped, the gate half-open. 'What makes you say that?'

'Nothing. It was just a shot in the dark.'

Malone had left the lights of the Commodore on. He was standing with his back to them; but Waring was brightly exposed. He was wearing a dinner suit, his black tie neatly tied, and he looked out of place, lost, even though he was standing in the gateway of his own property. He doesn't belong here any more than I do, thought Malone; and wondered if Waring realized it. He was one with the silvertail stockbrokers and entrepreneurs, who were feeling the pinch now but for a decade had flown high, who were photographed every week at expensive charity balls, who drank only vintage champagne, French, none of your native piss, who drove Porsches and Ferraris and Rolls-Royces, who stood on the top branches of the plum tree that they had thought would fruit forever. He decided he must look into Waring's background, find out if he, like Hardstaff, had secrets locked away behind his sternum. All at once he understood, if only vaguely, why the Waring marriage was falling apart.

'No,' said Waring slowly, 'there are no problems.'

'Just minor ones?'

'Such as?' Then Waring nodded, pushed the gate wide open. 'Oh, you mean finding the murderer?'

'Did you discuss that this evening?'

'Of course.' But somehow Waring made it sound as if the discussion had been perfunctory. 'Are you any further advanced than you were at my office this morning?'

'Of course . . . There's one thing, Trev. Curly Baldock says he's found someone who saw you driving through town last Monday night, going east. Did you go out to the gin?'

'What time is this supposed to be?'

'Around seven o'clock.'

Waring fiddled with his bow-tie; it suddenly came loose and he let it hang down his shirt-front. 'Well, yes. Yes, I did. Perhaps I should have mentioned it, but you know how it is . . .'

'How?'

'It –' Waring sounded as if he were trying to choose his words carefully; but the right ones wouldn't come. 'It would only have added suspicion to me. I was there twenty minutes, maybe half an hour, no more. That was when Ken Sagawa showed me the latest letter he had received. I didn't kill him, Scobie. He was alive when I left him. He said he'd think about my advice about going to the police.'

It was simple enough to be believable. 'Did you notice if he had a business diary on his desk?'

Waring frowned, then nodded. 'Yes, he did. I made a date for Gus Dircks, who was coming up from Sydney, and I to meet him out at the gin Friday evening. He wrote it down.'

'Doc Nothling wasn't to be there at the meeting? He's a shareholder.'

'No,' said Waring, choosing his one word carefully this time.

Malone said nothing, letting his silence say it for him.

Waring waited; then he said, 'I'll back my car out of the way. Thanks again for bringing Ida home. I hope you all had a good time.'

Malone nodded, turned to walk back to the Commodore in the moment that, right in front of him, one of the headlights went dark with a shattering of glass. Instinctively he dropped flat in the dust, shouting, 'Get down!' as a second, ricocheting shot went whining away into the darkness. He crawled up beside the car, reached up through the open front door, switched off the headlights and fumbled for the keys. Then, still flat to the ground, he snaked his way to the rear of the car, flinching as another bullet thudded into the fender right above him. He unlocked the boot lid, pushed it up, rose to his knees and groped frantically in the darkness for one of the guns. A fourth bullet hit one of the tail-lights and he felt a piece of the red plastic bite into his hand. Then he had both guns, had dropped flat again and rolled over, looking for the flash of the next shot.

He called out: 'Are you all right, Trev?'

'I'm okay.' He didn't know why, but he was surprised there was no hint of fear in Waring's voice. Unless he knew who was shooting and knew, too, that he was not the target . . . 'Where is he?'

Malone didn't reply at once; he was trying to stifle the doubts that kept recurring about Waring. He was becoming paranoid about him, as he had been about Hardstaff. Then he called out, 'I'm not sure. Somewhere over to the right. Have you got a gun?'

'There's a Twenty-two in the boot. I don't know if I can get to it –'

'Leave it there.'

Then he saw the flash out in the scrub an instant before the bullet thumped into the car right above him. He brought up one of the S & Ws and fired two quick shots, then he rolled away from the car, fearful that another shot might explode the petrol tank. He lay waiting for another flash in the darkness; the seconds seemed to turn into minutes, time stretching out like a rubber band; but he knew only a minute at the most could have passed before he heard the car start up out on the highway. He stood up, but he could see nothing through the trees that bordered the road. He heard the car accelerating, the hum of it coming distinctly on the still air; then he saw its headlights in the distance, the arrow of their beam growing thinner and smaller as the car, its sound now gone, sped away.

Waring, dusting himself down without looking at himself, staring off into the darkness, came up beside him. 'Is it any use going after him?'

'Forget it. Are there any back roads that'll take him back to town?'

'There are a couple. You think that's where he'll head?'

'The only other likely place out in that direction, other than your father-in-law's, is Noongulli. I don't think Chess Hardstaff or anyone working for him would be stupid enough to head straight for home.'

'Oh, for Chrissake! Chess? Shooting at you?'

Malone tried one for size: 'He could've been shooting at you.'

Even in the dimness of the starlight he saw Waring jerk. 'Me? Why me?'

He changed tack, another shot in the dark: 'Have you seen young Phil Chakiros since this afternoon?'

'Phil? You mean about the doping of my horse? Yes. But he's not a –'

'Killer? What did you tell him when you spoke to him?'

'I sacked him, told him he was on his own if there was an inquiry. If he's found guilty, then I'll sue him for the value of the dead horse. He has nothing, but his father can pay – he pays for everything for him. It's not the money I'm after . . . Jesus, do you really think Phil was out there in the scrub shooting at me?'

'I don't know. Him – or it could've been two or three other people.'

'But they were shooting at *you*. There wasn't a bullet came near me –' He stopped. 'You're having me on. What's the point of this, Malone? You're still trying to tie me in with the Sagawa murder, aren't you?'

'Forget it, Trev,' said Malone wearily, all at once wanting to be rid of the doubts; at least for tonight. 'Why did you have anything to do with Phil Chakiros in the first place?'

'He's a good trainer, he really understands horses. That's what he wants to do eventually, go down to Sydney, take out a licence for city tracks.'

'He can say goodbye to that ambition. Righto, move your car, Trev. Will they be worried if they've heard the shots up at the house?'

'Maybe, but I don't think so. 'Roo shooters often come out here at night. Saturday nights, too, we sometimes get the local louts, they drive out along this road shooting at the road signs. I've appeared for some of them in court.'

'Don't say anything, then. Lisa worries enough about me.'

'All right.' He went back to his car, stopped by its open front door. 'You still think I had something to do with the murder.'

'Did I ever say I thought that?'

'You implied as much. But maybe that's the lawyer in me. We're always looking for implication and inference.'

Waring got into his car and drove past the Commodore and up towards his house, out of sight behind the black screen of trees. Malone stood in the darkness, listening to the receding sound of the car till there was only the silence of the bush, that heavy hush in which any noise, the snapping of a twig, the call of a bird, is only an accent of the stillness. He felt himself tightening, the flesh contracting on his bones; he backed up against the car and looked around. He was used to the dark of city streets; his ears were attuned to city sounds. But there was a menace to this stillness, the aboriginal threat that the first explorers and settlers had found so unnerving, something primeval that the country's civilization had yet to conquer. Suddenly he felt his hands, each still holding a gun, begin to tremble.

He heard a rustling on the other side of the car and he swung round, both guns coming up. Then a kangaroo came out of the scrub and loped across the drive; then another and another. A dozen or more of them came out of the scrub and disappeared again into the darkness, ghostly and silent but for the faint thump-thump as they hit the ground in their unhurried rhythm, arrogantly unafraid of the threat of *him*.

3

Though it was one o'clock in the morning, the lights were on in the Chakiros home. It was a large one-storeyed house, built perhaps twenty years ago and undistinguished in style, the sort one saw in developers' brochures, stamped out like biscuits from a tract of dough. There were three cars in the driveway, Chakiros's Mercedes and two Fairlanes. Malone felt the bonnets of all three; they were barely warm, almost cold. Then he went up the three steps to the wide front veranda and rang the bell on the front door.

Philip Chakiros, in a fancy rollneck cardigan and jeans, came to the door. 'Yeah?'

'Could I see you out here, Mr Chakiros?' Malone could hear a chatter of voices back in the house, mostly male ones amplified by drink, and he didn't want to face a platoon of Ray Chakiros's mates from the Veterans Legion. With the enemy out here on the garden path, they might think they were back on the Kokoda Trail or the Mekong Delta.

Phil Chakiros hesitated. 'What d'you want?'

'Who is it, Phil?' His father came lumbering down the hall, dinner jacket and bow-tie now discarded, a beer can in his hand. 'Ask 'em in – Oh Christ, it's you! What the hell d'you want?'

'Just a word with your son, Mr Chakiros. Don't let me interrupt your party.'

'Come back at a decent hour. Shut the door, Phil!'

Malone, foot ready, waited for the youth to make a move. But young Chakiros just shrugged and stepped out on to the veranda. 'It's okay, Dad. Go back inside.'

'No, you come inside –' Chakiros was all belligerence, stoked by the drink he had had, ready for a small war right on his own doorstep. 'Come on –'

'Dad.'

Chakiros stared at his son, as if disbelieving that he had been given an order; then, like a good soldier, if a poor father, he turned and stomped off down the hall. His son stepped out on to the veranda and led the way down the steps and path to the front gate.

'Just in case he comes back. Dad's still a Wog father in lots of ways – he thinks he rules the roost.'

'Who does? You?'

'My mother.'

'You're not a Wog?'

The boy gave him a sharp glance. 'No. D'you think I am?'

'I don't put labels like that on people.' It wasn't always true; his own father, with his prejudices, sometimes spoke through his voice. 'Phil, where have you been all evening?'

'Oh Jesus! What am I supposed to have done now?'

'That doesn't answer my question.'

Young Chakiros leaned against the brick gate-post. It was not an arrogant pose, but rather one of weariness. Gone was all the smart-arse defiance of last night. 'I've been at the Legion club all night, till I came home about an hour ago. Dad and Mum called in there and picked me up. Why, what am I supposed to have done this time?'

'Do you have anyone who'll vouch for you having been at the club all night? Don't suggest any of your mates from last night. They'd bounce the truth around like a rubber ball if I questioned them.'

'You're like everyone else, you've got the wrong idea about 'em. They're a bloody sight more honest and law-abiding than some of the shit you have down in Sydney. They don't go around beating up old ladies, for one thing . . .' Then he sighed, as if he were weary, too, of defending his mates. 'Okay, ask the bar stewards, they'll tell you where I was. And some of Dad's mates. They're inside now, them and their wives. They didn't go to the ball, not the older ones.'

'Name one.'

'There's George Gillies –'

'Could you go in and ask him to step out here a minute?'

'Dad's not gunna like it.'

'I'll put up with that. I've put up with a lot worse since I landed here in Collamundra.'

'Okay, I'll get him.' He straightened up, walked a few paces back towards the house, then stopped. 'You still haven't told me what this is all about. I think I'm entitled to know.'

'Someone tried to shoot me tonight.' He decided, on the spur of the moment, not to mention Trevor Waring. Let Waring himself broadcast that *he* might have been the intended victim.

'Jesus!' His shock was genuine; there was no doubt of that. 'You mean you think I tried to do it?'

'Phil, you were carrying a gun last night that was fully loaded. You tailed me and Sergeant Clements for something like ten Ks. You told us you'd been out shooting kangaroos, but the gun hadn't been fired. You're an intelligent kid. Wouldn't you put yourself on the list of suspects when someone has a shot at me the following night?'

The boy had turned back to face Malone. 'No. You just said I'm intelligent – I am. Too intelligent to be that fucking stupid.' He was growing angry, genuinely so; Malone was sharp enough to recognize that it added weight to the boy's argument. 'I don't like you, Mr Malone, but you're wrong about me wanting to kill you. We had the gun in the car last night because we were gunna shoot out some road signs – we do it all the time.'

'Very intelligent.'

'Okay, so it's fucking dumb. I know that. But you get bored in this town, especially if you're as intelligent as you think I am. I can't wait to get out of the fucking place, but, I dunno, I get just so far and then I come back . . .'

Malone made a guess: life here as the spoiled son of one of the town's wealthiest businessmen, dull as it might be, had its easeful comforts.

'Where were you last Monday night? You didn't go to that concert at Bathurst, did you? Were you out shooting up road signs again that night?'

'No, we were over at Bathurst, like I said.' He sounded dogged now, as if he had made enough admissions for the night.

Malone let that one alone for the time being. 'Who sent you out to tail us last night?'

Phil Chakiros hesitated. 'Nobody. We just picked you up by chance.'

'You're lying, Phil.'

The boy was silent for a long moment; then he shrugged once

more. 'Look, don't take this any further, okay? I don't think he meant any real harm. It was my father. He's – well, he doesn't like anything going on in this town that he doesn't know about, that's all.'

Maybe. 'What he knows – who does he pass it on to? He just doesn't bring it home and you all sit around the dinner table and discuss it.'

'My mother wouldn't allow it. She hates gossip.'

'She sounds a nice lady. How does she feel about the mess you've got yourself into with doping that horse this afternoon?'

'She belted me.' He said it without smiling, a twenty-three-year-old who thought it the most natural thing in the world for his mother to hit him for doing wrong. 'She's old-fashioned.'

I wonder what you'd think of me? But would he belt Tom when Tom got to be twenty-three? 'She sounds nicer by the minute. Give her my compliments. You're going to be rubbed out, you know, despite anything your father might try to do for you.'

'I know. That's why I didn't go to the ball tonight – my mother wouldn't let me. She said she was too ashamed to be seen with me in public.' He turned towards the house again. 'I'll get George Gillies.'

'Never mind, Phil. You've cleared yourself.' Malone opened the front gate, went through and closed it behind him. He was aware of the smell of mulch on the garden and even in the starlit darkness he could see that the lawns were neatly mowed and trimmed. He wondered if Mrs Chakiros, an old-fashioned mother, made her son work around the house for what indulgences his father gave him. 'Good night. Pass up the road signs, Phil – there are better things to aim at. Oh, one more thing. When your father hears everything that goes on in town, does he pass it on to Chess Hardstaff?'

'Yes. How did – ?'

'How did I know? I think I'm like your dad, Phil. I'm getting to know everything that's going on in this town.'

4

Sunday morning Malone went to Mass with Lisa and the three children. She had brought them in in the Warings' Land-Rover; though Sean Carmody had once been a Catholic, it seemed that none of the Warings was. The church for the eight-thirty Mass was only half-full; some of the congregation, especially the men, also seemed half-full from last night's binge. The priest, an understanding young man whom Malone had seen at the races yesterday afternoon helping attend to the injured jockeys, kept his homily short and his voice low out of sympathy for the soft, sore heads in the pews. Malone had half-expected him to mention the Sagawa murder, at least to offer a prayer for the dead man's soul; but all the priest asked for was a prayer for the recovery of the injured jockeys; Sagawa was beyond recovery, being dead and a Buddhist. Malone waited for him to pray for the souls of the dead horses, being a true-blue Aussie, but no mention was made of them, though some of the congregation, being bereft owners and out of pocket too, looked disappointed. Malone's thoughts, as usual, wandered a long way from the purpose of the Mass. He was sure, however, that God didn't mind. He sometimes wondered if the Lord ever grew tired of the constant demands on His own attention.

As the collection plate was coming round, Lisa whispered, 'What's the matter with your hand?'

'I thought you were going to put something in the plate.'

'Not that, stupid. We all know how you can't put your hand in your pocket.' He was notorious for his careful approach to charity; he had once suggested that Peter's Pence should be split into farthings.

Maureen, leaning forward to hear this, nodded emphatically. 'Tightest fist in the West.'

Her mother clipped her, without taking her eyes off the Band-Aid on Malone's hand. 'How'd you do it?'

'I knocked it on the car door. It's nothing.' He had no intention of telling her of the shooting last night, and he hoped Trevor Waring would keep his mouth shut.

'Did you put Dettol or something on it?'

'Russ poured a beer over it. Relax. The priest is looking at you.'

Lisa and the children went up to receive Communion. Malone, after a reproachful look from Lisa, got up and followed them. He hadn't been to Confession in at least three years, but his sins, he figured, were minor; venial ones, as the Marist brothers at school used to call them. He was probably guilty of at least one of the seven deadly sins, but at the moment he couldn't think of any. He thought of them at random, gave his own judgement. Wrath: probably; Envy: no; Gluttony: no; Avarice: definitely no; Sloth: and still be in Homicide? Lust: well, maybe, but he had always kept it in hand (or maybe he should rephrase that). And last but not least, Pride: well, no, he didn't think so. If he had felt it, it was not large enough to be sinful. He stepped out of the pew and fell in behind Lisa and the children. A state of grace was a state of mind and he couldn't remember when he had last felt exalted enough to enter Heaven at a moment's notice.

Standing in the aisle he wondered if Sagawa's murderer was somewhere in the queue, his mortal sin expiated by confession to the priest and the Host ready to be laid on his tongue, all sin forgiven, even murder. He could see no one up ahead remotely connected with the Japanese; he wanted to turn his head to look behind him, but a woman pushed him in the back and whispered for him to get a move on. The Lord mustn't be kept waiting, not while you looked for a murderer in His church.

Coming out of the church he was surprised to see Narelle Potter rising from a back pew and going out ahead of them. He had not thought of her as a churchgoer; but maybe she was the town's Mary Magdalene, making a late penance.

'Are you coming back to Sydney with us tomorrow, Daddy?' said Claire.

'I don't know, love. I still have work to do out here.'

'Are you working today?' Maureen made a face when he nodded. 'Oh darn! Why do cops have to work seven days a week?'

'I think I'll work one day a week when I grow up,' said Tom.

'Just like the rest of the country,' said Lisa, who at times could be puritanical towards her adopted land. Immigrants make the best, if not the most welcome, critics. 'Will you be coming out for lunch?'

'I'll see how things go. I'll try and make it for supper, though, I promise.'

'We've been invited to a sunset supper out at the Nothlings'.'

Malone raised his eyebrows. 'Amanda Nothling's?'

Lisa nodded. 'I gather it's an annual thing to close out the Cup weekend. Not the whole town, just the élite.'

'We're élite?'

'I guess we are. Ida said they'd got their invitation and we're included.'

'Us too?' said Maureen, who never could and never would refuse an invitation: she would have gone to the razing of Carthage and the bombing of Pearl Harbor if she had been invited. 'Us too?'

'No. Whenever were kids an élite?'

'They are in American TV sitcoms,' said Claire.

'Sitcoms? Keep your jargon out of my hearing. There's your friend Mrs Potter.'

Malone grinned at the children. 'No time for jargon, but she loves *non sequiturs*.'

'What's that?' said Tom.

'I dunno. It's something she taught me.' He looked over his shoulder at Narelle Potter, who was standing at the church gate talking to a young couple. 'I think I'll walk back to the pub with her.'

'I knew it was gunna happen,' said Maureen, ham-acting. 'Leaving his wife and kids for another woman.'

'It's just a sitcom,' said Claire. 'It's not real life.'

'I don't think I'll get married,' said Tom, 'or have kids.'

'I'm glad to hear it,' said mother. 'Not for the time being, anyway.'

Malone belted each of his grinning kids under the ear, kissed Lisa, said he would call her at lunchtime and hurried to catch up with Narelle Potter as she went out the gate. 'Mind if I walk back with you?'

Her mind had been elsewhere; she looked startled. 'What?

No, not if you want to. Is that your family? Nice-looking kids.'

'They get it from their mother.' He was modest; which is close to a state of grace. 'You're a regular at Mass?'

'Are you?' That meant she wasn't. So what had brought her here this morning?

'When my wife and kids hold a gun at my head, yes.'

'So you go for their sake?'

Partly; but he also went for his own reasons. He had little patience for the trappings or bureaucracy of religion, but he needed religion itself; at least, some of the time. He was the sort of Catholic whom priests took for granted, not worth bothering about, because he would save himself when the time came.

'I go for my husband's sake, just occasionally. He was what they call a good Catholic, so I do it to please him. He wasn't a good man, but that's a different thing.'

He knew what she meant. 'I thought you loved him?'

'What gave you that idea? Never mind, you're only guessing. Yes, I did love him. But a man doesn't have to be *good* for his wife to love him. You'd know that, being a policeman.'

He grinned. 'Narelle, have you and I declared a truce?'

'No.' She didn't return his smile. 'Not yet. But you've been busting to know all about me and I thought I'd save you the trouble.'

'What have you got against me, other than that I'm a cop?' Which he knew was enough in the eyes of so many.

She walked some distance in silence. The streets were empty, all the stores but the newsagent's closed. A travel coach went through, bleary faces staring out through windows blurred by dust; they had no look of interest in what they saw, they had been on the road all night from Sydney and they still had a long way to go to wherever they were going. Malone felt that, metaphorically, he was a passenger on the same bus. He remembered, when young, travelling on a coach like that through a small town in outback Queensland where a sign described it as 'just east of too far west'. Some destinations were like that.

At last Narelle said, 'You're trouble. All you people from

Sydney are. Police, licensing inspectors, politicians, the do-gooders for the Abos, those stirrers who organized yesterday's demo. We're better off without you.'

'Gus Dircks, too?'

'Forget him,' she said contemptuously. 'He's useless.'

I agree; but for once his tongue didn't wag. 'Why is it that everyone in this town doesn't want to know who killed Ken Sagawa?'

'Everyone? Even the local police?'

'No, not them.' He had noticed a slight change in those at the station; nobody had rushed to help him and Clements, but they seemed less hostile and obstructionist. And there was the very noticeable difference in Hugh Narvo's attitude. He let his tongue wag: 'There's always the chance of a second murder.'

'Who? The other Jap?'

'I don't think so.' He debated whether he should let his tongue go further; then took the risk: 'Someone tried to shoot me last night on my way home from the ball.'

She had been about to step off the kerb to cross the main street to the Mail Coach; but she stopped dead, as if the traffic light had turned red and the roadway was full of menacing traffic. '*You?* Someone tried to *kill* you?'

He nodded. 'Just imagine what that would bring from Sydney. Collamundra would be overrun. I'm not that important myself, but the Police Department hates its officers being killed.'

She started off across the road and he had to grab her arm and haul her back; a car went past, horn blaring and a youth in the passenger's seat leaning back and yelling abuse. She shivered, her arm trembling in his grasp.

'Don't commit suicide, Narelle. I don't think it was you who tried to kill me.' It was cruel, but he had never been taught that the law had been designed to be kind and merciful. He sometimes tried to make it so, but more often than not it was a losing battle.

'Me? Kill you?' They were still standing in the gutter; she had the stunned look of a drunk who had woken to find herself there. 'You're out of your mind! God, why would I want to kill you? Shoot you? I'm scared out of my wits by guns – I always hated them . . .' Her face was stricken, all her looks drained out of the pale, strained flesh; she reminded him of some women athletes who aged twenty years in a twenty minutes' run. 'I was carrying the gun that killed my husband.'

'Yes, I know.'

Her look was jagged-edged. 'Is that why Russ all of a sudden cold-shouldered me? Or was it something else he'd heard?'

'Russ and I have never discussed you.' It was easier, and kinder, to lie. 'Narelle, where were you last Monday night?'

Her voice was sharp. 'Running the bar. I've already told Curly Baldock that.'

'Only after I sent him back to ask you, so don't blame him for leaning on you. But someone else has come up with the suggestion that you weren't in the bar all night.'

'Who?' They hadn't moved out of the gutter; the traffic light had turned green, then almost instantly red.

It had been Wally Mungle. 'Someone. Where were you, say between ten and eleven o'clock?'

The light turned green. They crossed the street and he took her arm to help her over the deep gutter to the kerb. She looked down at his hand, as if his gesture was satirical. He drew his hand away, almost angrily. The world had dropped down a deep dark hole from the one he wished he lived in, that he remembered dimly from other days. Everyone was suspicious of everything, even an expression of politeness.

'I went up to my flat and laid down. I had a headache.'

He looked at her quizzically. 'Narelle, that one's worn out. It's a woman's easiest excuse. It was the first thing Eve said to Adam when they got out of Eden.'

She didn't smile. 'I told you, I had a headache.'

'Brought on by what?'

'Men in general.' He could imagine that, with the bar full of them every night. 'The noise gets to me sometimes.'

'Just the noise? Not some man in particular?'

Another shot in the dark; he was becoming the world's best blind marksman. 'No.' But the answer was in her eyes, not in her voice.

'Come on, Narelle. Isn't it better I ask you than go around town asking other people?'

They had paused again on the corner, the Mail Coach stretching away from them at an angle on both sides. There were old-fashioned beer posters, behind glass, on the walls of the hotel, relics that she had somehow preserved: Walter Jardine paintings of footballers in baggy shorts, tennis players in long cream flannels, posters that his own father would have known in his youth. Narelle Potter had done a wonderful job of preserving the past in her hotel, but somehow she had let her life fall apart.

She said quietly but flatly, 'He's a married man. I'm not telling you his name.'

'So you did leave the pub for that hour or so?'

'Yes. I went with him to tell him I was breaking it off.'

'Are you in love with him?'

'Love?' She laughed. 'No. It was just – I don't know. Foolishness. Loneliness. I haven't thought what to call it.' She looked straight at him. 'But I can tell you one thing. He is not the sort of man who'd murder anyone. Either Ken Sagawa or you.'

'He's not the man you were with last night?'

'Bert Truman?' She laughed again, this time less harshly. 'Nobody in town would believe this, but Bert and I are just friends – we never do anything more than just hold hands. He was suddenly without a date last night, the girl he was taking to the ball didn't show up from Sydney, and he rang me and asked me on the spur of the moment. No, Bert wasn't the man.'

'Righto.' He could see that she was not going to give him the name of the married man; he would have to ask Curly Baldock to track him down. 'But getting back to who might've had a shot at me. Friday night you made it pretty plain you have no time for Japs or Abos. When I told you I wanted a room for Constable Mungle and Mr Koga, you acted as if I'd asked for a room for a couple of AIDS patients. Did any of those galahs down the bar, the ones who yelled to call out if you wanted help, did any of them offer to scare me out of town?'

'Inspector –' She had recovered some of her poise, though there was none of the hip-displacement swagger. 'I don't ask anyone in this town to do anything for me, not even the men who take me out. I've run my hotel on my own ever since my husband died and it's the best run one in town – your friends down at the police station will tell you that. Even the women who gossip about me will tell you, too. If I wanted to get back at you, I'd do it my own way. And it wouldn't be with a gun!'

They had moved along to the closed side-door of the Mail Coach. He had wondered for a moment while she had been speaking, why she didn't leave Collamundra. Now he realized this hotel was her castle and, despite her reputation, she was more secure here, *known*, than she would be anywhere else, where she would have to start all over again as a nobody. Men are sometimes given a second chance, sometimes several; women, never. Eve has a lot to answer for; or perhaps it is because the Bible was written by men. Malone wondered, however, how Narelle would feel in twenty, twenty-five years from now, when the castle had turned into a prison and men no longer found her attractive. By then she might be too old for the empty ecstasy of one-night stands, she might have a perpetual headache from loneliness.

'Fair enough,' he said. 'But you can't blame me for asking. It may surprise you, but I don't get shot at every day.'

She softened, smiled for the first time. 'Have you had breakfast?'

'I had it with Russ earlier. He's down at the station waiting for me.' He grinned. 'Were you going to ask me to have it with you? People would talk.'

'This may surprise *you*, but you're the first man I've ever asked to have breakfast with me, at least out in the open. I mean, since Bruce died. I'm indiscreet, I know that, but I never advertise.'

He broadened his smile, touched her arm; then just before he turned away he said, 'Narelle, have you made any guesses who might've killed Ken Sagawa?'

'Yes. But you'd never get me to swear to it.'

She opened the door to the private entrance, went in and closed it in his face.

He walked on and round to the police station. As he ascended the stairs to the detectives' room he could hear the shouts and complaints from the lock-up cells; there had evidently been a full catch of last night's drunks. A constable in shirt-sleeves, carrying two buckets of water, went through, shaking his head angrily as he saw Malone.

'Bastards, spewing all over the place!'

Malone gave him a sympathetic smile, went on up the stairs. That was one thing about homicide: blood, somehow, was less revolting than vomit.

Clements was alone at the desk he had been given, the running sheets laid out like a racing form guide in front of him.

'Picking winners is easier than picking killers.'

He had consumed his fair share of beer and wine last night, but he looked none the worse for it; this morning he had eaten a breakfast that might have made one believe he hadn't eaten since the same time yesterday. He had an indestructible stomach, a colon that worked like a never-failing flush valve and arteries that were flooding tunnels. The inner man of Clements suffered less than the outer, though hardiness had nothing to do with his soul. Clements never mentioned religion, unless prompted, and Malone stayed away from the subject.

'I've dug the bullets out of the car. Sundays the plane for Sydney leaves at nine, so they're on their way – I got one of the patrol boys to drop them off at the airport. Ballistics will have someone pick 'em up at Mascot and we'll have a phone report by midday. I've just been going through these again.' He held up the sheets. 'People questioned.'

'Let's hear them.' Malone took off his jacket and sat down.

'Okay, the whereabouts of Sagawa's contacts at the time of the murder, say from eight p.m. till midnight. Koga was at the movies here in town. The show came out at eleven, but I think we can eliminate him anyway. I wouldn't put him on my list.'

'Why not?'

'What would he have to gain? In a year or two's time, maybe he could want Sagawa's job. But right now, it's too soon, he's still not sure whether the natives are friendly or cannibals. There's no way he's gunna get the manager's job, not yet – and that'd be the only reason he could have for murdering Sagawa.'

'They could have had a blue and he killed him in anger.'

'Do you think Koga's got that sort of temper?' Clements

looked at him, knowing the answer. 'Forget it, Scobie . . . Barry Liss and the others out at the gin – I don't think so. All of them can account for where they were at the supposed time of the murder and their accounts have been corroborated. Again, what would be the motive? Aussies have never loved the bosses, but they don't go around murdering them. The union contingency funds don't cover that . . . Ray Chakiros and his jerk of a son? Maybe. I don't think the old man would pull a trigger, but the son might have. We'll put a tick against them.'

'I leaned on the kid last night over whether he and his mates were at that concert at Bathurst. I think they were lying.'

'I'm sure of it. I got Curly Baldock to check. They were still in one of the pubs, the Western Star, at eight o'clock – one of the uniformed guys saw them. If they'd left here to drive to Bathurst right after eight, they'd have got to the concert in time to hear James Blundell sing "Goodnight, Sweetheart".'

'Does he sing *that*?'

'Well, whatever.' Clements's own tastes ran to Broadway musicals; he was mired in the forties and fifties, caught between 'Oh What a Beautiful Morning' and 'Some Enchanted Evening'. 'Do you reckon young Phil and his mates went out to scare Sagawa and somehow killed him instead?'

'I dunno, Russ. They could've. Or maybe they were up to something else they didn't want us to know about. I'm inclined to believe the kid when he said he didn't kill Sagawa. You know, you get a *feeling*?'

Clements nodded. Twenty-three years' experience in the field gave you a feeling for reading the wind; without it, you might just as well sit at a desk reading papers. 'Okay, we'll put him on hold . . . Chess Hardstaff. We checked him ourselves, Curly and the others didn't go near him, and he has a coupla hours where he could of committed the murder . . . Waring, the same . . . Billy Koowarra's been eliminated –' Then he realized what he had said. 'Sorry, I didn't mean it like that . . . Your mate Fred Strayhorn.'

'He's not my mate. But you can scratch him off the list. He'd have no motive for killing Sagawa. He might've come back to Collamundra to kill Chess Hardstaff, but that's another matter.'

'Sure,' said Clements drily. 'Don't let's confuse things. So who else have we got, except those whose names aren't on the sheets, about nine and a half thousand other Collamundrans? There are the people who've got an interest in South Cloud. Doc Nothling and his missus, Amanda – but what motive would they have? Gus Dircks and his missus – no, we can forget Gus. He and his missus were still down in Sydney last Monday night – Mrs Dircks is still there, she didn't come home for the ball.'

'Why? The local MP's wife not coming home for the biggest event of the year?'

'I gather she can't stand a bar of Amanda Nothling. Any committee chaired by Mrs Nothling doesn't have Mrs Dircks on it.'

'Who told you that?'

'Ida.'

'She tell you anything else?' *About her husband, for instance?*

'No.' Clements looked back at his sheets, as if a clue had just peeped out from between the lines.

Malone let Ida slide out of the conversation, back to her unhappiness. 'What have we got on Narelle?' He told Clements of his walk back from church with Narelle Potter. 'She said Curly had questioned her, but I can't remember her getting a mention in the sheets.'

'She's not here. This guy she said she was with Monday night –' He paused, not wanting to say it; but he had to: 'I wonder if it's Curly?'

'We'll have to ask him, won't we?' It was a task neither of them wanted. They did not suspect Baldock of being implicated in the murder of Sagawa, they just did not want to question him about his personal affairs. If he was unhappily married and had been sleeping with Narelle Potter, then it was not police business. Except, Malone told himself, they were checking on Narelle, not on Baldock. Though Curly would hardly see it that way. 'Righto, what does that give us? Chess Hardstaff, Trevor Waring, young Phil Chakiros . . . I asked Narelle about her escort last night, the flash playboy Bert Truman. *He* drives a Merc.'

'Curly checked on him after you mentioned who owned Mercs.

Truman's in the clear. He was down in Sydney buying a plane – he takes delivery of it next week.'

'Well, someone's making money, then . . . Righto, we've got three possible suspects who could've killed Sagawa – though Waring and Phil Chakiros are in the clear as far as last night's crack at me is concerned. So that leaves only Hardstaff who might've killed Sagawa and then taken a shot at me.'

'Scobie –' Clements chewed his lip. 'I think you've got an obsession about Chess Hardstaff. Maybe he killed his wife – what? – seventeen, eighteen years ago.'

'I *know* he did. I've got the feeling.'

'Okay. But that's not our case. What would be his motive for killing the Jap?'

'He could've been trying to tell the Japs they weren't wanted.'

'Why?'

'So's he could take over South Cloud. Maybe he's changed his mind about not wanting to be in it, now he wants it all for himself. From what I hear, cotton's not like wool or wheat, its price doesn't go up and down like a yo-yo.'

'Does he have that sort of money to buy 'em out? Scobie, you're inventing motives. Sure, I know you wouldn't be the first cop who's done it. But you and I have never done it before and if you wanna start now, count me out.'

It wasn't the first time each had rebuked the other; but this morning Clements's tone had a bluntness to it. Malone, put in his place, backed down. 'You're right. But if Ballistics rings at midday and says the bullets you sent down this morning match the one taken out of Sagawa's body, what sort of headache does that give you?'

'That any one of nine-thousand-odd people in this town could hate both the Japs and Sydney cops. Or –' Then he shook his head. 'No.'

'No what?'

'I was gunna say Sagawa's killing could of been an accident. You told me at breakfast that young Phil said he and the other yahoos go out shooting up road signs at night. But if someone – not necessarily him and his mates – did shoot Sagawa by accident – the shot could of come from the main road, the bullet had lost most of its velocity by the time it entered his body – if his killing *was* an accident, then who took the shot at you last night?'

A light flickered at the back of Malone's mind. 'I think we ought to go back and see Doc Nothling.'

'Why him? Dr Bedi is the one who did the autopsy.'

'You said Nothling had been born in Rangoon. What if something happened there during the war that made *him* a Jap-hater?'

'He was just a kid then, he was born in –' Clements flipped through the pages of his notebook. 'In nineteen forty.'

'What if he'd lost a parent? Or both of them? Let's call him up. Do you have his home phone number?'

Amanda Nothling answered the phone out at the Nothling property. 'Oh, it's you, Inspector. I believe you're coming to our little party this evening. I'm looking forward to meeting your wife. You *are* coming, aren't you?'

'Yes, we're coming. Right now, though, I'd like to talk to your husband.'

'Police business?' Her voice hadn't changed, she could have been asking what he was going to wear to her party; but almost as if he were on the end of a video-phone, Malone could see her hand tighten on the receiver at her end.

'Not really. He's the GMO. We just want to check a few things. Where can I get in touch with him?'

She hesitated, as if debating whether she should tell him. Then: 'He's at the cotton gin with the Japanese. Do you still have your sergeant with you?' She said *sergeant* as if she had trouble recognizing such a lowly rank. He wondered how she had managed to stoop to talking to an inspector. 'Would you care to bring him with you this evening? Will he know what to wear? Just casual, but not thongs and shorts.'

'I'm sure Sergeant Clements knows. He'll like that.'

He hung up and Clements said, 'What will I like?'

Malone told him. 'Practise your manners and wear shoes. You'll be meeting the squattocracy.' He looked at his watch. 'Righto, let's go out to the gin. Nothling's out there. We'll be back in time in case anything comes in from Ballistics.'

They had reached the door of the empty room when Baldock, in thongs, shorts and a sweater, came in. 'It's my day off, like I told you yesterday, but I've got some papers I wanna take home –' Then he became aware of the awkward silence of the two Sydney men. 'Something wrong?'

Clements, glad for once that he was the junior man, left it to Malone.

'Curly –' He always hated these sort of personal questions. 'Curly, is there anything between you and Narelle Potter?'

Even Baldock's bald head seemed to frown. 'With Narelle? Christ, where did you get that?'

Malone explained, something he knew he would not have done if he had been questioning someone not in the force. 'I had to ask, Curly. You know her, you obviously like her more than a lot of people in this town do –'

'That doesn't bloody well put me in bed with her! Jesus, you're becoming paranoid!'

That was twice he had been accused of that. 'Righto, I apologize. But can you nominate someone who might be having an affair with her, a *married* man –'

Baldock brushed by them and went on into the room. 'I'll think about it!'

Malone looked at Clements, shrugged, and the two of them went down the stairs. 'Well, we buggered that one.'

'I think by the time this is finished,' said Clements, 'we won't have a friend in town.'

They drove out through another brilliant day, the sky absolutely cloudless, the horizon of low hills to the east as sharp as an etched line. Malone felt a certain comfort heading east: that way lay the known. Or at least partly known.

As they got closer to the cotton farm they saw the faint haze of dust; though it was Sunday, the harvesters were at work again. The Japanese bosses had to be impressed that they hadn't invested their money in a nation of bludgers. Of course they were paying double time for their confidence in the workers, but what the hell? Ray Chakiros would probably look on it as part of the war reparations, though Malone doubted that he would ever pay double time to *his* workers.

When Clements pulled the car up alongside the three vehicles, one of them a beige Mercedes, outside the farm office, they could hear the dull roar inside the giant thunder-box that was the gin. They saw Barry Liss come out of the huge shed, slip off his ear-muffs, recognize them and wave. Almost immediately he was followed by Koga, the three Japanese executives and Nothling. Liss moved into the annexe where Sagawa's body had been discovered, and the other five men came across towards the office. Nothling looked outsized beside the thinner and shorter Japanese.

'Morning, chaps!' The bonhomie washed over the two detectives like a wave. 'Even the coppers working on a Sunday? What's the country coming to?'

The four Japanese looked at each other, then at him. They looked like men who fervently hoped they would not fall ill, not if they had to have Nothling attend to them. He was their partner in the cotton venture and they looked as if they regretted that, too.

'May we see you a moment, Doc?' said Malone and made his excuses to the Japanese.

Nothling, the bonhomie suddenly falling away like a surgery gown he had discarded because the operation was off, hesitated, then nodded. Malone and Clements led him across to the Mercedes.

'Your car?'

Nothling was stone-cold sober this morning; there was no sign of hangover, he had not been at the ball last night. 'I told you, I drive an LTD. This is my wife's.'

'Oh yes, I forgot.' He hadn't. It had been a ploy to drain a little more of the confidence out of Nothling. 'How are the jockeys making out at the hospital?'

'They'll all recover. No thanks to the Abos. I understand you're not going to charge them?'

'None of the locals, no. That's Inspector Narvo's turf, not ours.'

'The territorial imperative, eh? We have the same thing in the medical profession. Very convenient at times. It's a pity it didn't prevail in the Sagawa case.'

Malone ignored that, decided to bowl at the wicket. 'Doctor, we understand you were born in Rangoon in Burma.'

Nothling's face went stiff; even the double chins seemed to firm. He had soft brown eyes that, in a thinner face, might have appeared large; now they narrowed. The more Malone saw of him, the more he wondered what Amanda Nothling saw in him. But he had long ago given up trying to look at a man through a woman's eyes. It was the worst sort of astigmatism.

'Yes. How did you get that information?'

'Is it something you didn't want known?'

'No-o. I just don't understand why it should interest you.'

'Did you spend the war in Rangoon?'

'No. My mother brought me out – I was only eighteen months old. We were on the last ship to leave. My mother took me home to England.'

'And your father?'

'He was manager of a rice mill up-country . . . Ah, now I'm beginning to understand.' Nothling looked across at the four Japanese who stood talking in a group outside the office door. '*They* don't know any of this.'

'Any of what?'

'Come on, old chap! Don't let us beat about the bush. My father was imprisoned in Mergui camp, he died there from ill-treatment by the camp commandant, Major Nibote. Who was tried and executed as a war criminal and who, into the bargain, was Mr Sagawa's father. But you know all that, am I not right, old chap?'

Malone glanced at Clements, then back at Nothling. 'No, we didn't know all of it, Doc. All we knew was that you were born in Rangoon and that Sagawa's father was a war criminal.'

'But you'd made an educated guess there might be more?'

'That's one of the things that keeps us going, educated guesses. That and luck.'

'A further educated guess is that I might have killed Ken Sagawa out of revenge for what his father had done to mine?'

'It's a possibility.'

'It's a flight of fancy.'

'They keep us going, too.'

'You're wrong, old chap. I'm not the vengeful sort. I don't fight other generations' wars.'

'Where were you last Monday night, Doc, between eight o'clock and midnight?'

Malone waited for Nothling to smile with wry amusement, which had been his tone up till now; but he didn't. 'Do I incriminate myself if I say I'd rather not answer any more questions till I've talked to my lawyer?'

'Not necessarily. Who is your lawyer – Trevor Waring?'

Nothling did smile then. 'Another educated guess? Or did he tell you he was my lawyer?'

'No. It's just that I wonder what all the other legal eagles in town do for clients. Trevor seems to have all the business that counts.'

'Yes, Trevor acts for me. He's the Hardstaff family lawyer. To answer your first question – I was at home last Monday night. All night.'

Drinking yourself into a stupor? But Malone couldn't ask that without incriminating Anju Bedi. 'Your wife or someone will corroborate that?'

'Oh, indubitably, old man. Wives always support their husbands, don't they?'

Malone noted a sudden change in the climate: as if Nothling had suddenly become recklessly relaxed. As if he didn't care what questions might be asked of him.

Clements had one: 'Did you blackball Mr Sagawa when he applied for membership of the Veterans Legion?'

'I don't belong to the Legion.' The momentary recklessness had gone as abruptly as it had come. 'I think I've had enough of this, chaps. I didn't kill Sagawa.'

Malone nodded, turned away; but Clements said, 'How well do you know Narelle Potter, Doc?'

Nothling, too, had been about to turn away. 'Only as a private patient. Don't tell me she's a suspect, too?'

'No. It's about something else.'

'I only know her as a patient, so anything I know about her is confidential. Now are we finished? This is getting tiresome.'

He sounds like his father-in-law, thought Malone. 'Thanks for your time, Doc. We'll see you this evening. Socially.'

Nothling raised his eyebrows. 'You're coming to our party?'

'Your wife asked us. Didn't she tell you?'

'I leave all that sort of thing to her. She's a continual surprise.'

He strode off towards the four Japanese still standing outside the office door. Malone said, 'Do you think he suddenly looked worried?'

'Something upset him. All of a sudden he looked as if he wanted a double whisky. Where do we go now?'

'Back to the station – wait a minute. Here comes Barry Liss.'

Liss, ear-muffs hanging round his lean neck like growths, came towards them. 'You wanna come with me?' he said and kept walking right past Malone and Clements; after a glance at each other, they followed him. Malone, looking back over his shoulder, saw Nothling and the four Japanese stop talking and stare after them.

When the two detectives caught up with Liss, Malone said, 'Your bosses don't look happy, Barry. You want to leave it and talk to us when you knock off work?'

'No worries, mate. They're never gunna fire me, not right now in the middle of the harvest. I'm the only one around here who's a mechanic, Mr Fix-it. It's not me who wants to talk to you, it's one of the guys on the harvesters. His name's Alf Pynchon.'

'Before we go over to see your mate, Barry . . . Were you at the Legion club last night?'

'Yeah.' Liss was puzzled by the question. 'Why?'

'How long? Say from eleven o'clock till one?'

'Yeah, the missus and me left when they closed down. That was one o'clock, it always is Sat'day night.'

'Was young Phil Chakiros there right up till closing time?'

'Phil Chakiros?' The lean face gullied with concentration. 'Yeah, yeah he was. Him and some of his galah mates. They're not my cuppa tea. I don't even pass the time of day with 'em. Why, what's he been up to?'

'Nothing,' said Malone. 'I guess it was a case of mistaken identity.'

'He's a pain in the arse. But then, so's his old man.'

They crossed the entrance road and entered the fields, walking between the rows, the unharvested white bushes stretching away on either side of them; it was like being in the middle of a frothing surf that had suddenly gone flat as the wind turned. They came to a harvester clacking its way through the bushes, its barbed spindles plucking the seed cotton from the open bolls. Liss waved to the operator in the high glass cabin and at once the man switched off his machine and swung down to the ground.

Liss introduced the two detectives, then said, 'I better get back to the gin. Don't make it too long, Inspector, just in case the Nips start cracking the whip. They already got the idea if you stop for a breather, you're laying down on the job. We got a long way to go to educate 'em. Hooroo and good luck. We all wanna see you nail the bastard who killed Kenny Sagawa.'

He left them on that and Malone and Clements turned to Alf Pynchon. He was as lean as Liss, but taller, with a long thin face, a long nose and skin scarred by sun cancers. He had the air of a patient man, one who had lived on the land all his life and knew Nature couldn't be hurried. Malone wondered if he was one of the small farmers on whom the banks had foreclosed, who was now reduced to working for someone else; worst of all, for foreigners. But he had nodded when Barry Liss had said that all the workers for South Cloud wanted the police to catch the killer of Kenji Sagawa.

'Last Monday night I was coming home from a pub in town – I live out there along the Bowyang road –' He nodded back over his shoulder to the east. 'I passed by here about nine o'clock, maybe a little later, I dunno. I seen a car parked just off the road out there, about a hundred yards along from the main gate. It was parked just inside the fence, up there where you can see those two she-oaks – there's another gate there and a track we sometimes use in the spring when we're planting. We've used it a coupla times this week to bring in the semi-trailers.'

'Was there anyone in the car?'

'I couldn't see, but, tell you the truth, I wasn't looking for anyone. It didn't sorta register, you know what I mean? I went past it and I only remembered it a coupla days later. It could of been just a couple having it off in the back seat.'

'What sort of car was it?'

Pynchon shrugged. 'Your guess is as good as mine. All I remember was it was light-coloured.'

'Beige? Could it have been a beige or fawn Mercedes? Like that one over there in front of the office?'

Pynchon squinted towards the office and the Nothling Mercedes parked beside the other vehicles. He was the laconic sort whose only expressive gesture was a shrug; he would answer kings, presidents and prime ministers with it; he used it again. 'I dunno. Honest.'

'Did the police interview you?'

'Yeah, Wally Mungle did. But, tell you the truth, I didn't think to tell him about the car. You know how it is.'

Malone knew, all right. The average person's memory was a waste-basket; one had to know what one was looking for amongst the trash. Wally Mungle, an inexperienced investigator, would not, as early as Tuesday morning, have been looking for a car parked somewhere amongst the cotton rows.

'Did Wally ask you where you were Monday night?'

'Nah. Why would he? Him and me have known each other for years.' It obviously had not occurred to any of the police that Pynchon could be a suspect. It was another form of cronyism, though that interpretation would not occur to them, either.

'Righto, Mr Pynchon, thanks. We'll go over there to those – silky-oaks?'

'She-oaks. Silky-oaks are the ones that line the main road as you go into town – they're not native to around here. They were planted by old Sir Chester Hardstaff. Hope I been some help.'

Malone and Clements walked away, cutting through the cotton rows towards the fence bordering the main highway. 'Silky-oaks?' said Clements.

'I was showing off. I read about silky-oaks once. But is there *anything* the Hardstaffs haven't had a hand in around here?'

They found the track and followed it down to the gate in the fence. It was a wire-netting, steel-framed gate, its chain hanging loose, and they swung it back and began to walk up and down, one on either side of the track, from the road to a distance of twenty or thirty yards into the cotton. Out on the highway traffic whirred and thundered past: cars, trucks and, once, three semi-trailers nose-to-tail, as threatening as a runaway train as they roared by, the tarpaulin of the rear trailer flapping wildly in the wind with a sound like gunfire.

'Here,' said Clements and opened up the grass to show a cartridge case. He ran his hands through the coarse dry grass beside the track but there were no other cases. 'Looks like a Twenty-two.'

'The only one?'

'I can't see any more. One shot – he must've been pretty good. Used a night 'scope, probably, like the 'roo shooters do.'

Malone carefully picked up the shell, tore a strip from his notebook and wrapped it loosely round the cartridge case and dropped it in his pocket. He wasn't hopeful it would lead him anywhere, but you always had to hope.

'We've got Buckley's chance of picking up any tire marks here. Those semis they brought in would've wiped them out.' He gestured at the wide, deep tread-marks, like some sort of tribal art in the dust. Then he squinted back towards the office and the parked vehicles outside it. 'Say Sagawa was outside the office when he was shot. How far would you say that was?'

'A hundred and fifty yards, maybe a bit more. If the lights were on in the office, he'd have been silhouetted against them. It's still a pretty good shot.'

'Why shoot him in the back?'

'Why not? Killers aren't fussy. This wasn't a duel.'

'I know that,' said Malone, testy for a moment. 'I'm just wondering about what you said – could it have been an accident?'

'And last night's shot at you was another accident?'

'That could've been someone else.'

Clements shook his head with slow impatience. 'Scobie, you're stewing your brain. If this keeps up you'll have enough theories to get you a job as a criminologist. Come on, let's go back to the station.'

They closed the gate and walked back through the cotton rows to the office. Pynchon was taking his harvester down the rows about fifty yards away; he waved to them from his cabin and they waved back. When they got to the office the Mercedes was gone and the Japanese were nowhere in sight. Then Koga came out of the office, blinking through his glasses.

'Dr Nothling's gone?'

'He said he had to go into town. To the hospital, I suppose. May I ask why you wanted to see Mr Pynchon?'

'Did Mr Tajiri ask you to ask that question?'

Koga shuffled his feet as if his shoes hurt, then lowered his voice. 'Yes, Inspector.'

'Tell Mr Tajiri we refused to answer, that it was police business. If he wants us to solve Mr Sagawa's murder, we'll do it our own way. Will you tell him that?'

Koga shuffled his feet again, then a smile flickered for a moment on his lips. 'No, Inspector. But I'll think of something.'

Malone grinned. 'Just tell him it was police business. Forget the rest. Are they going to be here at the gin for the rest of the day?'

'No, Mr Dircks has invited them out to the golf club to play golf. They are all very keen golfers.'

Bully for them. Malone wondered if they got double time while they were belting a little white ball round a golf course on Sundays. He also wondered if they would be looking over their shoulders in the middle of their swings for the bullet coming from the rough or some bunker.

5

He and Clements got into the Commodore and drove back to town. As they passed between the avenue of trees on the edge of town Clements said, 'Silky-oaks.'

'Up yours,' said Malone, but they grinned at each other, glad of the bond that bound them.

When they walked into the station the duty officer, a young policewoman, said, 'Inspector Narvo asked if you'd mind seeing him in his office. Would you like some coffee, Russ?'

She looked at Clements and Malone wondered if he would be included in the invitation. As they walked down the short hall to Narvo's office he said, 'When did you get so matey with the help?'

'This morning while you were at church. She's been off duty for the past three days, that's why we haven't met her. She thinks I'm Maigret, she wants to be a detective.'

'Well, don't start practising your French on her.'

They knocked on Narvo's door, went in to find him sitting behind his desk, not in uniform but in slacks, a button-down shirt with no tie and a pale blue pullover. The starch was fast draining out of him; Malone resisted the temptation to look under the desk to see if he was wearing thongs.

Narvo leaned back in his chair, linked his hands behind his head: Malone waited for him to prop his feet up on the desk, but that would be going too far. 'Wally Mungle has been in. He'd like you to go out to the blacks' settlement. His wife is there.'

'Ruby? I'd got the idea she'd turned her back on all that.'

'That's what I thought. Anyhow, she and Wally are out there now and she wants to talk to you.'

'Wally is one of your men, Hugh. Ruby should be talking to you or Curly.'

'I asked Wally if he'd mind if I came along with you and he said, no, he didn't think Ruby would mind. She just won't come in here. Do you mind if I come?'

'Hugh, this is your turf. Let's go out there now. Russ, stay here, wait for that call from Ballistics. Practise your French.' He grinned as the duty officer came to the door with two cups of coffee. 'Thanks, Constable, but I have to go out. Sergeant Maigret may ask you to join him.'

Her pretty face creased with puzzlement and as Malone and Narvo went out to the Commodore the latter said, 'What's that all about? Is Russ trying to put the hard word on one of my girls?'

'She wants to be a detective. She thinks Russ's middle name is Maigret.'

Narvo sighed as he got into the car. 'They all want to be in plain-clothes.'

'You never did?' Malone took the car out of the yard.

'No. It was always my ambition to be boss of this station and I knew I'd never be that if I went into plain-clothes.'

'You're in them this morning.'

'I'm off duty. I just came in to check if anything out of the ordinary had come in overnight.'

'Something out of the ordinary did happen last night. I got shot at.'

'I was reading that at the bottom of my copy of the running sheets when you came in. What do you make of it?' Narvo showed neither surprise nor excitement.

'What do you?'

'Someone's out of his twisted mind if he thinks that would stop the investigation. I'll ask for everyone that Sydney can spare, if you want me to.'

'No, leave it for the time being . . . You've changed, Hugh.'

They turned into the main street and headed west out of town. Church bells were ringing somewhere, a sound one rarely heard in the city any more, especially in the newer suburbs. The bells rang in Randwick, but it always sounded to Malone as a forlorn sound, a farewell to departed congregations. He wondered what the church attendance was in country towns these days.

'What do you mean?'

'You know what I mean. You're ready to make waves.'

Narvo was silent for a while, staring straight ahead; then he said, 'It was Chess Hardstaff at the races yesterday afternoon. Up till now I've – I'm ashamed to admit it, so it's just between you and me – I've bent the rules if he's leaned on me. Sometimes you have to do it in a country district. Nothing serious, just enough to, well, not make waves, if you like. I used to get angry with myself, sometimes I despised myself, but I put up with it. Then yesterday . . . Yesterday I finally had had enough. When he stood over me and demanded I arrest all the Abos, right there in front of them, I'd had more than enough. I didn't tell him to get stuffed, but that was what I was thinking and he knew it.'

'Did it make you feel better?'

Narvo smiled. 'It was like knocking over the school bully.'

They turned off the main highway and drove down along the river bank and into the settlement. There was a subdued air about the place; even the children were playing quietly with no shouting or laughing. Eight or nine older men sat in a circle under a tree, exchanging looks rather than words, as if everything had been said and now they were waiting for some resolution. They could have been a sculptured tableau of patience, but Malone wondered when the stone would crumble.

Wally Mungle came up from the riverbank, where Ruby sat on a fallen tree gazing out at the skin of the river being broken by the occasional leaping fish. He said hello to the two senior men and led them back to Ruby.

'It's about Chess Hardstaff,' he said and stood back, more like a policeman than a husband.

Ruby Mungle didn't rise from the tree-trunk but just looked up at the two white men. Her pretty face looked older this morning, as if a long sleepless night had aged her. Mungle, too, looked as if he hadn't slept.

'You wanted to see us, Ruby?' Malone remarked at once that Narvo had relegated himself to the background by stepping back a pace.

She glanced at Narvo, her husband's boss, then looked back at Malone. 'Yeah. I thought about what you said last night . . .' She stopped; but he held himself back from asking her to go on. Like the old men across the clearing, who were watching them closely, she was not to be hurried. 'I'll tell you what happened the morning Mrs Hardstaff was murdered.'

Out of the corner of his eye Malone saw Narvo stiffen. He said, 'Do you mind if I take notes, Ruby? I'll write a full statement later and Inspector Narvo can have someone back at the station type it up for you to sign.'

She turned her head towards her husband. 'Is that what I have to do, sweetheart?'

Mungle nodded; then decided to be husband and not policeman. He sat down on the tree-trunk and took her hand. 'It's gotta be done, love. Go ahead. Don't change your mind, not now.'

'What's it gunna do to you? I mean your job?'

Mungle looked back at Narvo. 'She's worried I might be transferred or something. We don't wanna leave Collamundra.'

'You won't be,' said Narvo quietly. 'I promise.'

Mungle pressed his wife's hand. She paused a while, then she began: 'That morning when Mrs Hardstaff was murdered, I'd got up early to go to the toilet. Us blacks had to use the outdoor dunny, Mum and I weren't even allowed to use the one next to the kitchen where she worked. Old Sir Chester insisted on that. When I come out of the toilet, Chess Hardstaff, *Young* Chess, as everyone called him, was coming out of the wing of the house where his and Mrs Hardstaff's bedroom was. He saw me and he ducked back inside. I didn't take that much notice, I was only eleven years old then and kids don't understand lotsa things adults do. But then I walked across to the kitchen, I dunno, I think I was gunna wash my hands or something, I looked back and he was running along the back veranda and around the corner of the house. Then I heard the Land-Rover start up and then I seen him driving away through the paddocks.'

Malone had been scribbling furiously in his own peculiar shorthand. 'Ruby, all this was – what? – seventeen years ago. I've got to say this – you're quoting a child's memory. That's not always the most reliable source.'

'Do you wanna hear this or not, Inspector?' She was not belligerent; more disappointed, it seemed.

'Yes, I do. But if this goes any further, there are going to be lawyers who'll tear your evidence to pieces. I've had it happen to cases of my own, where I thought I had everything sewn up.'

'Mr Malone, I *remember*. Mrs Hardstaff was the only one I liked on the whole place. She was kind to me and Mum, she treated us almost like – like *equals*. When Mum went in an hour later with her usual tray and she found her dead . . .' She stopped and, for some reason, gritted her teeth as if against pain. 'I *remember*, Mr Malone. I was right behind Mum with the teapot . . . I've only ever seen one murdered person. That was Mrs Hardstaff. I *remember*. There's nothing wrong with my memory about that morning – *nothing*. It don't matter whether I was eleven years old or a hundred and eleven. I *remember*.'

'Fair enough. I'm sorry.'

'Tell 'em the rest, love,' said Wally Mungle.

Above them in the red-gum that shaded them, a magpie

sharpened its beak on a branch, wishing it were spring and nesting-time, so that there would be a reason for dive-bombing the humans below and moving them out of its territory. A small boat, with an outboard motor fitted, came puttering down from under the bridge and went past, the man in it looking neither to right nor left: as if he doesn't want to see the blacks' camp? Malone wondered. If Chess Hardstaff was toppled on the evidence of a black girl, what would happen to the blacks here in the camp? Would they be run out of town as Fred Strayhorn and the communists had been all those years ago?

Ruby Mungle went on, 'Old Sir Chester come to Mum and told her he wanted her to take me into town, to bring me here –' She nodded back over her shoulder at the settlement; which in those days, Malone guessed, might have been no more than a collection of shanties. 'He said Noongulli was no place for me to be while the police were there and all, that it would be too upsetting for me.'

'When was this? Before or after someone had phoned for the police?'

'I dunno. It was after Mr Hardstaff, Young Chess, come back to the house.'

Malone looked at Narvo. 'You said the file's missing. So we don't know what time the call came in to the duty officer. Can you remember what time it was when you heard the call over your car radio?'

Narvo shook his head. 'I'd only be making a guess, it could be twenty minutes or more out. I'd have made a note of it on my board, but that sheet would have gone into the daily file. Seventeen years ago, that wouldn't still be around. When I took over the station, I decided we'd have a clean-up, the place was a mess. We burned a lot of old paper – Christ!' He shook his head at the stupidities committed in the name of neat housekeeping.

'Ruby, you said Chess Hardstaff came back to the house. How long was that after you'd seen him drive away in the Land-Rover?'

'I dunno, I'd only be guessing. It was after Mum and me had had our breakfast, before we went in to Mrs Hardstaff and found her dead. Maybe half an hour, maybe more. I know he was standing outside on the veranda when Mum screamed and we both came running out of the bedroom.'

She gritted her teeth again and Malone gave her a little time. 'Hugh, I talked with Fred Strayhorn, that old cove with the beard at the races yesterday, the one who's going out to see Hardstaff this morning.' He gave a quick explanation of the relationship between Hardstaff and Strayhorn; he noticed that the Mungles both sat up with interest. 'Sir Chester paid him to tell the police that Chess had been out at the site of the new dam with him –'

'I remember him now!' It was the first time Malone had seen Narvo show any excitement, though it would never get him arrested for riotous behaviour. 'They brought him in from wherever he was working on the property – I didn't do the interviewing, I was just the junior officer staking out the crime scene –'

'Well, anyway, I can get him to make a statement, I think . . . Ruby, did your mother ever say anything to you about the murder after that first day?'

She shook her head. 'We never discussed it. She brought me in here that morning and left me with her sister, my aunt – she's dead now, like Mum. But coming in in the back of the truck –'

'Who brought you in?'

'One of the station hands, I forget his name – he left the district ages ago, I dunno where he'd be now . . . Mum told me to forget anything I'd seen, not to talk to anyone about it, not even to my aunt. When I asked her why, you know the way kids do, she said we had to go on living out at Noongulli, that what the whites might do to each other wasn't no concern of ours. She loved her job as cook and she didn't wanna lose it. She didn't want me to grow up in the blacks' camp.'

And now here she was sitting on the edge of the blacks' camp telling her secret of so many years ago. 'Why'd you choose here to talk to us?'

'I wanted to come back and look at my people –' There was just a fleeting glance at her husband; Malone wondered if this was the first time she had ever used that phrase. 'Yesterday out at the racecourse I was *sick*, really sick, at the way Mr Hardstaff looked at my people, at the way he yelled for them to be arrested, as if he *owned* the district and everyone in it –'

Malone avoided looking at Narvo; but the latter said quietly, 'We understand what you mean, Mrs Mungle. Would you like to come back to the station now and make a formal statement and sign it?'

She looked at her husband and he pressed her hand. 'I think you better, love.'

'This is only the beginning, isn't it?' She looked around at all three men.

'Yes,' said Malone, 'but it could be the end of something, too.'

She stood up from the tree-trunk, still holding Mungle's hand; and at once two children came running towards her from a group that had been playing some quiet game with stones under a river-gum farther along the bank. They were a boy and a girl, about four and five, with dark curly hair, pale coffee-coloured skin and huge black eyes; they were beautiful but too young to be aware of it, still innocent of man's vanities and cruelties. Malone felt a sudden wish for his own children to be friends of these two, but he knew it would never happen. There were probably children as innocent and beautiful and shy in Redfern, no more than five kilometres from where the Malones lived, but they and his own children were separated by more than geography, by something that only tolerance and goodwill, notoriously unreliable transport, could conquer.

The children were introduced to Malone and responded with shy, polite smiles. Then the little girl said, 'Can we stay, Mummy? It must be nice living here by the river, all the kids to play with.'

Wally Mungle looked around at the settlement; then he ruffled the hair of his daughter. 'We gotta go, Kylie. Some other time, okay? Go and say goodbye to Granma. We'll follow you in our truck, Inspector.'

Driving back to town Malone said, 'Well, what d'you think?'

'I don't think you have enough yet to issue a warrant for murder, do you?'

'No.'

'This has got nothing to do with the Sagawa murder, you know.'

'Are you telling me to stay away from Hardstaff?'

'No. But if you don't wrap up the Sagawa case, but go back with Hardstaff indicted for a murder he committed seventeen years ago, what's Police HQ going to think? They don't like crossed lines. They like to keep everything neatly compartmentalized.'

'Do you?'

'I used to. But now . . . Keep digging. What's your next step?'

'I'll have another chat with Fred Strayhorn. Then we – you and I and Curly – can decide what to do? Okay?'

The car window was down and the slipstream was ruffling Narvo's hair. The neat, steam-pressed man Malone had met two days ago was gone; at least for the time being. 'Do you mind if we take the credit?'

'*That*'ll make waves. No, Hugh, I don't mind. It was never my case, anyway. I've just had a suspicion all along that Hardstaff somehow – I haven't got a clue *how* – had something to do with the killing of Sagawa. I still think he might have.'

'You're stretching it, Scobie.' But Narvo's argument was no stronger than that. He knew as well as anyone the web that bound men and their actions together. In one way or another the Hardstaffs had created Collamundra; it was not beyond the Hardstaff name, involuntarily or otherwise, to destroy it. He was not versed in history, but he knew the effects of human nature, which is much the same thing.

The Mungles arrived at the station almost immediately after Malone pulled the Commodore into the yard. Twenty minutes later Ruby Mungle's statement had been typed and signed and the Mungles were gone. The statement had been taken in Narvo's office, so it would not be overheard, and Clements, a quick if not expert typist, had come down from the detectives' room and typed it.

Curly Baldock had been called in again from home and he arrived just after the Mungles had left. This time he was no longer in shorts and thongs, but in slacks and shoes. Narvo told him what had occurred.

Baldock was still distant from Malone and Clements. He read the statement, then said flatly, 'You'll need more than this.'

'We've agreed on that,' said Narvo, at once catching the coolness in Baldock's attitude. 'But it's our case, Curly, not Scobie's and Russ's, and I've decided we should follow it up.'

'I'll try and get a statement from Fred Strayhorn.' Then Malone looked at his watch. 'Crumbs, is that the time? We're supposed to go out and see Hardstaff. I'll ring him and put him off. When I've got Strayhorn to put something down on paper, you can present it and Ruby's statement to Hardstaff and see if it scares him into a confession.'

'Do you think it will?' Clements looked at Baldock.

The local detective's coolness was lessening. 'We'll never scare Chess Hardstaff into anything. But it's worth a try. Who takes the blame for this, Hugh? I mean if it goes wrong. You or me?'

'I do.' Narvo leaned back in his chair, a sailor ready to take on the roughest waves. 'But you'll have to carry your fair whack. The only one who stays off this case is Wally Mungle.'

Baldock pondered a moment, as if wondering what life would be like if he were in the vanguard of a revolution against the King-maker and it failed. Then he nodded at Malone and Clements, all his coolness suddenly gone. 'Thanks for the leg-work. And for the kudos. It'll be a feather in our cap if we bring it off.'

Narvo smiled. 'A feather in your cap is no use if you've lost your head in the process. We'll just have to see that doesn't happen. In the meantime . . .' He looked at Malone.

'We still have to find out who killed Sagawa.'

'Clarrie Binyan phoned from Ballistics,' said Clements, switching back to basics. 'That bullet from last night's crack at you matches the one taken from Sagawa's body.'

'That means the murderer is someone from the district,' said Malone. 'How many gun dealers are there in town, Curly?'

'Just the one with a licence. He runs a general sports store.'

'Can you get him to open up his store today? Get him to go through his books, check on everyone who's bought any Twenty-twos from him over the past five years. Go back even further if he's still got the records. Check, too, if he's sold any 'scopes, especially night 'scopes. Russ will go with you.'

'What are you going to do?' Clements asked.

'I'm going out to have lunch with my wife and kids.' He grinned at Narvo, the other inspector in the room. 'Privileges of rank, eh, Hugh?'

6

That morning the two old men sat in the doorway of the big woolshed on Noongulli. It had once been the biggest shearing shed in the State, with a hundred and two stands, giving it one more than the shed outside Cunnamulla in Queensland that had claimed to be the largest in the whole country. Now there were only thirty stands that were still operated, but the long shafts, with their rusting wheels, still ran the length of the shed on both sides. The board floor was dark and shiny with a century of grease from the fleeces, but there were lighter patches where the shearers' sweat had bleached their own memorial marks. The huge shed smelled of wool, but it also smelled of something else: of history that was winding down.

The two old men now and again gazed westwards during pauses in their slow conversation, staring out at the illimitable distance that stretched, unbroken but for the occasional, unseen range or two of low hills, to the heart of the continent. Chess Hardstaff sometimes dreamed of what might have been, had his grandfather been farsighted and avaricious enough to have owned everything west of here, to have been king of the biggest livestock empire in the wide, wide world, to have owned more even than Kidman, the biggest king of them all. It was, of course, a madman's dream, but Hardstaff knew, as well as any psychiatrist, that one did not have to be crazy to have mad dreams. It was enough just to be greedy, and greed was not a certifiable offence. It was just one of the seven deadly sins and Hardstaff had never given much thought to such warnings. He recognized the existence of good and evil, but he left it to others to tell the difference; the difference, he reasoned, changed with circumstances. In the meantime he gazed westwards, especially now that behind him, to the east and south, in Sydney and Canberra, his power was waning.

'Do you believe in the existence of evil, Strayhorn?'

'I dunno, Hardstaff, whether I've ever thought of *evil*, I mean as evil. The world is chock-a-block with crookery and bastardry and skulduggery, though, and in some cases something a bloody sight worse. But yeah, I suppose I do believe in the existence of evil. Are you thinking of yourself or anyone in particular?'

Hardstaff smiled. 'You have a sardonic sense of humour. Is it natural or did you have to cultivate it?'

'I think it crept up on me, like old age and a cranky prostate.'

Hardstaff himself had driven into the showground to pick up Strayhorn. He had not trusted the latter to the care of one of the station hands, not because he thought the station hand might drive both of them off the road, though that might be a simple solution to what could prove to be a complex problem, but because he was afraid that Strayhorn might talk. He guessed now that Strayhorn would have held his tongue, not wanting to waste his dearly held secret on a stranger. On the drive back to Noongulli the two old men had said hardly anything to each other, more like old friends who had exhausted every topic than adversaries who had only one topic to discuss. Hardstaff rarely, if ever, spoke when he was driving and this morning he had not broken the habit.

'To answer your question, no, I'm not evil. I just work to my own design, not to some moral plan worked out by theologians who don't recognize the facts of life. God has never had to be political, that's one thing they'll never acknowledge.'

'What you did seventeen years ago, are you saying that was political?'

Hardstaff looked out across the pens and drafting yards, over the dipping troughs, all of them empty till mustering began and the shearing team arrived. In one of the far paddocks a willy-willy whirled up out of nothing, the spinning red-brown dust looking like a genie about to materialize; then it spun away into nothing again, magic dying before it could be called upon. Over towards the river, which here curled northwards, a station hand on a motorbike was herding some sheep towards a calico fold where a truck waited for them. In a solitary bluegum just beyond the yards a dozen white cockatoos, come up from the river, sat in uncharacteristic silence; then abruptly they took off with a loud screech, curling up like an explosion of white smoke. He remembered that that morning long ago the cockatoos had been out in force, shrieking at him as he had driven aimlessly along the river.

'I haven't admitted to doing anything seventeen years ago.'

'Chess – you mind if I call you Chess? What we're talking about is – well, pretty intimate. We're sorta old mates, at least for this morning. How does that strike you?'

'It doesn't make me jump up and down.'

'I don't think you ever jumped up and down, Chess. I'd say you were always a cold-blooded bugger. Who made you like that – your old man? He was cold-blooded enough, the way he paid me off that morning. Why did you kill your wife, Chess?'

It was the first time in all those years he had been asked the question; not even his father had asked, though he had known why. Neither had his daughters asked, though he sometimes wondered if Amanda had guessed what had happened. Rosemary had come home from London for the funeral, bringing with her her English friend Viola, but they had stayed only two days; Rosemary had shown some grief about her mother's death but no curiosity. She and her friend had walked about with their arms around each other, even Amanda excluded from their circle of two, and when she had left he had been no closer to her than he had been in all the years till she had grown up and left home at eighteen. Now a man he hardly knew, whom he had met less than half a dozen times in his life that he could recall, had asked him the bluntest question he had ever been hit with.

'Are you planning to blackmail me, Fred?' The smile was so thin it was no more than a flattening of the lips. 'Since we're sort of intimate.'

'But not old mates, eh?'

'No.' There had never been any old mates, not even in his political life.

Strayhorn smiled with genuine amusement, holding nothing back; it was almost a laugh. 'No, Chess, I'm not gunna blackmail you. I've done some dodgy things in my time, but blackmailing ain't on the list. But from all accounts your wife was a charming woman, everyone liked her, and you put her nightie around her neck and choked her to death. I'd just like to know why you did it?'

Hardstaff thought for a moment that he would not reply: he didn't owe Fred Strayhorn an answer. He put it off with a question? 'Have you ever been married?'

'No. I got close once or twice and I lived with a nice woman for some months up near the Snowy River – up there you need someone to keep you warm on winter nights. But no, I never married. I didn't like the thought of being chained up. Did your wife have you chained up? I'd of thought it was the other way around.'

'You don't have much of an opinion of me, do you?'

'No, Chess, I don't.'

'I'm held in rather high regard by the rest of the country. They may not like me, some of them, but they respect me.'

'Chess, that's your *public* figure. You don't believe in it any more than I do. Look at President Reagan. From what I read when he was in the White House, half of America thought he was the greatest public figure since Jesus Christ. But I'd bet New York to a brick that ninety-nine point nine per cent of the whole bang lotta them wouldn't have a clue what made him tick.' He paused, studied Hardstaff as if seeing him properly for the first time; the stare was not offensive, instead almost pitying. 'I think what makes you tick, Chess, is nothing but bloody pride. Well, it cometh before a fall.'

'You're going to contribute to my fall?'

'I'll be straight with you. I still ain't made up my mind. I come back to Collamundra this time, pretty sure I was gunna dob you in. You and your old man, Chess, you killed my mum and dad. You choked the life outa them, too, only you done it by degrees and it probably never crossed your minds that you done it. But you did. They were never the same again after you kicked us outa Collamundra and within four years of us leaving here they both died.'

Hardstaff forced himself to say, 'Sorry,' but he wasn't sure that he meant it. He could not remember the elder Strayhorns at all, they were faceless players in that opera on that Sunday afternoon too many years ago.

Then the old-fashioned box-phone on the wall just inside the doorway rang; it was an extension connected to the small switchboard in the homestead office. Hardstaff rose, feeling suddenly weary and – old? He had never felt like this before; at least not till last Monday night. 'Yes?' He looked at his watch. 'You're late, Inspector.'

'Something's come up, Mr Hardstaff. Will you be at your daughter's party this evening? Maybe we can have a talk then?'

'You've been invited?'

'I gather I'm eligible, despite the fact that your daughter thinks I'm a Commo, and I'm also a cop. I just hope it doesn't get around back in Sydney.'

'What – that you're a Communist?'

'No, that I've been to a Rural Party shindig.'

Hardstaff found himself smiling as he hung up. There were still some formidable opponents left to make life interesting, even though life itself was coming to a close.

He came back and sat down. 'That was Inspector Malone. Will you be talking to him?'

'He'll be the one, if I decide to say anything.' Strayhorn sipped the Scotch he had hardly touched. Hardstaff had brought over a bottle of twelve-year-old Glenfiddich, but he had soon realized he was pouring good stuff down the wrong gullet. Strayhorn had made no comment on it and the small omission had irritated Hardstaff, who hated wasting quality whisky on dull tongues. 'You said you were sorry about my mum and dad, Chess, but I don't believe you are. But it don't matter now. Your old man was the ring-leader that day and I dunno that he'd be sorry, either . . . I don't suppose you even remember what happened that Sunday?'

'No.'

Strayhorn sipped the Scotch again; then irritated Hardstaff even further by saying, 'A nice drop. It must be nice to be able to afford the good stuff like this . . . Maybe it's going back too far for you, since it didn't mean that much to you. It was just another Sunday afternoon outing. But you remember the morning you killed your wife, right? When we get on, Chess, sometimes we can't remember even yesterday. But long ago . . .' He smiled into the past, without pleasure. 'Long ago, it seems you can remember every detail of it.'

'So you'll go to Inspector Malone and tell him every detail of it, of that morning? It was a Tuesday morning, incidentally.'

'You remember the details, too, eh? Yeah, it was a Tuesday. Like this murder of the Nip, they found him dead on a Tuesday morning, didn't they? You didn't have anything to do with this latest one, did you?' The query was too casual, he was gazing out towards the paddocks, where the motorbike stockman had run the last of the sheep into the calico fold.

'No, I didn't.' Well, not directly, not till afterwards.

'I'm glad to hear that. You had anything to do with that and I think I'd be out on the road right now thumbing a lift back to town and the police. Two murders, that'd be too much, Chess.'

'So what's going to happen? You'll sit on your information till you feel ready to go to the police, is that it? You'll keep me turning in the wind?'

'I like the way you put it, Chess. But no, that wasn't the idea, though now you've thought of it, I might do it. I thought you were smarter than that, giving the other bloke ideas – you never done that as a political boss. No, the truth is, now I been back a few days, I think I'd like to settle down here till I kick the bucket. I've got a bit of money saved – I was never a big spender. I'm seventy-three years old, give or take a month, and in all the time I been coming and going, no matter how far I went, I always thought of Collamundra as home. I'm home now, Chess, and I think I'll stay. I might even come out here and ask you for a job as – well, I dunno, what d'you reckon? Companion? We could sit here the end of every day, like a coupla old mates, and talk about the good old days.'

'Jesus!' said Hardstaff, normally not given to oaths.

Strayhorn laughed. 'Relax, Chess. I was just seeing how you'd look turning in the wind.' He finished the whisky, put down his glass and stood up. He looked around him, down the length of the long shed. 'Y'know, the first time I come back here, I worked here in Down-in-the-Mouth Quinlan's team. You remember

Down-in-the-Mouth, most miserable bastard ever drew breath?'
'Yes, but the best shearing boss ever worked for us.'
'Neither you nor your old man recognized me. I worked on the third stand from that end. There were sixty of us, as I remember it, biggest team I ever worked on. Ah, Chess, it's all gone, ain't it? We'll never see the likes of it again.'

The two old men stood looking down the shed, hearing the echoes: the motors humming, sheep bleating, dogs barking, the bell for starting and stopping. Light gleamed on polished patches of floor and walls, turned into dim images: the bent backs of the shearers, the fleece flung into the air as it was tossed on the classer's table, the whirling arm of the handle of the wool-press as it was left to unwind. It still happened each shearing season, but the great days were gone: it was history.

And I myself might soon be, thought Hardstaff. 'You still haven't told me what you're going to do, whether you'll go to the police or not.'

'You still haven't told me why you killed her.'

'That would be a confession that I did it, Fred. And I'll never tell anyone that.' For that would mean a demolition of his pride.

'Well, then, you better get used to the idea of turning in the wind.'

Hardstaff sighed inwardly. A third murder might have to be committed.

SEVEN

1

After lunch in the Waring house Malone walked out and down to the yards. He stood leaning on the rail of a sand-yard, watching Tom, stiff with pride and some trepidation, trotting a horse in a circle. Then Claire came and stood beside him. He put his arm round her shoulders and felt her move a little closer to him, as if seeking his protection.

'How's your case going, Daddy?'

'We're getting there slowly. How's yours?'

'I don't know what you mean. I don't have any case.'

'I got it from a reliable stool pigeon that you had a case for Tas.'

She squinted up at him, making a face. 'God, there's no privacy in this family! If you must know, I don't have a case, as you call it, for Tas. It was just a – a phase. Have you seen his girl-friend? God, she's gross! She's got bigger boobs than Dolly Parton.'

'Do you mind? I'm your father, not a bra salesman.'

'Daddy, don't be so stuffy. Mum and I have discussed her figure – Mum agrees with me. They stick out in front of her –'

Crumbs, he thought, where did the little girl go who used to laugh her head off at Bugs Bunny and couldn't believe that I'd once done the same thing?'

'Well, don't say any more about Tas, please? Here comes TV Guide.' He pressed her shoulder, wanting to protect her against the heartaches of love, puppy or otherwise. Maureen sneaked in under his other arm as he dropped it from the rail.

'Daddy, come home with us tomorrow?'

'I can't, love. If I did, the Commissioner would either sack me or send me out to Tibooburra. How'd you like to live way out there in the Outback?'

Both girls made a face and Maureen said, 'I hate the country! All the flies and the snakes and things – urk! And there's nothing to *do*! They only get *one* TV channel out here. It's like living at the South Pole.'

'Tom looks happy enough.'

'He's a *boy*. He's a wally, anyway – he'd enjoy *anything*. I'm never going to move out of the city again as long as I live.'

Tom pulled the horse up in front of them, beamed down on them, the Man from Snowy River with green zinc ointment on his nose and a stockman's hat two sizes too large for him. There were streams ahead of him to be splashed through, fallen trees to be jumped, steep slopes down which he had to plunge: Clancy of the Overflow waited for him on the other side of a boy's river of dreams. He could be happy here, Malone thought. He reached across the rail and put a hand on his son's knee, suddenly sad that, not many years ahead, Tom would be leaving home, bound for a life in which he, the father, might not be needed. For a father, too, has a river of dreams which, too often, run dry behind him.

'Dad, can I have a horse for Christmas?'

'Don't be spack,' said Claire. 'Where would we keep a horse? In the pool?'

'Well, I think I'll stay here and be a tomeroo.'

'A jackeroo, you wally,' said Maureen.

'My name's Tom, not Jack.'

Malone welcomed the arrival of the Waring children who had now come out of the house. He saw Sean Carmody moving towards two chairs under a tree and he crossed over and sat down beside him. Carmody handed him a can of Aerogard and Malone sprayed himself against the flies that had followed him. Then he nodded enquiringly at a few clouds that were building up in the west.

Carmody shook his head. 'There's no rain out there. We're in for a long dry spell, I think . . . Trevor told me about last night's shooting.'

Malone tensed. 'Did he tell the women?'

'No, I gather you told him not to. You got any clue to who it was?'

'Not so far . . . Sean, did you know a local man named Frank Kilburn?'

'Of course. A nice feller, very quiet, except when he had a few in. Why?'

'Did he ever say anything to you about Chess Hardstaff and his war record?'

Carmody looked at him shrewdly. He took out his pipe, lit it unhurriedly and puffed on it before replying; the flies that hadn't been driven away by the spray now fled from the smoke. 'Who wised you up to that little bit of gossip?'

'Is that all it is – gossip?'

Carmody considered. 'No, I don't think so. Frank Kilburn wasn't a gossip-monger. But once or twice, when he was in his cups, he'd talk a bit more than was good for him. Or for Chess Hardstaff.' He puffed on his pipe again, then took it out of his mouth and let it start to die out. Malone waited, one eye on Tom, now trotting the horse once more round the sand-yard. At last Carmody said, 'Frank and Chess were in the same Air Force unit, flying Kittyhawks in North Africa. Chess shot down a German Messerschmitt one day and the Jerry pilot took to his parachute. Chess followed him down, playing him like a cat with a mouse, and shot him when he was about a thousand feet from the ground. Frank was the only one who saw it and he never spoke to him again – he wouldn't even back up Chess in his claim for the kill. He asked for a transfer to another unit and got it. When he came back to the district he wouldn't join the Legion in town because Chess was up to be president. If he came into town, he'd cross the road to avoid him. He lived on a property down south about twenty miles, it had been in the family for years, and after he came back from the war I gather he never really became part of the town's life. He was very bitter about Chess, said he was the most cold-blooded killer, that was what he called him, he'd ever seen.'

'Was he ever married?'

'No, not as far as I know.'

'I understand he died last year. What did he die of?'

Carmody smiled. 'Chess didn't kill him, if that's what you are asking. He died of pneumonia, something us old fellers are susceptible to. You're still chasing Chess over the murder of his wife, aren't you?'

'Not really. His name just keeps cropping up.' He stood up. 'Well, I'd better be getting back. I'll see you at the Nothlings' party.'

'I wouldn't miss it for quids.' Carmody knocked out his pipe on the heel of his boot, then stood up. 'Do you think Sagawa's murderer is likely to take another pot-shot at you?'

'It's possible. But keep it to yourself.'

'Does the thought scare you?'

'Sean, I'm not middle-aged yet. I've got a wife and three kids I love. I don't think I'm scared, but I hate the thought of some bastard wiping me out while I'm still enjoying what I've got.'

He went across to say goodbye to the children, telling them he would see them tomorrow at the airport, then he went into the house, collected Lisa and walked with her out to the Commodore.

'What's the matter with Trevor?' she said. 'He's been jumpy all morning and you saw what he was like at lunch. Didn't eat a thing.'

'Where is he now?'

'He's lying down. Ida's in with him. Have you been putting some sort of pressure on him?'

'In a way.'

'God, he's Ida's husband! The kids and I are guests in his home!'

'That's what he told me yesterday morning.' Better to take the blame for Waring's nervousness himself than to tell her about last night's shooting. 'I'm sorry, darl, but there were questions I had to ask him and he didn't like the answers he had to give. Now that's it, don't let's discuss it any more.'

'Now *you*'re getting jumpy.'

'It comes of being married to a policeman's wife.' He kissed her. 'I'll see you at the Nothlings'. Look your best.'

'Why, what competition will I have?'

He drove back to town, turning off into the showground before he got to the river bridge. The carnival and circus were in full swing; the town's children, if not their parents, were out in force. Malone found Fred Strayhorn at his stall, exhorting, without much enthusiasm, the locals to try their luck with his bamboo rings. When he saw Malone he handed over the stall to a youth, one of the carnival's roustabouts, and came across to join the detective.

'Let's get outa the crowd, Inspector. This is my last day with the show and I think I'm gunna be glad to turn me back on it. It's all too bloody noisy.'

'What are you going to do? Go back on the track?'

'No, I'm gunna stay here. Settle down. I'll check into a pub for a night or two till I find something, someone who wants to take in a boarder. Then I'll look around for a place to buy, something with a coupla acres.'

'Noongulli, for instance?'

Strayhorn grinned through his beard. 'I'd only be short four or five million, that's all. It's him you've come about, right? Chess Hardstaff.'

He pulled a couple of folding chairs out of the back of a five-ton truck and he and Malone sat down. Nearby two elephants, having done their act, were being hosed down by a small blonde girl in a spangled body-stocking that had a big hole inside each knee, as if she had worn it away nudging the elephants into whatever elephants were supposed to do in a circus ring. She looked across at Strayhorn and waved the hose; the sun caught the spray, turning it into a rainbow of greeting. Or perhaps of farewell: Malone wondered if the old man would miss any of these people when they moved on. Circus folk, he had heard, were supposed to be a family.

'I'd like a statement, Fred. I've got another witness who's already made a statement. The two of you are going to make life pretty difficult for Hardstaff. That's what you want.'

'I dunno that it is, Mr Malone. Now I'm gunna settle down here . . .'

Malone felt his temper rise. 'For Chrissake, don't pull that one on me! You can't suddenly become a local again, not after all these years, not after what Hardstaff and his old man did to you and your family!'

Strayhorn looked at him mildly. 'Keep your shirt on. I just have to do some more thinking, that's all.'

'Did you go out and see him this morning?'

'Yeah, he come in and picked me up. In his Mercedes, first time I ever rode in anything like that sorta luxury.'

'Did he offer to pay you off again?' As soon as he said it he knew it was a mistake; he threw cold water on his temper. 'Sorry.'

'So you bloody should be,' said Strayhorn, abruptly showing some temper of his own. 'Are you Crown Prosecutor as well as cop?'

'What do you know about Crown Prosecutors?'

'I told you, I been in trouble with the law. But that's all over now.'

'Righto, Fred, let's call a truce. I shouldn't have said what I did and I'm sorry. Now I want you to give me a statement about that morning when Mrs Hardstaff was murdered, just tell us what you told me yesterday morning. I appreciate it may be tougher for you if you decide to settle down again in Collamundra, but I think you may find more people will favour you than blackball you. Chess Hardstaff may be king around here, but he wouldn't win on a popular vote.'

'Kings don't need votes, son.' Fred Strayhorn, bachelor, had become fatherly. 'You should read more history . . . I'll think about it.'

'I wanted you to come in with me now to the station.'

Strayhorn shook his head. 'That's not on. Things are gunna be busy here till we close down tonight. I'll come in tomorrow, soon's I've helped them pack and they're on the road. I'll come in whether I'm gunna make a statement or not. It's been bloody years, another day won't matter.'

'You won't change your mind and shoot through on me?'

'Mr Malone, I've left Collamundra for the last time, that's a promise. Next time I go, I'll be in a pine box.'

As Malone drove out of the showground one of the elephants trumpeted shrilly and inside the circus tent a lion roared in reply.

He wondered if they were missing the jungles of Africa or if, like Fred Strayhorn, they had had enough of being on the road.

Russ Clements and Curly Baldock were waiting for him in the detectives' room. The look on Clements's face told him they had dug up a nugget; he just hoped it wouldn't be fool's gold. He dropped into a chair and said, 'Tell me.'

'We got Ted Hart, he's the local gun dealer, we got him out of bed. He wasn't too happy, he and his missus were in bed for their Sunday bit while the kids were out at the carnival. Anyhow, he came in and opened up his shop. We went through his registered sales for the last five years, that's as long as he keeps 'em. He's sold sixty-two Twenty-twos in that period, most of them Remingtons.

'Anyone who interests us on his list?'

'Practically everybody,' said Clements. 'Ray and Phil Chakiros, Trevor Waring, Chess Hardstaff, Bruce Potter, Narelle's husband – he bought one the day before he was killed. All Remingtons, except the Chakiros's guns, they're Brnos.'

'You've missed out one on our list. Max Nothling.'

'No, he doesn't own one. At least he didn't buy a Twenty-two from Ted Hart.' Clements looked at Baldock; they beamed like juveniles as they held out their nugget: 'But his wife Amanda bought two, a Remington and a Tikka. Plus a full set of 'scopes. For five years running, till she gave up the game two years ago, she was the Country Women's small-bore champion. Ted Hart, who saw her in action, said she could shoot the balls off a bull at two hundred yards.'

'The bull'd like that.' Malone looked at Baldock. 'You must've known that, Curly.'

Baldock was embarrassed. 'Of course I did! But I never give it a thought. Jesus, why would a woman like her wanna shoot Sagawa?'

Malone glanced at Clements, feeling their thoughts click into the same gear. Then he said slowly, 'Maybe Sagawa wasn't the target at all.'

2

'Why did you ask the Potter woman?'

'I wanted to see Max squirm. He knows it was because of her that I meant to shoot him.'

The Hardstaffs, father and daughter, were alone for a few moments, beyond earshot of the party crowd on the lawns. The Nothling homestead, east of the town and back in the slight rise of hills to the north, was another colonial relic, so beautifully restored that it looked better than it had in its original state. It had been featured in *House and Garden* and *Vogue Living*; the National Trust had placed its seal on it. No one ever mentioned the pioneer family, bankrupt and now forgotten, who had built it; sometimes even Max Nothling was not mentioned, because it was more often than not referred to as the 'second Hardstaff property'. Amanda was a Hardstaff, make no mistake about it. Her and Max's only child was registered as Chester Nothling-Hardstaff and he would inherit both this and his grandfather's property, the Hardstaff name carried on.

'Unlucky Mr Sagawa.' Chess Hardstaff didn't say, *Poor Mr Sagawa*. Sympathy, like forgiveness, did not come easily with him. 'I don't understand how you made such a mistake.'

'It was not an easy shot, not at that distance. Just as I pressed the trigger, Sagawa stepped in front of Max.' She said it so coolly that she could have been discussing a loose shot in some weekend competition. She regretted the death of Kenji Sagawa, a harmless little man who had paid her the proper respect on the few occasions they had met, but it was something that was distinctly apart from the anger and contempt she still felt for her husband. Later, she might feel guilt; but not now.

'You're sure she's not making *you* squirm?'

'Perhaps,' she admitted. 'But I'll never let her see it.'

'Were they together last Monday night? Max hasn't even mentioned her. Matter of fact, he's said hardly a word to me since that night. She could have been with him out at the cotton farm.'

He looked across the lawns to Narelle Potter standing beside a liquidamber. The garden lights had just come on and she was standing in the glow of one of them. She was a good-looking woman, he had to admit, but no man was paying court to her now; certainly not his son-in-law, who had removed himself to the far side of the lawn and had his back to her. 'Where was she?'

'He must have dropped her off somewhere. I'd been following them, but I lost them –' Amanda stopped, aware of his stern disapproval. 'I *know*. It's embarrassing and shameful, spying on one's husband . . .'

'I don't know why you didn't just kick him out, then divorce him.'

'And have everyone learn I'd lost my husband to the town bike? That's what you men call her, isn't it?'

'I use a more old-fashioned term.'

'Don't be so bloody pompous, Dad!'

He was suddenly aware of the tension in her; he had never seen her like this before. He wanted to comfort her, put a hand on her arm or round her shoulders; but he hadn't done that with her, or her sister, since she was a small child. It struck him, with shame, that he couldn't express sympathy properly even to his own daughter.

'I haven't thanked you for what you did last Monday night,' she said.

They hadn't discussed the murder till now; he wondered why she had chosen this awkward moment. Was she planning some spectacular confession? He hoped not. Confession was only good for the souls of those who heard it, it gave them a feeling of superiority without feeling sinful about it. All it gave the confessor was trouble.

'I had to do something. When Max rang me . . .'

He had been at home in Noongulli, listening to a Bach concerto before going to bed. He preferred the work of composers of the first half of the eighteenth century; the orderly architecture of their music suited his temperament. Then the phone rang and the night fell into disorder. It was his son-in-law ringing from the office at the cotton gin in a state of panic.

'But why call me, Max? Ring the police.'

'No, no! I know who shot him – it was Amanda!'

'What the hell are you saying? Just a minute.' He went across to the player and turned off the music. Then, unhurriedly, he went back to the phone. 'Amanda? You're not drunk again, I hope.'

'For Christ's sake, Chess! She's been following us – following me! She must have thought Sagawa was someone else –'

'Who?'

'Never mind that, Chess! Just come and help me – it's your fucking name that's in danger, not mine!'

'Where's Amanda now?'

'I don't *know*! For Chrissakes, hurry!'

Chess hung up, went out and got into his Mercedes and drove fast but with steady control into Collamundra and out the other side to the cotton gin. As he drove he thought of the madness of what he was doing, but, as always, he thought he could control it. Just as long as Max did not fall apart.

Nothling was waiting for him, the dead Sagawa lying between the Ford LTD and the Cressida. Max's panic seemed to have subsided, but there was still more blubber to him than bone.

'He's been shot in the back – the bullet's still in there. They'll trace it to her gun, won't they?'

'I don't know. I'm not experienced in police procedure – you're the government medical officer.' He looked down at the inert form of the Japanese. He felt more anger than anything else, an intense annoyance that something as stupid as this had happened. But, of course, it *had* happened before . . . 'What are we going to do with him now I'm here?'

'I've been thinking –'

Hardstaff looked at the darkened office cottage. 'Were the lights on when he was shot?'

'Yes, he was expecting me –'

'Go and put them on again. If someone drives past and sees three cars parked here and no lights, they'll wonder what's going on. If the lights are on in the office they'll assume we're having some sort of meeting.'

'But it's risky –'

'Do it!'

Nothling turned and went into the office and switched on the lights. When he came back he said, 'We have to hide the fact that he's been shot. We can take the body somewhere, out to the river, perhaps, and I'll try and extract the bullet, then we can throw the body in the river – Jesus Christ, what am I saying?'

Hardstaff said calmly, 'You are proposing a way of getting rid of incriminating evidence against your wife and my daughter.' He looked towards the cotton gin, a huge, black angular hill against the stars. 'Isn't there some way we can get rid of the body in *there*? All that machinery – it must have its destructive uses. Machinery usually does.' Unconsciously he had spoken like a Luddite, a thought which would have horrified him in a saner moment.

Nothling stared at him, his nervousness suddenly chilled by the cold calm of the older man. 'Christ, you beat everything, Chess!'

'Am I right? That's all you have to tell me. You know the workings here better than I do.'

Nothling looked towards the gin, said nothing for at least half a minute, then turned back to Hardstaff. 'Yes, there is a way. We could hollow out one of those modules that are ready to go into the feeder first thing tomorrow morning . . .'

It had taken them twenty minutes, working quickly but methodically, to bury the body and then re-pack the cotton around it. They were left with a quantity of cotton equal to Sagawa's bulk; Hardstaff, his mind even now acute to irony, wondered if Archimedes, turning from water, had considered such a principle. Nothling gathered up the surplus cotton and dropped it on a bundle of sweepings in the annexe.

They walked briskly back to their cars. 'What time did you get here?' Hardstaff asked.

'I'm not sure. About nine, I think.'

Hardstaff looked at his watch. 'It's ten fifteen now. Go home, find Amanda and tell her what we've done and impress on her that the two of you have been home all evening. Is your housekeeper home tonight?'

'No, she's away for two days in Bathurst, her sister's sick. What about yours?'

'She's in town at the films . . . All right, you leave first. I'll follow. And Max –' He could have been starting another political campaign; but, of course, it was a campaign, if not political. 'Get a grip on yourself. You're the GMO, you'll examine the body tomorrow morning when they find it. If that feeder back there works the way you say it does, there should be no need for an autopsy. Good night.'

'Will you talk to Amanda?'

'Not unless she speaks to me first about what's happened.'

Nothling had got into the LTD and driven away, going too fast and almost clipping the gates as he passed through them and out on to the main highway.

Hardstaff waited till he saw the LTD's tail-lights disappearing eastwards. Then he went into the office, went through Sagawa's desk and found the diary with Nothling's name marked in it for a meeting this evening. He took out his handkerchief, wiped where his hands had rested on the desk; then, on his way out, wiped the light switch where Nothling would have touched it. He did the same with the interior of Sagawa's car, just in case Nothling had sat in it with the Japanese.

He went out, got into the Mercedes and pulled away towards the driveway that led out of the farm. He had just turned on to the gravelled track when he saw the headlights turning in from the highway. His foot lifted for a moment, then he pressed it down again, switched his own headlights on to high-beam and went down the driveway towards the approaching car as fast as he dared. He went by it, spattering gravel, bounced over the cattle-grid at the gates, swung hard right on to the highway and headed west towards the town, home and safety.

He had, however, miscalculated; which was so unlike him. As a political boss he should have allowed more for human weakness; or anyway, for his son-in-law's weakness. Max Nothling had gone straight home, but it had taken him till the next day to tell Amanda what he and her father had done to cover up her crime. Instead, that Monday night he had got drunk, blind paralytic drunk, and next morning he had been in no fit condition to respond to the police call when the body was discovered. Dr Bedi had done the autopsy and then, slowly, everything had started to unravel.

Now here was Hardstaff on the lawns of his daughter's home, calmly discussing with her how and why she had murdered an innocent man whom she had mistaken for her husband's lover; the lover who now stood no more than thirty paces from them.

Then he was aware that Amanda had said something that he had missed. 'What?'

'I said, why did you kill Mother?'

It was the first time in seventeen years she had asked him that. He had expected to be shocked or frightened by the question, coming from her; instead, it was almost like the breaking of a boil, one he had kept hidden for so long. It was not a matter of conscience, he had never been troubled by such a weakness. There are just some secrets that, even in the most secretive of men, are cancerous.

'She was sleeping with Frank Kilburn,' he said.

'And he never said anything? Did he know it was you who did it?'

'I presume so,' he said calmly: Kilburn, too, was now dead and no longer to be feared.

'But why didn't you just divorce her?'

'Amanda, my dear –'

He raised a hand, but then it stopped in mid-air of its own accord. As if she understood, she raised her arm and put her wrist within the lock of his fingers, felt them close on her with what she knew was love. Max Nothling, watching from a distance, wondered at the gesture of affection, of intimacy, between the two people he feared and hated most.

'My dear –' There was no hint of tears; he was not capable of them. 'Pride. You and I both killed for pride.'

3

Malone was aware of the momentary hush as he and Clements appeared at the party. As they got out of the Commodore and joined Lisa and the Warings, alighting from the Mercedes, he felt the sudden chill come across the lawns from the crowd of fifty or sixty who were congregated between the swimming pool and the artificial-turfed tennis court. Faces turned towards them, small satellite dishes ready for any message the outsider cops might have brought with them. Then Max Nothling, face flushed from an early start to his drinking, came towards them.

'Welcome, welcome! I trust you and your colleague are off duty, Inspector? Oh, this is *Mrs* Inspector Malone? How can anyone so charming be married to a cop?'

'We're not married,' said Lisa, giving him what Malone recognized as her cut-your-throat smile. 'He's just my parole officer.'

Nothling recognized the smile for what it was; he showed some true charm by graciously retreating. 'I apologize, Mrs Malone. I'm not always the best of hosts, am I, Ida?'

'You do all right, Max,' said Ida, adding her own touch of graciousness. 'What's the champagne this evening, Aussie or French?'

'French for you ladies, local stuff for the natives. May I offer an arm to you both?'

He took the women away and Waring said, 'He spreads more bullshit than a yard full of Herefords.'

'He's as nervous as a bull that's just about to be turned into a bullock,' said Clements.

'You haven't come to arrest him, have you? Not at his own party?'

'No,' said Malone.

Waring, about to move away to greet another guest, turned back. 'Who *have* you come to arrest?'

'No one,' said Malone. 'Not yet . . . Before you go, Trev. How'd your meetings with the Japanese turn out?'

'I see them over there. Why don't you go and ask them?'

'No, Trev, I'm asking you.'

'I don't know that it's any of your business, Scobie. But if you must know – they're not selling. They are staying on. They set a price we just couldn't meet.'

'So they're not worried about the anti-Jap feeling?'

'Evidently not. But then, all that far away in Japan, they don't have to suffer it, do they? It's the consuls of empire who cop the spears in the back.'

Malone grinned. 'You haven't become anti-imperialist, have you?'

Waring smiled, the first time since getting out of his car. 'Lawyers have to believe in empires, of one sort or another. Otherwise we'd all finish up just working for Legal Aid.'

As he walked away, Dr Bedi came floating towards them, shimmering like a green-and-gold butterfly in another sari. She carried a small tray on which was a flute of champagne and two glasses of beer. 'Your wife told me you were both beer drinkers.'

'Are you a hostess?'

She put down the tray when the two men had taken their beers, then held the champagne flute in the long, elegant fingers which had none of the plumpness of the rest of her. 'No, I'm just standing in for the moment. Lady Amanda has just gone into the house with her father.'

'Lady Amanda?'

'A slip of the tongue. That's what the nurses at the hospital call her. Don't quote me.'

'How are the jockeys? Recovering?'

'Some of them are going to be out of action for quite a while. I believe they are going to sue the Turf Club for not policing the track properly – it's the Age of Litigation, sue anyone and everyone. We in the medical profession know all about that.'

'They're not going to sue the Aborigines?'

'What's the point? There's no money there.'

'Dr Bedi, if we come to you to make a statement about the Sagawa case, will you do it?'

She lifted her flute, looked at it as if it were a test-tube. Then she drained it in one gulp and said, 'No. All I'm going to say is what was in the autopsy report.'

'But that was signed by Dr Nothling.'

'Precisely.'

'We could report you to the medical ethics council, or whatever it is.'

'I don't think it would be worth your time and trouble, Inspector. You are not going to solve the murder that way.'

She raised the flute again, seemed surprised to find it empty, then turned and walked away, the sari fluttering about her like wings that couldn't be lifted to bear her away to somewhere where she would feel more at home. Because, Malone thought, I don't think she'll ever really be at home here in Collamundra.

The crowd had turned away from watching the two detectives and were intent on enjoying themselves. These people looked on themselves as the salt of the nation; Malone, grudgingly like a true city type, had to concede their right to their self-esteem. A great part of the country's export wealth still came, after almost two hundred years, from the efforts of these men and women on the land. But, like the Veterans Legion, they no longer had the political clout they had once had. The trouble was that the new rulers, the city bankers and entrepreneurs and developers, were going bankrupt and so, said the men and women on the land, was the country. Serves it right, they said, never loudly but emphatically. They, too, might go bankrupt eventually, but they would never starve. They would kill the fat lamb, slaughter the unsold beef, eat the grain the Wheat Board could no longer afford to hoard. All they had to do was stave off the banks when the time came. In the meantime they looked prosperous, kept a more watchful eye on the dry sky than on the banks and discussed the proliferation of taxes; the diminishing of subsidies; the price of wool, grain and cotton; and exchanged what gossip had sprouted since their last get-together. They discussed everything but the Sagawa murder, but occasionally some eyes would glance towards Malone and Clements, as if the grit of conscience had got under their lids.

'Well,' said Malone.

'Well, what?'

'Well, there's no point in putting it off. I think we'd better go in and talk to Hardstaff.'

'What, about Lady Amanda?'

'We don't have any hard evidence on her – yet. If she's as smart as I think she is, she'll have got rid of her gun.'

'She hung on to it after she'd shot Sagawa, at least till last night when she took the shots at you. Maybe she's held on to it to have another crack at you.'

'Why me? Why not you?'

'Privileges of rank, mate. What do we do? Go into the house uninvited?'

'I think the invitation said it was open house, at least for the élite. We won't have to break the door down.'

'That's good. I didn't bring the sledgehammer.'

4

Inside the house, in the large study-library, Amanda had just told her father what she had done last night. He was aghast, was *shocked*, a reaction so strange to him that for a moment he felt physically ill.

She saw how pale he had suddenly become. 'Sit down, Dad – you look as if you're going to faint. I didn't mean –'

'No, I'm all right.' He pulled himself together, settled his stomach with a dose of cold humour: 'Are you going to make a habit of it?'

'Don't joke. Last night I thought it would be a solution –'

He interrupted brutally: 'Killing a policeman? A solution? You were either drunk or mad!' Even in his own ears he sounded like the father of old, the one who had never had any encouragement for his children because he had never known how to express it without embarrassment. He retreated at once, not wanting to sever the tenuous bond that had been woven in the past twenty minutes: 'No, you're not mad. But you must have been drunk?'

It was almost a plea for her to say yes; and she obliged: 'I'd had too much to drink, more than I usually do. I was all of a sudden *afraid* of him, he's so – so tenacious. He'd never give up on trying to solve who killed Ken Sagawa, not the way the others gave up on Mother's killing.' She hadn't meant to be cruel and she hurriedly said, 'I'm sorry, I didn't mean it like that.'

'It's all right, I didn't have anything to do with that. It was your grandfather – I don't know whom he spoke to or what he said, but the police all at once stopped looking for whoever killed her. At least here in the district.'

'Malone is outside now. I saw him arriving as we came in here.'

'I don't understand why you invited him.'

'I think *you* invited him.'

He was puzzled. 'Me?'

'I mean that part of you that's inside me. We're alike, Dad, more than you know. Or perhaps you know it now. You used to invite your political enemies, the ones who wanted to kill you – politically anyway – you used to invite them to your parties at the national conference. It was almost as if you were betting that if you were close enough to them, you could see the knives coming. Inspector Malone isn't going to go away just because I turn my back on him.'

He had to admire her courage, even if it was reckless; after all, it was only a repeat of what he had done himself, a recklessness born of arrogance. He felt proud of her, in a *mad* sort of way. Then he decided it was time to start campaigning: 'Did you use the same gun?'

She nodded. 'The Tikka.'

'That wasn't smart. You should have used another gun, that would have confused them –' He was about to say he was disappointed in her; but that would have sounded like the old days. 'We'll have to get rid of the gun. Where is it?'

'There, in the rack.'

He went to the rack against the one wall not lined with books, where a dozen rifles and shotguns were stood like billiard-cues. He took out the Tikka. 'I'll get rid of it. Put it away somewhere till I'm leaving.'

He paused and looked at a framed photograph on a shelf above the gun rack. A much younger Amanda and Max stood arm-in-arm, smiling at the camera with genuine happiness; her figure had hardly changed over the years, but Max had not then become fat, was big but muscular and handsome. He thought it odd that the photo should be placed immediately above the weapons and he wondered who had put it there and when.

'Dad,' she said, 'don't put yourself at risk for me. Please.'

'Amanda –' He wanted to touch her again, but he was holding

the gun with both hands. 'Let me handle it my way. There'll be no risk, but if there is, whatever I do, don't interfere. I'm the boss, remember that. There's young Chester to be considered. I'm expendable now –' It would have rocked his enemies to their heels if they had heard him say that. 'But don't worry. We'll come through this all right.'

Then someone knocked on the closed door.

5

When Malone entered the house with Clements he saw Lisa at the far end of the long hall that ran right through to the rear. She was with Ida and he recognized what they were doing: the females of the species sticky-beaking in another female's lair. Lisa turned, saw him and raised her hand; her thumb and forefinger were linked in the circle of approval. *This will do me, hurry up and make Commissioner.* But one look told him no Commissioner would ever be able to afford this house, not an honest one.

A mixed-blood Aboriginal girl in a white smock came down the hall carrying a tray loaded with steaks and sausages for the barbecue outside. 'Where can I find Mr Hardstaff and Mrs Nothling?'

She jerked her head backwards. 'They're in the library. The fourth, no, the third door down.'

They walked down the hall, past the Rees, the Drysdale and the Whiteley hanging on the walls, and knocked on the third door down. There was no answer, but Malone sensed, rather than heard, the movement behind the door. He turned the knob; at least he and Clements were not using the sledgehammer. The door swung back and the first thing he saw was Hardstaff putting the gun back in the gun rack.

'Returning a borrowed gun, Mr Hardstaff?'

There was a moment's silence; then Hardstaff, not looking at his daughter, said, 'Yes. You seem to make a habit of barging in on other people's privacy, Inspector.'

'People expect their privacy to be respected, but they don't seem to appreciate that without law and order they wouldn't have much privacy.'

'This is a law and order intrusion, then? A nice distinction.'

'If you like. Can we see you a moment? Alone, preferably.'

'This is my house, Inspector,' said Amanda, 'not my father's.'

'I appreciate that, Mrs Nothling, and I apologize. But we'd rather talk to your father alone first. Then, if he wishes, we'll call you in.'

She looked at her father, who, his hands now empty, the gun back in the rack, put a hand on her arm. 'It won't take a minute, Amanda. Go out and take care of young Chester.'

His expression didn't change; but his message was clear. She hesitated, then she nodded and went out of the room, closing the door behind her. Clements took out his notebook and Hardstaff gestured at the large desk behind him.

'If you're going to make notes, Sergeant, make yourself comfortable. I'm sure my son-in-law won't mind. There's a dictionary there if you need it, and a thesaurus.'

Clements looked at Malone, shrugged and went and sat down behind the desk. Malone said, 'Don't waste your wit on us, Mr Hardstaff. We're not in the mood for it.'

Hardstaff sat down, suddenly feeling as old as he had this morning when he had been with Fred Strayhorn in the Noongulli woolshed. 'I'm sorry, Sergeant. For all I know, you may be a Doctor of Philosophy. Look at these books.' He waved a hand at the walls. 'Most people take my son-in-law for a drunken buffoon. He's read all of those, or most of them. At one time he used to quote them to me – Plato, de Montaigne, even Machiavelli. He used to say I could have taught Machiavelli a thing or two. I took it as a compliment. We did compliment each other occasionally in those days. But not any more. Nor do we quote anything to each other any more. A pity. He had wit, but he drowned it in Chivas Regal. *That men should put an enemy in their mouths to steal away their brains.* I'm not sure, but I think that's from *Othello*.'

'Are you a reformed alcoholic?' said Clements straight-faced.

Hardstaff looked at the big man as if he had not expected a whit of wit in him. Then he smiled. 'No, Sergeant. I've always known when to call a halt. Well, almost always.'

'Were you drunk the morning you strangled your wife?' said Malone.

Hardstaff looked at him, hurt, as if Malone had done something ungentlemanly. 'That's a low blow, Inspector. Why do you ask it?'

'We have two people who are willing to go into court and swear that what you told the police seventeen years ago was totally untrue.'

'Fred Strayhorn? Who is the other one?'

'No names, not yet.'

Hardstaff closed his eyes, as if looking for memory on the backs of the lids; then he opened them. 'Ruby Dawson. Ruby Mungle, as she now is.'

Malone went on, 'Then there's the Sagawa murder. We know now –' They didn't know; but you never told the suspect what you guessed. Machiavelli might not be quoted in the Police Department, but he had his disciples there. 'We know it wasn't Sagawa who was supposed to be shot.'

'Who was it then?'

'You'd know that better than we would.' He stopped being a fast bowler, bowled a wrong 'un: which is another word for a lie. 'Your Mercedes passed another car as you drove away from the cotton gin office around ten thirty last Monday night. You had your lights on high-beam, so the driver couldn't see you, but he recognized the car.'

Hardstaff shook his head. 'No, Inspector. On high-beam you can see nothing of what's approaching you. I've been blinded too often by fools who drive on our roads on high-beam, who never dip their lights when you approach them.'

'That answer's too pat, Mr Hardstaff. Have you been practising it?'

Hardstaff knew he had made a mistake; but he showed no sign of it. 'I think on my feet. When you've stood on as many campaign platforms as I have, you have to be quick. I'm an old-time political animal, Inspector, not one of these latter-day wimps who just want to talk to a television camera and not an audience.'

'Then it must have been your daughter's Mercedes. It was observed earlier in the night standing off the highway just up the road from the entrance to the gin. We understand she was a champion shot. Those are her guns?' He nodded at the rack.

'Not all of them. Some of them are her husband's.' He began to feel the ground shifting beneath his feet. He had never been a romantic, though he had never thought the end of the road would be at a cliff's edge.

'Does he own a Twenty-two?'

He was tempted. He had betrayed other men, it was part and parcel of the political life; but they had been sent only into obscurity, not to prison. 'No. The heavier guns are his.'

Clements got up from behind the desk and took the Tikka from the rack. 'When did you borrow this from your daughter? This is the one, isn't it?'

Hardstaff nodded. He was resigned now; all that could be saved was pride. 'Last Sunday.'

'Why? Don't you have guns of your own?'

'Yes. I just wanted to try that one. My own are Winchesters.'

'We're confiscating it as evidence,' said Malone. 'Write out a receipt for it, Russ.'

'Evidence for what?' But he knew he was just putting off the inevitable.

'Evidence for charging you or your daughter, or both, that you murdered Kenji Sagawa and that you attempted to murder me.'

'I thought you were investigating the murder of my wife?'

'Oh, we're sure you did that, too. But that's a case for the local District, not us. We'll turn over what we've dug up and they'll charge you, I've no doubt about that. But the Sagawa case is our pigeon. We'll charge you and probably your daughter – that will depend on our questioning of her –'

Hardstaff interrupted: 'Can they try someone for two murders at once, murders that are unconnected?'

Malone caught a glimpse of which way Hardstaff was hoping to go. 'No, I think the Sagawa case would take precedence, it's the more recent. Then when you've served your time for that, you'd be re-arrested and tried again. But that's unofficial advice. You'd better talk to Trevor Waring on that. He's out in the garden – do you want us to bring him in?'

Hardstaff shook his head. He knew he was beyond the help of lawyers; that is, if pride and Amanda were to be saved. All at once he wished for a sudden fatal heart attack; but he had the constitution of a Clydesdale, he was doomed to live too long. But not long enough to be charged with the murder of Dorothy: he would be dead in prison long before he had served the sentence they would give him for the later murder.

'No, there'll be time for him later. Yes, I shot Mr Sagawa and I attempted to shoot you last night.'

'Why? I mean, why did you kill Sagawa?'

'I don't believe I have to give you a motive.'

Malone had not really expected an answer; but he had had to ask the question, Clements would have had to make a note of it. He looked at Clements, whose face was blank. Both knew Hardstaff was lying, but all at once they had no desire to contradict him. But, again, something had to be said for the notebook: 'We think you're lying, Mr Hardstaff.'

'Prove it.' The old man's smile showed none of his teeth; it was the sort of smile that his defeated political enemies knew so well.

'You're protecting your daughter,' said Clements, but made no note of the question.

'Aren't you going to make a note of that, Sergeant? No, I don't think so. You don't want to prolong this case any more than I do. All the law ever wants is its pound of flesh. Perhaps you two want more than that, but you'll never be thanked for it. I confess to killing Mr Sagawa. Leave it at that.'

'We still want to talk to your daughter,' said Malone doggedly.

'No. I can't forbid you to do that –' He smiled again, a little less sardonically, almost whimsically. 'Not so long ago people did what I told them, at least the people around here and in the Party. But you're both Left-wingers, aren't you?'

'I think we're middle-of-the-roaders.'

'No place for an intelligent man to be. Someone once said that the middle of the road was occupied only by the white line and dead armadillos. I believe he was an American. Here it would be the white line and dead wombats . . . no, leave my daughter alone. You've got your pound of flesh. It's old and leathery, but it'll do for the purpose.' He stood up, surprised at how weak his legs felt. 'Shall we go now?'

Malone and Clements looked at each for a long moment, each waiting for the other to make the decision. They were just two men; rank meant nothing at this moment. Then Malone said, 'Hugh Narvo is outside, Russ. Go and get him. He and Curly Baldock can do the charging, it's their case.'

Clements went out of the room. The old man and the detective stood looking at each other in silence; they came from different worlds, more than just age separated them. Then Hardstaff said, 'You've chosen the best way out, Inspector. For all concerned.'

'No,' said Malone. 'I've chosen the easy way out.'

6

Two days later Malone and Clements drove out of Collamundra in the Commodore, heading east for Sydney and the punters who might have no respect for them but never thought of them as outsiders. Lisa and the children had left on yesterday's plane and Malone had been at the airport to see them off. Ida and the Waring children were there and Trevor Waring had arrived ten minutes before the plane was due to depart.

'I'm glad it's over,' Lisa had said. 'The murder case, I mean. But who would have thought *he* would have done it? How did you and Russ manage it?'

'Luck. An essential talent for a cop.'

He kissed her, then the children. Maureen was as loquacious as ever, glad to be going home to civilization and five TV channels. Tom was still wearing his stockman's hat, still determined to be a tomeroo, now reciting bush ballads that Tas had taught him, still droving cattle across the river of his dreams. Claire was out of love, returning to Jason or Ben or Shane, whoever had been the crush of a fortnight ago. Malone waved goodbye to them as they walked out to the plane and understood why Chess Hardstaff had pleaded guilty to the wrong murder. The hardest part to believe was that the arrogant, hard old man had had that much love left in him.

As Malone went to get into the Commodore to drive back to the police station, Waring came across to him. 'I've seen Chess. He's still refusing to offer any defence.'

'I think you'll just have to accept it, Trev. You can't win 'em all, not if your client wants to be a loser.'

'He's never wanted to lose before. He'd have killed to have won.' He didn't appear to have remarked the irony of his words; he seemed bemused by the stubborn silence of Hardstaff. 'The district will never get over this.'

'Have you talked to Amanda and Doc Nothling?' He had left the police questioning of them to Hugh Narvo. Pontius Pilate, he thought, had nothing on me.

'Not yet. I rang Amanda, but she refused to talk to me.'

'What about the doc?'

'He came in this morning.'

'How was he?'

'In a state of shock, I think. I got the feeling he knew more than he wanted to tell me, but I couldn't get anything out of him. He's asked Anju Bedi to take over for him at the hospital for a few days. I don't think anyone ever thought it was going to end up like this.' He looked in a state of shock himself. 'Not Chess. How long will they hold him over at Cawndilla?'

Hugh Narvo had thought it wise to move Hardstaff from Collamundra to District HQ at Cawndilla. 'That's up to you, Trev. If you can get the magistrate to grant bail, he could be out tomorrow.'

'Will you oppose bail?'

Malone held out the hands that had washed each other; but Waring didn't recognize the gesture, a strange lapse for a lawyer. 'That's up to Hugh Narvo and the locals.'

'I suppose you must feel pretty pleased with yourself?'

He looked for malice, but Waring's face was as bland as when he had first met him. 'Not really,' he said and left it at that.

Waring shook hands and Malone watched him till he had got into the Mercedes and backed it out of the small parking lot. He drove away, followed by Ida and the children in the Land-Rover. As she went out the airport gates Ida waved to him. There was something forlorn about the gesture and he wondered how much longer the Waring marriage would last.

He was about to get into the Commodore when the Mercedes coupé pulled in beside him. Young Chester Nothling-Hardstaff, wearing a hat with a school band round it, a school tie circling his neck, got out, said 'good morning' politely and went round to the back of the car and opened the boot. Malone hesitated, looking across the top of the Mercedes at Amanda.

'You've just missed the plane.'

'I fly Father's plane, I have a pilot's licence. Take the bags over, darling,' she said to her son. 'I'll be with you in a moment.'

The boy suddenly lost his politeness, looked belligerently at Malone, then slammed down the lid of the boot, picked up two suitcases and went across to a side gate beyond which were parked several light aircraft. A rifle in a canvas case was slung across his back.

'He's going to find it very rough at school for a while,' said Amanda.

'Especially if he arrives carrying a gun.'

'He's in the school cadets.' Her voice had iron filings in it.

'Where does he go?'

She named a school in Sydney, one of the State's oldest and most exclusive. 'His grandfather and his great-grandfather went there. He'll survive.'

'Because he's a Hardstaff?'

'Yes.' The pride was still there, despite the battering it would have taken over the past two days.

'Your husband didn't come out to see you off?'

'Don't be so casual, Inspector. Ask the direct question. Where is Max? I don't know. He moved out of our house on Sunday night. We are separating. There will be a divorce when all – when all this is over.' For just a moment her voice faltered.

'Are you staying on in Collamundra?'

'Of course!'

'Sorry. I should've known.' He had to admire her. 'Like you said about your son – you'll survive.'
'Yes, Inspector. Yes, I shall.'
She was challenging him; but the case was over for him, there was no extra time to be played. But he had to have the last word: 'Thanks to your father.'
He got into the Commodore, smiled at her through the open window, then drove out of the parking lot. In the driving mirror he saw her still standing by the Mercedes, staring after him, stiff and unyielding as an iron post, pride, arrogance and confidence in her invulnerability still intact. But time, as it had with her father, might eventually catch up with her. By then, however, Malone would be retired and there would be no satisfaction in it for him.
That evening he and Clements had a beer in the bar of the Mail Coach with Hugh Narvo and Curly Baldock. The others in the bar were quiet, looking sideways at the four policemen, not hostile but puzzled, as if not sure what the next step would be. They hoped none of them would be called for jury duty at Chess Hardstaff's trial and some of them were already dreaming up reasons to be excused, the Rural Party members of them looking on it as reverse cronyism. I'll bet I'm not the only Pilate in town, thought Malone.
'What will you do with Ruby Mungle's statement?' Clements asked.
'One thing at a time,' said Narvo. 'Curly and I have already had a word with Wally. He'll explain to her – not everything, but just enough. I don't think she'll mind. If she had testified against Chess for that old murder and he'd got off, she might've finished up back in the blacks' camp. Or I would've had to recommend that Wally be transferred. You know how things can go.'
'What about Amanda?'
'We'll keep an eye on her, that's all we can do.'
'Will you put in a report about her to District?'
Narvo took his time tasting his beer; he looked at Baldock over the top of his glass. Then he looked back at Malone. 'I think we've made enough waves, don't you?'

'My name's Pontius,' said Malone, smiling. 'What's yours?'

Curly Baldock, bald pate glistening under the lights, raised his glass. 'Here's to you two. We'll know where to come next time around.'

'No, thanks,' said Malone and Clements together.

Later the two of them had dinner with Sean Carmody in the hotel dining-room. 'I sent a truck in for Fred Strayhorn and had him out to lunch, after the carnival had gone. He's moving into one of the spare rooms till he finds something to buy. I think I may enjoy his company. He sent his regards.'

'Was he surprised the way things turned out?'

'Scobie, he's like me, we're of an age, maybe I'm a few years older. As far down the track as we are, there's a line from a Latin orator and poet that fits us both. *I am beyond surprise, but not beyond feeling*. The trouble is, with Chess being as old as us, I don't know whether to feel sad or angry. There are a couple of more lines from the same poet. *I shall go quietly, merely shutting my eyes*. The poet, incidentally, cut his wrists when he found everything stacked against him. Has Chess done the same?'

'Not as far as we know,' said Malone innocently and Clements, mouth full of sherry trifle, merely nodded.

Then this Tuesday morning, when the two detectives had come downstairs to check out, Narelle Potter, face pale and strained under her make-up, no bounce to her at all, all the hip-swagger gone, had been behind the tiny reception desk. Malone had signed the bill, promising she would be paid by the end of the week.

'Will you be back?' she said.

'I don't think so, Narelle. You won't want us back, will you?'

'No.' She had that frankness that the virgin and the whore share; at least with men. 'Not on official business, anyway. Maybe you'll come out next year for the Cup meeting and the ball.'

'Maybe.'

She shook hands with them; she held Clements's hand for a moment. 'Russ, you have a lot to learn about women.'

Clements glanced at Malone, then back at her. 'What guy doesn't, Narelle?'

And now, driving out past the bronze Anzac with his bayonet at the ready to be shoved up their rear, out past the silos and the railway siding and the last of the used-car lots, Clements said, 'How do you think Amanda Nothling feels about her father?'

'Do you mean is she grateful or conscience-stricken or what?'

'I dunno. That's the question.'

'If I think of an answer, I'll let you know.'

But he knew, in his heart, that in all probability neither of them would ever raise the question again. Not unless Chess Hardstaff, in a last-minute change of mind, pleaded not guilty and left the Sagawa case wide open again. But that was an improbability.

They passed the cotton gin and the farm, the harvesters still there in the vast fields, the foam of cotton almost gathered up now. Clements put his foot down and they drove east, towards the mountains and the city and the lesser sky, away from Collamundra and the never-ending plains and the crumbling edge of a changing world.